The scream appeared again, first as a small echo and then increasing in volume with every moment, with each second growing louder than before. A small mote of light appeared at the bottom of the pit, and as it rose it grew hotter and brighter. It flashed sunburst white, flame red, crystal green, lightning blue, and a black so intense that it cast shadows in the remaining darkness.

Suddenly it was even with them. It was a ball of fire with a human face. The face of the figure in the cage. It hovered over the abyss its face twisted in a mad parody of humanity.

"Treacherous mages! Die for your sins!"

Experience the Magic

MAGIC: The Gathering®

THE GATHERING DARK
ICE AGE CYCLE BOOK I

⚙ ⚙ ⚙ ⚙ ✳ ✿

Jeff Grubb

Wizards OF THE COAST®

The Gathering Dark

©1999 Wizards of the Coast, Inc.

Distributed in the United States by Holtzbrinck Publishing. Distributed in Canada by Fenn Ltd.

Distributed to the hobby, toy, and comic trade in the United States and Canada by regional distributors.

Distributed worldwide by Wizards of the Coast, Inc. and regional distributors.

Cover art by Gary Riddell
First Printing: June 1999
Library of Congress Catalog Card Number: 98-88151

9 8 7 6 5 4 3 2

ISBN: 0-7869-1357-6
620-T21357

U.S., CANADA,
ASIA, PACIFIC, & LATIN AMERICA
Wizards of the Coast, Inc.
P.O. Box 707
Renton, WA 98057-0707
+1-800-324-6496

EUROPEAN HEADQUARTERS
Wizards of the Coast, Belgium
P.B. 2031
2600 Berchem
Belgium
+32-70-23-32-77

Visit our web site at **www.wizards.com**

ACKNOWLEDGEMENTS

The world of Dominaria has many fathers (and mothers) and numerous doting aunts and uncles. The period of the Dark was first founded by the design team and authors of that card set–Jesper Myfors, Richard Garfield, Skaff Elias, Jim Lin, Chris Page, Dave Petty, Beverly Marshall Saling, Ron Richardson, and Rick D. S. Marshall. As one who has lived within the borders of these cards for several months, I thank them for their vision.

A particular debt is owed to Jesper Myfors; the original visionary who conceived The Dark. Jesper has been invaluable in providing background data and clarifying the original vision and intent of the card set. Jesper was the only one who could have proved that, regardless of what the final card text said, Barl the artificer and Mairsil the pretender were two different people, which turned soliloquies into dialogues. I hope that he (as well as the reader) finds this book true to the spirit of the age that he conjured.

Dedication:

To Steven Schend,
who kept a light burning in the window.

Prologue

The Cage

The temporal boundaries of the age known as the Dark are indeterminate. Trying to set down when it truly began and when it truly ended is akin to determining the exact moment that dusk begins and when the day finally and fully surrenders to night. Most scholars and theologians agree that the Dark began with the devastation of Argoth in 64 AR, and it extended several hundred years, until the continent of Terisia was at last firmly in the grip of its Ice Age.

None of those living during the time of this period would have identified themselves as living in a dark age, when civilization slipped from the golden days of the time of the Brothers. For them it was merely their everyday life, and if the days grew colder and the world more dangerous with the passing years, who could truly notice?

It was a time when the old nations collapsed, when goblins swelled their numbers in the hills, and when city-states quarreled and feuded under the onus of a tyrannical church. It was also the time when magic as we now know it came into full bloom; when the basic truths of modern spellcasting were first set down. During this ancient period the first true convocation of mages occurred, carrying on the spirit of Terisia City, combining their knowledge and encouraging their brethren in the exploration of this new art.

— **Arkol, scholar of New Argive**

In the depths of the catacombs beneath the Conclave Citadel, Lord Ith screamed in the darkness.

It was a ragged scream of lungs long since worn raw. He had been screaming for some time now, he realized, not knowing when one wail began and the last one had ended. Indeed, Ith did not know if his own voice was as loud as it seemed in his ears or if it was only the wheezing gasp of his breath against the silence that enwrapped him like a soft, muggy blanket.

Lord Ith, former ruler of the Citadel, former Lord High Mage, former supreme power of the Conclave, that collection of necromancers, thaumaturges, mages, and spell-dabblers, realized he was thinking about his screams, as opposed to just continuing to scream. He clung to the thought. Other thoughts accumulated around the edges of this first thought; fragile, flickering embers that could be nurtured, then banked into flaming moments, even hours, of lucidity.

It was futile, he knew, for the cage that entrapped him was draining his life, pulling away his power and his grandeur and his knowledge, wearing him down until exhausted sleep finally claimed what was left and the dreams rose within him again.

Worse things than Ith could ever have imagined or conjured while awake would come to torment him in those dreams. He would wake screaming anew and scream until the leeching effects of his prison would exhaust him again. It was an eternal cycle, one he had been unable to break, as strong and as eternal as the bars of his cage.

Lord Ith's cage was finely crafted of watersilver, its bars as clear and opalescent as a frozen waterfall. The struts were as thin as gossamer and as tough as steel. Lord Ith knew their strength, for he had railed against the bars in the long nights of his incarceration. Far above him, in the great banquet halls of the Citadel, the magicians and enchantresses dined on watersilver plates and cut their meat with blades made of the metal, but for Lord Ith the watersilver's purpose was to hold him tight, like an insect mounted for display and dissection.

The cage itself was strung on watersilver chains over an abyss, a blackness so deep that not even Ith knew of its true limits. The abyss had always been here, before the Conclave had been founded, before the now-vanished monks of artifice had made it their home, before the time of the Brothers and their unholy war that had wrecked the world.

The bars of the cage glowed faintly, a cold, pale luminescence found only in fireflies and certain varieties of mushrooms. Indeed, the bars shone with greater intensity than they had a moment before. His cage recognized when he was thinking, when he was sane, and reacted accordingly. Ith would eventually be too tired to think straight, and the exhaustion would take him, sending him down into the madness of his dreams.

It was always that way, in those few moments of lucidity. He would begin to think, begin to gather his thoughts, and the bars of his cage, carefully crafted and ensorcelled, would try to steal those thoughts from him. He had little time, he knew.

Ith cleared his mind for a moment and thought of lands above, of the sprawling castle that towered beneath soot-gray sky, of the great hills and marshlands that surrounded it. Once he had dreamed of a great labyrinth that would someday surround this domain and frustrate all but the most intent of travelers. That dream was dead now, as so many dreams had died. The bars of his cage grew brighter

3

for the moment, the watersilver already leeching his power from him.

Ith filled his mind with the memory of his lands, of his former lands, of the lands now held by the Usurper. A small flame of rage flared deep in Ith's soul at the thought of the Usurper, but the mage put down the thought and concentrated only on the lands he had not seen in years.

Once he had filled his thoughts with those memories, Ith unlocked a small parcel in the back of his mind—in that part that was still mostly sane—a part that the power of the cage and the things in his dreams had not yet reached. Lord Ith could feel the energy within himself rise, then peak, and then pass out of him as he sent a plaintive mental summoning out into the world.

The bars brightened momentarily, then faded. Ith could do nothing to affect his cage, and indeed his spells only strengthened their power. He had tried before and failed. No, this new spell reached beyond the bars. Ith could only hope that the enchantments of his cage would not suck all the power from his conjuration.

The spell stole precious energy from him, and for a moment Lord Ith blacked out. No, perhaps he only imagined he had blacked out. Perhaps he imagined he had cast the spell in the first place. The bars were already dimming again, and he noted dispassionately that his hands were clenching the metal spider's web before him, so that knotted muscles pulsed around his wrists.

Was it all a dream, wondered Ith, and he felt the darkness within himself rising again, threatening to overwhelm his tentative hold on consciousness. He let go of the bars and stood there, his fists balled now at his sides, his long fingernails digging into his palms. He felt the pain in his hands, and the pain drove back the darkness for a moment. It was good to feel anything at all.

Far in the distance there was the sound of a door opening, of keys jangling in the lock, of rusted hinges creaking as they flexed, and the soft whumping noise of an oak door striking a stone wall. Then another sound, this one the clipped noise of well-soled leather boots striking stonework, descending to where his cage hung above the abyss. The shadows cast by an approaching lantern danced along the walls.

For a moment he thought of his summoning, of his sharp, mental imploring, and allowed himself the luxury of thinking that the light was in response to his call. No, he corrected himself. The one he sought would not have needed keys to enter this place, nor worn hard-soled boots, nor needed a torch.

It was the Pretender. The Usurper. Mairsil. The one who had thrown Ith into his cage of mystic metal and taken over his position as Magus Alumni, as first among equals, as the ruler of the Conclave. The Usurper was the only one who knew where Ith was. The only one who could come visit him, unsummoned.

The darkness made an attempt to seize Ith's mind and drag him back down into madness. It keened and wailed, imploring him to let go of the light of lucidity, to flee into its warm heart of insanity. Ith imagined physical gremlins hovering around him and seeking to protect him from Mairsil, to drag him back to safety in the depths of his tortured dreams. The old mage fought off the temptation—at least he thought he had fought off the temptation—though when his mind grew clear enough for him to focus again, the Usurper was standing just a few feet away.

Mairsil the Pretender was dressed sumptuously, as if he had just left a feast, which he likely had. His cape was made of cloth of gold and trimmed at the neck and sleeves with ermine. The shirt and pants beneath were made from velvet of a hue so deeply purple as to appear a part of the night sky. His face was masked, and Ith remembered with a start that masks had been in fashion when he had been first imprisoned. The Pretender's was made of gold, and it encircled his eyes and covered his nose making him look like a predatory bird. Spikes from above the eyepieces followed his high brow into the long dark hair that was swept back over his shoulders. Again, it made him seem like a bird of prey.

"It has been a while," said Mairsil his voice smooth and soothing.

Ith noticed that as Mairsil spoke he stroked an oversized ruby on his right ring finger.

"Nearly a year since you were last well enough to chat. We had feared we lost you entirely."

Ith said nothing. In his mind he would play out such conversations—conversations where Ith reduced Mairsil to emotional rubble with nothing more than a few choice phrases—but when Mairsil came to visit the words and venom within the older man boiled up to the surface so fast that he sounded like little more than a dog barking. So Ith now held his tongue.

"Not that anyone has been asking about you really," continued the Pretender in the face of Ith's silence. "Most have forgotten about you entirely. Its been over a decade, you know. But I remember you Old Friend." A warm, quicksilver smile blossomed beneath the hawkish mask, "Oh, yes. I remember you."

Ith realized that his hands were still clenched, and he

slowly, purposefully opened them. He regarded Mairsil as one would regard a venomous serpent.

"I knew you'd be up and around though," continued the Pretender. "I could feel your power flicker through your toys."

He reached beneath his robes and pulled out a wand. Its handle had a grip like that of a saber and was crafted of the same alloy of watersilver that now held Ith in place. At its tip the wand pulsed with a pale piece of quartz. No, not quartz, thought Ith, the memory bubbling up from the base of his brain, but a powerstone, one of the few that had survived the Last Battle, when Urza and Mishra had attempted to destroy the world.

Ith thought he had held himself motionless, but something must have given him away, for Mairsil laughed, a raucous laugh like that of a crow.

"Ah, you recognize your toys, Old Friend? Then you should know that this one has been most useful in ferreting out dissent and prompting confessions. That is how I know that no one truly misses you, and most have forgotten that you were even here."

Again the Pretender laughed. The pale pinkish power stone flashed briefly, and then it was gone, the wand squirreled away beneath the opulent cape.

"But I remember. Oh, yes. I still remember enough to keep a close watch on you."

It was meant to be a haughty taunt, but Ith saw through it. After all these years, Mairsil still feared him. Mairsil had felt the softest tugging of Ith's magical power far below and had come running to make sure that his former mentor was still imprisoned.

That warmed Ith's heart a little. Trapped in a cage above a bottomless pit, buried beneath the catacombs of his own castle, he still frightened the Pretender. It was small solace, but it was enough, and for the moment it kept the darkness at bay.

"I take it you haven't given any more thought to my offer?" said Mairsil, his face suddenly stern and his manner direct.

Ith blinked and searched his mind for any such offer. All he found were wide, blank spaces of darkness. Parts of his memory, he thought, that had already been eaten by the gremlins from within his dreams. Motionless and silent, he just stared at Mairsil.

"It would be such a simple matter to tell me, you know," said Mairsil, his voice a little tenuous, "to buy your freedom with a few simple words."

Ith continued to stare at Mairsil. His voice was raw from screaming, so that his throat hurt even to breath, but he felt no need to scream, not now.

"You can't save yourself," said Mairsil crossly. He was fidgeting with the great red gemstone on his ring again. "All your knowledge will die with you if you continue to act like this. Come on, Old Friend, I know you better than this. I was once your student, and you trusted me in all things. Give up! Don't let your pride kill your knowledge! Tell me what I want to know!"

Ith could feel the gremlins moving about at the base of his brain, but he kept his jaw shut and his eyes leveled on the Usurper. Ith knew he would not last much longer, before the darkness spread into the rest of his mind and dragged him back down into sedate madness.

"I have your citadel," said Mairsil, and suddenly the wand was out again from beneath his cloak, its gemstone tip now glowing like blood. "I have your weapons, your followers, your magics! What do you have that I cannot obtain? Your very existence is being sucked dry! I could spare you all this! Tell me what I need to know! Tell me Urza's secret!"

The words were like a key to the last of Ith's sanity, a great iron key scraping as it turned in a rust-pitted lock. The tumblers, oiled but unused for years (it seemed), clicked and fell into place, and Ith knew what Mairsil was seeking. What Mairsil, who controlled everything that had once been Ith's, had been denied. Again Ith knew why he had been trapped in his cage, but not slain when the Pretender had usurped his title and his position at the head of the table.

Ith now remembered what Mairsil wanted.

The former Lord High Mage stared at the Pretender, and the corners of the older man's mouth drew upward a fraction. It was only the merest shadow of a smile, but it was a smile nonetheless.

Mairsil saw the smile and cursed, his mouth a twisted sneer beneath the golden mask. He raised the wand, and lightning danced around the tip. Then the lightning sprang to the cage, its electrical fires twisting and spinning around the watersilver bars and jabbing into the old mage's flesh. Ith howled as the power of the wand coursed through him and around him. Yes, that was how these conversations usually ended, the gremlins at the base of his mind whispered. He would frustrate Mairsil, and the Pretender would take petty revenge on Ith's flesh.

Ith blacked out. It was a dreamless state, safe from both Mairsil and the gremlins. It was merely oblivion, and as Ith slowly regained his senses, he realized that he missed the sensation. Perhaps provoking Mairsil was worth something after all.

How long Ith remained unconscious he did not know.

What he did know was that when his mind finally cleared again, Mairsil was gone. He had not heard the Pretender's boots strike against the stonework as he stormed out of the catacombs, nor heard Mairsil's curses, nor heard the far-off door slam hard into its jamb. He could imagine all that happening, and that was enough.

Unless, he thought, he had imagined the entire discussion in the first place.

No, Ith reassured himself. Mairsil the Usurper had been here, filled with pride and foolishness as always. The old mage's hands still hurt from where he had grabbed the bars, from where the dancing lightning had scarred him. Mairsil had been here.

Now someone else was here as well.

It took a moment for Ith to realize that he was not alone. The newcomer stood motionless where Mairsil had been moments (hours? days?) before.

He was a tall, lanky imitation of a man, a man who had been stretched on a rack and healed in his now-lengthened form. The creature's wrists hung down to his knees, and his head slouched forward from huge, humped shoulders. He was wrapped in old clothes and rotting rags, layer upon decaying layer. The creature's fingers were pale and blue, but his face was hidden beneath the folds of his hood.

He was waiting for Ith to speak. It took the former Lord High Mage a long time to realize that this was the being he had cried out for with his plaintive spell. Ith himself had called this ragged creature forth from his hiding place. More keys turned in his mind, and he remembered who and what this creature had once been and how it served Ith now.

Ith struggled. The encounter with Mairsil had taken

too much out of him. Already he could feel the darkness at the bottom of his brain surging upward, eager to claim him into its form of oblivion. Exhaustion had made him weak, had made him vulnerable, and sleep would claim him soon. For Ith, sleep meant not the peace of unconsciousness but dark visions of deadly things—things that, once thought of, would drive the thinker mad.

Ith had been thinking of those deadly things a great deal of late.

"Help me," he rasped to the creature, his voice as leathery as the tattered boots the rag creature wore. The creature made no move, for he was as powerless against the cage as Ith.

The captive mage shook his head, trying to keep the darkness at bay through sheer force of will. It would not be denied.

"Seek help," he said instead to the rag-cloaked man. "Bring me one with the key. Bring me one who carries the secret. Bring him to me, so he may set me free."

The ragged creature nodded, or at least looked as if he nodded to Ith, and turned away. But Ith was already slipping back again, into the madness that haunted him. He began to slip through the darkness, into the dreams where gremlins conspired to steal away every trace of reality and threatened to destroy all memory of what had come before.

Already the events of the recent past were fading. Ith wondered if he had imagined the ragged figure, or the conversation with his former, traitorous student or even the cage that held him. Those images blended with the dreams of dark-fleshed gremlins that now seemed to burrow out of his skin.

Deep beneath the Citadel of the Conclave of Mages,

Lord Ith let out a high, keening wail of madness as the darkness consumed him. Once begun, it seemed that he had been screaming forever.

1

Memories of the Land

Through the centuries there are a number of legendary figures that have come to us from the time of the Dark— figures, such as Ith, the horrific Rag Man, Vervamon the Elder, and Tivadar of Thorn. Yet one figure is an enigma among these enigmas. Time and again throughout the period of the Dark—and up to the end of the Ice Age itself—there is reference to a folk figure known as Jodah. It has been suggested that Jodah is the surname of a family of sorcerers, or a honorific title of respect, or that Jodah is a previously unknown Planeswalker. The fact remains that Jodah (be he one or be he many) is today regarded as one of the founders of magic as we now know it.

—**Arkol, Argivian scholar**

"I'm cold," said Jodah, huddled over the unlit fire pit.

"You're always cold," replied Voska with a laugh, rubbing his hands together for effect over the gathered collection of dry twigs and leaves in the stone-ringed pit.

"It's always cold," replied the youth. "The whole world is cold."

"Well, it's not going to get any warmer," said the teacher, "so you might as well give in and show me that you know what to do about it. Light the fire. Banish the cold." He waved an arm over the fire pit, his worn sleeve flapping in the chilly evening breeze.

Jodah stared at the lumpish bundle of tinder with something that felt like hate. Hate of the cold. Hate of his present situation, far from civilization, far from family. Hate of Voska for putting him in his present circumstances, for taking him on this god-forsaken route. And hate for himself for going with this self-described wizard in the first place.

The bundle of tinder at the base of the shallow pit remained untouched by his anger. If sheer force of will determined how magic functioned, then Jodah would already be a powerful mage, more powerful than Voska, more powerful than Jarsyl, the legendary wizard in his family tree and more powerful than even Urza and Mishra, the bringers of the Devastation.

More powerful than anyone.

But mere willpower, or anger, or hatred did not unleash magic, Voska would say (and he would say it, Jodah realized, if Jodah did not try something fairly quickly). There were other paths that led to magic, and his time as Voska's apprentice taught him that much at least.

Jodah attempted to unfurrow his brows. He knew that Voska could light the fire with but a few words and the errant wave of a hand, but that wasn't the point, was it, now? The idea was for Jodah to light the fire without flint or tinder or anything other than his own mind.

It was a test, and Jodah hated tests more than he hated the cold.

Jodah straightened his shoulders and shook his head, trying to clear the irritation and anger from his mind. His dark hair, long and worn loose since they had fled from the coast, grazed his cheeks, as he moved, in a tender caress. The motion did little to unclutter his thoughts, but the action felt good. It felt right. That too was one of Voska's instructions about how magic worked—it felt right.

Jodah took a deep breath and let it out slowly.

"Whenever you want to start," said Voska, leaning back and regarding the dark-haired lad through slitted eyes. Jodah wondered if the older man was laughing at him. Probably. Voska was regularly amused by most things he encountered, particularly Jodah. The lines at the corners of the old man's face showed that he laughed regularly.

"I'd like to cook these hares before the witching hour strikes," said Voska, offhandedly, motioning at the skinned and cleaned rabbits laying out on a flat rock, waiting only for the kiss of a flame.

Jodah stared at the bundle of tinder again, but now he was not looking at it. Instead he was looking beyond it and was thinking of the land. That was one of the keys to magic, Voska had stated early in his apprenticeship. The land held its power close to its bosom, the older man had said, and waited only for one with the talent and the will and the patience to call it forth. That involved memories, coming to know the land as one knew one's own self. Better, perhaps, in Jodah's case.

Jodah thought of the mountains above the ancient family estates. Memories of the mountains held great power, Voska said, of flame and of storms. Fire was from the mountains, and memories of those mountains could be harnessed to create flame. Jodah had seen Voska do it a hundred times. He had been walked through the process, step by step, on chilly nights such as this one, but this was the first time Voska had expected him to do it on his own.

The memories of the mountains would not come. The haze-tinted ranges were visible from his family's lands, but they were always remote, always standing sentinel on the western horizon. They were the lands of the dead dwarf kingdoms and new tribes of goblins and orcs. The mountains were recognized and respected, but they were also feared. Voska had no fear of the mountains. He claimed to have been raised among the Kher peaks, and the mountains were his home.

Instead Jodah thought of his homeland, many leagues behind them. He thought of the farms and orchards and gardens of Giva province. When his great-great-grandfather, the mighty Jarsyl, was Jodah's age one could ride a full day in any direction and still encounter landholders who owed fealty to their family, and the manor grounds brought rich harvests of apples, cherries, and cranberries. Even when his grandfather Thargrin was alive, the harvests were plentiful, and tithes brought by the farmers were enough to enjoy a good life. Yet by Jodah's lifetime the family orchards were overgrown with weeds, and the surrounding farms were mostly barren, overfarmed during the increasingly short summers and for the most part turned into pasture. The manor house had been built by Jarsyl's mother after the Devastation, but the passing of time had done it in. When he last saw it, on the cold rainy day when the family finally abandoned it, its supports had rotted dangerously, and its slate roof bowed precariously in the middle.

Part of Jodah's mind told him he should put aside the thoughts of the manor and the old farms, for the fire magic he sought lived in the mountains. Yet once begun, he could not break away from the reverie of home. He would never see that home again, he knew, and he would probably never see his surviving family either.

Yet from the memories of his homeland there came a light, like a door opening in Jodah's mind, or a dream remembered. That was the magic, he knew, the mystical wishing power that drove all spellcasting, the stuff that fed the engines of dreams. It was not mountain magic, filled with heat and angry stone, but rather that pouring from his memory of the surrounding farmlands and plains. Jodah could smell the winds of a brief, warm summer sweeping over the sun-dappled fields of grain, and he heard the scream of a lonesome summer hawk.

It was the wrong type of energy for lighting fires, but it was all he had, and it came unbidden now. To contain it, to deny it, would damage him, Jodah knew, for that was another of Voska's first lessons. Jodah pulled on the energy, drawing it from his memories like a spinner pulls thread from the wheel. Part of his mind saw the tinder in the fire pit, but part of his mind was elsewhere, back on the family's manor, listening to his grandmother speak of the days when the land was in its glory. He gathered it together and focused it on the gathered clump of leaves and small twigs. Then something inside him, at the base of his brain, *moved.*

Across from Jodah, Voska was viewing the lad through half-closed eyes, half expecting the boy to suddenly shake his head and admit defeat. Voska remained silent through Jodah's preparation and meditation, though usually he would seek to coach, focus and direct the boy's thoughts.

If the lad could light the fire, then he had learned his lessons well. If he could not, well, they were far enough from civilization not to attract too much attention and close enough to get Jodah to a church healer if he did damage himself.

Voska wanted the boy to succeed but did not want to walk him through the entire process, not this time. He had told Jodah for the past year and a half that a wizard should think things through and not depend on anyone, not even his teacher. Voska felt the lad had promise, though he started his studies extremely late, at the age of fifteen. Still, Jodah showed an aptitude to the craft, and had the blood of old Jarsyl in him, and Jarsyl was a legendary wizard in his own right.

Voska started from his reverie as Jodah's eyes suddenly widened within his lean, boyish face. The young man rocked forward, his hands splayed wide. That was not how this spell was supposed to be cast. Something was wrong

A great ball of light incandesced around the bundle of tinder beneath Jodah's hands, glowing hotter and whiter by the second. Voska shouted a warning, but his voice was drowned out by a crackling, not of lightning, but of light itself, sparking and feeding on the air in the heart of the fire pit. The light bleached all color from their surroundings—the trees, the stones, even Jodah's faded silk vest was reduced to a series of white patches and black shades.

In another moment the light rose from the fire pit like a phoenix ascending from its flaming nest, burning its way through the canopy of trees above them. The ball trailed a plume of light and rose perhaps twenty feet. Then it exploded, soundlessly, in a still brighter flash. Voska threw an arm up in front of his face, his eyes screwed tight, and still he could see the flash of the glowing ball as it detonated.

The afterimage of the light ball still burned Voska's eyes, and he had to blink away the bluish flash from his vision. When he had regained his vision, he saw that the slender young man was already hunched over the pit, studiously feeding the flickering flames at the base with small bits of kindling. The passage of the light ball through the fire pit had ignited the tinder.

Voska scowled and opened his mouth to reprimand the boy but did not know what to say. Jodah *had* lit the fire after all.

Finally, he said, "You weren't concentrating on the mountains, were you?"

Now it was Jodah's turn to blink.

After a while, the younger man nodded and said, "It felt right. Isn't that what you always said—that it should feel right?"

Voska looked stonily at the boy, then said, "I said that once, back when I still had my sight. Now, feed the fire while I finish preparing the hares. Unless your little display brought them back to life and frightened them away in the process. Then after dinner we'll talk about this."

Voska turned away from the young man, half to fetch the hares and half to conceal the broad smile that threatened to break across his weathered face. Voska was sure that as soon as his back was turned, Jodah was smiling as well.

* * * * *

"How does a mage keep track of his spells?" said Jodah, after they had finished the hares and dug the last of the new potatoes from their shallow graves beneath the fire pit.

It was dark and starless, the continual clouds reducing the world beyond their fire to varying patches of blackness. Most nights were overcast and starless on Terisiare these days.

"Wizards keep track in a number of ways," said Voska. "Some mages wrap them within songs and verses that hold mnemonic clues. Some attach mental significance to various items on their clothing. There are mages along the southern coast, near ancient Almaaz, who wear large vests festooned with buttons. They continually fidget with the buttons, reminding themselves of every spell they ever cast. Some chaos wizards don't bother to remember at all and call up the spells as they need them. I've done that on occasion."

There was a pause as the young man digested the information. "What about books?" he said at last. "My grandmother once said that her grandfather had a number of books on the subject, though they've long since disappeared. Can you write your spells down?"

"Yes and no," replied Voska, warming to the conversation. "Writing down a spell is like trying to write down a dance. It can be done, capturing every nuance of the dancer, but it does not translate well from the stage to the written page. The same applies to magic. You can describe it, you can attempt to explain it, you can even teach it, but without the magic itself present, you cannot truly utilize it. I've seen a number of magical texts over the years, and they range from scholarly tomes on the nature of mana and its connection to the land to useless collections of folk rumors and superstition. The most useless are volumes that explain magic to those who already understand it. A book like this is as valuable as a text that teaches a fish to swim. All such tomes, of course, are banned by the church."

Another pause, then Jodah said, "How do *you* keep track of your spells?"

Voska allowed himself a sly, almost wolflike grin. "I imagine a large tower, set among the Kher Ridges where I grew up. Each of the rooms of my mental tower has a balcony overlooking the mountains, the mountains from which I draw my power. And in each of the rooms I keep one of the spells I use."

Jodah thought about that for a moment. He thought of the old manor house, settled among cracked flagstones and weed-choked gardens. He thought of the entranceway, a broad expanse of yellowed granite and cracked jet that had seen generations of muddy feet. He placed his spell, the light ball, at the foot of the wide staircase that had been built with the house itself. He mentally closed the door of the memory house again.

Voska reached over into his saddlebag and pulled out a small silvery disk, about the size of his palm. He offered it to Jodah over the fire, and the younger man took it carefully.

In the light of the fire Jodah could see his own reflection in the disk, long black hair swept loosely back over his ears, black eyebrows over piercing dark eyes. He looked closely at the stubble on his face, the first attempts at a beard and mustache framing his thin-lipped mouth. He pursed his lips into a thin line.

"It's a mirror," he said simply.

"Observant as ever," said Voska, a smile in his voice. "It predates the Devastation, which is true for almost all things that are worth half a damn these days. The hedge-wizard who first taught me magic gave it to me after I cast my first real spell. Now I'm giving it to you for the same reason."

"Is it magical?" Jodah's eyebrows peaked above his narrow nose.

Voska laughed.

"Everything is magical," he said. "The skein and the weave of magic flows through us, like it flows through the land."

"But does it work magic?" said Jodah.

Voska replied, "Depends on the magic you want to work. Some mirrors are used for divination. Some are used for meditation. And this one . . ." his voice trailed off.

"What do I use it for?" prompted Jodah.

"Reflection," said Voska, and laughed again.

Jodah felt the blood rush to his face, and Voska added, "Don't be angry, lad. That's the same thing my first teacher told me. Well, he told me a lot of things, like the mirror being part of a machine found abandoned in the desert, or that it had come from Ashnod the Uncaring's slave pits. But I found it was good to see myself as others see me, on occasion, and I think it will be good for you as well."

Jodah looked at the mirror again and saw the reflection of a young man, not quite a boy any longer but not quite an adult. Voska meant well, but his small jibes still bothered Jodah. Regardless of its heritage, the mirror was solid and cool and unlike anything made in these days.

The boy nodded and changed the subject. "Why are books about magic banned?" he asked.

"Ah," said Voska, finishing the last of a potato and looking around to see if any had escaped their feast, "that would be the church. They do the banning."

"But why does the church ban them?" pressed Jodah.

Voska flashed a grin again. "The church wants to ban everything," he said. "It gives them something to do with their priests."

Jodah said nothing, instead staring into the embers of the fire.

Voska added softly and seriously, "They are afraid of magic, you see. They try to ban what they cannot control."

"We control magic," said Jodah, "or try to."

"But they don't control *us*," said Voska, "and they are afraid of what magic can do to them."

Jodah closed his eyes, trying to parse out Voska's logic. "But we aren't a threat to the church. We don't care what they do."

"They don't know that," said Voska, "and what they don't know they are afraid of."

"That makes no sense," said Jodah, sighing.

"Neither does the Church of Tal," said the older man, smiling as if Jodah had made his point for him. Then he added, "You know of the Devastation."

Jodah felt as if he was being treated like a child. "Everyone knows about Urza's Devastation," he said curtly.

"Also called Mishra's Devastation," said Voska quickly, "also called the Brothers' War, also called the Antiquities War."

"I know the stories," said Jodah, and the hurt did not disappear from his voice.

"Then you tell me a story," said Voska, in the dying light of the campfire. "Tell me what happened."

Jodah was quiet for a moment, then said, "There were these two brothers. Urza and Mishra. They fought each other, trying to rule the world. And they changed the world in the process, devastating it. Destroyed the land. Sank whole islands. Burned whole cities. The world is colder and darker and more dangerous now because of what they did. Some stories say they killed each other. Others said that one killed the other, then went insane and fled to find new lands to destroy."

"They were powerful wizards," said Voska.

"They weren't wizards," said Jodah. "My grandmother told me the stories, and she said they weren't wizards. They were powerful, and they had great machines, but they weren't wizards. Wizards are different."

"Ah, that's the point," said Voska, "they were powerful, and they were different and had abilities beyond most people, and that's why everyone *thinks* they were wizards. *That's* why the church seeks to burn the magical books. That's why they hound the mages and put wizards and artificers on pyres."

Jodah looked up from the fire. "Because they are afraid someone else will get as powerful as Urza and Mishra?"

Voska nodded. "Someone that powerful would be a big challenge to the church itself. And the Church of Tal does not like competition."

Something soft and heavy tripped over a tree root slightly downhill of their encampment. There was rough, throaty laughter, followed by numerous shushing noises. Then more guttural laughter, this time muffled.

Jodah looked quickly at Voska, and the older man rose quickly, more quickly than Jodah had seen him move in a year and a half. The older man's face was no longer smiling, and his hand strayed to his hip, as if to grip a sword that no longer hung there.

"What's . . ." Jodah started to ask, but the old wizard waved him curtly to be quiet.

"Goblins," said Voska in a voice no more than a whisper. "Move uphill behind me and keep quiet."

He bit off the last words sharply, and Jodah nodded and quickly scrambled uphill into the brush, slipping the mirror inside his high-topped boot as he did so and pulling a short knife from that same boot in the process. He knelt down beside a large-bowled, twisted trunk of an ancient oak.

Down the hill there were more voices, rough and guttural, trying to form human speech without the proper vocal chords. "Oi, the fire!" said one at last. "Annyboda home?"

"Hello, the darkness," came Voska's voice in return, strong and confident, the smile in his voice again. "Only a simple traveler who desires his solitude. Nothing more or less."

There was rough laughter again from down the slope.

Jodah stared into the darkness, straining to see the green-skinned creatures. He had seen goblins before, or rather their skins, stretched over wooden frames as hunter's trophies in Giva. No matter how many had been killed, there always seemed to be more of them. Goblins usually stayed in their mountains, unless they were on a raid, and the nearest human farmstead had to be miles away. Why would they . . . ?

Jodah's heart dropped into the pit of his stomach. Of course. They saw the light. The goblins were going to a raid, or returning from one, and saw the beacon he had created rising above the forest. They had seen his light, and they had followed it to the source.

Followed it to them.

The voice from down the slope was talking again. "Yu got anny fud for us?"

Voska laughed, and it was the easy laugh he used with bureaucrats and merchants. "I had some rabbit earlier, but you're too late, I'm afraid. I have a small fire here, if you're cold, but otherwise there is nothing here that would interest you. You'd best be on your way."

There were some mutterings downslope, and Jodah poked his head farther around the tree. Voska was standing calmly, his back to Jodah's hiding place, the fire pit between himself and the goblins.

"Mebbe there ain't nuttin' for us," said the voice, "an' mebbe there is. I tink we wanna come find out."

"You are not welcome," said Voska simply, "and you have been warned."

Again the laughter, and there was motion among the brush, and the first of the goblins stepped into the firelight.

The goblin was a mockery of the human form, naked to the waist and wearing rags around its hips. Its skin was green and warty, and unlike the leathery hides Jodah had seen in the cities its tough flesh was stretched smooth and tight over well-muscled sinews.

The creature was shorter than Jodah, but stockier, with hunched broad shoulders and arms that almost dragged on the ground. It carried a cudgel in both hands, and Jodah noted that the tip of it was smeared in some dark, sticky-looking substance.

The goblin's mouth dominated its face, more of a muzzle than a mouth, and was filled with sharp teeth that splayed in random directions. Heavily muscled brows shaded deepset, bloodshot eyes, and its ears were like a mule's, jutting in opposite directions from the top of its head.

"You're not welcum eeder," said the goblin with a snarl, "and dat is yur warning." Other shadows began moving out from the among the brush.

Voska made a single motion with his hand, waving

outward, palm up, like a farmer sowing a field with seed. Yet instead of crops there blossomed hundreds of small jets of flame from the ground, at the feet of the lead goblin and around his compatriots. The lead goblin squealed as its rags caught fire, and it dropped its weapon and began slapping at its thighs and groins in a desperate attempt to quell the flame. The others were daunted by the fire's effect, and by the flames themselves, and pulled back.

"Kor!" bellowed one of them, "Itz wizars. Itza wizar there!"

Voska chuckled and pointed a finger at the leading goblin. A single line of flame jutted from his finger and flew unerringly to strike the goblin in the chest. Green flesh crackled, and the goblin screamed as the fire fed off the creature's flesh.

Jodah could not take his eyes off Voska. The elder mage made it look so easy—the choice of spell, the recalling of the memories of the land, the few hand motions that unlocked the power and the effects of the magic made visible in fire. Jodah knew how difficult it was, and Voska carried himself effortlessly. Later the mage would be exhausted, but now he turned aside a company of goblin raiders with ease. The lead goblin was now little more than an animated fireball, cascading down the side of the hill, scattering its fellow creatures in its wake.

Then everything changed. There was a twang of a bow from down the hill, and the shaft of a goblin arrow blossomed in Voska's shoulder. Voska raised his hand to his shoulder and cursed, his concentration suddenly gone, his spells made useless. The surviving goblins saw this and gave a deep-throated cry.

Jodah shouted as well, clutching his knife and rising from his position. He made two steps, them pitched forward into the soft, cool moss beneath the brush. Something had tripped him, Jodah realized. He spun as he landed, half-expecting some goblin scout to loom over him, ready to slit his throat.

Instead there was nothing. No, not nothing, there was a motion back near the tree line, of a tall figure. Not a goblin, it was far too tall for a goblin. A hooded figure dressed in dark gray and black. The figure lingered for only an instant, and then it was gone.

Jodah raised himself up and tried to leap forward to aid Voska, but others were converging on the scene now. There was the sounding of a horn to his right, close and clean and bright. It was a human horn, a hunting horn. That was followed by the ratcheting sound of crossbows unleashed, at least twenty, cutting the thick foliage with their passage like angry hornets. As Jodah watched, two of the goblins collapsed, white-feathered arrows in their throats and chests. The remaining creatures hesitated for a moment, then fled—their morale shattered—following their flaming leader down the hill.

Then their rescuers were in the glade as well. The newcomers were dressed in fitted armor plates and stopped only briefly in the clearing to wind their crossbows or draw their weapons. Then they disappeared in pursuit of the goblin raiders down the hill. The tunics worn over their armor were white, and their capes purple. Jodah realized they were from Alsoor, the next major city state along the coast.

One of the soldiers paused long enough to look at Jodah as the apprentice pulled himself from the ground. Jodah expected the soldier, a blond-haired young man, no older than Jodah himself, to pursue the goblins. Instead, he motioned with the crossbow for Jodah to join his master. A bolt rested in the groove of the crossbow, and its string was pulled taunt and cocked.

Jodah got up slowly and moved toward the wounded Voska. The older mage had pulled the goblin arrow from his arm and was pressing a blood-stained hand against the wound.

Another man entered the clearing. This one was tall and walked with a stiff gait. He was unarmored, and his tunic was marked with twin sunbursts—the symbol of the Church of Tal.

Voska was already speaking. "I cannot thank you enough for the timely rescue. We were camping here when the goblins . . ."

The unarmored man lashed out, striking Voska square across the jaw with the back of his fist. The older man staggered under the blow, and a trickle of blood dripped from the corner of his mouth.

Jodah shouted and stepped forward, but the young soldier's gauntleted hand came down squarely on his left shoulder. It felt as if a vise had been attached there.

The unarmored man was speaking. "You stand accused of the use of sorcery in the lands of Alsoor."

"There were these goblins, dear sir," said Voska, his voice bubbling with blood.

"The lands of Alsoor are under the spiritual protection of the Church of Tal, and it is under those laws that you are hereby arrested, and under those laws you will be tried. I am Brother Tanar. You will accompany me back to Alsoor for trial." He turned and motioned for trumpeter to sound recall and bring the pursuing troops back.

"We got what we came here for," said Tanar, regarding both Voska and Jodah with a stony gaze.

Voska rubbed the bleeding corner of his mouth with

the back of his hand. "I think," he said, loud enough for both Jodah and the guard to hear, "we were better off with goblins."

2

Inquisition

One of the most powerful forces during the period of the
Dark was the Church of Tal. Its origins are thought to have
been in a union of two small sun-worshipping cults among
the early Yotians, though the church itself, at its height, went
out of its way to erase all traces of its humble beginnings.
The church also went out of its way to erase all traces of
magic and magicians during this period as well. While magic
would survive and eventually triumph against such oppres-
sion, the same cannot be said for those most unfortunate of
sorcerers who were brought before the inquisition of the
Church of Tal.

—Arkol, Argivian scholar

The chamber was relatively opulent, at least by stan-
dards of the modern day and age. It had an internal fireplace, and the walls beneath the thick tapestries were
made of stone. Jodah noticed the heavy tables and chairs
made of solid wood, and thick curtains partially covered a
leaded window to keep the night air at bay. Most of all,
Jodah noticed the large number of metal pokers and tongs

that were resting with their tips in the fireplace itself. The tips glowed red like goblin eyes.

The trip back to the walled city of Alsoor had taken most of the rest of the evening, and it was now only hours from dawn. The best time for an inquiry, Voska had noted with sarcasm, since most executions were scheduled to take place as the cloud-filled sky lightened with the promise of a sunrise that would never come.

Voska had been manacled by Brother Tanar with ornate bracers fastened at the wrists, so he had to hold his arms crossed in front of him. The bracers looked like cast iron, but were inset with a spidery pattern of a silvery metal. The pattern looked like spun sugar set into the darker metal.

Early on, Voska had wiggled his fingers, and the tracery glowed with a dull silver light. Voska choked back a scream and fell to his knees, putting his head against his manacled wrists.

"Don't try that again," said Brother Tanar as he hefted Voska to his feet. Jodah thought he knew what the "that" was—any attempt to mentally tap the magical forces of the land. The manacles apparently had some type of anti-magic property. How else would you imprison a magician, if you had no magic yourself?

They did not manacle Jodah but marched him alongside Voska, a pair of guards behind them. They did not seem to care what Jodah did or said, as long as it did not involve escape.

"Where are they taking us?" Jodah had asked softly.

"Alsoor," replied Voska. The older mage's voice was thick and syrupy, and the blood had dried in a dark river stemming from one side of his mouth. The soldiers had bandaged his wounded arm but left the damage inflicted by Tanar untended, as a warning.

"The church is strongest in the cities, and we are being taken to a church court."

"Why a church court?" asked Jodah.

"Because magic is a crime against humanity," said Voska with a soft chuckle that belied his current state, "and only the church is powerful enough . . . and wise enough . . . to rule on such crimes."

Jodah dropped his voice a little. "But why didn't they chain me up as well?"

"Because," Voska said, and the amused tone was back in his voice, "you were not witnessed casting a spell, and until you do, you are innocent under church law. They would not chain the innocent, only the guilty. They are not animals, you know."

There was another small chuckle and a hint of triumph, however minor, in Voska's voice.

Jodah was unsure about the comment about the Alsoorians not being animals. The guards had returned from their pursuit of the goblins with a collection of grisly trophies—heads and hands, that were dumped into a bag and brought along with them. Jodah noted that at least one of the trophy heads had the hair burned from it, and he wondered if Voska would be credited with the kill.

Now, in the enclosed chamber on the second floor of the church Embassy in Alsoor, Jodah looked at the heated tongs and pokers in the fireplace and wondered again about the humanity of the Alsoorians. He felt a shiver run up his spine which had nothing to do with the cool, evening air leaking through the curtains.

"Lovely decor," muttered Voska to no one in particular. "Love what you've done with the place."

There was another breeze as a door to their right opened and closed. A massive priest entered, followed by a pair of female scribes. No, the massive figure was a priestess, though she looked large enough to beat the Alsoorian guards two out of three. She was broad shouldered and tall, with a lantern jaw and heavy, brooding eyes that seemed twisted in a perpetual scowl.

She took long, heavy strides to the desk, the hem of her habit gliding along the hard stone floor and sounding to Jodah's ears like a legion of snakes. Her robes were white and marked with the double sunburst of Tal. In the firelight her garb was the color of pale and corrupted flesh.

The huge priestess sat down on a massive chair behind the desk. Jodah thought Voska would mention that the chair, a huge, ornate monstrosity, looked as if it was constructed specifically to hold her frame, but the older man said nothing. The priestess rested her elbows on the oak desk, templed her fingers, and regarded the prisoners.

Jodah felt another shiver as her eyes swept over him, regarding him and discarding him in the same instant. It felt as if she could peer into his heart, exposing any sin, real or imagined. As he shook, he felt her eyes leave him and pass on to Voska. She stared at the older man for a longer time, then asked in a gravel-throated voice, "What are the charges?"

One of the scribes, a plain girl who had to hold her tablet close to her face said, "Sorcery, Your Grace."

The heavy-set woman let out a grunt. "And are there witnesses to the crime?"

Brother Tanar spoke up now. "Aye, your Grace. My company was tracking a group of goblin raiders through the northern hills when we witnessed a fountain of unnatural light springing from one of the hillsides. When we arrived, I and my men were witness to a battle between this sorcerer and the goblins. The wizard set his opponents alight from a distance with hellfire and witchcraft. My men charged into the battle and dispatched the goblins and then arrested the sorcerer."

Jodah opened his mouth to speak, to contest the charge, but there was suddenly a heavy, gauntleted hand on his shoulder. The gauntlet belonged to the guard behind him. He looked at Voska, and the older man just shook his head at him.

"Are the brother's charges true?" said the priestess to the older mage.

"Well, that depends on your definition of truth, my lady," began Voska.

The priestess interrupted, slapping a meaty palm down on the table, "I am *not* your lady. I am Primata Delphine, in the service of the Order of St. Zil, most revered be her name. I have full authority in matters of rooting out sorcery in the eastern city-states, so toy with me at your risk. You will call me Your Grace, or Primata Delphine. Am I understood?"

Voska nodded slowly, carefully digesting both the primata's words and her heated tone. "I understand."

"You understand what?" snapped the primata.

"I understand," said Voska, pausing only a moment, "Your Grace."

"Again I ask you," she said pressing her fingers together, "are the brother's charges true?"

"They are true in that there was a fountain of light on the hillside," said Voska solemnly, "and that it was likely sorcerous in nature. Indeed, my companion and I saw it as well and went there, much like the goblins and Alsoor's own noble knights, to investigate it."

"And the charge that you attacked the goblins with hellfire?" prompted Primata Delphine, her tone as level as a stone crypt.

"I would hesitate to say that I attacked anyone," said Voska, warming to the tale, "rather, that the goblins attacked me, or rather us. I had taken the precaution of scooping some hot coals into a cup and tossed them at the goblin leader when he charged toward me."

"Your Grace," said Brother Tanar, "the goblins burst into flame at a wave of the sorcerer's hand!"

"I had no idea that goblins were so . . . flammable," Voska managed a brief shrug, despite his wound and manacled hands.

Jodah had seen Voska's act of innocence before, a play usually presented for the benefit of a rent-demanding landlord or an outraged patron. Often his glib, easy lies brought a smile and occasionally got them off the hook.

The priestess sat there stone-faced. "Are you saying that a brother in the holy church was wrong?"

"Wrong?" said Voska, blinking innocently. "I cannot imagine a servant of the holy church *ever* being wrong, as they are guided by the light of Tal. I merely state that the illustrious brother, in his zeal and holy fervor, might see one thing and conclude another."

The corner of the primata's mouth tugged, and Jodah thought that as close to a smile as the large priestess was capable of.

"Your wits are nimble," she said, "and it takes quick thinking to be a sorcerer. You do not do your case good by being quick with your mind. Or by being glib with your tongue."

"I understand, Your Grace," said Voska, bowing slightly, "and I appreciate your understanding and wisdom in preventing an innocent man from being accused of a horrible crime."

Primata Delphine made a noise that was halfway

between a chuckle and a grunt. She turned to Jodah. "And you, boy. Is what your friend says true? Or does Brother Tanar speak the truth instead?"

Her eyes bored into him, and Jodah felt his throat constrict and his mouth turn suddenly dry. "I . . . " the young man began, then coughed. "I saw what my friend Voska says. I also saw what the good brother described. I can understand why the brother feels that there was magic involved, for it seems miraculous that a single man could stand up to a company of goblins."

"A miracle," added Voska, seizing on the word. "Surely the Book of Tal speaks of miracles, and perhaps the good brother was witness to one here."

"*Silence*," snarled the primata, and Jodah knew that Voska had played one card too many in this particular game. The priestess' eyes remained focused on Jodah. "Your accent in strange lad," she said. "You're a northerner?"

Jodah nodded slightly and responded, "I was born in Giva Province."

"Yes," said the primata, "that would make sense. That is a heathen province, filled with hedge-wizards and sorceresses. You never had school, did you?"

Jodah opened his mouth to protest, then halted himself.

When he did speak, he said, "I never went to a church school, if that's what you mean. I was taught at home." To himself he added, by those who knew more than you ever will.

Primata Delphine shook her head sadly. "We see so many of you these days, refugees from Giva. The cold and the snows and the goblins drive so many of your countrymen south into the civilized lands. And here you are lost, like goats in need of a herdsman. The church," she added, "can act as that herdsman. As a guide for you."

She rose from behind the desk and slowly walked around it, speaking as she lumbered forward. "Long ago, before the Devastation, Giva Province was called Argive, and it was the home of Urza and Mishra. You *have* heard of them, of course." She paused long enough for Jodah to nod, "Giva was a heathen place then, believing in no gods but the dark gods of magic, and the Brothers' battle began there. Much of the world is still tainted by the Brothers' spells, and the Book of Tal tells us that we have yet to pay the full price for their deviltry."

Primata Delphine was in front of the desk now, and looked directly at Jodah again. "Urza and Mishra used magic. Magic is a crime. Worse still, it is a sin." Her features softened for a moment. "The sinner may be forgiven, but the sin must be purged. Do you understand?"

Jodah nodded, but slowly this time.

Primata Delphine gave a tight-lipped smile. "Then answer me truthfully and free from fear—did your companion here use sorcery?"

Jodah did not look at Voska but looked straight at the priestess instead. "No ma'am, he didn't."

The primata nodded, and Jodah's belly exploded in pain. He doubled up from the force of the blow, and was pulled upright by the guards behind him. Stars danced before Jodah's face, but beyond the stars he saw Brother Tanar, pulling his fist back for another swing.

"Your Grace," said the priestess, leaning back on the desk. It groaned beneath her weight. "Not madam. Address me as Your Grace, or as Primata Delphine. I ask you again. Did your companion here use sorcery?"

This time Jodah looked at Voska, but the older man's face was deathly pale and his brows drawn. "No, Your

Grace," he started to say, and was rewarded with another hammer punch to the belly before he got the third word out.

Repetition did not make the assault easier. Jodah tried to cover his stomach, ward off the blow with his arms, but strong hands held him tight by the wrists and shoulders. A short eternity passed as the stars faded from the corners of his vision.

"For the third and last time," said Primata Delphine, with as even a voice as if she were discussing the purchase of grapes in the marketplace, "did your ally here use sorcery?"

Jodah looked at Voska, and all blood seemed to have drawn out of his face. "No," he said simply, and winced in anticipation of the blow. But Brother Tanar did not hit him again. Instead the churchman moved back toward the curtained window.

"I understand," said the primata, "and I am saddened to see how far the corruption has spread. Have you known your ally long?"

Only for the past year and a half, thought Jodah, but he said, "Only a few weeks."

"And how did you meet?" she said.

My mother died, and the family had finally abandoned the old manor, thought Jodah, when the land finally gave out. When the snows lasted until mid-year's day, one brother went to sea, one went exploring north, and before she died Mother had made Voska promise to look after Jodah—to teach him proper magic—a year and a half ago.

He said, "We met on the road."

"From Giva?" asked the primata.

"Yes," said Jodah.

"Many walk sorrow's path," said Primata Delphine,

sounding as if she was quoting someone. "Many bring •
their sorrows with them." Then she said, "So you met him
on the road."

"Yes," said Jodah.

"You were found far from the road," said the primata.

"We thought there was a short cut," said Jodah, then
remembered Voska's own tale, "and we saw a light."

"Ah yes," said the primata, "a light. The light that
Brother Tanar and the goblins saw as well?"

Jodah shrugged. "I suppose so."

The primata shook her head. "Did your companion
mention magic during your travels?"

"No, Your Grace."

"Did he cast any spells? Summon any creatures of the
pit? Invoke any foul beings?"

"No, Your Grace."

"And did he teach you any magic?" she said.

Jodah looked up and found the eyes boring into him
again. "No, Your Grace," he managed, but his voice
sounded as weak and false as a tin coin.

"Michelle," said the primata, and the near-sighted girl
set down her tablet and went to the fireplace. She pulled
the poker from the flames and walked to the priestess. The
tip of the iron spike glowed like an orange-red star.

Primata Delphine grasped the poker by the grip, and
walked toward Voska. "Did you pollute this lad's mind
with magic?"

"No, Your Grace," said Voska, but his voice was hollow
and his eyes never left the tip of the poker.

She waved the hot tip inches from Voska's face. "I ask
you again, have you taught the boy magic?"

"No, Your Grace," said Voska.

The tip of the poker edged closer. "For the third and

last time, did you teach him any of your hellish magics?"

Voska swallowed hard, and gasped, "No, Your Grace."

The primata stepped back, and regarded Voska carefully. Then she raised the poker again and without looking, pressed it slowly toward Jodah's face.

Strong hands were again on Jodah, and the young man tried to lean away from the out-thrust instrument. He could feel the heat growing as it approached his face and felt the tears well up in the eye closest to the heat. It already felt as if his cheeks were on fire. Another few inches and . . .

He heard Voska's voice gasp, "Stop!" and the heat receded slowly.

Jodah looked at Voska, and the older man's shoulders were slumped in defeat.

"Do you have a statement to make?" said Primata Delphine, her eyebrows raised, the corners of her mouth tugged back in a false smile.

Voska was silent, and the priestess repeated herself, "Again, do you have a statement to make? A statement about magic?"

Voska looked up at Jodah and chewed on his upper lip.

"A third time I ask," said the primata, grasping the hot poker tightly. "Do you . . ."

"Jodah," said Voska, in a voice that seemed to issue from the grave, "show her."

"Show her?" said Jodah, blinking in disbelief. If the one sure way to condemn yourself was to cast a spell, asking him to cast a spell before these people was suicide. Did Voska suddenly want company on the martyr's pyre?

Then Jodah realized what Voska was really asking, and he understood. "If that is what you wish," the young man said simply, sounding as defeated as Voska appeared to be.

To the primata he said, "Your Grace, I will need a bit of space for this—" he looked at Voska—"demonstration."

The priestess of the Church of Tal smiled fully for the first time, and Jodah thought her smile more frightening than anything he had seen in his young life. She reached out and handed the poker to Michelle, who dutifully returned it to the fireplace. Primata Delphine said, "Give him his room, but stand ready."

The heavy hands released him.

Jodah knelt on the floor and realized that part of it was carpeted, a thick, heavy carpet from the north, perhaps from Giva itself. He smoothed out a patch of the rug in front of him, and began drawing—first squares, then circles, then squiggles in the rug's pile with his finger.

"Take careful notes," said the primata to the one scribe, who was diligently attempting to record all of Jodah's nonsense inscriptions.

Jodah's hands flew over the rug and then left it entirely, tracing symbols in the air. There were trees and butterflies sketched out in the air, along with more squares, and for a brief moment, rude words spelled out quickly.

Now Jodah's mind was no longer on the movements of his hands. He was thinking of the manor lands again. He was thinking of home and unlocking the magic held in the memories of those lands.

He could feel the power burning, the same power he had felt earlier that evening, in the dying light of the day, before he had encountered the goblins and the soldiers, and particularly before he had encountered the church. He conjured in his mind the map of his house, and he was there, standing in the doorway, on the entranceway of white granite and jet. He leaned forward and grasped the spell that he had left there.

The motions of his hands grew more frenetic, and Jodah began to whisper something. The primata, the guards, the scribes, even Brother Tanar, leaned forward to catch his words. Voska looked away.

Jodah closed his eyes tightly and hoped that Voska would do the same. With a final flourish, Jodah unleashed his spell.

Even through eyes screwed tightly shut the light was intense, filling his vision. Jodah could imagine it spouting upward like a fountain, smashing into the ceiling and spreading outward in an intense column. It only lasted a moment. A moment of intense brilliance, and then the radiance was gone.

Jodah opened his eyes to find the primata and most of the others on the ground, shouting and pawing at their blinded eyes. Voska had been ready for the spell and was now running at full tilt toward the curtained windows.

Jodah suddenly realized that the older man was not alone. He was driving the massive Brother Tanar before him, half-guiding and half-carrying the big man. Tanar had one hand clamped tightly to his eyes, and the other waving desperately around looking for something to grab hold of.

Voska and the holy brother hit the curtains and the window beyond. The window leading snapped and shattered under the blow, and in an instant both men were gone, along with the window and a large amount of the curtain, leaving only a huge gaping hole. The night air whipped in through the hole, flapping the remaining curtains in a bitter-cold breeze.

Jodah ran to the jagged opening and looked down. The older mage had used Brother Tanar as a cushion to soften his landing. The brother was sprawled face up on the cobblestone street, but Voska was already rolling free.

"Come on!" shouted the old mage, "they aren't going to wait all morning for us to escape!"

Brother Tanar, still blinded, roused himself and reached out toward the sound of Voska's voice. The older man wheeled and clubbed the holy brother with his manacled wrists. The brother went down again on the cobblestones.

Jodah looked back at the wreckage of the room. The primata was already on her feet, leaning on the desk, cursing as tears streamed down her cheeks. Then Jodah looked back down at the street. It was still well before dawn, and the houses were shuttered and silent.

Jodah jumped.

He landed hard, and rolled forward slightly. Voska was at his side at once, helping Jodah to his feet.

"You have to get moving."

"Where are we going?" said Jodah.

"*We* are not going anywhere," said Voska quickly, but firmly. "*You* are getting out of here as quickly a possible. Steal some clothes, smuggle yourself out. I don't know how, but you're to get out of Alsoor. I, on the other hand, am going to go find a blacksmith." He held up his chained wrists and shook them for emphasis. "Provided I can find one who does not believe too strongly in the Mother Church."

"I'm going with you," said Jodah.

"No," said Voska sharply. "Together they will spot us a mile off. I promised your mother I would protect you, and I'm going to do that, even if it means that I have to lead the church hounds away. Do you understand?"

"But . . ."

"No arguments this time," said Voska, and Jodah saw that the older man meant it. "The next big city-state is Ghed, three days to the south and west. It's a port city. I'll meet you there, at the Harp and Peacock, in five days' time. If I'm not there by the sixth day . . . "

Voska paused, and cocked his head to listen for approaching guards. The only sound was the primata's distant cursing.

"Listen to me. If I can't make it, there is a group of magicians. They are teachers and students, and they try to keep the flame of knowledge alive in these dark times. I want you to search them out. Do you understand?"

Jodah could feel tears beginning to well in the corner of his eyes again but from a new type of pain. He just nodded.

"Good," said Voska, with a smile in his voice. "You can do it, lad. You have the gift, the same as your great-great-grandfather. You get out of town, and I'll join you in Ghed. All right?"

Brother Tanar stirred at their feet. Voska looked down at the bruised and battered brother, and with a heavy foot booted him solidly across the face.

"It's a sin to strike a holy man," he said with mock-seriousness, "and it's also a crime. But you know, right now it just feels *right*."

* * * * *

The pair stayed together for a block, passing shuttered windows and closed doors. The air puffed white in front of their mouths, and from far-off there were the first sounds of the city awakening.

They came to a Y-shaped intersection. Voska went right, pointing for Jodah to take the left-hand fork. Both knew that within a few minutes Alsoorian troops, under the firm command of the church, would be swarming through the streets.

Jodah hesitated a moment and saw only Voska's retreating back. The older mage did not look back.

Jodah took the left-hand fork.

There was no immediate sound of pursuit behind them, and Jodah willed himself to slow to a walk. A running man was always guilty, or at least remembered.

Around him, the city was starting to come alive, and Jodah was heading toward one of the market districts. Already some of the merchants were stirring, opening the heavy overhanging shutters of their shops to catch the early risers. There was a yeasty smell of bread in the air, and the first pony carts passed him on the street.

The sky was lightening now to the gray dawn that seemed to forever hover in skies over Terisiare. Somewhere else in the city, those accused of crimes against the church were being led out to wooden posts set in the square and bundles of wood piled around their feet. Jodah wondered if Primata Delphine was overseeing that important ritual.

No, he decided, she would be shouting at Brother Tanar for his clumsiness and barking orders that the Alsoorian troops should find the prisoners and return them. How hard could it be to find a shackled old man and a stripling boy?

All too easy, thought Jodah, as more people began to fill up the streets. He felt simultaneously protected and vulnerable. His presence on the streets of a city in the early morning would be less questioned, but any one of the people on the streets might remember him and pass on that recollection to the guards who would come looking for him.

They would have his description, both his and Voska's. Jodah would have to steal different clothes, he realized, and probably shave off his beard and mustache. The last one was a blow against his vanity, for it had taken him a month to get even the sparse growth he had managed, but Jodah would rather be alive and unfashionable than look good for the inquisition's burning stake.

He knelt down and checked his boots. The dagger had been confiscated, of course, but the other boot still held the mirror that Voska had given him. Delphine's inquisitors had thought so little of him that they had not even searched him for additional weapons.

When Jodah looked up he saw the guards. There were a pair of them, lounging outside a vendor's booth, their pikes leaning against a wall. One of them was laconically chewing on a dried apple while the other was talking, apparently about the weather, staring at the lightening sky and squinting, looking for some hint of the sun.

They did not look like soldiers intent on a city-wide manhunt. Indeed, they did not look like they were intent on anything more than breakfast and the end of their shift. Still, Jodah could not afford to be spotted.

He rose slowly and backed up, first one step, then a second. Of course the guards were not hunting him and Voska. Where could the two fugitives go? The city-state of Alsoor was surrounded by walls ten feet thick and gates mighty enough to withstand all the other city-states combined, it was said. The primata did not have to send troops looking for her prisoners. She could wait until Voska and Jodah tried to leave the city and arrest them at those gates. Or the escapees would have to stay within the city walls and wait for inevitable recapture.

Jodah took a third step back, and one of the guards glanced up from his apple. A young man walking backward would be suspicious, and Jodah froze, and tried to look at a point five feet to the left of the guardsman. The guard surveyed the area over the dried remains of his apple, then went back to his meal as his partner still watched the sky for a break in the cloud cover.

Jodah spun on his heels and headed in the opposite direction, looking for the first alley to dodge down and hide himself in. There would be more guards in the merchant districts, he realized, as the various businesses would be accepting shipments and readying their stock for sale. The worst place for a wanted, escaped prisoner, and a would-be clothes thief. Better find somebody's newly washed clothes hanging out and do it soon, Jodah thought. Disguised, he might be able to try passing unnoticed out of the heavy gates of Alsoor.

Despite himself he looked back, long enough to see the one guardsman toss the core of his apple aside. His partner had gathered their short pikes, and apple-guard took his from his companion. Then the pair of them headed down the street.

Toward Jodah.

A thin alley appeared on his left, snaking though a collection of fishmongers' shops, and Jodah dodged down the narrow passage. He was convinced that the guardsmen had spotted him and were now following, waiting for the right moment to strike. Full flight was now the only option.

Jodah ran two steps down the alley and slammed into something hard. He rebounded, falling backward on the fog-dampened cobblestones.

The something he slammed into was covered with thick cloth, but beneath the cloth was the unrelenting firmness of granite. Jodah looked up into the cowl of a hooded figure and wondered if he had run into a statue that had been wrapped for transport.

Then the statue moved, and Jodah tried to scramble backward away from the thing. It was taller than Jodah but hunched forward. Its shoulders were at the same height with where its hidden ears should be. It's face was partially concealed beneath a long, drooping cowl, but all Jodah could see beneath the cowl were more rags wrapped around its face. It was robed in dark, grayish rags the same shade as the sky above them.

The same colors Jodah might had seen the night before, when something had tripped him in the forest.

The ragged man held a long, blue-white, thin-fingered hand out, palm down, fingers splayed. Jodah froze in place.

The ragged man brought his other hand toward what would be his face, a single elongated finger raised toward his hidden mouth. Jodah stopped breathing.

With his first hand the ragged man pointed toward the narrow entry of the alley. The two guardsmen walked past. One was walking slowly, the other still staring at the sky. Neither looked down the alley.

Jodah let himself start breathing again. He looked at the ragged figure in the alley.

In the increasing light the figure seemed to grow less imposing. He was tall but more emaciated than powerful. He seemed solid, but the morning breeze tugged at the frayed hem of his robe. His arms were too long and too thin to be human.

"Who are you?" Jodah said in a gravely whisper. He cleared his throat and asked again, "What are you? Can you help me get out of the city?"

The ragged man pointed toward the entrance of the alley, and Jodah slowly rose and crept along the wall to the main thoroughfare.

Across the street was a fishmonger's stall. Its overhanging shutter was already open, and both husband and wife were laying out the wares—salted fish, likely from the port city of Ghed. They were arguing as they laid out the dried shad, shark, haddock, and eel on low wooden tables in front of the shop.

Of greater interest to Jodah was a small wagon in front, hooked to a pair of old, worn-out horses. The wagon was half filled with barrels, three feet high. As Jodah watched, one of the other workers in the shop rolled another barrel out of the doorway and hefted it, unaided, onto the back of the wagon.

Empty barrels, then, thought Jodah. Salted fish had to come overland from Ghed, and they wanted the barrels back to use again.

Empty barrels. Heading for Ghed.

Jodah turned to ask the ragged man what he thought, but the creature was gone. Only the gray walls, the shade of his tattered clothing, remained.

There was a crash behind Jodah, from the direction of the fishmonger's shop. Something in the back of the shop had fallen, and both husband and wife bustled back to the scene of the disaster, leaving the front of the shop unguarded.

Jodah crossed the street, and looked both ways. The street was still mostly deserted, for the moment, save for a few merchants worrying about their own stock.

The young man clambered onto the wagon and pushed down on one edge of a barrel lid. The other end raised. It had not been set firmly, because it carried nothing important. The unpleasant aroma of concentrated salt and ancient fish burned in Jodah's nostrils.

He looked around, and there were no guards, no one

paying attention, no one who apparently thought he was anything more than a workman rearranging the barrels. Jodah stepped into the barrel and crouched down, re-fastening the lid as he did so.

He lost the last bit of light as he heard the returning voices of the fishmonger and his wife. His barrel rocked as similar barrels and additional crates were loaded onto the wagon. After a short while, there was the cry of the teamster, and the wagon lurched forward.

They moved agonizingly slowly at first, threading their way through the streets of Alsoor. Twice they stopped, and Jodah was sure that they were at the heavy, mechanically powered gates of the city, but each time they started up again after a brief interruption.

The third time they stopped it had to be at the gates, for there were indistinct voices beyond the barrel. One was rough and guttural—the teamster himself. The other was equally rough, but authoritarian—perhaps the captain of the gate guard.

Then there was the hollow noise of an empty barrel being thumped, sounding like a toy wooden drum, then another, then another.

A cold drop of sweat ran down Jodah's back—the guards were checking the barrels. A Jodah-filled barrel would sound very different from one containing only the odors of salted fish.

The thumping got nearer, though it was erratic. Were they checking every barrel? wondered Jodah, or were they checking only the ones that they could reach? Despite himself, he stopped breathing again.

The barrel next to him was thumped, for Jodah could feel the vibrations through the wooden sides of his hiding place. Then there was a pause, and Jodah could hear only his heart pounding. Then another thump, this one on the other side of him, and continuing thumps as they moved away from him.

At last there was the authoritarian shout, and the wagon began to lurch forward again. Only then did Jodah take a deep breath, and he had to fight to contain the gagging cough from inhaling bits of particulate salt and fish that had been within the barrel for far too long.

Jodah would get out of Alsoor. He would be able to creep away from the wagon and reach Ghed. Voska would find him, and the pair of them would take a long sea trip, hopefully to someplace where the church was not so powerful.

But the first thing Jodah would do once he got out of the barrel, he resolved, was to wash the stench of salt and fish off him, even if he had to bathe in ice-cold water to do it.

3

Alabaster Potions

*The elder nations from the time of the Brothers—Yotia,
Ancient Argive, and Korlis—were decimated by the Devastation of Argoth, and much of what is known of those times is
now lost. In their wake, small independent city-states arose
under the all-seeing eye of the Church of Tal. Each city-state
was an autonomous entity, claiming fields and farms to supply
their burgeoning population. The bulk of that population lived
tightly packed within the city walls, so that plague and disease
were more the norm than the exception.*

—**Arkol, Argivian scholar**

Voska did not show up at Ghed within the week, nor
within the week following. By the third week Jodah was
sure that something had gone wrong, and if there was no
word by the fourth he would go back to Alsoor, primata or
no, and find out what had happened.

Then the spotted plague hit Ghed, and the city was
sealed.

As plagues go, the spotted plague was more of an incon-
venience than a pestilence, but it was enough to grind the

city to a halt. One's joints swelled up, one's brow grew warm, and the skin erupted in a myriad of pin-sized red dots. It did not kill anyone, at least not directly, but it left its victims weak and unable to protect themselves from other diseases. So the city fathers closed the gates, sealed off the districts within the city, and in a few cases quarantined and burned several afflicted households.

The plague had several effects within Ghed. First, it was assumed that it was brought from without, and since there was no sign of that particular disease from Alsoor or the Giva Provinces it was settled that it had to be from far-off Almaaz. Several Almaazi traders were stoned to death in the streets before the city's noble council banished natives of that nation, for their own protection, and shipped them out. As a result, there would be few ships from Almaaz for a while.

Second, the Church of Tal experienced an influx of new members as many stragglers of the holy flock suddenly recalled their devotion and crammed the temples and cathedrals in order to ward off the disease. Of course, some more cynical citizens noted that close proximity with other plague victims might increase the chance of getting the spotted plague. Said cynical citizens also noted that, were they in the position of the church, they would deliberately spread such minor plagues to encourage the faithful. Of course, such heartfelt cynics said such things very, very quietly, and only to other cynics whom they knew well and trusted.

Thirdly, there was an influx of enlistment in the armed forces of Ghed. With the harbor and the gates closed, a lot of young men were no longer needed for the docks and fishing boats. Worse yet, the granaries were steadily dropping, and the army promised two squares a day, and that was one meal more than most young men were expecting in the first place. The army also had church healers and miracle workers who could keep the brunt of the plague at bay. And finally, most of the citizens (especially the cynical ones) agreed that once the plague was mostly passed, there would be maneuvers to grab as much farmland as possible before the harvest set in.

There was a fourth effect of the plague, and one that most of the citizens would not speak of. With the plague, there was an increase of talismans, witch-wards, plague-wheels, and curatives within the city walls. All manner of potions, infusions, and poultices were used by the populace to stem the tide of the plague. Rune-carved gems were sold that guaranteed the safety of the water or wine, and scriptures written on thin scraps of goblin skin were wrapped around the joints to ward off swelling. There were a thousand homemade remedies, bits of folklore, and invocations to forgotten gods that all promised some relief from the spotted plague.

The church took a very dim view of all this, of course, so that any such home remedies or folklore cures were carried out away from official knowledge. All the potions, poultices, periapts, and phylacteries were sold quietly and delivered in the dead of night.

There was an ancient crone in the city named Mother Dobbs who, the neighborhood legend went, had "the sight" and, for a small fee, would concoct a potion capable of curing the spotted plague, or create a charm that would protect one from being struck down with the disease. Yet those desiring the curatives might be unwilling to visit her house and set down their money. A go-between was often needed—someone who was unafraid to walk the plague-haunted, night streets of Ghed.

That someone was Jodah, for the time being. At least until the plague flag over the gate was removed and he could travel to Alsoor. At least until he found Voska again, and at least until he had saved up enough money to bribe his way on a ship out of the harbor.

Each night he would take Mother Dobbs's folk cures around to those who were too timid or prudent to fetch them for themselves. He would pick up the packages as the old woman retired for the evening and set out promptly on his rounds. Well, almost promptly. Of late he had taken to examining the potions himself, in his quarters in the attic of Mother Dobbs's house, before starting to deliver them. At first he sought to understand the cures, but later, aided by his knowledge of how spells truly functioned, he began to try to improve upon them. Up till now, no one had complained.

Jodah had three deliveries this evening, for each of which he would be paid a few coins, and sometimes an extra copper bit or two for his trouble. He always nodded in thanks and blessed the buyer for his gracious donation, but he knew that a few extra bits of copper would not aid him if the church caught him walking the streets with packages of folk curatives tucked beneath his shirt.

Each of the packages contained a gypsum bottle, wrapped in a bedding of wool, set inside a box made of thin wood and the entire package wrapped in brown paper and tied with string. Within the bottle was a viscous mixture of white, yellow-white, and gray-white fluids that, if left to themselves, would settle in three bands. For that reason Mother Dobbs instructed Jodah to shake the package hard, before passing it along, and instructed the buyer to consume the concoction as soon as he opened the package.

The first package was to be delivered to an address uncomfortably close to one of the numerous temples of Tal. It was one of the townhouses that might be owned by a successful merchant or a minor bureaucrat. Jodah had learned not to inquire too closely about who lived where in Ghed, particularly since these people tipped well.

This delivery came with instructions. He was to come to the back entrance, knock thrice, count to five, and then enter. Jodah found such arrangements irritating, as if the potions were thought to be delivered by some magical pixie as opposed to a tattered, bearded youth. Still, such buyers often tipped well for Jodah's indulgence in ritual.

Jodah took out the first package and shook it hard. He knocked three times slowly, then counted to five quickly. He threw the latch and opened the door to what seemed to be a servants' kitchen.

The room was empty, the tables and cabinets cleared in anticipation of preparing the morning meal in a handful of hours. A work counter was set in the middle of the room, and the lone door out of the kitchen was opened a crack.

There was money on the counter. Jodah knew what to do.

He set down the package on the counter and started to sweep the coins into his hand. Then he stopped. The money here was twice the normal price that Mother Dobbs usually charged. Was there a mistake, wondered Jodah, or had Dobbs raised the prices of her mixtures without telling him? Or was the rest supposed to be a tip?

He paused for only a moment, and there was a voice from the cracked door. "Is there a problem?" The voice was soft and warm and feminine.

Jodah jumped at the sound of the voice, and looking up he saw the door swing the last fraction of an inch shut.

Then he shook his head, swept the rest of the money into his hand, and left. He closed the door behind him and was three steps away when he heard the bolt solidly shut home.

Jodah looked at the kitchen entrance of the town house for a long moment then moved on to his next delivery.

The second package was to be delivered down by the docks. It was the area hit hardest by the plague, which was one of the reasons why the Almaazi traders were blamed for the outbreak. He had to detour twice to avoid patrols of the Night Watch. In normal times, these consisted of two guards in black armor with green capes, generally bored and easily bribed. These were not normal times, however, and each Night Watch patrol was accompanied by a Priest of Tal. This resulted in less boredom and less bribery, both of which disappointed the watchmen to no end.

As he moved toward the docks Jodah passed the first of the quarantine signs. If all the members of a family succumbed to the plague, the church reserved the right to mark the house as quarantined and was forbidden to make any outside contact. Those within the house were left to survive as best as they could or to die of the disease. Then the house would be burned or ritually purified for future occupation.

Jodah noted that most of the quarantined houses were in poor areas, and that there were few in areas that were loyal to the church. The wealthy could afford the priests' blessing, and if everyone in the house was stricken, they could simply hire more servants.

It did not surprise him that the address he was given was marked with a quarantine letter, the official document stamped with the double sunburst of the Church of

Tal. In the darkness the symbol looked like a blood-red set of eyes.

Jodah walked past the address, then doubled back. There was no one on the street, not even the occasional drunk. The priests had little love of the poor, so patrols were few and infrequent.

He saw a flicker of motion out of the corner of his eye, and Jodah turned. There was nothing there, but the hairs on the back of his neck rose. Since his escape from Alsoor, he half-expected his ragged guardian angel to reappear at any moment, but for the past few weeks everything had been quiet. Was the figure that he had seen in Alsoor (and had seen in the forest, he was now convinced) more than just a chance encounter? He had looked for the ragged man among the beggars and cripples of Ghed but had seen nothing that resembled him.

Jodah leaned up against the wall across from the address and waited for a full five minutes, but the figure that had flickered across the corner of his vision did not reappear, if it had existed at all. Then he crossed, removed the package, shook it, and quietly knocked on the door.

The door opened immediately about a foot. A warm blast of air tumbled out and wrapped Jodah within a soft, enticing fog. Jodah fought the urge to inhale the contagious air of a plague house. Slender, palsied hands, shaking from fever, appeared out of the darkness and grasped the package, trying to tug it weakly from Jodah's grasp.

"Payment first," said Jodah, his voice low.

One hand let go and retreated into the darkness, then returned with a pair of coins.

"That's only half," said Jodah, fighting the building urge to inhale and wanting to be away from the door when he did.

"Please," said the voice, cracking wetly like a boil breaking open, "my boy, he's nearly dead. He won't live through the night without this."

"That's only half," said Jodah again.

"I've nothing else," said the wet, fluid voice. "When he's better, we can get the rest. Please."

Jodah thought for a moment. The take from the first house would cover both that package and this and leave him a handsome tip as well. But what if Mother Dobbs had expected more money from the first house? Then it would be Mother Dobbs's fault for not telling him to charge the rich more.

Jodah took the coins, and the package disappeared within the darkness of the plague house. He turned away and took three large steps before allowing himself to inhale.

Turning away, Jodah again caught a fleeting glimpse of something darting around the corner, something that was watching him, something that pulled back as he approached. He walked toward the corner, but when he reached it, whatever it was that was watching had disappeared.

The last drop was a merchant's shop, one that Jodah had visited time and again. Jodah was sure the merchant was not using the potions herself but rather selling them again, at inflated prices, to other victims and potential victims. Jodah would find the money in a wood box behind the main dwelling, near the midden, and leave the package in the box.

However, now he was sure he was being followed, but he did not know if his pursuer knew that he knew. It could not be the Night Watch—they blundered down the streets and alleys as if they owned the city. A cutpurse?

There were better targets elsewhere, even in these near-empty streets. A spy for the church? Mostly likely, Jodah decided. Some concerned citizen, probably, who was following him, ready to report any violation of the law to the church: like visiting a plague house.

Like carrying forbidden magics.

Jodah lengthened his pace, and now he heard footsteps as well behind him. Soft footfalls, like feet in slippers, taking two steps to his one, struggling to keep up.

He abandoned his intention of making the third drop, instead placing the package within his shirt. Jodah took a right at the next corner and then a right again. The footsteps kept up with him. He paused at an alleyway, then dodged down it, confident that his pursuer was behind him.

The alleyway was narrow and descended almost immediately down a flight of stone steps, their centers worn by the passage of many feet so that it looked as if the blocks themselves had melted. Archways littered both sides of the alley, with doors set deeply back from the stairs. Early upon his arrival in Ghed, Jodah had slept in such doorways. Now he pressed himself against a shadowed archway and awaited his pursuer.

He did not have long to wait. There was a long shadow from the entrance of the alley, that slowly moved toward him. The shadow diminished as it neared, until it was smaller than he was. Jodah nodded to himself—at least it was too short to be his ragged guardian angel. Slowly and carefully, Jodah's pursuer walked right by him.

Jodah lunged out of the doorway and slammed into the figure with his shoulder, hard. It was his intention to knock his unknown pursuer to the ground, then hold him down until Jodah found out why he was being followed.

That was his intention, but his pursuer was too quick. The young man caught a portion of the figure's cloak, and then his pursuer wheeled, dropping neatly out of the way. Jodah's own momentum threw him forward and down a few stone steps. He shouted as he tumbled and struggled to regain his balance. He finally slammed against the far wall and felt something crack. A warm wetness dribbled out of the package held against his side, staining his shirt.

He wheeled in place, but his would-be target had not moved from the spot. Instead, his pursuer stood in the darkness, waiting for Jodah's next move.

Jodah shook the stars from the corners of his eyes and cleared his mind. He thought of his homeland and pulled from those thoughts the energies to power his magic. He had been practicing in Mother Dobbs's windowless attic, and could now pull the power of the land and think of his spell at the same time. He reached into the entranceway of his mental manor house and pulled forth the spell.

And was too slow. As he readied the spell the very ground seemed to slip away from him. It was as if the alley was a long rug, and his pursuer had grasped one end of it and shook it up and down, sending a quick series of waves down its length. Jodah's eyes told him that the alley was not moving, but his stomach heaved and pitched from the feeling that he was being violently battered.

All thoughts of his own spell were lost at that moment. Jodah shouted and gripped the sides of a door archway in a desperate attempt to stay upright. Only slowly did the world stop spinning around him.

The shadowy figure took two steps forward and held a hand, palm-up, between the two of them. A small blue light flashed in the cup of that palm, illuminating them both.

Jodah saw a young, female face, framed by dark hair that was cut in bangs. The skin was smooth, the features pleasing, and if Jodah were somewhere else he would have thought to compliment the young woman, particularly if she was pursuing him. However, at the moment the woman's soft lips were pulled back in a snarl, and her gentle brows were knotted in fury.

"Who in Mishra's name are you?" she snapped. "What do you think you're doing?"

"Doing?" said Jodah. The world still rocked around him, and it was the best reply he could manage.

"The potions, you idiot child," said the young woman. "What do you think you're doing with those potions?"

Jodah blinked. "I just run deliveries. Don't know anything about . . . "

Then the young woman balled one hand into a fist (the one without the blue flame) and stomped her foot on the paving stones. "Don't play the fool with me, child. We don't have time for it."

"I don't know what you're talking about," managed Jodah, wondering if he could talk and call on his magical energies at the same time.

"Do you know what is in one of Mother Dobbs's 'potions'?" she said, her voice dripping with venom. Jodah flinched at the mention of the name, and she continued. "Yes, I know who you work for. I purchased one directly from the old woman a few days ago."

Jodah shrugged, and she continued. "Mare's milk, mineral oils, and the yolk of an egg. It could clear out your lower track, but that's all. But do you know what the potions you deliver do?"

Jodah's back stiffened, and a line of sweat dripped down his spine. He had been found out.

"There's an odd difference between the potions the old woman sells and the ones that are delivered in the dead of night. The ones you happen to deliver *really work*. They cure the spotted plague, or whatever is afflicting the drinker!"

Jodah mentally cursed himself, but it had seemed so obvious to try and help Mother Dobbs' potions with a little magic of his own. He had hoped to just make them drinkable. He had never thought the difference would be so incredible or so obvious.

The woman was talking again. "And if I can figure this out, you can bet the *church* can figure it out." Again she made the foot-stomping motion. "Who taught you to cast magic?"

Jodah blinked, suddenly realizing that he was being asked a non-rhetorical question. "Pardon?" he managed.

The pursuer leaned close, and the light crackled in her palm. To Jodah it no longer looked like a flame but rather like a bit of a lightning bolt. "Spells. Who. Taught. You?" Her face was as stern and cold as a statue's.

Jodah leaned back "I am Jodah of Giva Province. My master was Voska . . ."

Now it was the woman's turn to be surprised. The dark eyebrows raised and disappeared beneath the bangs. "Voska? Where is he?"

"I don't know," said Jodah.

"Feldon's Cane and Crutches!" she snapped, "where *is* he?"

"I don't know!" said Jodah, realizing that he was shouting now. He lowered his voice but did not soften his tone. "We were captured by the church in Alsoor and escaped. We split up. He was supposed to meet me here. He hasn't shown."

"Alsoor," she said, bitterly. Then she turned slightly

and looked back toward the alleyway entrance.

When she turned back, her face had changed—still serious but not as angry.

"We have company. All your shouting, no doubt. Stay put, I'll lead them off. I'll contact you later."

With that the blue flame was extinguished, and the woman became a cloak-shaped shadow again. She waved her palm upward toward Jodah's face, and Jodah caught a bright flash of blue light at the corners of his eyes.

Then she was gone, almost flying down the broad steps of the alleyway.

Jodah tried to stand and follow her but found that he could not. Whatever spell she had worked, it had robbed him of his ability to stay upright. He felt as if he was in the grips of a three-day binge without even the benefit of tasting the alcohol. Jodah's stomach tried to climb up his windpipe, and he knew he would be looking at his evening meal if he moved too quickly. It seemed to be a localized version of whatever had knocked him off his feet earlier. Extremely localized and focused entirely on him.

Defeated, Jodah cured up in the doorway, hoping the world would stop spinning again soon enough.

That's when he heard the feet—heavy boots on the paving stones. He did not have to look up to know that the Night Watch was coming down the alley. He could not do anything about it, even if he wanted.

The voices of the watch drifted up toward him like bubbles.

"What's this one?" said one of the guards.

"Drunk," said the other, "or maybe drugged."

"No," said a third voice, "something else." This voice was as sibilant as a snake's, and Jodah shuddered as the sound of it.

There was a hissing noise. No, thought Jodah. Sniffing. The one with the third voice was sniffing the air. Had he thrown up already and not realized it?

Finally the third voice said, "Sorcery. There were spells here. This way."

The first voice spoke up. "What about this one?"

"Leave him," said the hissing one. "The church cares naught for victims. Only for sinners."

They were gone, the noise of their boots clattering down the alleyway.

A small eternity passed. Nothing else thundered through, screamed at him, or otherwise inverted his world. Jodah concentrated on long, deep breaths, pulling the cool night air into his lungs. Finally he dug out the mirror from his right boot.

Even in the minimal light of the alley he looked horrible. His face was pale and sweaty. His beard and mustache, filling out nicely, now looked like a black square framing cracked lips and a dry mouth.

Jodah stared into the mirror until his face regained something akin to a natural color. Then he slowly pulled himself up and staggered back toward Mother Dobbs's.

The church was there ahead of him. There were guardsmen in the black and green uniforms holding back the crowd as two priests escorted the old crone out of her home. Trapped between the two heavy priests, Mother Dobbs looked confused, unable to understand why the church had come for her now. She always made it to services, she tried to explain. Everyone knew about her little folk medicines. Why did they come for her now?

Toward the back of the crowd, Jodah knew. The church left her alone as long as they knew she was a fraud, a seller of useless nostrums to a gullible public. The moment the potions really started to cure people . . .

Thanks to him, he realized. Thanks to his own meddling.

The priests helped Mother Dobbs into a donkey cart. Some of the people watching jeered at Mother Dobbs. Others just looked stricken, as if one of their favorite pets had been dragged away. Or, more likely as if her customers would be the next occupants of the donkey cart. One of the priests cracked a whip, and the mule lurched forward, carrying off the confused old woman.

The other priest nailed a quarantine sign on the front of the door, emblazoned with the double sunburst of the Church of Tal—the seal was fresh and ran like wet blood. Then he followed the cart, intoning the praises and wisdom of the holy church.

Jodah watched them go. Surely, he thought, they would let her go. They would find out she had no wizardry in her. That her potions and nostrums were fakes. The magic-sniffer would get nothing out of her but a bad headache from all the incense she surrounded herself with. They would have to let her go after a few days. Wouldn't they?

Jodah realized that once they knew that Mother Dobbs was harmless, they would go looking for the real wizard in the area. Her suppliers. Her friends.

Her delivery boy.

Jodah looked at the blood-red seal of the church and bit his lower lip. The next morning, under an assumed name, he enlisted in the Ghed Army, and within the week, when the plague flag was finally pulled down, he was marching with a military unit north, toward Alsoor.

4

Spoils of War

The city-states of the Dark were autonomous, independent entities, each one vying for power against the others. There were twelve major city states and a host of minor ones throughout the period of the Dark. All of them maintained their own armies, often at great expense. Early historians state that this was to fight the goblins, but in actuality most of their battles were against other city-states. The church, more concerned with spiritual matters and willing to see the individual city-states spend their time battling each other to their own detriment, turned a blind eye to the continual infighting, until it was too late.

—*Arkol, Argivian scholar*

A month later, Jodah staggered, alone, through the wreckage of a forgotten and abandoned city. Occasionally he would pause, and cock an ear to the wind, listening for pursuit, then would press on again, limping through the weed-choked streets of the city. His armor and weapons were gone, as was all of his company.

The city was on no map that Ghed had, and Jodah wondered briefly what its name had been. Perhaps it dated back to the time of the Brothers' War. Perhaps it was some rival of Alsoor or Ghed that was defeated in combat, or had its trade routes choked off, or was just abandoned to the cold.

Jodah shook his head. Most of the buildings were still standing, which was unlikely in the case of a war. Much of the furnishings were still in the houses, though they had rotted to uselessness. Something had swept through here—some magical or a disease or a combination of the two—and removed every living thing.

Not every living thing. There was a flurry of beating wings above him. Jodah ducked instinctively, and a flock of pigeons banked overhead, disappearing behind the roof of one of the taller buildings. There were no people, or dogs, or horses, but there were birds. At least he wouldn't have to worry about starving. Provided he could catch them.

Provided that he avoided the goblins, of course. If not for them, Ghed could have taken Alsoor itself, and he could have found Voska.

* * * * *

The war did not start out as a war, at least not to the participants. With the lifting of the plague warning in Ghed a week after Jodah joined up, and with a large number of men under arms, the city-state's aristocrats had determined that the army should provide a show of force to the north.

"Of course," Togath would note, privately over the fire, "this also gets a large number of men foraging off the land as opposed to suckling at the city's granaries."

Togath was twenty years older than most of the other men in the unit and as such had been made corporal. He was also an affirmed cynic, becoming more cynical with every mile they put between themselves and Ghed.

Togath also pointed out that most of their maneuvers were through lands where the farmers were unsure about whether to sell their upcoming harvest to Ghed or Alsoor. A large military force in said farmers' back yards might tip the balance one way or the other.

Jodah nodded but said nothing, noting that Togath's insightful comments on Ghed intentions and tactics were never voiced when they were around the upper ranks.

For the first week or so there was a lot of marching, interrupted only by relatively good eating provided by the local farmers who hoped that the army would eat and move on.

The army was relatively good to Jodah. His unit was made up of general outsiders—natives of the southern coast and refugees from Giva province and other northern regions. It was sprinkled with a few raw recruits filled with excitement and empty of knowledge, and leavened with what professional soldiers could be dragooned into serving as officers.

The food was good—fresh breads and meat-laden stews made with supplies "donated" by loyal farmers, fish from the rivers, and game from the forests. Jodah himself brought down a deer still in its winter coat, a rarity this late in the year, and they made jerky of the venison left over.

Discipline was present, but minimal, as long as they put on a good show in the black lacquered armor and green capes at infrequent parade marches. They drilled and marched and drilled some more, then ate.

And, best from Jodah's viewpoint, was the total lack of priests in the army. While the church was apparently concerned about the morale and morals of the men within the city-state, that concern ended as soon as they started marching around and sleeping under the cold starless skies.

"It would seem like they were playing favorites," said Togath, "if they went out with one army and not another."

"Why not go out with all the armies?" asked one of the young hotspurs.

"Because then," Togath said with a deep frown, "they might get blood on their nice clean robes when we start fighting. And it is a when, not an if. It's only a matter of time. Nobody builds an army without intending to use it."

* * * * *

Jodah slowed his painful walk, limping from one side of the street to the other. His wounded leg was on fire now, and he tried to put as little weight on it as possible. If he could find some mare's milk, an egg, and some mineral oil, he might be able to whip up something that could aid him, he thought. Or at least take his mind off the pain.

Many of the roofs of the buildings were sagging from rot, and in several places had caved in entirely, but there were enough still standing to see that it had been a serviceable city. Save that its inhabitants just left one morning, never to tell anyone of its existence.

There was something else odd about the city that Jodah could not put his finger on immediately. Then it came to him—the city had no walls. He had seen small communities, like his old family manor, which did not have any walls, but something this large, surviving without

71

protective stone between it and the outside, was beyond his comprehension.

Or not so strange. There was nothing in the city now. So the lack of walls might have been the reason they abandoned it.

A weird feeling crawled up Jodah's spine. He had become separated from the other survivors in the fog and soon afterward found the first buildings of the city. The buildings loomed in the mist like great, gray shadows, resolving themselves only as Jodah drew nearer. First one, then another, then a third, and then several aligning themselves in the fashion of a street. Then patches of paving stones appeared among the grass and hard-worn dirt.

Side streets appeared and arched away on both sides. Jodah realized that the city was laid out like a circle, with the wide main streets leading to something at its center.

Jodah stayed to one side of the street now, taking comfort in the solidity of the buildings, and limped toward the city's heart.

* * * * *

Indeed, Togath was right, for while the Ghed army was drilling, a similar force in Alsoor was also being readied. The presence of a major Ghed force was a threat to Alsoor, even though its walls were ten feet thick and it boasted mighty gates that (some said) dated back to the time of the Brothers. The idea that some of the farm communities along the river might send their harvest south rather than north to Alsoor was intolerable, so the Alsoorians marshaled their own force, stiffened with a healthy dose of elven mercenaries from the Shattered Islands.

Having collected this group, resplendent in their purple and white, the rulers of Alsoor sent their army on maneuvers as well.

It was only a matter of time before the two forces collided. The spark that lit the flames of war was set over a few barrels of wine. Jodah heard the tale later from Fendah, a former ropemaker from the south who was a fertile source of the military grapevine.

A unit of Ghed cavalry was scouting and scavenging and came upon a winery. The workers were busy loading several casks of the recent vintage into a wagon. The lieutenant asked where they were shipping the casks. The vintner explained that there was an encampment of Alsoorians nearby and that he was sending the wine, with his compliments, to their commanding officer.

The cavalry lieutenant explained that the wine would better be served on the tables of the Ghed forces. The vintner, faced with a dozen armed men on horseback, quickly agreed and offered to deliver an equal amount to the Ghed command, with his compliments.

It would have been a simple matter of military procurement, had not a unit of Alsoorian horsemen ridden up, resplendent on their white horses. This unit was to provide an escort for the vintner's wares, their commander explained loudly, since it was known that there were Ghed robbers in the area.

Harsh words were exchanged, and then blows. Swords were drawn and blood and wine spilled on the vintner's doorstep. The end result was that the Alsoorian horsemen were put to full retreat, while the Ghed forces regrouped back at their base, spreading word of the Alsoorian invasion of Ghed-loyal farms.

Within the day, Jodah, Togath, Fendah, and the rest of

the unit were marching northward, seeking to block off an Alsoorian retreat at the Great Bridge where the main route between the two cities crossed the Alamar River.

The going was slow and unpleasant. The weather had turned, and the skies unleashed a merciless pounding rain, cold and so hard that it would strike the ground and rebound, splashing those marching through it from below as well as above. The units quickly were strung out as they pressed forward, and some disappeared, never to be heard from again. Fendah said he understood that those units had been caught by Alsoorian outriders or nether-spawned creatures summoned by foul wizards who had supposedly allied with Alsoor.

Jodah bit back his tongue at the rumor. First, his time in Alsoor showed them to have no more interest in magic than Ghed. And second, the idea that magic was used primarily to summon evil and destructive creatures rubbed him raw. This was the type of ignorance that the church encouraged and fed on, that allowed the inquisition to proceed without impediment. Still, it was not to Jodah's advantage to admit that he had been in Alsoor recently nor to confess to a sympathy to magicians, and as such he remained silent.

Togath took up the challenge of Fendah's rumors, however, and pointed out that during every war rumors had circulated about the opposite side consorting with demons, from eldritch followers of Urza or Mishra, to the monstrous Eaters of the Dead that scavenged the battle-fields, looking for the wounded and crippled to feast upon. Ever pragmatic, Togath believed that the missing units had gone rogue and would eventually turn up as merce-naries in the employ of some petty noble or another within a fortnight.

Jodah concentrated merely on placing one foot in front of the other. He considered fading into the driving rain like the lost units but decided against it. His ultimate goal was Alsoor, and they were already heading that way. Besides, Fendah might be right about the Alsoorian outriders.

In the end, they lost the race. Enough of the fleeing Alsoorian units reached the bridge in order to secure it, and they brought up fresh reinforcements from their side of the river. The Ghed units ahead of Jodah's force did catch their foes by surprise, but the Alsoorians, after a brief battle, conducted an ordered retreat across the huge stone bridge and dug in. By the time Jodah's unit arrived a grave pit had been dug, and the fallen from that first battle had already been burned, and armed pickets had been constructed on both sides of the bridge.

Jodah's unit rested for the night, footsore, exhausted, and disappointed. Fendah spent the early part of the evening away from their bivouac, and when he returned, he was spitting nails. The rumor mill said that command knew about a ford several days' travel up the Alamar. With the morning sun they would be ordered to march there and hold it against the Alsoor forces.

Fendah was wrong. It was two hours before sunrise that the order came down, and they were rousted from their blankets and told to prepare for the march. When the sky finally lightened enough to be considered sunrise, they were already five miles up the river. The rain, which had slackened to a mere drizzle through the night, now greeted them anew with a cold torrent that hid everything beyond a few feet from view.

Jodah kept his head down and concentrated on putting one foot in front of the other.

* * * * *

As he neared the center of the city, Jodah heard the splashing of water, like a series of waterfalls. The fog was clearing now, and he could see both sides of the street. Above, the sky was a white dome.

The roads converged at the city's heart in a great circle, a circus of hard, plate-sized paving stones. Grass had sprouted in the cracks between the stones, and numerous pigeons were strutting around, picking at the seeds and blades of grass. But the heart of the city was dominated by a fountain.

It was twice as tall as Jodah, with a wide basin and a lip that extended back two feet over the fountain's inner edge. Rising from the center of the fountain was a pedestal, and mounted atop the pedestal were four lion heads, one for each of the cardinal directions. Each of the lion heads issued a healthy spout of water that sprayed out, almost reaching the overhanging edge of the basin's rim.

Jodah approached the fountain, and the pigeons took note of him. They exploded in a burst of wings, only to swoop down again on the far side of the circus and resume their seed-picking activities.

Jodah looked over the wide rim. The water looked mountain-fresh spewing from the lion's mouth, but the basin was filled with a thick growth of algae. The bottom of the basin had filled with muck, and greasy-looking plants jutted from the water, spreading wide, foul-smelling leaves. The foaming waters of the fountain collected near these stalks in strings of bubbles, and several dark shapes that Jodah chose not to identify floated in the water.

Jodah looked around. There was motion to his right. He started and turned, and there was a figure at the edge of the circus, just where the fog began to thicken again. At first he thought it another soldier, either from Ghed or Alsoor. The figure was dressed in dark robes and had a hunched profile, its shoulders even with its ears.

Jodah slowly turned fully toward the figure, fearful that this vision would evaporate if he moved too quickly. It had to be his dark guardian angel, the ragged man. Once was coincidence, twice was fate, Voska had once said. Thrice was a lead-pipe cinch.

Jodah took a step toward the ragged figure, and it glided smoothly to one side, into one of the buildings, as if it was a ghost. Jodah shouted and started limping toward the building, a hundred feet away.

That was when he heard the rough laughter of the goblins coming into the central plaza.

* * * * *

On the fourth day north their company captured a spy. An Alsoorian soldier caught on the wrong side of the river was discovered sneaking around the encampment, apparently trying to gather information. He was quickly put under a light guard in one of the supply tents. Fendah broke the news over mess that evening.

Togath noted that if the spy was in the supply tent, then he had better accommodations than they had. For effect, he wrung out his blanket and slapped it against a tree. The rain had finally slackened, but it had left behind a thin, wispy mist that covered the land, and seeped into every item of clothing the soldiers had.

In the morning they would be on the march. Fendah

figured that they would reach the ford ahead of the Alsoorians. The spy would be shipped back to Ghed, pumped for information, and then eventually turned over to the church. By that time, the war would be over.

Jodah thought the spy was getting the better end of the deal in this war, but he said nothing. That evening, after the others had bedded down, he slipped out of the encampment and headed for the supply tents.

The Alsoorian must not have been an important spy, for they left a young boy to guard him. The youth was more slender than Jodah and had to be at least four years his junior. He looked like a child playing soldier in his oversized greaves and tunic, clutching onto a pike that towered over him. Yet there was something in his manner, something in the way that he drew himself up as Jodah approached, that said this one, despite his age, had seen more fighting than Jodah, Fendah, and Togath combined.

"I'd like to see the prisoner," said Jodah, returning the youth's salute.

"Do you have permission?" said the youth. His voice was still childlike, not even cracking with the first hints of maturity, but was filled with iron.

"No, but I can get it if need be," said Jodah. Half a lie was better than none, he reasoned. Still, it did not feel comfortable lying to a child.

"I'm not supposed to let the prisoner speak with anyone unobserved," said the youth.

Jodah cocked an ear at the boy's thick accent and said, "Northerner?"

The younger boy almost blushed, but nodded.

Jodah said, "I'm from Giva province."

The younger boy allowed himself a small smile. "I'm from Thorn. I've heard of Giva."

"Then you know that men of Giva are honorable and honest." Jodah paused for a moment. "For the most part, at least. I need to ask the prisoner a question or two."

"I am not supposed to let the prisoner speak with anyone unobserved," repeated the child.

"Then come and observe," said Jodah.

The boy hesitated for a moment, then nodded. "All right. This way."

The makeshift holding area was a clear spot in the tent. Casks and bags had been pushed aside, and a heavy wooden spike had been driven into the center of the cleared area. A short chain, no more than eight links, had been fastened to the spike with the other end attached to the prisoner's manacles, so that he was forced to stand hunched over, squat, or lie down.

The prisoner was lying down, and Jodah could see why they felt comfortable leaving a boy to guard him. The spy was emaciated to start with and badly beaten during his capture. His face was a mass of bruises, and one eye was totally shut from the swelling. Blood crusted on both sides of the prisoner's mouth, and his once-white tunic was dirty and bloody.

To Jodah it looked as if the prisoner had not arrived in camp to steal information but more likely to steal bread. The prisoner looked up with his one good eye and croaked, "Whad now?"

"Just a question or two," said Jodah. "You are from Alsoor?"

The prisoner gave a chortle that threatened to become a body-wracking cough. At length he said, "Sure. Why not?"

"You are from Alsoor," repeated Jodah.

"Yeah," said the prisoner through swollen lips, "whad about it?"

"I need to know about a man named Voska," said Jodah.

"Watah," said the prisoner in a throaty whisper.

"No, Voska," said Jodah.

"No, I need some watah," said the prisoner. "In the barrel, over there."

Jodah looked at the young guard and raised his eyebrows in a question. The boy nodded and went to the barrel, pulling out a broad-bowled ladle. He took it to the prisoner and tipped it slightly. The prisoner cradled the bowl of the ladle in his manacled hands and drank deeply.

"Voska," prompted Jodah again.

The prisoner coughed, and it was a wet, throaty cough this time. "Never heard of him," he said. He smacked his lips, moistening them with his tongue. "Hold on. This Voska was a sorcerer?"

"A spellcaster, yes," said Jodah. The young guard had replaced the ladle in the water bucket and was now looking intently at Jodah.

"Church has him," said the prisoner. "Yeah, that's where I heard the name. Supposedly he was caught performing sorcery. Raising spirits, sacrificing farm animals, that sort of thing. But instead of just killing him, they've got him locked up in Alsoor. Inquisition business."

"Is he still there?" asked Jodah, aware of the anticipation in his voice.

"Dunno," said the prisoner, looking up with one good eye. "You'd have to ask the churchmen about that."

Jodah thought about it a moment, then turned away.

"Hey," said the prisoner, "I told you what you wanted. You gotta tell me one."

"What do you need to know?" asked Jodah.

"I heard a rumor," said the prisoner, "you Ghed-heads

have black wizards working for you. You've raised a nasty spirit of your own, an Eater of the Dead. Is that true?"

"No," lied Jodah calmly, "we have *three* of them, all lusting for Alsoorian blood."

Before the prisoner could react to the statement, Jodah turned and walked out of the tent. A young voice called from behind him. The boy-guard came up, his brow a single dark line over his eyes.

"Who is this Voska?"

Jodah didn't want to lie to the boy but didn't want the youngster to have unanswered questions, questions that he might seek answers to elsewhere. "He's a wizard," Jodah said simply.

"I heard. What is he to you?" said the boy, and the iron was back in his voice.

Jodah took a deep breath and plunged fully into the untruth. "I lost my family thanks to this Voska. I have my own reason to reach Alsoor, you see. I have a personal reason to find this wizard."

The boy looked at the ground and spat. "It's such a damned waste," he said.

"Wizards?" said Jodah.

"Fighting," said the lad. "I mean fighting between the cities. They're all human, all real people with real lives. Meanwhile the goblin raids are getting worse and worse."

Jodah nodded. "You'd think with all the people coming south the church and the city-states would realize where the true threat lies."

The boy snorted. "I hope I live to see that day."

"I hope we both live to that day," said Jodah.

The boy smiled and held out a hand. "Tivadar," he said.

Jodah took the small, strong hand and gave his assumed name and his unit and asked the lad to keep the matter of his inquiry quiet. Then Jodah left Tivadar the child-guard behind and headed back to his unit's encampment.

* * * * *

The goblins entered the center square, singing lustily. One of their numbers shouted for the others to pipe down, or he would do some piping himself on their flat heads.

"Yaheard dat?" said the one shouting for quiet. His voice carried even over the thundering roar of the fountain.

"Yahear what?" said one of the others.

"Yaheard somebuddy shout?" said the first one.

"Yah, you!" came another rough voice. "Dere's nobuddy here! Softskins left this place yearzago!"

"But dey left dere stuff," came another voice, this one snuffling and nasal, "I never knew dey'd ever leave dere stuff!"

"Dat's bad," said the first voice. "Dat means dere comin back soon."

"We'll be ready for 'em" shouted another, which kicked off another round of shouts, songs, and rude threats.

Beneath the overhanging lip of the fountain, Jodah clung to the inside wall of the basin. The turgid water was higher than his chin, and he had to tip his head back in order to breath. Muck seemed to crawl over his legs and ankles, and the ice-cold water tingled against his flesh. He was already losing the sensation in his toes, and considering what might be in the water, that was for the best.

The one who's voice Jodah heard first, the apparent leader, was speaking again.

"Yeah, yeah," he bellowed, "we'll be ready for 'em, just like dah last time!" And there were more cheers.

Beneath the rim, Jodah hoped that they would move on, camp in some other part of the city or just move away from here. The cold, clammy feeling was creeping up his legs as the water stole the warmth from him. His wounded leg, which had earlier seemed to be on fire, now felt as if it had daggers made of ice jammed into the wound. The cold reached his loins and stomach. He wondered if he was turning blue. He tried to shift slightly from his crouch but was rewarded with a painful set of needles along both legs.

He shifted again, then halted entirely, stopping himself from even breathing. There was a shadow on the water in front of him. Something was directly above him, sitting on the rim itself. The shadow wavered in the churning waters of the fountain, but he was sure that it had mule-shaped ears on either side of its pointed head and a heavy, underslung jaw.

"Whaddaya doing?" came a voice from nearby.

"Thursty," said the shadow about Jodah. "I wanna drink." And with that the goblin muzzle leaned down directly over Jodah's hiding place to sip from the fountain.

Jodah took a deep breath, and slid beneath the greenish water, hoping he could hold his breath until the goblin was done.

* * * * *

The united armed forces of Ghed reached the ford first and dispersed a token garrison left by the Alsoorians, a garrison that had been unaware of the state of war between the two city states until the first cavalry units thundered across the shallow crossing, screaming and putting those who fled before them to the sword.

The bulk of the army crossed without incident and encamped on the far side, in Alsoorian territory. Scouts reported that the main body of Alsoor's forces was two days away. Their choices were to dig in on the soft earth surrounding the ford or to try to seek out the Alsoorians in the surrounding hills.

Jodah's feet felt as if they were as thick as leather boots, and his legs felt like lead. So naturally the decision was to meet the Alsoorians in the hills, and they marched again, into the fog-shrouded hills

On the morning of the second day, an outrider brought news out of the fog. The Alsoorians were just south, in the next valley over. They were still in marching formation. They had no outriders of their own, and as such were unaware that the Ghed forces had beaten them to the ford. They were vulnerable to an ambush.

The Ghed forces, aided by a thick blanket of morning fog, would top the low line of hills that framed the Alsoorian line of march. The commanders deployed their heavy cavalry to the left flank to ride down on the enemy's rear echelon, while the rest of the Ghed army engaged the Alsoorians along the length of the line of march. At least that was Fendah's idea of what was happening, and for once Togath had no response.

Jodah knew little of the full plans of the Ghed commanders. All he saw was a blanket of white on all sides, through which moved the shadowy forms of other Ghed foot soldiers. They were moving shoulder to shoulder up the hill. Togath was on one side, Fendah on the other. Beyond them were other members of their unit, becoming misty and indistinct in the fog, grayer and grayer until they vanished entirely in a field of white

They ambled in a rough line to the top of a hillock,

some of the ragged forms reaching the crest before others. Just as Jodah reached the top there was a shout from his right and the distant blast of a trumpet. Then everyone on his right and left was shouting and running down the opposite side of the hill, charging full tilt into the thicker fog beyond that hid the Alsoorians.

For most of the descent there was nothing, only other Ghed soldiers running alongside Jodah through the fog. Then shapes loomed up ahead of them. The shapes clarified into desperate Aloosrian foot soldiers trying to pull themselves into formations capable of receiving the Ghed charge. Pikemen still tried to form protective squares as the first attackers were already among them. Then there was just pandemonium on all sides as the armies met.

Jodah had his sword out in front of him, and he ran with the rest. He paused only briefly whenever a shape rose in front of him. If it wore the black and green of Ghed, it was a friend. He hoped that the other fog shape would recognize they were on the same side. If it wore any other colors, Jodah waved his sword in front of him, hoping to force any opponent back or at least convince his foe to go attack someone else.

Shadows and silhouettes danced all around. Ahead of him the mist cleared enough to show a figure wearing enemy colors, purple and white. The enemy raised its blade over its head and charged forward. Jodah swung his blade around in a long, lazy arc.

Jodah's blade struck something hard, and when he pulled it back it was coated with blood. The figure had charged past him and was swallowed again by the fog. The idea that it was someone else's blood on the blade trickled dully into his brain as another shape, also not wearing black and green, lunged into view, brandishing a spear.

Jodah ducked under the thrust point of the spear and came up hard with his sword. His arm tensed under the jolt as his blade bit deep into the attacker, and then the spear wielder was gone as well.

About this time Jodah stopped thinking, at least in terms of who was doing what to whom. He was concentrating on only hitting that which was not black and green and avoiding being hit himself. A rain of javelins came from somewhere and fell among his company, bringing down several of his fellow troops. One stuck dully into the soft ground next to his left foot. Jodah stared at it a moment, then was caught up as another opponent lunged at him.

It took a few moments for Jodah to realize that he was no longer fighting other humans. Rather, these were more slender, whitish creatures with elongated faces and scaled armor shaped like oak leaves. Elves. They were fighting elves, and he remembered Fendah's story about the hiring of mercenaries from the Shattered Isles—elven mercenaries, who delighted in battling against the humans who broke their civilization centuries before.

Jodah saw Fendah, briefly, on the ground, the ropemaker's head lying there, a wide smile across his face, his body nowhere to be seen. Something soft and snakelike uncoiled in the pit of Jodah's belly, and for the first time he smelled the scent of human blood on the wet, fogbound grass.

There was another opponent and another, and Jodah fought like an automaton, warding off the worst of the blows. Something, a dagger or a short, thin blade rattled across his lamellar armor, but there was no sign of his assailant. There were shouts of victory and death all around him, but he had no idea which side they belonged to.

There were shouts to his left, and Jodah assumed that was the Ghed heavy cavalry finally smashing its way up the length of the enemy line. A horseman in Ghed armor almost rode him down, and Jodah fell backward over a pile of bodies, human and elven. When he arose, his armor was coated in slime and mud.

More shouts, and these sounded like shouts of victory. There were more people in the fog wearing armor like his, so he assumed they had won. The slender elves and the humans in bloodied white and muddied purple were in full flight now, ceding them the battlefield.

That was when the goblins attacked.

Again, Jodah was not aware of what had happened at first, only that the shouts of triumph had died and were replaced by panicked screams. There were drums in the distance, great kettle drums not used by human armies. The elves and men of Alsoor were no longer fleeing them but were now running toward them and past them. Out of the misty fog behind the fleeing forces appeared a new set of shadows—bunched together so thick that they seemed to be a single creature—spreading from the right edge of Jodah's vision to the left.

Goblins appeared out of the mists, dressed in ragged armor looted from raids on other human encampments or abandoned battlefields. Most were the green-skinned beasts that Voska had fought, but among them there were ones whose flesh was bone-white. These creatures fought like madmen with swords clenched tightly in each hand, not caring for their own injuries. Some of the goblins were sinewy and thin, like parodies of the elves that they brought down with stone-headed clubs. Behind the goblin line, larger, giant-sized shapes, that Jodah could not completely identify, loomed through the fog.

The goblins crashed into the human forces and threw them back, like an ocean wave striking a sand castle. Jodah felt as if he was carried physically backward as opposed to fleeing of his own volition. He slashed at a few of the goblins, and they disappeared, to be replaced by others. A riderless horse, bearing the livery of a Ghed commander, thundered through the goblin lines, its flesh striped with numerous cuts, its eyes wide with fear.

The two warring human armies rallied and unified against the goblins, forming knots of humanity as the goblin tide surged forward. Jodah found himself on a low hillock, flanked by an elf on one side, an Alsoorian on the other. Half the elf's face was slick with blood, and part of his ear was missing.

The boy-guard Tivadar would be so pleased, thought Jodah bitterly. Everyone was united to fight the goblins.

Then there was a fiery explosion not too far to their left, a reddish hue that spread out through the fog, bearing light and screams. Jodah thought at once of magic and wondered if the goblins had their own spellcasters. There was little time for such thought, for a wave of goblins was upon them again. They were driven from the hillock, and the elf disappeared beneath the swords of the goblins. Something bit into his thigh, and Jodah lashed out automatically, cleaving something that screamed in an inhuman tongue and then was silent.

They pulled back slightly, up the side of the valley. Then they retreated. Then they were routed, casting aside their weapons and their armor in the dim hope of outdistancing the goblins. Jodah remembered that the hillside seemed smaller on the way down. Now its seemed like a cliff, covered with wet, greasy grass that denied any proper flight and threatened to spill Jodah and the others back into the laps of the goblins behind them.

There were others with Jodah—blind-eyed in panic and uncaring as to what lay ahead of them as long as it was not what lay behind them.

The ground in front of him leveled out, then descended again. He half ran, half tumbled down the slope, the screams and shouts of the goblins and men and elves dying behind him. Still he ran with the others up another hill and down again until at last exhaustion and the blood leaking from his leg stopped him, and he collapsed in the wet grass. The world spun around him and then closed around him as he felt unconscious.

Jodah did not know how long he slept, only that he had been unconscious a long time. His leg felt as if it was on fire, and the world around him was still fogbound, still wrapped in cotton. There was no noise, and Jodah had no idea where he was.

He guessed, from the general brightness of the sky, which way was south and began limping north and slightly west, hoping to reach the ford and find other members of his unit or even other humans or elves.

He met no other survivors in his flight, not even bodies left from the assault. The going was slow and eternal, and he felt as if he had been abandoned in a small universe of his own, a universe bounded only by his fog-limited vision. Bounded by that and by the growing pain in his leg.

He came upon the city later that day.

* * * * *

The lead goblin smacked his companion, almost knocking him into the fountain's pool.

"Whaddayah, Stoopid?" he snarled.

The other goblin snapped back, "Whaddayah mean, stoopid?"

"You ain't gonna drink dat!" said the lead goblin.

"Why not? Its just wadder," said the goblin.

"It's dirty wadder," said the lead goblin.

"So?"

"So look at all dah mud an plants an stuff. It's palluted."

"So?"

"So lookadda pigeons," said the lead goblin, sounding exasperated.

"Whadaboutda pigeons?" said the other one.

"So da pigeons do what da pigeons do in dat wadder," said the leader. "Youwanna drink *dat?*"

There was a long moment of silence, then the goblin said, "I guezz not."

"You are *so* stoopid, sometimes," said the lead goblin.

There were some shouts from across the plaza. The lead goblin bellowed, "Whadday see?"

Another throaty bellow came back "Something's moving down here!"

"Whatizit?"

"Dunno!" came the answer. "Come look!"

"Let's move it," said the lead goblin.

"But I'm still thirsty," said the other goblin.

"We find a stream lader," said the leader. "Lesgo!"

The two padded away, taking the other goblins with them. The fountain remained unguarded for a moment, the only sound being the thunder of the water from the lion's mouth.

Then Jodah broke the surface, spitting and gagging. He had remained underwater until his lungs had nearly burst and still inhaled a fair amount of the particulate-laden waters. Now he sputtered and coughed, aware that any goblin within ten yards of him would be able to kill him like a kitten.

Jodah inhaled again, deeply, and coughed again, but there were no goblins around to hear. He wiped the muck and algae from his face and looked around. He was alone again in the central plaza.

Slowly he pulled himself out of the ice-cold water. He would have to find shelter and then escape the city. No, escape the city center first, then make a fire—dry himself off. His magic was good for that, at least.

He felt chilled to the bone as he staggered out of the square, heading the direction that the goblins had originally come from. Only later, once he had built a fire in one of the outlying buildings and dried off, did he realize that his leg no longer hurt and the wound had closed up entirely.

5 ☾

Sima

Most of the histories of the Dark portray the Church of Tal as a monolithic, single-minded faith ruling over, and often contending against, a double handful of rebellious city-states. While it is true that the church was more unified and organized than the city-states, much to its advantage, it was not a single monolithic structure. Records of the period indicate that it was a confusing tapestry of smaller saint-faiths, usurped local religions, and holy cults of personality. Add to this the wide variety of divided dogmas and outright heresies within the Church of Tal's ranks, and it becomes obvious why the inquisitions, and the later crusades, were formed. Of course, it should be equally obvious that those inquisitions and crusades were infested with the same disputes over dogma, cults of personality and outright heresies as the rest of the church hierarchy.

—Arkol, Argivian scholar

Jodah found his way back to the Alamar River and began following it south toward the Great Bridge. He considered heading north, far from the madness of the warring city-states, particularly since his wounded leg was feeling better, but the need to find Voska was too great.

He moved quietly, keeping the languid flow of the river to his right as he moved south during the morning and afternoon, finding shade in the heat of the day. He used his spell of light sparingly, to light fires in the evening and once to stun a river rat long enough for him to catch it for supper. He found he developed greater strength and control over the light as he repeated the process of casting the spell. Yet, his achievements would mean little if he could not reach Alsoor.

He was hampered by the fact that he did not know who, if anyone, was winning the war. He met no one along the river's side, but found a large amount of abandoned equipment, enough to deck himself in Alsoorian garb and still carry the fragments of his Ghed armor in his backpack. He had also found among the castoffs a bottle made of carved crystal, filled with rum. Regardless of who controlled the bridge, he would be prepared.

In the end it did not matter. When he arrived at the bridge on a gray, overcast morning, Alsoor forces controlled the northern end of the Great Bridge, and Ghed forces the southern. Neither seemed particularly pleased about the presence of the other, but there seemed to be a lack of unsheathed weapons, and traffic moved effortlessly from one side of the bridge to the other. Indeed, a large caravan was encamped on the far side of the bridge in Ghed territory.

Jodah stopped an ostler who was bringing up fresh horses and asked what had happened in his absence.

"War's over," said the stableman. "Church negotiated a peace treaty between the two after the Battle of Pitdown. Stragglers like you have been coming in for about a week now. You were there?"

"I'm afraid I was," said Jodah.

The ostler sucked on his teeth and said, "I heard it was bad."

"Bad enough," said Jodah. "So one can travel to Alsoor, then?"

"One can," said the ostler, "but unless one feels like camping outside the city walls, one shouldn't."

Jodah raised a tired eyebrow at the other man.

"The plague flag flies over Alsoor," said the ostler, "like it did earlier over Ghed. The cold grippe, or something like that, this time. Nasty bit of work, I hear. Your stomach freezes into a solid lump, as I understand it, and you die trying to pass it out of your body." The older man shook his head sagely at the encampment on the far side of the river. "That's why this lot is heading south to Ghed. Can't say I blame them."

Jodah raised his head and poked a chin in the general direction of the encampment. "And who are 'this lot'?"

The stableman leaned forward in a conspiratorial fashion, "Churchmen," he said simply.

"The church?" Jodah blinked. "Since when does the church leave a city, even one with the cold grippe?"

"Part of the treaty, I hear," said the stableman. "They have a cartload of heretics, wizards, and sinners that they're going to burn in Ghed."

"I see," said Jodah, thinking at once of Voska. Would he be among the prisoners?

"They're going to tie them to stakes and set them on fire, the first morning they get there. Burn them alive!" said the ostler with a grin. "Sort of a 'welcome to the neighborhood' party!" He broke down in a wheezing laugh.

"Charming," said Jodah. "And they're heading for Ghed."

"Indeed they are, goodsir," said the stableman, "indeed they are."

Jodah let the stableman go about his business and paused only to change out of the tattered remains of his Alsoorian uniform and into the tattered remains of his Ghed armor. The Alsoor guards sneered at him but let him pass.

The Ghed guards, on the other hand, challenged him as he approached. He gave his assumed name and his former unit.

The commander of the bridge guards checked a large board. "You're a survivor of Pitdown?" he asked in a nasal braying.

"That's what they call it, I suppose," said Jodah, trying to remain professional. His eyes swept the church encampment. Could he find a way to join the caravan south? Should he?

"That was over a week ago," said the commander, an accusing whine in his voice.

"I was separated from my unit," said Jodah, and shrugged. "I didn't have a map with me."

The commander made a dismissive snort and hooked a thumb toward the encampment. "Join up with the Church Guard. They'll be escorting Her Grace Primata Delphine and the holy prisoners to Ghed. Then you'll be reassigned once you get there, or discharged. War's over, you might have heard."

Jodah stared at the bridge guard commander in disbelief.

"Is there a problem soldier?" said the commander, his whine growing indignant.

Jodah snapped back to reality. "No sir! Thank you sir!" Gathering his backpack, Jodah may his way to the church encampment.

The encampment was nearly packed and ready when he arrived and was a hive of activity. Jodah looked for someone in charge but without luck. He also looked for where the "holy prisoners" were but with similar lack of success.

Somebody behind him shouted something, but Jodah continued to scan the crowd. There were a number of Ghed soldiers, and some of them had a wide-eyed, slightly terrified visage. Other survivors of Pitdown he guessed. He wondered if he too had that painfully honest expression on his face. He felt the mirror on the inside of his boot but did not reach for it.

Someone shouted again, but Jodah's blood ran cold when he saw Delphine, primata of the Order of St. Zil, being helped onto her horse. Her mount was a huge white gelding set with an ornate, boxlike seat that allowed the large woman to sit sidesaddle. Despite himself, Jodah felt like turning away. Surely his beard and ragged attire would disguise him after all this time.

The primata looked up, and for a moment Jodah thought their eyes locked. His blood froze, and his heart dropped into his boots. But the primata's face remained impassive (or at least no more irritated than she normally seemed), and she gave no hint that she recognized Jodah.

Then a heavy hand was laid on Jodah's shoulder, and he jumped three feet in place, twisting to face his assailant as he did so.

Togath backed up three steps, taking his hand off Jodah's shoulder as he did so. "Did the battle leave you deaf, man? I called you, and you seemed lost in your own little world! Tal's Book, it is good to see that you survived the battle!"

Jodah took a deep breath and tried to calm his thundering heart. Togath had called him by his assumed name, the one he had enlisted under, and he had ignored it.

"I'm afraid I've wandered a long time to get here," he said.

"You and I both," said Togath, then lowered his voice. "Though there should be few more boring jobs than guarding Our Lady the Overstuffed Suet-Bag. At least we deserve the rest, eh?"

Jodah smiled and was rewarded with another slap on the back.

At last the company formed up. Jodah and Togath's group was assigned to the rearguard, which meant that the rest of procession had to pass before them.

First came the vanguard, the fresh troops sent from Ghed, their lamellar armor waxed a lustrous black, and their freshly laundered tunics as green as a sun-dappled forest. Then came the outriders, similarly outfitted and colorful. Then the primata's horse, followed by a number of lesser church officials, either mounted on horseback or in personal carriages. Then a lumbering wagon, which, Togath mentioned, contained either the church treasury from Alsoor, or several thousand copies of the Book of Tal, or both. Then another unit of footmen, this group more ragged and practical looking than the vanguard. Then came several wagons holding the holy prisoners, then Jodah's units in the rear.

The wagons holding the prisoners were only a little larger than the donkey carts that hauled Mother Dobbs away. They were stuffed with prisoners who were manacled and hobbled, and the manacles of a few were tied to the railing of the wagon.

They were an uninspiring group. If the church was to be judged on the strength of those who opposed it, there was little that could be said on its behalf. Indeed, it looked as if the church had emptied Alsoor's gaols and dungeons in order to provide a sufficient stock of sacrifices. Togath could note (but did not) that the prisoners were examples of the enemies of the church in the way poverty, dirtiness, sickness, and famine were considered enemies, for they were all clear examples of those traits.

Jodah scanned the prisoners, looking for Voska's face, then goggled in surprise. At the prow of the third wagon, her wrists manacled with ornate chains, was the blue-clad woman from the alley! Her garb was tattered prisoner-gray now, but her heart-shaped face and bangs were unmistakable.

Jodah stared at her, she turned slightly, and her eyes met Jodah's. As with the primata earlier, he got the feeling that she saw him looking at her, but this time there was the feeling that she recognized him. Her head bobbed just a bit, and she allowed herself a small smile, and she turned back to face the direction of the procession.

The last of the prisoner wagons rumbled by. There was no sign of Voska among the prisoners.

Togath elbowed Jodah and said it was their turn, and they collected in the back of the van with the other shabbily dressed survivors of Pitdown, bringing up the rear.

* * * * *

It had taken little effort to volunteer both himself and Togath for guard duty (except perhaps Togath's unwillingness to get only a half-night's sleep after marching all day). It took a bit more persuasion (and the salvaged bottle of rum) to arrange to be assigned to guard one particular prisoner.

Most of the sinners, criminals and ne'er-do-wells scheduled for the inquisition pyre were put into one large tent for the evening. Those who might provide particular problems were given their own quarters and their own guards. So it was that Togath and Jodah ended up in the early hours relieving the guards of the blue woman's tent. Jodah noted that the church was much more serious about its prisoners than the Ghed military was—two guards were posted to each tent and told in no uncertain terms to keep all outsiders out until relieved.

Jodah waited until most of the guards were changed throughout the camp and the area began to settle down. Then he said, "I'm going to go into the tent, Togath. I want you to stay here."

There was silence a moment, then Togath said, "So that's what this is all about."

Jodah looked at the larger man quizzically.

Togath shook his head. "All this effort, for a bit of fluff? Can't you just wait until you get back to Ghed? I know of a very good house in the docks district . . . "

Jodah understood what the guard was saying and shook his head violently. He could feel the blood rushing to his face in embarrassment. "That's not what I meant. I need to talk to this prisoner."

Togath blew out his cheeks in a derisive snort, "Yeah, that's what I always said, too. Just wanted to talk. Never ends up that way, though."

Jodah felt his face grow hot. "I'm serious, I'm looking for somebody. . . ."

"So are we all, lad, so are we all," said Togath, then gave Jodah a long, steely look. "Go on, then. I don't think the church will care, and she'll be kindling in another day. I'm going to move off a little, here and keep lookout for the watch commander. Just keep it down, if you don't mind?"

Jodah wanted to argue with the other guard but instead just shook his head and unbuttoned the tent flap.

As he slipped in, Togath gave one last shot. "And don't take too long. I think I might need a good long 'talk' as well in a couple hours." He punctuated the remark with a nasty laugh.

There were supplies in the tent—shoved against one wall, with a cleared space in the middle. In the center was a great iron peg driven into the rocky soil, and a short chain linked the peg to the prisoner's manacles. It was similar to the method that the Ghed military had used to keep their captured spy, but the iron peg, the chain, and the manacles themselves were inscribed with a spiderlike tracery of thin silver lines. Similar, Jodah noted, to the manacles that had bound Voska.

"It's about time you got here," said the blue woman, now dressed in gray.

Jodah scowled a hand out, palm down, motioned for her to lower her voice. He didn't trust Togath to not stand by the tent flap and listen to what was going on.

"I need some information," Jodah said in a level tone.

The woman raised her crossed and bound hands, "What, no rescue? And here I thought you'd come to free me." She shook her head, and her hair swept across her face like waves. "Sorry I didn't contact you sooner, Jodah of Giva Province. I've been a little busy." There was not a hint of apology in her voice.

"I want to know about Voska," said Jodah, kneeling down opposite her, figuring how long the chain truly was and staying outside her range.

The woman held up her wrists again. "Free me first."

Jodah shook his head. "Information first. You left me puking in an alley last time we talked."

The woman's eyes narrowed, and for a moment it felt as if she was trying to carve her way into Jodah's soul. He sat there, unmoving, waiting for her to make her decision.

At length she licked her lips, shut her eyes, and said, "Voska is dead. I'm sorry." Her shoulders slumped slightly forward as she said it. That did sound like an apology.

The bottom dropped out of Jodah's stomach at her words, and he felt dizzy for a moment, a repeat of the feeling he had in that alleyway. It was not magic that brought on the vertigo, but fear. Fear that the woman was speaking the truth.

"No," he said at last in a whisper. He should have gone back to Alsoor immediately after he escaped that city. He never should have left Voska behind. He never should have split up from Voska in the first place.

He never should have cast the spell, the spell that brought the church and the goblins.

"I am sorry," said the woman, raising her crossed wrists again, "but we don't have time for this. You have to get me loose."

Jodah shook his head again. His mouth worked, but there was no sound for the moment. Finally he managed, "How? How did he . . . "

The woman settled back on her haunches, and her face was a combination of concern and impatience. "That doesn't matter. No, I'm sorry, it does. Short version is all I know. They apparently caught him soon after you got away. He put up a fight. They shot him with crossbows. That's what I put together, after they caught me."

"No," said Jodah firmly, "we captured a spy from Alsoor. He said that Voska was alive. That the church had him."

"The church put out that information," said the woman quickly. "They were hoping you would hear and

101

come back to rescue him." She paused a moment, then added, "They caught me, when I came looking, instead."

There was a long silence in the tent. Jodah's face felt flushed, but not from embarrassment. Voska was dead, and it was his fault.

The woman waited for a moment, then in a low, stern voice said, "You understand what happened? They put out a false rumor in hopes of getting you to come back. They wanted *you*. I think they still do, from the questions they asked." She held out her wrists a third time. "Can we go now?"

Jodah blinked back the wetness at the corners of his eyes. Could he trust this woman? Was Voska really dead, or was she just telling her own story to get him to free her?

He looked into her cold, blue eyes and saw that she was serious. And there were a dozen other stories she could have told instead.

Voska was dead, and the church was still looking for him.

He looked at the manacles. "I don't have the key," he said. "I don't know . . . I mean I can't . . ." he stammered.

The woman sighed impatiently. "Of course you can. I can't, because they are welded onto *me*. If I try, the feedback will overwhelm me. You can. Just open them with a spell."

Jodah looked at the manacles carefully now. They had a thin joining line along one side but no sign of a lock or catch. "I don't know how," said Jodah in a small voice. "I don't know that spell."

"So make it up!" hissed the woman. "What's your color?"

Jodah looked at the manacled woman with disbelief. "My what?"

"Your color!" the woman strove to keep her words to a whisper, but it seemed a losing battle. "I don't believe that Voska never . . . Okay, we'll take it from the beginning. What spells do you know?"

"I can make bright light appear," he said. "Bright, hot light."

"And I take it that's what got you away from the primata in the first place," said the woman. "Apparently that put a real wrinkle in her wimple. What else?"

"I can make potions, with the right material," he continued, then spread his hands out wide. "You know that as well. I haven't been doing this very long."

"I can see that," said the woman, with a bit of ice in her voice.

Jodah looked in her eyes and thought he saw gears turning as she strove to figure out what to do next. At length she said, "When you cast a spell, what do you think of?"

"Think of?" said Jodah, then realized what she was saying. "I think of my home, where I grew up, in Giva."

"Mountain, plains, seacoast?" prompted the woman.

"There were mountains in the distance," said Jodah, "but it was mostly farmland. Orchards. Vineyards. Gardens."

"Plains, then," said the woman. "That fits with the curative magic and the light balls. All right, here's what we can do. I want you to pull out the magic of your land. You know how to do that?"

Jodah nodded, and closed his eyes. He was back in Giva, back at the family manse. Slowly he pulled the energies from those memories and shaped them into a glowing white ball in his mind.

"Good," said the woman, "what are you envisioning?"

"I am thinking of a white ball of light." said Jodah.

"That ball is the *mana*, the magical energy," said the woman. "Now I want you to keep thinking of that ball and open your eyes."

Jodah did so.

"Now I'm going to tell you how to shape that mana. I can't be a hundred percent accurate, because it can't really be put into words."

"Like writing down a dance," said Jodah, feeling a fresh twinge of regret for Voska.

The woman almost smiled. Almost. "Close enough. Now I want you to shape the ball into a disk. Flatten the poles, and imagine the edge of the disk is so narrow that it can easily fit into the seam of these manacles. Can you do that?"

"I can try," said Jodah, flattening the ball in his mind. Then he asked, "Have you ever done this before?"

"Made a spell on the fly?" asked the woman. "Yes. One time I had to do it for another mage who had his hands trapped like mine."

"Did it work?" said Jodah, the disk of mana was a spinning vortex, and he imagined it moving toward the manacles.

"Sort of," said the woman. "He casts spells one-handed now. Easy! Just let the disk slide into the joint and move along the length of the manacles. Yes, that's it . . . "

* * * * *

Togath had wandered a few feet away initially, but curiosity had quickly gotten the better of him. By the time he was back into hearing distance, the voices were soft and indistinct.

Maybe the lad had been telling the truth, thought the older guard. Maybe he just wanted to talk to the woman.

Waste of an opportunity, he thought, but every man has his own desires.

The soft murmuring went on for a few moments, and there was the flickering of light within. Indistinct shadows formed on the walls. The murmuring voices stopped.

The lad was getting careless now, thought Togath. One thing to leave one's post for a bit of personal excitement. Quite another to light a lantern and call attention to the matter. He'd better stop Jodah before he roused the whole camp with his foolishness.

Besides, thought Togath with a grin, it was his turn.

The large guard pulled back the tent flap and said, "Lad, I hate to interrupt, but if you've had your fun . . ."

His words died in his throat as he saw the pair kneeling on the dirt floor of the tent. The woman's manacles were laying to one side, and she was rubbing her wrists.

Both the lad and the woman looked up at once. They had the look rabbits get when you surprise them. Then the woman raised one hand and balled it into a fist.

Togath felt something warm and wet spread over the front of his brain. Then the woman pulled her fist toward her, and the wet something seemed to be pulled through the front of his skull. It was as if she had dug a fishhook into his brain, and just . . . pulled.

It happened very quickly. Togath managed to say "What the . . ." before slamming into the soft earth.

* * * * *

"What did you do to him?" said Jodah sharply.

"A spell of amnesia," said the woman in a matter-of-fact manner. "He'll wake up in an hour with no memory of having seen us. We'll be gone by then."

"Gone?" said Jodah.

"Gone," repeated the woman. "We're going to put as much distance as we can between us and this camp. I know of a safe place we can hide, then I can take a ship west."

The woman started for the tent opening, but Jodah remained still. "No," he said.

The woman blinked, then her brows narrowed, "What do you mean, 'no'?"

"I mean there are others who are prisoners here." said Jodah, "Prisoners of the church. We have to free them too."

"Free them too?" the woman choked on her voice. "Are you insane?"

"Insane enough to try to free you," said Jodah, his voice stern and level.

The woman's face tightened, "I could leave you here."

Jodah nodded, "You could. But you said the primata's trap caught you when you went looking for Voska. You went after Voska for a reason. I think that same reason will keep you from abandoning me now."

The formerly blue woman balled one hand into a fist and stomped the ground. She looked as if she was going to curse, but instead she said, "How do you want to do this?"

Jodah breathed a sigh of relief. "Are there any other spellcasters in the group?"

"Real wizards, like you and me?" questioned the woman. "Most of them are just penny-ante alchemists and fortune tellers. One or two scholars who are guilty of just asking the wrong questions. There's one who claimed to be a necromancer, but he's just crazy. He's probably also the only one who can really cast spells."

"Go get him first then," said Jodah, "and try to free as

many of the others as you can. I'll make a distraction on the other side of the camp. Can you use your induce vomiting spell?"

"Induce vom . . ." said the woman, then almost smiled. Almost. "You mean the Unbalancing, the one I used in the alley. Yes I can use that spell, but I can't do it all that often. We could use it to clear the way out of here."

"Good," said Jodah. "Wait fifteen minutes after I leave, then get to work. The horses are staked just west of here, on the side of the hill. Meet me there."

"Fine," said the woman, clearly uneasy. "You have any weapon I can use? I could take your friend's sword, but that will likely attract too much attention."

Jodah reached down in his boot and pulled out his dagger and Voska's mirror. The woman took the dagger, but her eyes were locked on the mirror.

"Hold onto that," she said simply, nodding to the mirror. "It will probably be useful."

Jodah headed for the tent flap and paused to look at Togath, sprawled out on the floor of the tent.

"It's better to leave him inside than out," said the woman, seeming to read Jodah's thoughts. "If we succeed, there's going to be too much confusion for anyone to think of questioning him. And if we fail . . ." She let her voice trail off for a moment. "You really want to do this? You don't know these people?"

Jodah snorted. "I don't even know *your* name, and I helped you."

The woman straightened, stung by Jodah's words. Then she said, "Sima. I am Sima of the City of the Shadows. And don't worry, you can count on me to do my job. I'll free the other prisoners and be along presently."

Jodah looked at the woman, nodded, and was gone.

* * * * *

Slowly, Jodah moved through the camp, weaving slightly, looking like nothing more than a slightly inebriated soldier returning from a session of gambling in one of the tents. He moved carefully though the various units, taking note of which troops were where. They were well within Ghed territory, and except for the guards on the prisoners, there were few pickets.

The great wagon filled with books (and or treasure) was parked near a great white tent. Earlier in the evening the tent had been illuminated from within with a pale light, but now it was dark, and the guards nodded off at the doorway. Jodah looked up at the overcast sky, took a deep breath, and conjured the memories of the land.

He took the memory-energies, the mana the woman spoke of, and concentrated them into little seeds, each seed no larger than his thumbnail. He kept the memories alive as he moved around the perimeter of the great tent, dropping a seed to the ground, then stepping on it, then moving on. No one seemed to notice him as he did so.

The memories grew hot in his mind and started to burn, to sear the edges of his imagination like hot coals dropped onto velvet. He had never held the memories, called upon their power without using them, for this long before. As the back of his mind grew warmer, he wondered how badly he could hurt himself casting spells.

He finished his orbit of the command tent and wandered toward the wagon. His mind was aflame now, and he thought he could smell ammonia in the back of his nose. A husky shape, another guard, loomed up out of the darkness.

"You're out of quarters," said the soldier. "Report at once to—"

There were some shouts far away, coming from the prisoner tents. The soldier looked toward the shouts, and his hand drifted to his sword.

That was when Jodah released the power of the mana-seeds he had planted.

Light erupted in glowing fountains around the command tent and the wagon, sparking upward like hot, white fireworks set in the ground. The soldier who had accosted Jodah had been directly above one and now clawed at his face as small embers of light glowed brightly in his beard. The command tent was already smoldering from the heat, and there were shouts from within. A few feet away the first tongues of flame licked the underbelly of the wagon.

Books, thought Jodah as the flames spread into the wagon itself. It was carrying books, not treasure.

The casting had exhausted him, and Jodah now just wanted to curl up and sleep, but the camp was up and swarming like an overturned beehive. Instead, he ran for the center of camp. There were screams and shouts around him and orders barked as the commanders sought to protect the churchmen, extinguish the fire, and chase the prisoners all at once.

Jodah took a deep breath and bellowed, "Goblins! We're under attack! Goblins!" and rushed toward the perimeter of the camp. Several of the would-be firefighters charged out into the darkness as well, ready to engage an imaginary enemy.

Jodah circled around, his breath ragged and hoarse in his ears. Twice he passed small squads heading out into the night, seeking to find the supposed enemy. Others had quickly picked up his cry, and soldiers were now hopping out of their quarters half-dressed but looking for the goblins. Jodah headed through the confusion for the prisoner tents.

A pack of prisoners, still manacled together but unhobbled, lurched into view, then froze at the sight of him. Jodah pointed away, a direction out of camp, and the prisoners, like some multilegged monster, shuffled quickly out of sight.

Jodah smiled grimly. Apparently he could count on the woman named Sima to do her job.

There was the sound of swords striking each other in the distance, and Jodah wondered if some of the prisoners had armed themselves. Instead he briefly caught a grim tableau—a unit of soldiers locked in battle with what looked like animated skeletons. The skeletons fought silently, their long, curved blades drawing blood from their assailants with every strike. The soldiers' blows chopped off hunks of bone, but the skeletons would not stop attacking until they had been totally dismembered.

The supposed necromancer, Jodah realized. Apparently he had the ability to cast spells after all. Jodah felt empty, exhausted, but clutched onto Voska's mirror as a talisman while he moved through the camp. The various unit commanders were regaining control of their troops. Regardless of the situation, the prisoners had only minutes to make good their escape.

Finally he reached the paddock on the hillside, overlooking the camp, where the horses had been staked. Most of the guards had been called back into the camp, and the horses, smoke in their nostrils, were pawing the earth and pulling at their tie ropes.

Jodah stopped and took a deep breath. Sima came loping up the hill, breathing hard, her face as haggard and exhausted as Jodah felt.

She turned slightly, waving at the pandemonium in the camp beneath them. "Happy, now?" she said.

Jodah nodded, and said, "Now we can leave, milady."

"I think not," said another voice, stepping out from behind the horses. "Aiding sorcerers is a sin. And a crime. Your journey ends here, my children."

Jodah looked up and saw the massive form of Primata Delphine emerge from the shadows. The big woman was sweating profusely, and Jodah knew that she had probably run here as well, hot on their heels.

"The light of Tal illuminates all," said the priestess. "When the attack came my first concern was for the books, but they are already lost. Then I realized that any attacker would likely think of gathering the horses. The wisdom of Tal lead me to you."

Jodah clutched his sword with one hand, Voska's mirror with the other. He searched his mind but could not concentrate on the land, could not count on the memories. His mind was exhausted.

The primata was quoting scripture now. "Bathed in the hallowed light, the infidels looked upon the impurities of their souls and despaired." As she spoke, her form began to glow, first like a tent lit from within, and then bright enough to bathe the entire hillside in near-daylight. The horses, with the exception of the primata's own ivory-shaded mount, thundered their hooves against the ground and tried to uproot their stakes.

Jodah turned to Sima and said, "Can you do that Unbalancing . . . ?" but the question died in his throat. The woman from the City of Shadows was already doubled over, clutching at her belly, her face worn and white in the luminous glow of the priestess.

"She is unworthy of Tal's beneficent light," said Primata Delphine, "as are you." Again she quoted scripture, "And I will take a sword to the infidel and the unbeliever, and my blade shall shine with the fire of righteousness." The primata raised a hand, and the air seemed to coalesce into a flaming sword in that hand.

That was enough for the horses. Wide-eyed and foam-mouthed, they ripped their ropes from the earth and were gone into the darkness, running all directions. The only one unfazed was the white gelding, Delphine's mount.

Primata Delphine pointed the flaming blade at Jodah, and white-hot fire leapt from the tip, arching toward him. Jodah reached into his mind and found nothing—no memory, no ready spell, only a regret that he would never see his family's manor again. Instinctively he threw up his hands to ward off the blow, the mirror and the blade striking each other as he did so.

The flame from priestess's sword struck the crossed mirror and sword, hesitated for a second, and then doubled back, leaving Jodah unharmed. The holy fire struck the primata in the chest, and her robes now glowed of a new radiance, of the crimson flame of burning cloth. The primata screamed, and her flaming blade disappeared, and she dropped to the ground, rolling to extinguish the blaze, the slope carrying her down the hill.

Jodah lowered his arms, then looked at the blade and the mirror. The mirror was magical after all and had the power to turn the church's work against it. He gripped his sword and began to chase down the hillside after the smoldering form of the priestess.

He got no more than ten feet when he saw a line of

human shapes in black and green armor coming up the slope. They scattered as the flaming priestess rolled down among them, then, realizing who was on fire, chased after her. Cursing, Jodah climbed back up the hill where the primata's gelding still stood, nibbling at the grass.

Jodah grabbed Sima's shoulder and dragged her to her feet. He half led, half shoved her toward the primata's horse.

The horse was laconic as Jodah hoisted the other spell-caster onto its back. The activity was enough to rouse her fully, and Sima pulled him up behind her. From horseback they looked down on the camp. There were a number of fires within the camp now, but it seemed that matters were slowly being brought under control. The collection of green and black figures had stopped the tumbling fireball that was the Primata Delphine, and half the force remained with her while the rest of the soldiers were working their way up the hillside toward them.

"Time to leave, Goodlady Sima," Jodah said, and he jammed his heels into the flanks of the horse.

The gelding leapt forward, both Jodah and his companion hanging onto its mane for dear life. Direction did not matter to Jodah as much as distance.

Exhausted and hungry, they rode until the early morning hours, when the eastern sky shone red with the promise of a sunrise that never seemed to come. Only then did they halt long enough to let the horse water.

"Where are you going now?" she asked.

Jodah shook his head, "I don't know. I stayed here because Voska . . ." His voice died, "I don't know if I can go home, either."

The woman nodded sternly, "Then come with me. There is a safe house we use south of here. I could use your help in reaching it. And you need some real training in magic."

Jodah turned over the woman's words in his mind, looking for some slight against Voska's training. It was there, he realized, but he decided it was better to ignore it.

At length he said, "I think that would be best, after all."

6☾

Voyage and Storm

Enigmas seem to attract enigmas. Viewed from our safe position in the future, the Dark was but an instant, a short prelude to the Time of Ice, and it makes perfect sense that Vervamon should have known Primata Delphine, who should have known Tivadar of Thorn who should have known the Rag Man. In reality, the continent is wide and the years long, and few if any of these people ever met, regardless of the later legends.

One exception to this may be the Jodah figure and the mysterious City of Shadows. Numerous individuals and places are credited as being Jodah's "teacher," but this secretive group surfaces again and again, and there may be some truth to the claims that they were the first to show the Jodah (or Jodahs) the nature of the third path.

—**Arkol, Argivian scholar**

"What did you mean when you asked what my color was?" said Jodah, basking in the sun.

The sunlight was a rarity for him, and he could not remember the last time he had felt its warmth. They were miles from shore, and a stiff ocean breeze moved spotted clouds overhead. Inland, it was continually overcast, gray, drizzling, and miserable. Yet on the open ocean, far from the land, there was sunlight.

They had ridden south for several days to the coast. There a small village brooded by a tidal mud flat that extended to the southern horizon. Once, Sima had explained, it had been a fishing village, but after the Devastation of the Brothers, the tide went out and never came back. She knew an innkeeper there, and he provided separate rooms for them.

Each night, the innkeeper climbed a narrow staircase to a tower, carrying a lantern with a bit of red glass in the lens, and shone the lantern out across the flats. The first two nights, there was no response in the darkness. On the third night, low on the horizon, there was a responding light, equally red.

Before morning Sima and Jodah were loaded into a wide, broad-bottom skiff and poled out across the flats. It was slow going, and the eastern sky was already beginning to lighten as they reached their goal—a round-hulled cog at anchor, its dark gray sails furled against the night breezes.

Conversations were short and low-toned. Sima and Jodah came aboard. Several bales of some sweet, tangy-scented material were loaded into the skiff from the cog. Then the skiff pulled away, and the ship raised anchor, riding with the tide to deeper water.

The captain, a rough-hewn man with an unkempt black beard, made the pair welcome—they were welcome to sleep on the quarter-deck at the rear of the ship, welcome to leave the crew alone, and welcome to not go below decks or inspect the cargo too closely, otherwise they would be welcome to walk home.

Sima agreed to the captain's terms readily, and surprisingly to Jodah, even humbly. The blue-clad woman later explained that the captain was as superstitious as all seamen legendarily were but understood something of the magical craft and tolerated spellcasters. That made him a valuable asset to mages such as herself, and she was willing to follow his demands and turn a blind eye to his other activities.

The captain's mate was an elven woman who said nothing but regarded both the new passengers with a sneer that made Jodah wondered if he had stepped in something before coming aboard.

The first days, as they fled on horseback, Jodah and Sima said little to each other, so drained they both were from the battle, and so worried were they about recapture. Once they had reached the village by the flats, Sima cautioned Jodah against asking too many questions—the inn-keeper was an ally but not a particularly trusted one. Only now, out of the sight of land, under the first sun he could remember in a year, would she answer Jodah's questions.

"Color?" said Sima. She was dressed in blue again, a dark blue gown slit up along both sides to the hip, with blue leggings beneath. She wore no jewelry save for a golden comb used to gather her hair back. At the moment, she was leaned back against the railing, holding the comb in her hand, letting the breeze tug at her hair, so that it looked like a dark banner.

"You asked me what my color was," said Jodah. "Does magic have color?"

Sima shifted her position to regard the young man. "What color is the mana when you summon it?"

Jodah shrugged. "It's white."

"Is it?" she said almost smiling. Jodah found the smile a bit patronizing but let it pass.

"Why wouldn't it be white?" he asked.

"Can you see it?" she asked, "with your eyes?"

"Well, no." said Jodah, "but I can imagine it with my mind. And in my mind it's white. And when I form the lights, those are white as well."

"You see it in your mind. So can you have color without vision?" said Sima.

Jodah shifted his position, stretching out his legs. "If you feel the color a certain way, I suppose. I don't think I'm making much sense, but yes."

Sima gave a knowing nod. "You're correct, and it *does* make sense. You can have color without vision, and it is that type of color that I'm talking about when I'm talking about mana. It was discovered early on that different types of memories unlocked different types of mana. Different flavors. Different colors."

"Which is why you asked what I had thought of when I summoned the ener . . . the mana," said Jodah.

"Right," said Sima leaning forward off of the rail. "Those pulling from open countryside—the farms, the fields, even large grasslands, their mana tends to be white. Those who remembered the mountains tend to think of their energy as being red. I often see the energies as a blue ball, and my memories are of my home as well, which is an island community. Those who live within forests have green mana, and those whose memories are of swamps, fens, and bogs have black mana."

Jodah digested her words. It sounded as if she had everything figured out. "Are there only five types of this mana?"

Sima replied, "As far as we have determined, there are

five discrete types that are tied to the land." She held up a hand, and touched each finger in turn, starting with the thumb. "White, blue, black, red, and green." Then back to the thumb. "Plains, islands, swamps, mountains, forests."

Jodah shook his head. "What about a forest with a swamp in it, or a mountain on an island?"

Sima responded, "We aren't fully sure, but it seems that one particular memory can be used for a number of different types of mana, provided that it has the feeling, the essence of that type. That's what we think, at least."

"And who is the 'we' that is doing all this thinking?" asked Jodah.

Sima almost smiled. Almost. Instead she said, "Each color seems to have its own natural affinity, or tendency. Red, for example, tends to be a destructive color—think of volcanoes and fire and storms. It seems to be chaotic and disorganized and as such capable of inflicting great amounts of damage very quickly."

"Voska," said Jodah, quietly.

"From your description, quite likely," said Sima. "Destructive, from what he could do with fire, and disorganized, since he never really taught you about the true nature of magic." Jodah scowled, and Sima quickly added, "and probably didn't think much about it himself. There are all manner of hedge wizards and wild talents in the world, who have discover this ability, and never go any further than using it to light fires and scare away enemies."

Sima paused but Jodah said nothing, so she continued. "You on the other hand, remember the plains. Big open territory, usually settled by humans. Farms, cities, and fields. Your color, of course, is white. Organized, unlike red, and restorative in nature. That's why you could make Mother Dobbs's phony potions work, which is how you came to my attention in the first place."

Jodah looked out the stern, wondering if Mother Dobbs had been freed. He had assumed she had been. Perhaps she had been burned by the church as well. The thought made him very uneasy.

Sima continued, "Green is the color of nature, and those who imagine this color seem to do well with plants and wild animals. The connection with the forest seems to be key here. Gardeners with a 'green thumb' may manipulate this color unconsciously. Black is the color of decay and is connected with the balance between life and death. The crazy necromancer, once I freed him of his bonds, whipped up a dozen skeletons, did you know that?"

Jodah nodded and said, "And blue? What is your color?"

Sima leaned back against the rail.

"The mind," she said, "thought. Creation. Emotion, and control."

"Control?" Jodah shifted uneasily. "What kind of control?"

Sima looked out over the stern. "Watch," she said, standing up and walking to the rear rail.

The dark-haired woman pulled her hair back in a tight bun and secured it with her comb. She looked much more severe and matronly as she did so, Jodah thought. With her hair down she seemed only a few years older than Jodah, but when she put her hair up again, she appeared older, more formidable, and more unforgiving.

Then she leaned on the rail with both hands and half closed her eyes.

Jodah waited, and nothing happened for a long while. He looked out over the wake of the ship. The ship was reaching, sailing at an angle with the wind, so that the sails caught most of the moving air. The ship's wake formed two long, rounded waves that spread out behind them.

Something moved along one of those waves. Jodah blinked and missed it. Then another something. Then a third. Small triangular fins appeared along the wake of the ship.

Jodah opened his mouth to say something, and one of the fins erupted, pulling up from the water, showing a rounded back and a thin snout shaped like a bottle. Another of the creatures broke the surface of the water, and then two more. Now they were leaping in the wake of the ship, playing and squealing in high, clicking voices as they chased them.

Their presence did not go unnoticed. The crew apparently thought these creatures were a good sign, and there were shouts from among the rigging and from those swabbing the deck. The captain and the elven mate came up on the quarter-deck, and the captain surveyed the leaping creatures with his glass, smiling and totally ignoring Sima's presence. Even the mate managed a grim, tired smile when she saw the large fish flashing in the sun.

Jodah looked a question at the first mate, and immediately the smile faded, replaced with the same disdainful sneer the elf had before.

"Dolphins, Land-Child. They're dolphins." And then she stomped back down the ladder to the main deck, shouting orders and obscenities at crewmen as she did so.

The display lasted for another few minutes, the dolphins launching themselves into the air. They were huge fish, as large as Jodah himself, yet they could pull themselves entirely out of the water in a single leap. They crossed each other in the air, and splashed, one after another, into a single spot. Then, as quickly as they arrived, they were gone.

The captain returned to his maps and left Sima and Jodah alone. After a few minutes, Sima opened her eyes and wiped the sweat from her brow.

"You did that?" said Jodah.

Sima nodded, fighting a smile. "Yes."

"You controlled them?" asked Jodah. "You called them?"

"I . . . I think," said Sima. "That's one of the problems with magic, Jodah. We aren't quite sure of everything it can do, and we aren't quite sure how it does what it does. At least not yet. When I was a girl I watched the dolphins play, following the fishing boats, so I know dolphins well. I don't know if I call them to me, or control their actions, or even cause them to come into being. It's just something that we are still working on."

"Again, there is a 'we' involved," said Jodah.

Sima paused, as if thinking of a response. She said, "We are unsure about so many things. Are creatures summoned by our call or called into being? Can we create matter, or are we just borrowing from some other location? What happens to the energies we unleash with a spell? Why are some mages better with one type of magic than another? Is there something about our very natures that directs us to one color of magic or another?"

"And what kind of magic does the church use?" said Jodah.

Sima blinked, taken aback by the comment. "I cannot believe the Church of Tal would ever use magic, under any circumstance. They speak of miracles and the 'Will of Tal,' but they hate magic with a passion."

Jodah looked puzzled. "Then what did the primata use against us, that night in the camp? She called a flaming sword out of nowhere, and threw a fire bolt at me. Isn't that magic?"

Sima thought for a moment, then shook her head.

"The church hates magic in all its forms," she said again. "The primata probably had some artifact that allowed her to do that. Any artifact that's powerful enough seems like magic to the uninformed."

Jodah cocked his head. "Artifact." That made sense. Jodah remembered the stories from his grandmother. Mishra and Urza were not magicians but artificers. That made sense. More importantly, it felt *right*.

Jodah let out a deep sigh. "I'd like to see an artifact that powerful."

"You already have," said Sima primly. "Voska's mirror."

Jodah looked surprised, then bent down and fished the mirror out of its holding pocket in his boot. It was cool and smooth. He held it up, and his face—reddened by the sun, looked back at him.

"Then this truly *is* magic?" he asked.

"Possibly," said Sima. "It was fortuitous that it cast Delphine's miracle back at her and thereby allowed us to escape. And it has an aura about it, almost like a taste. Once you have studied enough magical items, you get a feel for that. But I don't think it is magical in and of itself. I do think it can affect magic, which is one reason we should take a good look at it when we arrive."

"And where will we be arriving?" said Jodah sternly. "Several times you have talked about 'we' in terms of you and me, and then in terms of you and someone else. Who

123

is this other 'we' that you keep mentioning? You mentioned a City of Shadows as being your home. Is that where we are going?"

Sima licked her lips. "You know how the church feels about magic?"

"All too well," said Jodah.

"Well, as a result, many wizards have formed secret communities to better teach and understand magic. They hide behind their magical wards in concealed or secret places of the world and strive to figure out how to control the forces of mana," she said.

Jodah thought about Voska's mention of such groups when they parted. "And you are from one those groups?"

Sima nodded. "Ours is a very old school of magic. You know of the Brothers?"

"Everyone knows of the Brothers," snorted Jodah. Now she was treating him like a child.

"The founders of our school fought in the Brothers' War." said Sima, with a touch of pride in her voice.

"That was centuries ago!" said Jodah.

Sima nodded again sagely, even smugly.

Jodah hated to reveal his curiosity, but asked, "Who did they fight for, Urza or Mishra?"

"Neither," said Sima, "they fought against both, and they won."

Jodah made a rude noise, and Sima cocked an eyebrow at him. "Are Urza and Mishra still around, that you know of?"

Jodah had to admit that he had always assumed that they had died in the Devastation.

"Our school did survive," said Sima, almost smugly. "I would consider that to be 'winning' the war, wouldn't you?"

Jodah thought about it. He nodded again, slowly, despite himself.

Sima continued, "Our founders followed what they called 'the Third Path,' the one that was neither Urza nor Mishra. That path became what we know now to be magic. Real magic."

Sima turned to Jodah. "Our school began in secrecy, hidden from the world. It has grown over the years, but it remains a city of shadows, hiding in many ways from the merciless light of the church. On occasion, members of our group pass into this dark world, looking for old artifacts from the time of the Brothers. Looking for knowledge of spells now lost. And looking for talented individuals who can cast those spells."

Sima paused for a moment, and Jodah said, "Voska. You were seeking Voska, to bring him into your group."

"Aye," said Sima, "we . . . the mages of the City of Shadows, of our school of the unseen, are not too proud to realize that we don't know enough about this new force, about magic. So we study, and we collect, and we train."

"And you want to bring me to your scholars?" asked Jodah.

"Yes," said Sima.

"Me," he said, his eyes narrowing, "or do you merely want Voska's magical mirror?"

Jodah expected the woman to stammer, perhaps to deny and dissemble—anything to rock her from her self-important perch. Instead she turned serious, and said, "We want both. Capable spellcasters are as important as magical devices. And our school has always sought out powerful artifacts."

Jodah brightened slightly, "You think me a capable spellcaster?"

"I *think*," she said, stressing the second word, "that you have *potential*. I'll take you to my city and present you as a candidate for proper training. I promise you that. Which means you have to start treating your magic with more seriousness. Fortunately, we have several weeks before we make landfall, and I can work with you. But you will have to let me be honest with you and be able to take criticism."

"I can do that," said Jodah, mildly stung by the idea that he could not take her comments, or could not learn from her.

"Fine," said Sima, "then let's begin."

* * * * *

By the end of the first day Jodah was irritated with Sima. By the end of the second day Jodah had passed irritation and was well into full-bore infuriation. By the third day, the quarter-deck had become a battlefield between the two.

Like rival cats trapped in the same closet, they hissed and nipped at each other continually. The captain no longer took his readings on the sun from the quarter-deck, and even the elven mate avoided them as they squabbled.

"Your breathing is all wrong," Sima said sharply.

"I can only breath one way," replied Jodah irritably.

"Well, it's wrong," said Sima with a prim certainty. "You are breathing in when summoning the mana to you. That tenses you up. Breath out when you do it."

"It doesn't work when I try it that way!" snarled Jodah.

"Then you're not trying!" said Sima. She clenched her fist and stomped the deck hard, but her face was a stern mask.

"Urza's blood!" cried Jodah to the ever-blue sky, "According to you, you have to do *everything* perfect in order to cast a spell. You have to be perfectly at ease *but* also be completely aware of your surroundings. You have to avoid concentrating *but* know exactly what you are doing. Each action should be both natural *and* precise. Jodah! Let yourself go loose *and* remember to keep your fingers spread slightly apart. And most of all, Jodah, remember to breath differently than you breathed all your life!"

Sima scowled and took a deep, an almost theatrical breath, then raised both hands, palms upward. "I realize this is difficult. You have to unlearn a lot of bad habits Voska let you accumulate."

"Voska was a *great* teacher!" Jodah was verging on shouting now.

"I'm sorry, but the idea of putting spells in mental locations, like some type of filing cabinet, was the wrong way to look at it," said Sima hotly, ignoring Jodah's growing ire. "You will someday find yourself mentally riffling through imaginary bric-a-brac, looking for the correct spell for a situation, when you *really* need to understand the nature of magic itself and how you can bend it to your needs."

"My way works for me," shouted Jodah.

"But this way is *better*!" shouted Sima back.

"Not for me!"

"Then you're just beyond hope!"

The two stared at each other as the deck rose and fell beneath them in a soft, easy rhythm. Both had their jaws and fists clenched, and were glaring daggers at each other.

Sima closed her eyes and drew a deep breath. "Very well," she said finally, "let's not fight about this. Keep track of your spells however you want. It's a personal decision, after all."

Jodah continued to glower. "I am *not* beyond hope."

Sima bit her lip, then said, "No, you're just very frustrating. No, don't bridle. I may be expecting too much too soon. Just listen as I explain the theory behind it, and I'm sure you'll understand why I want you to do it a particular way."

Jodah grimaced and envisioned reams of papers and scores of books piled up in some subterranean library listing all of "Sima's theories" of why magic worked the way it did. The concept of five colors seemed fairly sound, but why only five? And how did artifacts fit in? Or holy relics? And the church's miracles? Did they fit in at all? There were tales of steam-driven beasts before the Devastation. Were they part of the five colors? Did the five colors truly exist before Urza and Mishra? Were they created as a result of the Devastation? Was the light he created by his spells truly little bits of matter or was it movement among bits of existing matter?

Sima did not seem to have the answers to any of the important questions, to Jodah's mind. All she had was ritual and repetition and studies and most of all, theory. He nodded sternly and sagely as Sima expressed the purpose of proper breathing, but inwardly he had already reduced her voice to be at the same level as the squawking gulls, and thought it just as relevant.

There had been a time, when the pair of them were fleeing the church encampment on the back of the primata's white gelding, when Jodah felt Sima's warm, greyhound-thin body pressed against him and thought normal thoughts of one his age regarding young (and less-than-young) women. Now, Jodah looked back to those musings and shuddered. If they *had* done anything, he knew, they would then have to sit around and *talk* about it. Jodah shook his head in disgust.

The storm between the two of them, abated for only a moment, began mounting again as Sima droned on. This time Jodah's irritation was mirrored by the seas themselves. Clouds started to pile behind them on the horizon, and the sea had turned a greenish hue, flecked with whitecaps. The captain made an appearance toward midday. He surveyed the choppy horizon and addressed the pair.

"It's going to be a bit of a blow, and a nasty one at that," he said, interrupting one of Sima's diatribes. "If you need the shelter, come to the helm directly below this deck, where we tend to the rudder. It opens onto the main deck, but it'll provide some protection for you."

Sima nodded quickly and waved the mariner off, returning at once to her lecture on interrupting a casting with another, shorter spell. The captain gave Jodah a sighing, sympathetic nod, and headed back down the ladder to the main deck.

Jodah for his part practiced his patience, though every jibe from the woman seemed to dig into his flesh. Then came more practice, and with it more of Sima's comments and sniping. About his pose. About his actions. About his breathing.

As the day wore on, the clouds continued to mount, changing from inconsequential balls of lamb's wool to a massive wall stretching along the horizon from one side to the other. Small tongues of lightning were already clear along the dark hem of this storm. The wind picked up, and the cog ran before the storm. The captain bellowed for the crew to furl the mainsail and ship the crosspieces of the mainmast, else the force of the wind would bring it down.

Jodah's own anger and irritation was rising again with the storm. He had hit the limit when he asked about removing an enchantment, and Sima corrected him by saying he meant to say that he would, in that case, be removing the power of that enchantment instead.

"It's the same thing," said Jodah hotly.

"It's not," responded Sima frostily. "When you disenchant you negate the spell itself forever, while when one disempowers one merely dampens it for a short time by preventing it from accessing its magical energies. But that's probably beyond your abilities at the moment."

Jodah stared angrily at Sima, wondering if, lost in her world of spell theory, she had any conception of the effect she was having on her would-be student. Finally, he looked down at the deck and said, "Maybe this was a mistake."

"It's a simple mistake," said Sima. "You just don't know the difference between disenchanting something and disempowering . . ."

"No, not that," said Jodah, angrily, "a mistake to think that you can teach me your type of magic in a matter of weeks."

Sima's face clouded. "Well, if you would *just* listen and not argue so much . . ."

The ire now cut loose again, and Jodah was shouting now. "Listen? I feel like I know less than when I started! Maybe I *am* beyond hope! You seem to think me some type of . . ." He clawed his wrecked mental mansion for the right word, and finally settled on "dunderhead!"

"Dunderhead?" Sima spat back, matching Jodah's anger. "You're probably the most capable student I've seen! You've got more natural talent than you know what to do with! If you would just calm down and try to do things the right way, you'll be amazed with what you can do!"

Jodah stared at Sima. "Was that finally a compliment?" he asked.

Sima balled one hand in a fist and slammed it against her thigh. She opened her mouth, but her words were drowned out by the sharp patter of rain slamming into the deck. Jodah looked back, and a black wall of rain was catching up with their ship from astern. The storm had broken.

Then it was upon them, and there was no more time for argument. The ship was swept up in a great swell and catapulted forward with the leading edge of the storm.

Jodah and Sima scrabbled to get down the ladder to the relative safety of the helm—little more than a covered porch open on three sides—directly beneath the quarterdeck. As he scrambled down the ladder, Jodah noticed that some of the crew had already tied themselves to their posts with stout cables. The captain was bellowing something, but Jodah could not hear—the young man's ears were filled with the sounds of the storm.

The ship rocked precipitously, and despite himself, Jodah reached out to snag Sima as she stepped off the ladder. She pushed back against him, and the pair of them slammed against the port railing. Then Sima was up again, clawing for the railing, making for the relative safety of the helm's back wall.

There was the sound of tearing cloth, and looking upward, Jodah saw one of the sails ripped away by the wind. It took flight, like a large canvas bird tumbling end over end until it was lost in the raging storm.

Jodah's hair stood on end, and he looked up to see lights dancing around the remaining mast. They were glowing balls of energy, and idly Jodah wondered if they were made of mana, or if they were some natural phenomenon summoned by the force of the storm.

Jodah reached the captain, who stood at the tiller, both hands gripping the heavy beam controlling the ship's rudder. Sima and two other sailors were holding to the beam's length. Jodah shouted and pointed at the balls of energy that swooped and bobbed over the deck.

The captain gave a wide grin. "Good Omen!" he shouted. "Now man the tiller and keep a straight course! If we turn abeam of the storm, we'll be scuttled!"

Jodah grabbed the tiller, replacing Sima. Her gown was drenched now, as were they all, and she moved to one side of the helm, holding tight to the side railing. Jodah grunted and felt he was trying to turn the boat by himself, as the captain bellowed orders.

The battle to hold the ship to a steady course lasted about thirty minutes, and Jodah's arms felt as if they had been strained past human ability. Then there was a visible drop of the wind. He could feel the resistance in the tiller-beam slacken against his reddened palms and the pressure lessen in his ears; though the rain continued to lash at the deck around them.

"We're going to make it!" shouted the captain. "Steady now!"

Jodah looked up at the mast, and the glowing spheres were still there, a mated pair orbiting in a dance around the main mast. The surviving sail, farther toward the bow, was holed and torn, and the spheres dodged around the tattered remains.

Despite himself, Jodah reached into his boot and took out the mirror. Voska's mirror. If these balls were mana-based, perhaps he could use the mirror to attract them and perhaps control them like Sima had done with the dolphins.

The rain was a solid wall that bisected the ship, but already Jodah could see that some of the men had unlashed themselves and were now moving on the deck.

Then he realized with a start that the forms moving on the deck were not quite human. They were more slender than the crew, as slender as elves, and had great crests of hair that swept behind them like manes. And they had no legs, only the bottom quarters of dolphins, and they thrashed as they moved forward on the decks.

The cries went up simultaneously. There were two sets, from different locations.

From the deck there came the cry, "Captain, we've been boarded!"

From below deck there came the cry, "Captain, we've been holed!"

The elven first mate let out a cry of "Merfolk," and drew a thin blade that was almost as long as her arm. Jodah moved the mirror to his other hand and drew his own sword.

The first wave of boarders were on top of them—their lower quarters moving like snakes and their bodies raised above, armed with clubs and three-branched spears. They were human from the waist up, though totally blue. One of them hissed at Jodah and swung a thick, heavy club made of coral. Jodah danced away from the blow then came back with a slash of his own. A ragged, blue-green streak appeared in the center of the mer-creature, and it fell away.

Jodah looked for Sima, and saw her, along the far railing on the starboard side. The storm had torn part of the starboard railing away, but she had hooked her leg around a splintered post and was now standing, effortless and calmly as the gale tore at her hair and gown. She held up both hands, fists upward, and pushed them forward, flicking her fingers as she did.

A wave rose from the rain-drenched deck itself, a wave of blue-green water that spread along the width of the ship and powered itself toward the bow. The merfolk in its path were swept up and carried overboard by the tidal force.

Magic, thought Jodah, intending the word as a reprimand. He was supposed to be casting spells, but he reached for his sword at the first real threat. Part of him wondered if any of his light-fountain spells could be useful here, and he cursed himself for not thinking of it sooner.

There was a crack of lightning, and the crossbar of the remaining mast crashed to the deck in front of them, bringing down a maze of rigging with it. Merfolk attackers were already clambering over the fallen mast, and for the first time Jodah noticed that the ship was riding perilously low in the water, so that swells were now coming up to the level of the deck.

The ship had been boarded. They had been holed. The merfolk attacked from above and below, and now the ship was sinking.

Jodah stood and meant to stumble over to Sima, to ask if she had any spells that could keep them afloat, but as he released his grip from the rail, the ship veered to the port side, and a great swell crashed over the larboard. The wave swept Jodah off his feel, and he lost hold of both his sword and the mirror.

The deck pitched downward toward Sima, and Jodah fell forward, out of control. He, his sword, and the mirror were all sliding sideways across the ship's deck. In front of him the white-churned ocean filled his vision.

From the corner of his eye he saw a flash of blue, and Sima sprang from her position along the splintered port railing. She skidded along the deck through the water, moving with great speed.

Magic, again, thought Jodah, and lunged out to grab her as she passed, but he was not fast enough, and she had leapt too high along the cascading deck. She passed a good foot above Jodah's outstretched fingers, and the young man continued to dive along the overturned deck toward the waiting sea.

Jodah tuned his head and had a chance for one last glimpse of Sima. She almost skated across the deck, reaching down and grabbing something shiny and round and smooth that glittered as she snared it in elegantly long fingers. Then she was gone, colliding with the mass of fallen and torn canvas that had been the forward sail.

Jodah was gone as well, as the deck finally ended, and he shot out over the water. The starboard side came up and the ship righted itself, but Jodah was moving so fast that he was launched in a short arc into the downpour.

He hit the water hard, his body twisted and unprepared. It knocked the wind from him, and when he drew a breath, saltwater coursed down his throat. He broke the surface of the water and sputtered, his hair matted against his face, his wet clothing pulling at him like an anchor.

He was trapped in a world of gray ocean swells and cold rain. He could see no one else among the choppy, white-pointed waves. The ship was gone. Sima was gone. Everyone was gone, and he was left alone to die.

Jodah's heart sank as he realized that Sima had not tried to save him. She had leapt across the deck to save Voska's mirror. He was incidental. She acted to save the artifact.

A cold hand closed around Jodah's heart. Then other hands, beneath the surface, latched firmly onto Jodah's arms and legs. Jodah had a moment to let out a shout of surprise as they pulled him underwater, beneath the churning waves.

And then Jodah did not think again.

The Drowned Mage

What we call the history of the world is usually the human history of the world. In our pride and arrogance we assume that ours is the only tale worth telling. In doing so we ignore the heritages of the elves, the minotaurs, the merfolk, and yes, even the goblins. Who knows what kingdoms rose and fell among the merfolk during the Dark, or what dark pacts the elves made for their own survival. The history books, the human history books, are mute on the subject, save where their stories cross our own.

—**Arkol, Argivian scholar**

On a lonely beach, the sun setting behind him, the Rag Man waited.

The sand blew around his feet and caught in his tattered garments, forming fine traceries where the dark bandages met. Occasionally, a good burst of wind would send a spinning sand-dervish along the length of the beach, shoving grit into the Rag Man's face. If the being had eyes in the conventional sense, he would have been blinded, but instead he stood there.

Waiting.

The tide was coming in, each wave traveling slightly farther up the wide, tilted expanse of the beach. In another hour, the Rag Man would be forced to retreat up the beach, taking his package with him.

That would be in another hour. For the moment, the Rag Man stood on the beach, watching the fiddler crabs move from hole to hole. Watching as the waves exposed the sand fleas, that would then burrow again in the loose muck, only to be exposed again by the next wave.

Waiting.

Shadows appeared in the water, no more than the heads and shoulders of creatures coming out of the sea. One, two, four, then seven. Their skin was a dusky blue, and they wore their long hair like lions' manes. They moved toward the shore, toward the Rag Man.

The Rag Man waited, giving no sign of noticing them.

The merfolk reached the breakers now, and as the storm-swollen waves crested, they slid into the beach, letting the waves carry their streamlined bodies. Six of them remained where the waves crashed and hissed up the beach. One of them, the leader, raised herself in the thin tidal waters and half crawled, half slithered forward.

The merfolk leader curled up on her piscine hindquarter and hauled herself to her full height, still shorter than the Rag Man. The mer-creature said something in a garbled, throaty language.

The Rag Man nodded.

The merfolk leader said something else, more emphatically.

The Rag Man nodded again.

The merfolk leader motioned with her arm, and two more of her people splashed ashore, carrying a bundle between them. The bundle was wrapped in a net made of cord woven from kelp.

The commanding merfolk gargled something else, and the two bearers unwrapped the net to reveal a young man, his face pale and his skin slightly bluish. The young man did not move. He had a gag made of seaweed fronds clamped across his mouth.

The merfolk leader looked at the Rag Man. The Rag Man merely nodded.

The merfolk leader gargled something else. One of the other merfolk pulled at the frond over the young man's mouth. It came away easily. The young man still did not move, and his chest was still.

The merfolk leader struck the prostrate body in the ribs.

The young man coughed once, and water spilled out of his throat, then he inhaled, in a deep, ragged breath—coughed again—and continued to breath. His chest rose and fell normally now.

The Rag Man nodded and reached for his satchel.

The black-wrapped creature picked up the canvas bag and pulled from it a helmet. The helm was made entirely of orange coral and looked as if it had been grown into that shape instead of fashioned by human hands. He presented it to the merfolk leader.

The merfolk leader bared her fangs and said something else in her garbled, throaty language.

The Rag Man merely nodded.

The three merfolk raiders half crawled, half slithered back to where the combers were breaking. Already the other merfolk were fleeing the shore. The two bearers followed, diving in without looking back. The leader looked back one last time, then dived in as well, following her brethren away from the beach.

The Rag Man waited until all the merfolk had departed, the sky darkening behind him. Then the ragged creature picked up the young man and pulled him free of his kelp-woven net. He grasped the young man by the neck of his shirt and dragged him up above the high tide mark, where even the storm-swollen waves would not touch him, to a small divot between two dunes. Driftwood had already been stacked in a shallow pit, and dried salt grasses had been added as tinder.

The Rag Man laid the young man's body out and touched the side of his cheek with the back of a skeletal hand. The young man's flesh was already warm, when moments before it had been as cold as ice.

The Rag Man reached inside his robes, reached inside his chest. There was a cracking noise as the being snapped off part of his own rib cage. The manlike creature withdrew the bone and held it up in the moonless night. The ragged edge of the bone glowed of its own volition, a corpse light powered by undead wizardry.

The Rag Man knelt down and used the sputtering corpse light to set fire to the driftwood. Their position between the dunes would keep the light from being seen from afar.

The Rag Man checked the young man's body again. It was warmer still. He moved the lad slightly closer to the flames—not so close as to singe the clothing, but close enough to warm the young man.

Having done so, the Rag Man watched the tableau he had created—the body, now breathing steadily, the fire in its pit, and himself, all set between the dunes in a moonless sky.

The Rag Man nodded and walked fifty paces away. Then he stopped, turned, and faced the fire.

And the Rag Man waited.

8☾

Safe Havens

Better known than the enigmatic City of Shadows was Ith's Councilhouse, also called Mairsil's Citadel, or the Magician's Conclave. At a time when all the rest of the world was plunged into darkness and ignorance, the Conclave served as a beacon of magical thought. Here was the home of Ith, and Mairsil, and Barl, and Shannan and a host of other names that are invoked by mages to this day. Here was the true flowering of magic, where the persecuted spell-casters could find a place to work, to research, and to study, and they came from all over Terisiare to benefit from this magical renaissance.

—Arkol, Argivian scholar

Jodah awoke, spitting sand out of his mouth. He opened his eyes and saw a screaming gull wheel high in the air over him—apparently it was sizing him up as refuse and disappointed that he proved to be still alive.

The young man pulled himself to a sitting position. Every joint in his body complained from the effort, and his flesh felt as if he had been battered by a gang of assailants and then left to die.

Then he saw the waves breaking down the beach, a long tidal flat between him and the combers. He remembered what had happened—the ship, the storm, and Sima.

A cold fury gripped his stomach. Sima had abandoned him. She could have saved him, and she had not. She rescued the mirror and not him.

The gull screamed again, and Jodah looked out over the ocean. It was slate-gray now, almost merging with the sky in a single, overcast expanse, rolling out to the horizon and then rolling back over his head. Sima had not saved him, but he had somehow survived.

And now Sima was probably dead, along with the captain and his elven mate and likely anyone else on-board the ship. Like Mother Dobbs. Like Fendah and the other soldiers, both Alsoorian and Ghed, at Pitdown.

Like Voska.

The gull settled down above the waterline to contest some surf-deposited object with a black-headed tern. Jodah rose slowly, his joints still ringing from the movement, his flesh feeling like heavy clothing. He shooed the birds away, hoping that perhaps they fought over some clue to the fate of the others.

What they had been fighting over was the decaying corpse of a fish. A long, slender eel that had been pulled from its deepwater home in the storm and dashed on alien shores—just a bit of flotsam, like himself.

Jodah stripped and bathed in the surf, the cold water bracing his skin and anesthetizing the pain in his joints. He dusted the bulk of the sand out of his clothing and dressed again, all too aware that he would be feeling bits of grit beneath his shirt and pants for days. He replaced the heavy boots and for a moment had a vision of them filling with water, dragging him down beneath the stormy waves.

Had he survived by miracle or by magic? he wondered. Did it truly matter? The rest had died, and he had lived and what was the point of wondering why that was so?

Sima would have provided a reason, easily and effortlessly, but she was dead. That did not make the ache of her betrayal any less.

When Jodah turned back toward the inland he saw the ragged figure in torn scraps and tatters standing on the dune, a lantern in one hand and a satchel in the other. The sea breeze caught the ends of the figure's robe and bandages and turned them into dark pennants against the cold gray sky.

Jodah blinked, and the ragged man did not disappear. The tattered creature did, however, turn away and descend the far side of the dune.

Jodah shouted and began running. Running in the loose sand above the tide line would be slow going under the best of circumstances, and it was made more difficult both by exhausted muscles and heavy boots. When Jodah crested the first line of dunes the ragged figure was gone.

No, his quarry was a few hundred yards away, on the other side of a low marsh of sea oats, standing on a second line of dunes. Again, the figure turned and disappeared slowly as Jodah ran forward. The footing was better among the clumps of yellow-brown weeds, and he reached the top of the inner line of dunes, scanning the horizon for the mysterious figure.

Inland of the second line of dunes was a meadow overrun with purplish flowers. At the far end was another low hillock, this one carved with the perfectly round opening of a burrow; about the size of a man. The ragged creature was standing next to the entrance of this cave, and, as Jodah spotted him, the figure turned and walked inside.

As Jodah neared the entrance, the burrow itself was lit from within by a pale, reddish light.

Jodah slowed and carefully approached the entrance. Within was a small cave, running no more than twenty feet back into the low hill with sloping walls like a tunnel. There was space to stand in the center, and the sides had low rows of packed earth fashioned like benches.

The ragged figure released the lantern and raised his arm. Something glowed a sickly white in his hand, a wan companion to the warm crimson shades of the lantern. As Jodah entered, the figure dropped the bone-white stick and crushed it, firmly, beneath his heel.

"Who are you?" said Jodah.

The ragged figure went to the far wall and sat on the earthen bench.

"I said, who are you?" repeated Jodah.

The figure pointed to a similar earthen bench on the opposite wall.

Jodah entered the small cavern warily. If he had a weapon, Jodah would have bared it. Even now he regretted not pausing to grab a chunk of driftwood. "Three, maybe four times you've shown up in my life. Always when there's trouble. What are you? A ghost? A dream? A trick of the light?" ranted Jodah.

The ragged figure said nothing but maintained his pose on the earthen bench, thin blue-tinged hands clasping his knees.

Jodah crossed the cavern in a rush. "Why don't you answer me?" he shouted.

Jodah intended to reach up and rip the rags covering the creature's face, to tear back the cowl and reveal the features beneath. Part of him thought he might know the face if he saw it. Part of him thought there would only be a skull beneath the robes. And part of him thought his hand would pass through the robes, rags, cowl, and all, and the ragged figure would fade from view like a fever dream unmasked.

Jodah did not even see the creature move. Suddenly one thin hand had raised from its position on the creature's knee and grasped Jodah's hand firmly around the wrist—Jodah's fingers mere inches from the cowl. Jodah felt icy cold from the fingers reach up his arm, but his wrist was locked in an unyielding grip. The ragged creature twisted his arm slightly, and Jodah's entire body twisted to the left, following the motion of his trapped hand.

There was a momentary pause, and the intense grip lessened, apparently to give Jodah the chance to pull away, to flee. Instead, Jodah tried to swing his body around and grab the ragged figure with his other hand.

Again the ragged man was too fast for him. His opponent redoubled his grip on Jodah's wrist and brought the trapped wrist forward, and then down, and then flung it and the body it was attached to across the room. Jodah slid across the earthen floor of the cave and smashed into the far bench.

Jodah slowly picked himself up off the floor. The tattered figure motioned to the bench, then raised a single finger to his unseen, covered mouth.

"Sit down and shut up," said Jodah, more to himself than to his companion in the cavern. "I think I get the message."

The ragged figure said nothing.

Jodah pulled himself up on the earthen bench and regarded the tattered figure. His companion in the cave was covered head to toe in ragged bandages, even beneath its robe and cowl. The ragged being's fingers were bare, but they were no more than long, whitish talons, little more than spurs of bone. Was this thing human? Was he magical?

One thing for certain, Jodah thought, rubbing his sore shoulder, he wasn't a dream, and he wasn't a trick of the light. For the moment, that discovery seemed to be enough.

The ragged figure sat immobile, across the earthen burrow, on a bench of packed earth, skeletal hands on his knees. Jodah watched, one foot raised on his own bench, his back against the soft earth of the cave wall, waiting for the rag-wrapped being to take any action. The only movement in the cave was the flickering of the wick flame in the lantern by the ragged creature's side, and their own shadows following that flickering, locked in a tight and exact dance.

After fifteen minutes Jodah felt drowsy. After twenty he realized that he should be anywhere else but in a burrow with some inhuman creature. At twenty-five minutes he realized that the tattered human thing across from him could have killed him three or four times over but had so far only provided help. The thing had been his dark guardian angel.

At thirty minutes Jodah was asleep, his head dropped to his chest, snoring softly.

Across from him, the Rag Man waited.

* * * * *

Jodah awoke at the Rag Man's first movement. The creature of rags and tatters stood up, his slumped shoulders barely grazing the interior curve of the cave.

Jodah's eyes were open at once, and he brought up his hands immediately to put them between himself and the tattered black figure. The ragged creature merely hunched over and picked up the lantern by its oversized loop.

He walked to the entrance of the small cave, turned back slightly as if to invite Jodah to follow, then left. The light went with the ragged man, and Jodah followed.

The air was odd. It was colder than before, in a world where everything seemed to be either cold or colder, and the smell was wrong. The smells of the ocean, of salt and things dying on the beach was missing. Instead there was a cool, sharp tang carrying just a hint of distant smoke.

Jodah reached the entrance of the cavern and saw that he was now very far from the beach. The cavern entrance was not on the side of some purple-flowered hillock but instead carved into the side of a great black mountain. Steps, worn by the passing of many feet, led down from the dark hillside. Ahead of him, the ragged figure walked slowly down the stairs, holding his lantern ahead to guide his path.

Jodah shook his head. He looked back into the cave. It was the one he had entered before, the one by the beach. Yet now it opened out to a completely different part of the world.

Sima had talked of magic having flavors, tastes, and smell. This definitely had the feel of magic, and it had a smell, one that Jodah could not put his finger on.

Jodah turned and followed the descending lantern-light, finding his footing in the dying light of the day.

The sky was red with sunset to his right, and a shoulder of the black mountain cast a shadow that consumed him and his guide. Ahead of them, across a low, flat plain was another shoulder of the mountain, thrust out and farther away from its parent. On that out-thrust shoulder was a great castle.

Castle, yes, though a large one, larger than most towns, with a huge central keep and numerous towers. The towers were tipped by ornate iron frameworks that looked very much like a collection of holy symbols welded together at random. Equally ornate balconies with iron railings dotted the towers. Flying bridges and curved battlements spanned the spaces between the towers and the central keep.

In the waning light Jodah could see that the complex sprawled out and downward over most of the mountain's shoulder. Portions of the great building hung over the cliffs beyond, suspended by buttresses, and it would seem, aided by spells and wishful thinking.

For its part, the central keep was dominated by an ever-higher set of peeked roofs, some of thatch and wood shingles, and some of multicolored slate that caught the last glimmers of the evening light. There were lights in some of the upper windows, and even from this distance Jodah could hear the sound of people laughing.

Jodah caught up with his ragged guide, who was moving slowly and methodically across the plain. At first Jodah thought that the patch of land they were crossing was some type of abandoned garden, like the ones he knew in Giva Province, given up to rot and weeds. There were low walls everywhere, overgrown with dark ivy and glory-plants. The glory-plants had withdrawn their flowers with the loss of the light and would bloom again only in the morning. The walls were tumbled and decayed and snaked in all directions.

A labyrinth, Jodah realized. It was like a garden maze

built in front of a manor house, but this one was huge, and had been abandoned. No, he corrected himself, it had never been finished in the first place. Someone had intended to fill the plain with a great maze and had stopped halfway through the process.

His guide moved silently. Was this castle the place of the creature's master, Jodah wondered? Or was his dark angel merely guiding him to a safe haven? He followed the ragged man cautiously.

The evening light had faded entirely behind them as they neared the causeway to the castle's main gate. As Jodah watched, small fires appeared along the lines of the battlements, but there was no sign of movement along those walls.

The lanky hunched figure stopped and set the lantern on the ground at Jodah's feet. The figure pointed at the main gate.

"You're not coming with me?" said Jodah, his brows lowered in concern.

The ragged figure placed both hands over the center of his chest, palms inward. Then he raised a finger to his hidden mouth.

Jodah nodded. "You don't want them to know about you," he said. "But is it safe there?"

The ragged figure did not respond but was moving off, back to the unfinished labyrinth.

"I asked . . . hey!" said Jodah, and bent down to grasp the brass lantern. When he rose again, lantern in hand, the ragged figure was gone.

Jodah muttered a curse under his breath and looked at the causeway. He had no weapons, no food, and no idea where he was. The only way to go was forward.

He crossed the causeway and rapped hard on the main

gate with the fleshy part of his palm. The door thundered under his knocking.

The great gate itself was made of two halves, so that when it was fully opened a full-sized giant could stride through without stooping. On one half of the gate was a smaller door, and in that door there was a slot covered by a sliding piece of wood. The piece of wood slid open with a resounding clack, and Jodah walked over to it.

"Who are you?" said a voice on the far side of the door. It sounded bored and disinterested.

"I am Jodah," said the young man simply. "Where am I?"

The voice on the far side ignored him. "Why are you here?"

Jodah took a deep breath and said, "I seek a safe and warm place. Would you turn away a tired traveler?"

The voice said, "Are you a wizard?"

Jodah looked at the eyes on the other side of the slot and thought of the church. "I don't know if I want to tell you that," he said.

There was a chortle. "Well, when you decide you are, sonny, you be sure to knock again. I'll be here all night." And with that the shutter of wood clattered shut with a final click.

Jodah stared at the door and carefully counted to ten. Then he counted a second time. The third time he started at ten and worked backward.

Then he took a deep breath and cleared his mind. The path for this spell was now as well-worn as the steps leading down from the mountain, and he did not need to fully think of it as he called it from the depths of him memory.

He knocked on the small door with one hand and placed the other, palm outward, on the small sliding shutter. Nothing happened. He knocked a second time.

"You still here . . . ?" said the peeved voice on the other side, sliding the shutter open.

There was a shout of surprise as Jodah unleashed the blast of light in the doorkeeper's face. The main portion of the light was white, but Jodah had included small stream-ers and balls of green, red, ebony, and blue radiance as well.

"I thought about it," said Jodah to the door, "and I suppose I *am* a wizard after all."

A weak voice answered from behind the shutter. "Then enter, friend wizard." There was a pause, and then the voice added, "I'll open the gate for you as soon as I can see well enough to find the door handle."

* * * * *

In his luxurious study, Lord Mairsil hunched down before his clockwork creation. It was too wide to put on a shelf and just tall enough to make putting it on a work-bench unfeasible. He would have to have the servants build a special low table for it, eventually, but for the moment he had a greater problem with it than just aesthetics.

He ran a long, elegant finger over one set of cogs, then another set, tracing the motion of the clockworks from one set of gears to another. The gears were made not of metals but of minerals and stone. The largest wheels were slate and marble, the ones that were smaller were made of quartz and mica, and the smallest and most vital pieces of the device were carved from rubies and sapphires. One small, rune-covered plate near the heart of the construct had been fashioned of rare and perfect obsianus, and others were made of platinum, rustbane, and watersilver.

He tapped one particular cog and nodded, then went to his workbench, bringing back the smallest of his hourglasses. He turned the hourglass over as he passed his hand over the a rune-carved gem on the clockwork itself.

The clockwork sprang to life, its gears and cogs glowing of their own radiance. The tie-rods of graphite spun in time, and the golden cords hummed through jasper pulleys. Within the dim light of the study the gems bathed Lord Mairsil in an ever-changing glow.

Lord Mairsil paid no notice. Instead he was lost in thought, idly twisting the ruby ring on his right hand.

The last of the sands of the small glass ran out, and as it passed through the narrow neck of the timepiece, Mairsil reached his hand out. He touched the rune-inscribed gem just as the bit of white sand joined its fellows at the base of the glass.

There was a soft, firm rap on the doorjamb of his study.

"The calendar is fast," said Mairsil, looking up.

"My Lord Mage?" said the stocky figure at the doorway. Barl, chief artificer of the Conclave, entered the room. He was the only member of the Citadel who would dare to knock on Mairsil's door when he was involved in an experiment.

"I said, the calendar is fast," said the master of the Conclave, rising from his crouched position, "half a tick over fifteen minutes. Expand that out to weeks, months, even years, and that is intolerable."

Barl let out the sigh of a man who had heard this type of news before. "I will check the parts . . ."

Mairsil interrupted. "It's the jadeite cog, the third smallest of the set. It is wearing too fast. Replace it with one made of nephrite."

Barl bowed and replied, "Your words become my deeds."

"As always," said Mairsil. "Why have you come?"

"A new arrival," said Barl, "a potential initiate."

"It's late for any new arrivals," said the Lord. "They normally arrive with supply caravans and the like. Any ability?"

"Likely," said the artificer. "He blinded the doorman with a flash of light."

A smile gently grew across Mairsil's face, tugging at the corners of his thin mustache. "Indeed? Industrious sort."

"You wished to be notified. Handle him as normal?" said Barl, folding his hands in front of him.

"Yes," said Mairsil, looking back at the clockwork in front of him. "Interview and audition. Find out if he has any magics on him, or if he knows where to find them. Then give him something challenging. I think . . ." he looked at the stocky man. "I think it would be a good thing to bring out one of the old toys. Yes, if he's using light, he's likely a white, then one of the old toys would be best for him."

Barl bowed and touched a hand to his wide forehead. "As you wish, my lord."

"Send a runner for me for the audition," said Mairsil, absent-mindedly. "I feel the need for a little diversion coming on."

Barl gave a solemn grin. "Of course, My Lord Mage." He turned to go.

"And Barl?"

"Yes, My Lord Mage?"

"You didn't carve the jade cog yourself, did you?"

Barl paused, then said, "No, My Lord Mage, a student of mine did. He is a promising student, and I thought he could handle it."

Mairsil nodded. "The promise is unfulfilled. Tell him

that I am displeased. And break two of his fingers as punishment. On the left hand, of course."

Barl paused again, then said, "Of course, My Lord Mage. Your words are my deeds, as ever."

"I thought it was lesser work," said Mairsil. "I can always tell when one of the apprentices does it. Sloppy. Hopefully your next apprentice will be more careful in such matters."

"Yes, My Lord Mage." Barl was gone. Mairsil knelt down again next to his gemstone calendar. With one hand he flipped the hourglass, and with the other he touched the rune-gem that brought the device to life.

He leaned back as the magical colors played out on his lean face, and he twisted his ruby ring as he watched both the device and the hourglass.

* * * * *

Deep beneath the castle, Ith fought the darkness and his own madness.

He could feel the darkness surging up from beneath him, from the depths of the pit. The pit had predated the Citadel and indeed likely predated the monastery that had once stood here. The pit was eternal, and from the pit rose the darkness that clawed at his thoughts. Hideous creatures thrived in that darkness.

Sometimes he envisioned the thought-creatures as being great jellyfish, rising like balloons from the depths of the pit, trailing poisonous tendrils made of spun gold. Sometimes they were spectral dragons the size of bats. Sometimes they were skeletal bats the size of dragons. Sometimes they were gremlins with pitchforks. Always they called to him, always they entreated him.

Always they tempted him.

They could free him, if he would only free them. He was there as a lens of power, magnifying Mairsil the Pretender's abilities, swelling the usurper's source of mana. But he was also a gate, a doorway between the real world and the things that lived within the pit—or beyond the pit.

He dreamed of a man made of wires and bone, with snakes growing from the back of his head. The wire-man whispered horrible truths about Mairsil, about the Conclave, about the ever-darkening world.

When Ith awoke, he knew it to be more than a dream, but he was unsure if he had awakened to his life or only to another dream. Then he began screaming, and the madness took hold of him for a long time. The madness seemed to be a bulwark against the dark, but he needed to be sane. At least he thought he needed to be sane.

On occasion the watersilver in his bars would glimmer with power as Mairsil pulled more of Ith's energies upward—to be harnessed in the usurper's spells and devices—and in doing so he weakened the wall against the things in the pit even more.

Ith felt a scream rise within him, and he fought that as well as the temptation of the darkness. He tried to maintain his grip on the real world, but he had forgotten why doing such a thing was important. It was what he had always done, and so he continued.

Something in the real world moved, the movement of soft cloth against stone. Like a swimmer seeking fresh air, his lungs bursting, Ith forced his mind through the black waters around him and finally emerged into the real world.

He was back. Back in his watersilver cage. Back in the safe blackness of reality, and he was not alone.

His servant stood on the edge of the abyss. Had the Rag Man been there long, or had he just arrived? Had Ith not just sent him away, that last time? Had he gone away? Ith could no longer tell.

Ith's voice rasped in the darkness. "You. Are back."

The Rag Man bowed slightly at his master's voice.

"You have brought aid?" said Ith, his hands wrapped around the bar. Even the touch caused the watersilver to glow.

Again the Rag Man bowed.

"Where is it?" said Ith.

The Rag Man held out both hands, skeletal and empty. Then he pointed above, to the lands where Mairsil had taken Ith's place at the head of the Council, where the wine ran free and the mages wasted their talents at fripperies.

Salvation lay above him. It was not here yet. So close, and yet so far.

Ith nodded wearily and slumped back into his cage. In the back of his mind he thought he heard the rich laughter of the creatures from the pit. For the first time, Ith was tempted to join them. He felt the madness and the darkness claw at him.

"So," he said in a throaty chuckle, "it begins."

Interviews and Auditions

The thing to remember about the mages of the Dark era is that, despite the name, this was a time of discovery and enlightenment. The borders of magic were being pressed back by bold individuals who did not think in terms of traditional dogma or boundaries or balances or limitations. Spells were cast for the first time there by wizards who never thought of the full potentials of their actions. Or, by the same token, the full repercussions.

—Arkol, Argivian scholar

The guard closed the gate door behind Jodah, feeling his way to slam home the bolts, and bellowed for another servant. One appeared, a portly man dressed as a butler, who then escorted Jodah down the main hall. Jodah left his lantern with the door guard and added that if the guard blinked often, his sight would return faster. The guard thanked him for this information, his eyelids fluttering wildly.

The hall itself was wide and sumptuous. The ship that had sank beneath Jodah's feet could have fit comfortably inside this hallway, and its masts would not have even grazed the ceilings. The floors were marble but covered with thick rugs of ornate design. Jodah looked at them, and the name of the weaving came to him—Fallaji. They were Fallaji rugs, though there had not been any Fallaji for hundreds of years.

The walls were hung with thick draperies of rich, dark velvets. Occasionally they would be parted for a doorway, or, just as often, for a large portrait.

Jodah noticed that both the door guard and the portly servant wore torques—metal collars that were open slightly at the throat. The door guard's torque had tips that ended in round spheres, while the butler's ended in wolves heads, leering at each other across the front of his thick neck. Both were made of dull metal and had a familiar spider-web of silvery material spun across them.

The butler motioned for Jodah to sit down on a velvet-covered chair, and the portly gentleman assured him that someone would be around to see to his needs shortly.

There was a painting directly across from Jodah which, even given the width of the wall, loomed over him. It was a full-body rendering of what Jodah assumed to be one of the castle's inhabitants or even a noble ancestor. The figure in the painting wore a dark silk shirt and dark pants. He was festooned with a gold brocade vest, over the shirt, which bore large, crystalline buttons. He held in one hand a hat, wide-brimmed with a golden feather, and his other hand rested on the hilt of a rapier.

The portrait's face was calm and self-assured. The figure had dark hair, with only a few streak of gray at the temples, and a thin mustache that framed a hard, unyielding mouth. He wore a jeweled cuff in the right ear, the left being hidden in the portrait and a huge ruby-stoned ring on his right index finger.

The portrait's eyes were particularly striking—they seemed to look to the bottom of one's soul. They were very much like Primata Delphine's eyes, and that made Jodah very nervous.

Jodah was staring at the portrait so intently that he didn't notice that he was no longer alone. Only the laughter woke him from his revelry.

"Could this be a new pupil?" said one man's voice.

"Or a new servant," said another male voice. "It's so hard to tell when they've just gotten here. Until they are properly torqued."

"It's been so long since we've had either," said the first. "Student or servant, that is."

There were three of them, two men and a woman. The men were dressed in a similar manner to the figure in the portrait—slacks, shirt, and vest. One was dressed entirely in red, down to his boots. The other male was in green, though he had a purple vest that was marked with all manner of arcane symbols. The second male was fatter than the butler, and it was clear that his purple vest had not closed in some time.

The woman was a peacock by comparison. Her gown was a radiant collection of blue and green silks that seemed to shimmer as the light reflected off of them. Her gown was opened at the front, and a torrent of ruffles spilled from the top, matched by a similar train dropping from her hips behind her. Her skin was dusky, the color of coffee. Her hair was black and frosted and piled up on top of her head, held in place by numerous combs and what looked to Jodah like several serviceable weapons.

Jodah noticed that none of them wore torques.

The woman leaned down over Jodah, and he caught a heady whiff of her perfume. "So tell me, child," she purred in a fluid, strangely accented voice, "are you *Inn* or are you *Jinn?*"

Jodah's eyes watered at the sharp smell of musk. "I'm sorry?"

The fat man laughed, and his red companion said, "Our friend Drusilla here fancies herself to have a touch of the desert in her heritage. She wants to know if you are mortal or mage."

Jodah blinked back the perfume. "Both, I suppose." Then he added defensively, "I can cast spells."

"As can we all, my boy," said the fat one, slapping his companion on the back. "See, I told you! New one, fresh in from the hinterland with a dream of power, a glimmer of magical ability, and no idea what to do with either. Well, lad," he turned to Jodah and patted his expansive belly, "you'll find out soon enough if you measure up to our requirements and join the Conclave of Mages."

Jodah tilted his head slightly and said, "Requirements? What requirements are you talking about?"

"Yes, Friend Lucan," said a new, powerful voice from behind the fat man, "which requirements *are* you talking about?"

The fat man stiffened, surprised at the sound of the voice, and quickly stepped to one side. Drusilla and the red-dressed man had already stepped back as well, revealing the new speaker between them.

The arrival was a stocky, muscular man with a thin, neatly trimmed beard. His hairline had receded to produce a wide patch of forehead, now furrowed. He was dressed simply, in leather leggings and a white, ruffled shirt, which did nothing to conceal the muscles of his arms and legs. He wore no jewelry. Jodah noticed that he wore no torque as well.

Jodah also noticed the new one's eyes. They were blue and as sharp as daggers and locked on the fat one, Lucan, who now was caught in a long, stammering apology.

"I was speaking in jest, Friend Barl," managed Lucan finally.

"Of course," said the one called Barl in a clipped, direct tone, "I would assume so, Friend Lucan, since you would know better than to share secrets with any stranger." Barl was not looking at Lucan but rather regarding Jodah. Jodah thought of him as a butcher sizing up a cow but returned the newcomer's gaze calmly.

For his part, Lucan blanched, the blood leaving his face entirely and heading for other parts of his body, "Of course, Friend Barl," he gasped. "I know better than to share secrets."

"You have other matters to attend to?" suggested Barl.

Lucan's face relaxed. "Of course! Why, yes, I *do* have other matters to attend to! And with your leave, Friend Barl, I will attend to them, forthwith!"

Barl nodded imperceptibly, and Friend Lucan was already down the hall, a great ship carried by unseen winds, Friend Drusilla and Friend Dressed-in-Red in his wake.

Jodah watched the great form in its purple and green retreat and then turned to look at the man the others had called Barl. The stocky man was regarding him, but it was no longer the "butcher-sizing-up-cutlets" look.

Jodah said, "I'm sorry if my arrival created a disturbance."

Barl turned slightly, then said, "Come, let us move to a quieter study for our talk."

Barl passed Jodah, and the younger man rose and followed. Jodah noticed that he was taller than Barl—indeed, Lucan and the others were taller than the muscular, simply dressed man as well. Yet Barl radiated his own aura of confidence and power that made him seem much, much larger than he was.

They passed several more doors and numerous portraits, most of them of the man with the mustache, like the one in the main hallway. Behind one door there was the sound of music and laughter, but Barl did not slow. He came at last to a small door, set with a silver rune in its center. He touched the silver rune, then opened the door.

"Come in," he said, "and make yourself comfortable."

The room consisted of a sideboard, a large desk and two chairs. One was positioned behind the desk. The other was much smaller and simpler and set to one side. Jodah took the smaller chair as Barl walked to the sideboard. He produced a piece of parchment, a vial of black ink, a quill pen, and what looked like a beetle. He sat in the larger chair behind the desk and laid all four items in front of him.

"Just a moment, and then we can begin," said Barl. He opened the back of the beetle and poured the ink into it. Then he set the plume between the beetle's jaws, and the pincers closed on it, holding the pen between them. Then he placed the beetle—still clutching the pen—on the upper left corner of the parchment.

"Interview with a prospective adept," said Barl, leaning back slightly in the chair. "Barl, artificer to the Conclave, reporting."

As he spoke, the beetle moved across the parchment, inscribing deeply in the surface and filling the carved lines with ink. The result was extremely small, extremely readable printing.

Barl mentioned the date and the time as well, but Jodah was watching the pen. Only when Barl said something else, and Jodah read, upside down, the words, "And your full name is?" did he realize that Barl had asked him a question.

"Uh, Jodah," said the young man, "Jodah of Giva Province."

As he spoke, the beetle moved to a new line and dutifully took down his words, including the pauses.

"Don't worry about the recording scarab," said Barl. "It takes down everything, or tries to. Use it on someone with a bad cold and it produces all manner of interesting spellings."

Jodah looked at the stocky man and just nodded. Barl gave a slight, tolerant smile.

"Why are you here?" he said.

"Pardon?" said Jodah, aware that that was being recorded as well. He took a deep breath and said, "Excuse me?"

"What is your purpose here?" repeated Barl, with the calmness of a man who seemed use to such discussions.

"I came . . ." He thought of the ragged man and the warning for silence. "I felt a need to be here. There is strong magic here," he added, thinking that sounded vague enough to be true. "It felt *right*."

"And you arrived how?"

"By the front door," said Jodah.

"Before that," said Barl, waving his finger horizontally in a circular motion for Jodah to roll back the time.

"I . . ." Jodah wondered how much Barl knew. "I wandered into a cave. The next thing I knew, I was here."

"And have you used a haven before?" said the stocky man.

"Haven?" said Jodah.

"The cave," said Barl. "We use them to move across long distances."

We use *them*, thought Jodah. Instead he said, "I didn't know what it did."

"And did you do anything while you were in the haven, in the cave?"

Jodah thought of the brief fight with the dark guardian, "I fell asleep. That is all."

Barl was silent, looking at Jodah and stroking his beard. He did not have the piercing stare of Primata Delphine. Instead, Jodah got the feeling that this small man was trying to see him in totality, to see him from all sides at once. If anything, it was more disconcerting than the primata's gaze.

"I'm sorry," said Jodah after a moment.

Barl leaned forward. "Nothing worth apologizing for. You have magic?"

"On me?" said Jodah, "no. I had a mirror that might have been, but I . . . lost it." He looked at the beetle, writing upside down, and noticed that it had paused where he had.

"I meant, do you have the capacity to cast spells?" said Barl, his brow furrowed slightly.

"Oh," said Jodah, "yes, I guess so. White mana, as one would say. I can make curative potions and produce light."

"So Alex at the door attested to me," said Barl, and the thin smile had returned. "He has got most of his vision back, by the way."

Jodah was unsure what to say in response. "That's good," was what he finally settled on.

"Yes," said Barl. "So you are a White Mage?"

"Yes," said Jodah.

"And your teacher is a White Mage as well?"

"No," said Jodah, "red. I mean I think he was a Red Mage. Used red mana."

"Was?" said Barl.

Jodah took a deep breath and wondered if the beetle would record the wait. "He's dead," he said at last. "The church . . ."

"We know a great deal about the Church of Tal here," said Barl, making a sour face. "A great deal indeed. Then your master is dead?"

"Yes," said Jodah.

"And you found your way here by means of which you are not certain?" said Barl.

"Yes."

"What was your teacher's name?" said Barl, raising his eyebrows slightly.

"Voska," said Jodah. "His name was Voska."

Barl the Artificer said nothing but slowly shook his head. The name obviously meant nothing to him. "Any other wizards that you know that might speak of your abilities?"

Jodah thought of Sima very briefly but said nothing. He just shook his head, then added, "No," for the benefit of the scarab.

"Any relatives skilled in the magical arts?" said Barl, cocking his head slightly.

"Not really. I had a great-great-grandfather, Jarsyl. He was supposed to have been a wizard." Jodah looked hopeful.

Barl shook his head slowly again. The name seemed to carry no more meaning to the artificer than had Voska's. He said, "I suppose that this Jarsyl is dead as well."

"I suppose," said Jodah in a tired voice.

"Anyone else who might come forward with tales of your ability?" said Barl.

Jodah shook his head. "There are some members of the church who might have a few things to say."

"Not a group we can contact directly," said Barl smiling grimly.

The beetle had reached the bottom of the page and chirped expectantly. Barl took another piece of parchment and put the beetle on it. The beetle waited patiently for his next words.

"Why?" he asked.

"Why?" said Jodah.

"Why?" repeated Barl. "Why did you come here? Why do you want to study at our Conclave of Mages?"

Jodah stammered, aware that his words were being taken verbatim, then stopped and took a deep breath. Why was he here? Because some ragged figure led him here? Because he was pursued by the church? Because Sima and Voska and everyone else he knew were dead?

At last Jodah said, "Because I am tired. I am tired of being cold all the time. Tired of being hunted. Tired of being hungry. And I think magic can change that."

* * * * *

The rest of the conversation covered minor matters—what Giva Province was like, his mother's maiden name, and the like. They spent a long time talking about Jodah's encounters with, and opinions of, the church, and Barl seemed amused by Jodah's description of Primata Delphine. Jodah mentioned the ragged man not at all, Sima only in passing, and never as a spellcaster in her own right. Barl added another sheet of parchment and in the end had three pieces, all printed with small, legible hand-writing.

Barl put the parchment sheets in a folder and returned the scarab, ink, and pen to the sideboard. Then he said, "Do you know who I am?"

Jodah looked at him, "Your name is Barl. You said you were an artificer. You dress like a servant, but you don't wear a metal band around your neck. The others in the hall seemed to be afraid of you. They call you "Friend," but they don't seem to mean it. You call them "Friend," but you don't mean it either."

The stocky man gave a gratified smile, the first one that seemed to have real emotion behind it.

"My name is Barl. I am the chief artificer for the Lord High Mage Mairsil, the master of the Conclave. Only servants wear the torques—magicians do not. Though I know naught of spells as you and the others do, I work my magic in my own special way. The others *are* afraid of me. 'Friend' is a token of respect—all mages are equal here within the Conclave's walls, and considered friends."

"Including your Lord High Mage Mairsil?" asked Jodah softly.

"I consider him my friend," said Barl, "and he considers me his." He turned toward the door. "This interview is over. If you wish to join our conclave as a student, you must pass one last challenge."

Jodah rose, but did not move toward the door. "And if I don't want to join as a student?"

Barl turned back to him and said, "If you choose not to, or if you fail the challenge, you will be fitted with a torque and join us as a servant. Answering the door for other would-be mages, carrying pots, and cooking. Yes, we can make you do that. Shall we go?"

Jodah followed.

Barl led him down the main hallway, and through an archway. Behind them there was the sound of laughter, the crash of glassware on stone tiles, and more laughter still. Through the archway they descended a staircase of white marble that turned into a staircase of gray stone and at last into a stairway of black iron. They spiraled their way downward a short distance and at last came to a great set of oak doors set with steel bands.

Barl picked up a sheathed sword from a rack of similar weapons and handed it, hilt first, to Jodah. Jodah grasped the hilt, and Barl pulled the sheath back, releasing the blade. It was a broad blade, made of some coppery metal, and had inscriptions along its length.

"You might need this," he said.

Jodah looked at the inscribed weapon. The runes seemed to dance along its length. He nodded.

Barl opened the door and ushered Jodah beyond it. Jodah stepped through, and Barl shut the door behind the young man.

Jodah found himself in a narrow passageway that opened out on a larger space ahead of him. Where the passageway opened outward there was a portcullis, now draw up. The floor was dark, damp earth.

It always came down to tests, thought Jodah, and he hated tests.

Jodah moved forward and saw that beyond the portcullis the passageway opened into a narrow stadium, no more than fifteen feet across and fifty feet from end to end. The opposite end was marked with another gate, also raised fully. Beyond the other gate was darkness.

On all sides were stands, stone benches piled one upon the other until they were twenty rows high. There were a few people in the stands—a large woman in flamboyant dress, sleeping, her swan-shaped hat laying to one side. A drunken man, wearing a crimson mask, who regarded Jodah with weaving, unsteady eyes. Another old man, frail and gray, who was reading a book yawned and put his text aside as Jodah entered.

Barl appeared at the top of the stands and made his way down to a point equidistant between the two gates. Ceremonial bunting had been hung over the rail here, though it had been spattered by blood and covered with dust. Barl turned to Jodah.

"Are you prepared?" he asked.

Jodah didn't know what to say, so he just raised his sword and saluted.

Barl dropped his chin slightly in a bow. "Let the challenge begin, then."

There was a glimmer at the far entrance, and Jodah stood his ground as his opponent entered the area.

It was not human—in fact it was more insect than any living thing Jodah had seen before. It stood nearly as tall as he and had an almost triangular helmet tipped with large, beetlelike eyes at the corners. It was encased entirely in bronze-colored armor, and it creaked as it walked, a high-pitched whine that tugged at the sides of Jodah's brain. Jodah noticed that one arm of the creature was slightly larger than the other, and the armor along that arm was of a slightly different alloy, more tarnished and pitted.

More importantly, that arm also wielded a great axe. The axe's handle was made of silvery metal, but its blade seemed to be made of glass or crystal.

Jodah expected his opponent to bow, to nod, or give some recognition to himself or to Barl. Instead it charged forward, immediately and wordlessly, each foot firmly planted in the soft, dark earth, gaining speed with each step.

Jodah smiled slightly and cleared his mind, pulling up the memories of the land as easily now as a weaver would pick up the strands of thread from a loom. He did not even need to imagine the old house, the entranceway, the spell that he sought. He just knew that he needed it, and it appeared, the mana building within him.

He shifted the sword to his left hand, then raised his right. He pointed at the creature's head and mentally released the latch that held back the spell energies. The creature's head was encased in a ball of brilliant light.

It did not slow down in the slightest.

The smile faded from Jodah's lips as the creature continued to charge, unaffected by the glowing brilliance that wrapped its head. Jodah moved to one side, hoping the blinded creature would still charge right past him, but as it approached the bronze-armored, insect-warrior raised its glass axe high and brought it around in a long, level stroke, about chest high.

Jodah stumbled backward, falling as he did so. The blade passed inches in front of his face, and he was suddenly on the ground. Jodah twisted to the right, and the metallic creature's second blow smashed into the dark earth where he had been seconds before.

Jodah leaped up, hoping for a moment to regain his composure. His opponent would not give him that moment. Instead it lunged forward, leading with the dull head at the top of the axe, and caught Jodah in the stomach. Stars danced in front of Jodah's eyes, and he staggered back another few paces but did not lose his balance this time nor his sword.

He brought the blade up to meet the axe's next chopping blow and found he could not stop the heavy weapon, but he could turn it aside. His opponent's head looked like an angel's, its triangular shape surrounded by a now-soft, almost holy glow. It recovered from the parry and brought down another chop identical to the first. Again Jodah took a step backward and turned the downward swing aside. The armored creature recovered and chopped again, each thrust parried in turn, but each thrust also driving Jodah farther back.

Barl watched the slow erosion of Jodah's position through half-shut eyes and shook his head slightly. He frowned. There was a shadow to his right, and he looked up.

"My Lord Mage," he said.

"How goes this one?" said Mairsil, watching as Jodah continued his slow retreat. "Have we found a diamond in the rough?"

"Promising at first," said Barl with a sigh, "but he looks like he is a one-trick hedge mage, now out of his depth. Here is his file." He passed the folder to the taller man, but his half-closed eyes never left the field.

The Lord Mage's robes hissed over the stone as Mairsil sat down next to Barl. The taller man opened the folder, ignoring the battle beneath them and stroking his thin mustache. He nodded twice as he read the initial statements. At the bottom of the first page his mustache twitched.

"Something?" said Barl, not turning from the match but catching Mairsil's sudden tic nonetheless.

"It says that the young man's ancestor was Jarsyl?" said Mairsil offhandedly.

"Yes," said Barl. "I did not recognize the name. Should I have?"

"No," said Mairsil. "I do, though. Do you think he will survive this little encounter alive?"

Barl frowned as Jodah took another step back. He had retreated most of the way across the arena already. Chop. Parry. Retreat. Chop. Parry. Retreat.

"Unlikely," he said at last.

"Pity," said Mairsil. "I think he could have been useful, in the library."

"Should I stop the challenge?" asked Barl gruffly, but the Lord High Mage was already shaking his head.

"Of course not," said Mairsil with a wicked grin. "*That* would be cheating."

On the dark earthen floor of the arena, Jodah was nearly at the end of his tether. The armored creature had given him no respite since the initial attack and seemed not to be fazed in the slightest by the lights that danced around its eyes. The creature moved relentlessly, its axe pistoning up and down tirelessly. Jodah himself was near the breaking point, and sweat coursed down the sides of his face and into his eyes.

Didn't it get tired? he wondered. How could it keep up the assault like that without ill effect? It was as if it was some sort of unliving creation, programmed to respond to his actions in a certain way. As long as he parried the blow, the next blow would be identical, wearing him down.

Jodah grinned grimly as the realization dawned on him what exactly he was fighting. The armor was not armor covering a living creature but the outer skin of some man-made construct. A device, like they spoke of in the old books, before the Devastation. One of Urza's or Mishra's creations.

The metallic man-insect chopped again, and Jodah

parried and danced back. He knew what he fought, now. The only question was how to buy himself the time he needed to defeat it.

You may need this, Barl had said when he gave him the sword.

But not as a weapon, answered Jodah. With the next chop, Jodah flipped his arm upward as he parried the blow, letting it be carried by the axe. The crystalline blade of his metallic opponent brought the blade back up toward its own face. It stepped backward for a moment, released one hand from the axe, and brushed the spinning sword aside, sending it clattering against the far wall.

It had taken long enough for Jodah to regain both his wind and his concentration. As the creature raised the blade over its head to bring down one more blow, Jodah raised a hand, pulled the memories forward, and placed his palm against the beast's metallic chest. The plates of its chest felt warm as Jodah sent his power through the creature's limbs and joints.

The creature halted in the middle of its upswing. Then, overbalanced, it slowly tipped backward and thundered onto the soft dark earth of the arena floor.

Jodah dropped to one knee, almost immediately afterward, breathing hard.

He looked up at the stands. The resplendent woman was still sleeping, and the drunk had slipped into a coma. The old man with the book had returned to his text.

Jodah thought someone had entered during the fight, someone who had talked to Barl, but now the short, stocky man was alone at his seat. He clapped softly.

"You removed its enchantment," said Barl.

"I . . . removed . . . its access . . . to that enchantment," said Jodah breathing hard. "Slightly . . . different spell. I thought . . . you might want . . . to use . . . the machine again . . . later."

Barl smiled, and it was a warm smile. The artificer seemed relieved that Jodah had succeeded. "Indeed we might," he said. "Now, lets get you cleaned up and ready for presentation."

10 ☾

A Dance of Many
(Part 1)

The thing that confuses most conventional historians about the period of the Dark is that they assume there must be only one story that encapsulates the entire period, much like the rivalry of Urza and Mishra dominated the times of the Antiquities. Instead it was a gathering of multiple threads and varied individuals—church and goblin lord and crusader and mage. There were those seeking to return to the glory of the Age of the Brothers, those seeking to crush out the light of magic, and those who cared not one way or the other. Only when these varied threads intertwine with each other do we get a full view of the tapestry of that dark time.

—Arkol, Argivian scholar

Sima stood on the beach, looking at the remains of the fire pit. It had rained hard the night before, and the pit had turned into a shallow pond, bits of charred wood floating on its surface. Already sand fleas were burrowing along its ash-strewn bottom, and crabs scuttled around its perimeter.

Voska's Mirror had led her here but led her no farther. The merfolk had called off the attack as soon as they had emptied the hull from below. In the teeth of the storm, the captain, elven mate, and the surviving crew had taken to the ship's small boats, and she stood on the prow of one such vessel as the storm washed over the quarterdeck, and the shattered mast disappeared beneath the waves. It had taken two more days to reach a safe harbor.

An enchantment on the mirror, so recently in Jodah's possession, assured her that he was still alive. A second enchantment, more obscure and draining to cast, led her to this beach, but here the trail stopped. Sima knew that Jodah had spent some time here, at least a night, but where he went afterward the enchantment had left maddeningly unclear.

She sat by the shallow pool and watched her reflection, first in the water, then in the mirror itself. A heart-shaped face crowned with thick, black bangs stared back at her accusingly. She stood up and paced around the pool. Then she looked down again, but the same accusing face stared back.

She could abandon him, she knew, to whatever fate had claimed him. There were enough mages lost everyday—to stupidity, to fear, to the church. She would not be the first adept to have returned to the hidden city of magic with empty hands and a mournful story.

But she had told him truly that he was a quick learner, and she hoped that he would come back with her to the City of Shadows; to help her and the other mages push back the boundaries of magic just one inch farther. If he could control his temper and just learn to concentrate, she thought, he would have been a capable wizard. Now he was gone, and all she had was the mirror.

At least she had the mirror. Jodah could have saved himself from the storm, she had thought at the time (and, if the spells she cast were accurate, he had indeed saved himself). The mirror however, the mirror he had foolishly taken from its secure pocket, would have been washed overboard and lost if not for Sima's intervention.

If only he had not pulled it from his boot! Her soft mouth hardened at the thought, and she stamped a foot in the sand. For all his potential, the youth was still a fool!

There was another spell she could cast now, the most powerful of the three divinations she knew, but she was loath to unleash its power or to pay the price it demanded on the mage who cast it.

She could return with the mirror to the City of Shadows. She could tell them the tale of Jodah and Voska and the church and leave it at that. They would have the mirror and the regrets of one mage who died and another who was lost.

But then, she thought, she would never truly know what had become of him, would she?

Sima sat again at the edge of the pool and gathered her thoughts. She thought of the fishing village that was her home, of the islanders in their wide-gunnelled boats, heavily laden with nets. She thought of the islands and reefs that she had sailed to as a lass. She thought of her mother's boat, of the days spent helping to fix the netting. She thought of the times she set out the long lines tied with clay pots that were used to snare octopi. She thought of the islands of her youth.

She thought of one island in particular, one with beaches of the darkest volcanic sand. They had beached the craft in the face of mounting clouds from the east that never quite manifested into a full-blown storm and spent the evening around a bonfire, serving up the fresh catch with berries found inland. Several of her mother's sisters had beached their boats with them. One aunt had a small shell ocarina, while another always brought a bit of rum with her when they went to sea. By the end of the evening they were all singing and dancing, the sand beneath them as dark as the starless sky above, suspended between the heavens and the sea.

She thought of that island and inhaled and could almost hear the crackle of the fire and her aunt's piping music and smell the smoky scent of the roasting fish and the pungent tang of the rum, for it was the first time Mother had let her try any (that Mother knew of, anyway).

She nodded and thought of the other islands of her youth, more quickly and mechanically, as a mage should. She pulled the mana from those memories and from the memory of that night on the black sand, and she poured it into the shallow pool of ash-strewn seawater.

As she poured the memories out, the magic of the evening of the black sand poured with her, into the pool. She could feel it pull away from her mind, like an octopus releasing its grip.

Sima shaped the energy into a small, tight, blue ball and asked the ball one question: Where is Jodah now?

The pond was murky for a moment, then it rippled and distorted, opening a window into another part of the world. It was overcast wherever Jodah was, but most of the inlands were overcast these days. Dark mountains loomed up on all sides, and in the distance there was a large citadel or monastery of some type, hunched on the shoulder of one of the larger peaks.

The vision cleared, and Sima was suddenly swooping

among those peaks. She thought she might be looking through the eyes of a bird, and indeed there was a flutter of black wings at the corners of the pool, at the edge of her vision. She neared the dark monastery.

Ornate iron turrets and glass windows dotted the monastery. No, Sima realized, it once had been a monastery. Others had expanded upon it, adding towers and flame-lit battlements where none had been needed before. The former monastery was now a sprawling mass of linked buildings, dotted with balconies and parapets, slowly moving down the shoulder of the mountain to a cold gray sea.

Her heart sank as she realized what she was looking at, and she hoped the spell had somehow misfired and showed her a false vision, but this was not the way the spell worked.

The crow vision wheeled over one of the parapets and showed two men standing on the exposed stonework, near a railing carved in the shape of black lions. One, a stocky man in simple dress, was motioning toward the surrounding countryside. The other was younger and thinner, dressed in a rough, brown robe, like a monk, and had a beard that was just starting to darken fully.

The crow must have cried, for the bearded face looked up. The younger man was Jodah.

Sima leaned back from the pool, and the vision faded, the window into the other realm returning to mere water and chunks of burned wood. She sat back on her haunches and shook her head.

The Conclave. Jodah had fallen into the hands of the Conclave. Their citadel was impossibly far to the north, she knew, and built on the wreckage of an old monastery that was ancient before the Brothers battled. They were the dark side of her city, the lair of dangerous wizards and magic run amok.

Jodah was in the midst of it.

Sima rose and looked to the north. She remembered, from the tales of her mentors and from the old maps, where the Conclave was supposed to be. It was horribly far, she remembered, even with the help of magic. She had no idea how Jodah had gotten there, nor how she would reach it herself, but she remembered that she had made a promise to bring Jodah to her city. That promise now drove her northward.

She remembered the maps, she remembered the tales, and she remembered the warnings. She remembered her promise to Jodah. The only thing she could not remember now was the evening on the black sands of that island in her youth. She had sacrificed that memory to power the spell.

A lone tear ran down the side of her face as she looked northward, though she could not tell anyone why.

* * * * *

"We get a lot of crows," said Barl as the black raven spiraled above them. "All manner of scavengers—ravens, raptors, and even the occasional vulture. There seems to be more of them in these dark days. Indeed, if anything, they've been getting larger over the years. I saw one recently, a hawk, that was bigger than you are."

Jodah nodded. His grandmother had spoken of warm summers as a girl, and now there was snow in the uplands of Giva province even in high summer. The world was indeed changing and not for the better.

After the initiation challenge they had provided him

with a set of dark brown robes, like that of a religious monk, to cover his tattered, sweat- and salt-stained clothing. Now, in the high tower of the Citadel, the wind still cut its way beneath the folds, and he shivered. It smelled like snow, and Jodah thought they must be fairly far north indeed. Barl was dressed as he was always dressed, in his simple shirt and slacks. He seemed unfazed by the chill weather.

"This was once a site of a holy order, now forgotten," said Barl. "Its practitioners died out or were killed or abandoned the place during the Brothers' War or shortly thereafter. The Lord High Mage's mentor found this place and deemed it to be as suitable as any for founding his council house, his refectory, his hiding place for the Conclave."

Barl motioned to the mountains. It was midday, and Jodah saw that the dark peaks were topped with snow. The peak whose shoulder carried the former monastery was the runt of the litter, and the mountains became higher and more imposing as they marched south, their peaks finally piercing the cloud cover and becoming lost to view. Barl pointed directly ahead.

"To the south and east, the mountains—the last sentinels of the Sardian range. Here is were the caverns of safe haven carry those who know their secrets across the land," Barl raised an eyebrow at the youth. "But you already know that, I suppose." He turned slightly to the left, to a grayish blotch to the northeast at the foot of those mountains. "The Tanglewoods," he said, "not as impressive as the Scarwoods or the Savaen Expanses but still a deadly place of man-eating vines and carnivorous plants."

He turned to the north, and pointed to where the

woods ended. Much of this expanse was rolling hills, bare save for brownish grass.

"To the north, plains," said Barl. "Open lands that are dominated by savage horsemen and superstitious townsfolk. They are lesser beings, without magic. We don't worry about them overmuch."

He pointed west and still a bit north, back to the tower itself. "On the other side of the citadel, we have the ocean—a wide bay that was once dotted with islands, but as time has passed the level of the sea itself has dropped, and the islands have joined in larger masses and shallow flats. Blue is not a popular color among the mages here, and that is one reason."

Finally he pointed to the south and west, and said, "Where the sea met the land there were farms and orchards, but now there is only marsh and bog. It's a damp, fetid place, neither entirely of the land nor of the sea. Some believe there are banshees, undead, and other evil spirits lurking out there." He turned to fully face the younger man. "Do you understand what I just said?"

Jodah nodded.

"Then tell me. What did I just say?"

Jodah pointed to each of the directions, following the same order Barl had just done. "Mountains, Forest, Plains, Islands, and Swamp. Red, green, white, blue, and black. The lands of magic. The colors of magic."

Barl smiled in satisfaction, and Jodah asked, "What color is your magic, Friend Barl?"

The smile faded only a trace. "I have no magic, or no magic as you understand it. My magic is of things, of artifice, and of gears. I study forces in play and weights reacting against each other and items dropping from a great height. And because I do not work with your type of magic I am freed from its requirements and dangers. I serve as Lord Mairsil's firm right hand. He trusts me, and I make things happen for him."

"Including teaching the new students, Friend Barl?" said Jodah.

The smile regained its brightness. "No. We have no official teachers here. If you want to learn magic, you must go out and learn. Come, we should go down now."

The stocky man led the way back into the tower and down a lengthy spiral staircase. They came out two floors above the main hall. Jodah was perplexed by the architecture and the way rooms related to each other within the sprawling complex.

They paused out in front of a set of double doors. Behind it there was the sound of music and laughter. Barl turned to Jodah and said, "You know what will happen?"

Jodah took a deep breath and nodded.

The stocky artificer grasped the golden door handles and twisted. Both halves of the door swung inward, and he entered, Jodah in his wake.

The room was a riot of color and noise. There were revelers in all manner of costume—rich vests and velvet capes for the men, wide silk skirts for some of the women, clinging gowns for others. There were numerous masks and several faces that Jodah hoped were masks. The walls were brilliant white and were hung with golden draperies showing dragons and knights battling.

In his simple brown robes, covering water-stained and ripped clothing, Jodah felt like a beggar who had somehow stumbled into a royal ball.

There were no musicians, but the music stopped as soon as Barl entered the room. A ripple of silence began at the door and worked its way outward, Jodah and Barl at its center. As the circle of silence expanded, the various party goers quieted. Small conversations stopped, or in some cases were finished off with a few whispered words.

Everyone was staring at him, thought Jodah. He straightened, refusing to be cowed by such a large gathering.

A voice behind him, rich and strong, said, "Now that we have your attention, we can begin."

Jodah nearly jumped at the sound of the voice. It was not Barl's but was instead more fluid—more practiced and elegant. He was about to turn, when the speaker moved forward. Jodah had been positive that no one was behind them when they entered the room. Barl stepped aside to let the speaker pass.

The figure was tall and powerful, dressed in a black shirt and slacks with a golden capelet hanging halfway down his back. He held a walking stick of dark russet wood with the polished white head of a carved skull on the end, but he showed no need of it. The figure wore a giant ruby ring on his right hand.

This was the figure in the portrait from the hallway.

"We have a new arrival," said the tall figure, addressing the crowd. "One who has shown the talent and passed the initiation and wishes to be admitted into our brotherhood of equals. What is the name of this new brother?"

Barl nodded at Jodah, and the young man said, "Jodah." His voice cracked as he said it.

"Louder lad," said the smiling figure. "I don't think everyone heard you!"

"I am Jodah," said Jodah feeling as if he was shouting it, then adding, "of Giva Province."

One of two of the women in the crowd smiled at Jodah's northern accent, but the tall figure took no notice of it. "And are you willing to become a part of our Conclave, Jodah?"

"Yes." Jodah tried to look in the taller man's eyes as he said it, but the speaker was too fast for him and was back scanning the crowd even as he spoke.

"Do you promise to devote your energies to uncovering the secrets of magic, as we here have done?" said the speaker.

"Yes."

"And do you promise to aid your fellow mages, and treat each one as a friend?"

"Yes."

"Has the candidate passed his challenge?" said the tall speaker.

"He has," said Barl, in a clear, calm voice.

"Does any here present know why this candidate should not be admitted?"

There was a heartbeat of silence, no longer than a short intake of breath.

The flamboyant speaker smiled again. "Then with the powers of the Lord High Mage of the Conclave, of the first among equals of the Council, and holder of the vision of a world free for magic, I, Lord Mairsil, induct you into our ranks, Candidate Jodah. Please step forward!"

Jodah took a step forward toward the taller man. Mairsil raised a finger and a single spark danced on the fingertip.

"Do not fear," he said in the casual manner of a barber or dentist. "This will not hurt."

Jodah nodded. Barl had mentioned this part of the initiation to him. Mairsil's enchantment would protect him from detection and keep the secret of the Conclave of Mages a secret.

Mairsil touched Jodah's forehead with his sparkling finger. The spark disappeared, and Jodah felt almost as if it passed within him, nestling at the base of his brain.

"Welcome to our Council, Friend Jodah!" said Mairsil. To the crowd he said, "Friend Jodah will be assigned to the library, initially."

Jodah looked past the tall mage and at the crowd for the first time. Some looked simply bored. Others looked mildly amused. One or two shot venomous glances at Jodah, and one of those darkened further at the mention of the library.

"Welcome to your new home!" said the taller man, striking Jodah on the back with an open palm, just hard enough to stagger him forward. Jodah turned to thank him but Mairsil's back was already to him, and the tall mage was towering over the smaller artificer in some private conference.

Neither took further notice of him. He was abandoned to the crowd.

"You are Friend Giva, then?" said a white-haired young woman, pressing a narrow glass into Jodah's hand as he turned back toward the room. The glass was filled with something cold and bubbling that smelled of strawberries.

"I am Jodah. I am from Giva Province, yes," he said, grasping the glass with both hands, as the other option was to let it splash down the front of his robes.

"Ah," said the woman, with a slight bow. "Friend Jodah from Giva, then. You have powerful wizards in Giva?" The white-haired woman's eyes were extremely wide and blue and seemed to suck Jodah in. Her accent was strange and lilting.

"Um, I don't know," said Jodah. "I mean, wizards are not horribly common there or always welcome. . . ." He ran out of things to say and took a large, hard pull on the narrow glass. The woman's eyes brightened as he drank.

His throat caught on fire, and Jodah immediately doubled over, coughing. His eyes watered from the strawberry-flavored incendiary, and he fought the twin urges to flee the room and to collapse entirely.

Through teary eyes, he looked around to see if he had made a scene. No one was looking at him, not even the white-haired woman, who had moved on to another victim, pushing another narrow drink into the hands of a small man with an inordinately long beard.

Barl was at his side, and said, "You have had a long day. Perhaps you should get some rest."

Jodah knuckled back the tears in his eye and looked at the bubbly concoction. "Perhaps I should," he said, putting the liquid inferno on a sideboard and hoping that no one else would mistake it for a real drink. He added, "The Lord High Mage, is he still . . ?"

"Mairsil has little time or interest for social events, though he attends them when his schedule permits," said Barl, "Let me guide you to your quarters."

Jodah scanned the room for the tall mage in black and gold, but he was gone from the party. Jodah nodded, looked at the volatile drink one last time and already felt his stomach rumble in rebellion. To Barl, he said, "Perhaps you'd better take me to my quarters."

And then Jodah was gone from the party as well.

* * * * *

"What do you mean, *gone?*" snarled Primata Delphine.

The miracle worker looked helplessly with unseeing eyes at the large priestess from across the sacrificial altar.

"I thought I had a fix on the sinner's position, Your Grace, but he suddenly vanished." The slender woman in green robes raised her hands, each hand extending its fingers as she did so. She added, "Poof!"

"Was that 'Poof' as in he died suddenly and messily," said Delphine, "or 'Poof' as in he detected your miracle and raised hell-spawned magical defenses against it."

Sister Betje raised her shoulders in a shrug, and raised her hands again, fingers splayed. "Just Poof! And he was gone."

The primata looked across the brazier, wishing she could look in the miracle worker's face fully. Miracle workers of Order of St. Nanta wore red scarves across their eyes, and, it was widely known, saw truly without truly needing to see. The primata had heard that they accepted voluntarily blindness in their order and had the eyes gouged out and the sockets filled with hot gold, but she never wanted to ask. The varied practices of other orders within the Church of Tal interested her not in the least.

She had waited a week for one of the Order of St. Nanta to arrive, and another three days afterward for the altar to be purified and the sacrifice, a white lamb without blemish or scar, to be sanctified, slain, and at last burned. Now the supposed miracle worker told her that suddenly her quarry no longer existed.

"Poof," said Sister Betje once more for effect.

The primata rubbed her temples with her fingertips, then said, "Try to find the other one, then."

"Excuse me?" said the Sister.

"The *other* one," said Delphine. "The woman he escaped with, the one we trapped in the first place. Find her."

The Sister was silent for a moment. "That may take

some time," she said at last.

"Time?" snarled Delphine. "What kind of time do you need?"

"Ideally," said the blind Sister, "we should begin again. Re-consecrate the altar. Gather new woods and herbs. Select a new lamb without blemish or scar . . ."

"You have all that here!" thundered Delphine. "We've done all that! Just look for the woman, instead!"

"The heavenly hosts are not to be ordered around casually," said Sister Betje, fire in her voice.

"The heavenly hosts stiffed you on your first request," said Delphine, her voice dripping with irony. "See if you can get them to pay off in an alternate sinner!"

Sister Betje's shoulders stiffened, and her mouth became a thin line. "Don't blaspheme. The hosts are not merchants, to be haggled and bartered with at one's whim."

A messenger arrived at the doorway of the shrine and waited nervously. Primata Delphine took a deep breath, then let it out. "Of course," she said to the blind woman sweetly. "Approach the heavenly hosts in the manner you think best, and see if, in their bounty, they will grant you a vision of the woman in question. But do it *now*, before your sacrifice is a *pile* of *cinders!*"

With that the Primata Delphine spun on her massive heel and stomped out of the shrine, leaving the blind priestess chanting lowly over the smoking lamb. Delphine almost ran over the messenger, a young man who leaped to get out of the way.

She wheeled on the messenger. "What is *your* desire, my child?"

The boy bowed low. "Your Grace, the lord guardian will see you now."

189

The primata stifled an unladylike and unTal-like curse, nodded, and motioned for the boy to lead her to the Lord Guardian's presence. As they walked through the high-vaulted passageways of the temple, Primata Delphine mentally composed herself, reeling in those large portions of temper and harsh words that she had so willingly dealt out moments before.

The boy opened one half of a great set of double doors, and Primata Delphine paused for a moment, straightened her robes, tucked a bit of stray hair back under her cowl, and entered the reception chamber.

The chamber consisted of a short hallway ending in a stepped circular dais. At the foot of the dais was a desk of white painted wood, where a stenographer sat, his head down, his quill pen at the ready. Atop the dais was a high-backed throne of red velvet, trimmed with gold, and seated upon throne was the lord guardian, the highest ranking church official in this part of Terisiare.

As custom demanded, Primata Delphine paused three times as she walked down the red plush carpet leading to the dais. Each time she placed her forehead against the floor in obeisance, and each time she struggled to get back up again on her feet. Finally, on the bottommost step of the dais, she knelt.

The lord guardian was a fat, balding, little man. However, within the Church of Tal to say he as fat was pejorative, and as such heresy. And to say he was balding would imply that he was aged and infirm, and as such was heresy. And to say that he was little would be to diminish the entire church, and as such was heresy.

Primata Delphine thought none of these things but did wonder if his lordship was sleeping, for his eyes were closed.

The eyes did not flicker open, but the lord guardian spoke clearly. "You seek a boon, my daughter?"

"I do, your lordship," she responded. "Of late our most holy lands have been plagued by—" she paused for effect— "sorcerers."

"Many lands are," said the lord guardian. "They of the vermin of these cold and dying times. How are you particularly plagued, my daughter?"

"Lord Guardian, I have been relentless in my pursuit of those that use foul sorcery," said the primata, almost bowing to touch the floor with her forehead. "And have proved both worthy and effective in my pursuit of sorcerers, wizards, other hellspawn spellcasters. Yet two have eluded me, and I seek permission to seek them out and punish them, and the blessing of the church to aid me."

"Why do you seek these particular two?" said the lord guardian, not moving except for his lips. "Will not the wisdom of Tal and the heavenly hosts, not to mention the foul forces these wizards themselves serve, eventually bring about their destruction?"

"Lord Guardian, this pair of sorcerers blinded me and my fellow priests, defeated my loyal warriors, and stole my horse. The burned me, so that our healers had to labor mightily to salve my wounds and restore me to health!" As she spoke, she could feel the heat rising in her face.

The lord guardian could apparently feel it as well, and said, "Anger is a sin, Primata. Remember that,"

Delphine nodded, chastised. "They are the only two that have escaped the judgment of the church under my watch. They are a smudge on my otherwise perfect record."

"Pride is a sin as well," said the lord guardian, not opening his eyes.

The primata took a deep breath, then said, "My Lord Guardian, I fear that these two adepts may seek out other sorcerers and pass on their knowledge to them, so these other sorcerers will be emboldened to attack the church as well."

There was a long pause, and for a moment Delphine feared that the lord guardian, Lion of the Church, had fallen asleep or been finally taken to his spiritual reward. Then, just as she was forming a new question, he said, "You have our permission child. A document will be drawn up indicating that all good churchmen and church-women should lend you what aid you demand in order to allow you to bring this pair to justice."

The Primata Delphine rose unsteadily to her feet, her left foot having fallen asleep in the proceedings, and bowed. "Your wisdom is unmatched, my Lord Guardian."

"Do you know the mysteries, daughter?" asked the lord guardian. "Can you protect yourself from these sorcerers?"

"I know the prayers and the psalms, my Lord Guardian," said the primata. "I know how to make the holy wards to keep me proof from their magical entreaties, and the prayer to reduce their hellspawn artifacts to dust. I know the ritual of holy light to make their souls quail and may call upon the sword of justice to execute them in the name of Tal's Wisdom. I fear no evil magic, for I have the power of the Book of Tal within my heart."

"Tell me, Daughter," said the lord guardian, "why do you seek these two with such intensity? Why do you hate spellcasters so much?"

Primata Delphine pulled herself up to her full height. "My Lord Guardian, mages are an affront to the natural order and the wisdom of the Book of Tal. The very presence of magic is foul and unclean, something that no sane person should be involved with. The work of hated Urza and damned Mishra was magery most foul, and almost destroyed all of us. I will not rest until I have put every wizard to the torch, burned every demonic book of spells, and rooted out every vestige of magery, regardless of where it may be found."

The lord guardian gave the most imperceptible of nods. "Your righteousness is to be commended, Daughter, and may your holy fire burn bright as you pursue and punish your escaped sorcerers."

Primata Delphine retreated, bowing, though not kneeling, three times as she retreated. The messenger, leading Sister Betje, met her at the door. The primata closed the door behind her and turned to them sternly.

"The hosts have smiled upon your enterprise," said the blind woman without preamble, and for a moment the primata thought she meant her meeting with the lord guardian. "For while one demon is lost to us, another stands revealed. She is to the west of us, by the coast of the Shielded Sea, and she is moving north, slowly.

The primata smiled, and though the miracle worker could not see it, the messenger quailed at the sight of the smile. "If I find one, I shall find the other. Come, good sister, we have begun our own crusade against unholy magic. It will be glorious."

Back in the reception hall, the lord guardian said in a languid voice, "Read that last part back for me. What she said just before leaving."

The recorder straightened his papers, then said, in a level voice, "I will not rest until I have put every wizard to the torch, burned every demonic book of spells, and rooted out every vestige of magery, regardless of where it may be found."

There was a long pause, then the lord guardian gave a hiccuping chuckle. Then he was silent again.

"Lord Guardian, if I may speak?" said the clerk.

"Of course, my son."

"Her Grace. Does she not know?"

There was another brief silence, then the lord guardian said, "The mysteries of the faith are mysteries for good reason, my child. Not all can comprehend their immense grandeur. The primata knows what she knows, for if she knew less she would be less effective. And if she knew more, she would be less than useless."

"I see, Lord Guardian," said the clerk. "Thank you Lord Guardian."

There was silence again in the reception hall, broken only by an occasional hiccuping chuckle.

A Day In The Life

One of the great misconceptions, from the days of the Brothers themselves to today, is that magic is somehow marvelous and wonderful and that being a mage is some type of glorious adventure. In truth, magic is just a study in forces, albeit forces that are undetected by the common man. And most of the work of a mage is not involved in deadly spellcasting duels, but in wearisome study, tiresome memorization, and unending research.

—Arkol, Argivian scholar

Barl led Jodah to a small room off the main hallway. The room contained two beds, and Barl informed Jodah him that the other bed would be for another first-year student, should one suddenly present himself at the gate. Barl ordered measurements to be taken by the torque-wearing servants for proper clothing, and he left the youth to bathe and prepare for bed. A pitcher of warm water and a bowl had been provided, along with towels, and Jodah scrubbed himself mercilessly to rid himself of the last of the salt and grime before climbing between the fresh-ironed sheets and falling fast asleep.

He awoke to find both his robes and his tattered, ragged garb missing, replaced by new garments that fitted him well but not snugly. There was a blue shirt made of what felt like silk, and slightly darker pants made of light wool. A vest of purple was provided, with large copper buttons. The quiet and effective servants had left his boots but had cleaned them of the mud and dried them thoroughly.

Jodah stuck his head out the door and looked around. The interior hall was windowless, but small lamps were set in alcoves every few yards. At first Jodah thought them to be candles in glass chimneys, but closer inspection proved them to be nothing less than imitations, their wicks and flames instead being teardrop-shaped gems that glimmered with their own lights. Jodah found the idea fascinating, and he did not hear his assailant until it was too late.

A massive hand impacted on his right shoulder, nearly forcing Jodah into the wall. As he stumbled forward, another meaty palm raised up to steady him.

"Didn't mean to surprise you," said his attacker, cheerfully, sandwiching the young man between his huge paws.

His assailant was a huge man, but, just as Barl was small and had an aura of largeness about him, this one was big and looked less impressive for his size. His belly spilled over the top of his belt, and his untucked shirt strained at the lower buttons. He had more of a beard than Jodah, in that it covered most of his face, but it seemed less since there were huge bald spots and areas covered only by one or two strands of overlong hair. The dirty-white hair on his head was stringy and drooped down in front of his sparkling eyes. Indeed, his eyes seemed like the only parts of him that were fresh and awake.

"They sent me up to wake you and drag you down to

breakfast! Come on!" He let go of Jodah and quickly trundled down the hall. Halfway to the stairs, he shouted over his shoulder, "They're serving ham!"

Jodah blinked and, unsure of himself, padded after his cheerful compatriot. By the time he was halfway down the hall, his new friend was at the stairway, and as he reached the stairs Jodah could hear the large man slapping the bottom steps with his oversized boots. It was fortunate that the staircase let out directly on the dining hall, or Jodah would never have found breakfast at all. By the time he arrived, his new companion had already plowed through the buffet line and was ensconced behind a heavily laden platter of biscuits, gravy, griddle cakes, eggs prepared any number of different ways, and berries that clung to sides of the towering mass of food like mountainclimbers fearing an avalanche. And there was ham, of course.

Jodah took a few pieces of the ham, a soft roll, and two griddle cakes. He considered the thick, syrupy coffee but settled for an infusion of sweet-oak leaves, poured by one of the torqued servants. As he moved away from the line, Jodah looked for somewhere to sit among the populated breakfast tables. He caught a now familiar flash of dirty-white hair but had no time to react, because his large assailant was waving with both arms, on the off chance that Jodah did not see him.

Jodah set down his plate opposite the huge man, who he had already mentally dubbed the Happy Juggernaut. The man shoved the remains of a gravy-soaked biscuit in his mouth and held out a sticky hand. "Buddaway, Aimchunnon!" he burbled, the crumbs dripping down his shirt.

Jodah looked at the hand, and the other man realized

his *faux pas*. He quickly grasped a portion of the tablecloth (his napkin having vanished, presumably eaten), swallowed, and tried again.

"By the way," he said, "I'm Shannan. I was told that you were the new kid and I should help you settling in. You want that roll?"

Jodah said Shannan could take it, and it was a good thing because the large man had already taken possession of the pastry before Jodah had finished giving permission. Nothing short of a fork in the back of the hand would have driven him away from the biscuit—if that.

Jodah introduced himself and asked what sort of help a new student, such as himself, might need that Friend Shannan could provide.

"Make sure you know where the meals are, and the heads," said the Happy Juggernaut, mixing his words with the energetic chomping of his breakfast.

Perhaps they closed the hall after an hour, thought Jodah, and that was why he had to eat so fast.

"And get you to the library. They told me that as well. You're working in the library."

"Do you work in the library, Friend Shannan?" said Jodah, almost fearing the reply.

Shannan, his mouth filled with several somethings, shook his head, then held up a finger for Jodah to wait until he managed to swallow his mouthful down.

"I work for Barl. Well, actually for one of Barl's assistants. I just got promoted. I'm working on making little gears out of nephrite. That's a harder type of jade, you know."

Jodah nodded, then asked, "Why are you making jade gears?"

"Nephrite," said Shannan. "I don't know, but Barl

wants it for something big. That's the way it is around here—there's always something going on around here, and we only get to know the small bits. But if you listen, you can pick stuff up. Look over there."

Jodah followed the sausage-sized finger to where two figures in robes, male and female were speaking in low whispers.

"Ophenia and San-Lo," Shannan said, not bothering to explain which was which. "Two months ago they hated each other, to the point that everyone feared that open spell combat would break out in the halls, or at least an official challenge in the arena. Then Barl comes back from one of his trips with a magical whatsis, a dark sphere made of unknown wood. San-Lo wants it, but Barl assigns Ophenia to research it, *but* all the books that Ophenia needs are in Lo's private stock. So the two of them have been playing kissy-face for the past couple weeks, with one trying to get the books and the other trying to get the sphere. Won't last, of course, but I think Barl was hoping to get the two to stop acting like rival cats. Worked, at least so far."

Jodah looked at the table. All he saw was two people, male and female, talking over small cups of coffee. He saw neither fighting cats nor kissing faces but took Shannan at his word.

Exhausted by the long dissertation, Shannan plunged back into his meal, surfacing only to deliver some other bit of gossip.

Drusilla, according to Shannan, attained the color of her night-black hair through use of certain plants growing in the southern swamp. Dorine was the name of the white-haired woman, and she had a taste for young male servants. So did Lord Dervish, but he had better taste than she did. Jonko, a red mage who was not present at the moment, had a talent for humiliating the staff publicly. Orm, also absent, was said to be wasting away in his study, refusing all meals in a quest for a higher consciousness. And Lucan, the fat man whom Jodah had met the day before in the hallway, was by general consensus a blatant backside-kisser.

Jodah noticed that there was nothing about Barl or Mairsil in Shannan's listing of gossip.

"It doesn't pay to talk about one's boss," Shannan patted the last of the gravy from the corner of his mouth, missing some and smearing the rest in his patchy beard. "Besides, Barl's the one that makes everything work around here. He's the chief artificer, but he's also the one who makes sure that everything in functioning properly. If something or someone needs to be replaced, he does the replacing. He gave me this task, making the gears, after the last guy had a nasty accident. Broke two of his left-hand fingers in a vise."

"What about the Lord High Mage?" said Jodah. "He's not your boss."

"He's my boss's boss, so what I said is doubly true," said Shannan, "but there are things that one knows, if one knows how to listen." He paused for moment, trying to effect a knowing grin but only managing a sloppy leer, then said, "You want the rest of your ham?"

Shannan finished the last of Jodah's breakfast, and Jodah thought his large, cheerful companion might charge the buffet to get seconds.

Instead the huge man said, "Come on, I'll show you the library. You gotta have a good memory around here, because the rooms make no sense whatsoever, and Barl forbids maps."

Jodah shot Shannan a puzzled look, which brought about another story.

"The way *I* heard it is that two white mages were mapping the place, starting at opposite corners. When they got to the center of the old monastery nothing matched up, and they got into a fight. They were finding bits of the two of them for weeks afterward in the halls. Anyway, that's the story I heard. So, Barl says, no maps. He's got a gift for simple, straightforward solutions that way. Here we are."

The library turned out to be the common or shared library for the Citadel. Most of the established mages had their own private libraries, as well, Shannan noted, and guarded them like rabid wolves. In the shared library were the materials that where held in common stock—books that were obviously nonmagical, general references, and items newly recovered from the hinterlands or left to the shelves by departed mages.

Shannan abandoned Jodah to the care of a deeply wrinkled woman who ruled the library from behind a redoubt of potted plants set on her desk. She said her name was Nedda and informed him that it was short for Nedastophalites. She paused for a moment, as if expecting him to recognize the name. When he didn't, her eyes narrowed, and Jodah had no doubt that her opinion of his intelligence dropped by at least ten points.

"You'll be working in the Scriptorium," said Nedda sharply, walking toward the back of the library.

"I'm not very good at writing," volunteered Jodah.

Nedda pulled up short and gave him that same intelligence-shrinking look.

"Writing isn't necessary. You know how to work a scarab?"

Jodah stammered for a moment, then said that he had seen one work but had not used it himself. She nodded and walked over to a side desk, pulled out a scarab, a quill, and ink. She showed him in short, deft movements, how to fill the scarab, where to place it on the paper, and how to deactivate it when he was done. Some scarabs made a noise when they reached the bottom—a buzzing or a peeping. These didn't, so you had to watch them out of the corner of your eye, or they would just stop when they ran out of paper.

The big thing, she said, was to not hem and haw and not to stutter.

"You don't stutter, do you?" she said, her eyes narrowing again in challenge.

Jodah said no, and she brightened just a touch.

"Good. Had a stutterer once. Worked here three months before we figured out no one could read what he had dictated, and we only found out because one of the red wizards blew herself up going through one of the texts he had transcribed. Damned fools, both of them."

She led Jodah across the room to beneath a great window made of panels and prisms of glass. The window overlooked the forest, or it would have if there was not a pounding rain at the moment that rattled the glass in its fixtures and threatened to break in at any moment.

Stacked at the base of the window were books of all shades and sizes—large elephant folios and tiny pocket books, ancient scrolls and runes carved into clay tablets. Some were incised on bones, and several were scribbled on metal disks. There were all manner of traditional books as well, bound in leather, cloth, metal, and several substances that Jodah could only guess at.

Nedastophalites set down the scarab and the ink and

opened a drawer in the table to reveal a deep bin of parchment.

"You read aloud, the scarab writes. You finish the book, you go to the next one."

Jodah looked at the huge mound of books. "Where should I start?"

Nedda shrugged. "Start anywhere. They all have to be done, eventually." And with that she wheeled and went back to her desk.

Jodah looked at her retreating form, then at the pile of books. He picked up one volume, but the handwriting was badly crabbed, and had water stains along the bottom, rendering it almost unreadable. He set that aside and chose a smaller tome. This one was filled with a more elegant hand and seemed to be a diary of some type.

He returned to the table, set up the scarab to record his words, and started to read.

It took a little time to get used to. He had to speak loudly and clearly enough for the scarab to register, without undue pauses or using the wrong word or stuttering. Jodah made a few mistakes early and put aside one entire sheet that was too error-filled for him to tolerate. About mid-morning the scarab ran out of ink without him noticing it, and Jodah had to re-read a section again after making that discovery.

Nedda came over twice. First she reviewed a finished page and made Jodah record it again. The second time she just gave an approving snort and retreated back to her plants.

About the time his stomach started grumbling, around noonday, Shannan reappeared with a hearty smile and a sack full of food. Nedda gave a glare that went past disapproving and ventured into the realm of homicidal, but the

Happy Juggernaut ignored her gaze entirely. He set the sack down on the table, upsetting the scarab in the process and smearing the page. Jodah sighed and asked what was going on.

"Lunch," said the artificer, the fresh stains on his shirt bearing witness to that basic truth. "It's catch-as-catch-can around here, but there will always be something in the kitchen. And if you're involved, you can always ring for a servant to bring you something."

Jodah looked at Nedda for confirmation of that fact, but the woman sat there stone-faced, glowering at the huge invader to her realm.

"You sound a little hoarse," said Shannan, digging through the bag. "Scriptors usually get that way, so I brought some hard candies. They're real good, and they help." A rainbow of sweets clattered to the table.

Shannan also brought some biscuits, ham slices left over from breakfast, some dried fruits, and some slices of black bread with raisins as well. He consumed half of what he had brought as Jodah ate his portion.

When the food was gone, Shannan pushed himself away from the crumb-laden table and declared, "Back to gears for me! I'll stop by before dinner to get you. And don't let Our Lady of the Potted Plants work you too hard. The rule here is that you should work at your own pace, as long as the work gets done."

And with that Shannan was gone, leaving Jodah to regard the huge pile of unread tomes. Jodah sighed, swept the crumbs from the table into his hand, disposed of them, then returned to his work.

Jodah took two breaks in the afternoon. The first was to find the nearest water closet, and the other was to check something in the history section. The books on the shelves were roughly grouped by subject, with histories in one area, diaries in another, spell texts in a third, and an over-stuffed, abandoned area labeled "holy texts."

Jodah finished the slender diary that afternoon and went on to a larger text about shipping in the Shielded Sea. As he read aloud, his memory slipped back to the storm and to the merfolk and to Sima. He suppressed a shudder as he thought of the cold water closing over him and had to check the scarab to make sure that his reaction was not committed to paper.

The second text contained a number of foreign words that Jodah did not recognize, but he found that if he spelled them out, the recorder would handle them. That made him feel better as well.

The book was intriguing but long, and Jodah was only half done before Shannan arrived to drag him to dinner. Jodah placed a marker in the book and cleaned the scarab as Nedda had instructed him, and then he packed it away.

On their way out of the library, Jodah paused by the plant-strewn desk. He said, "Nedastophalites was the last warrior-queen of now-lost Zegon, before they were ruled by a council. She died fifty years before Urza was born, and her reign was regarded as a golden age of the Zegoni people, winning them their freedom from the main Fallaji rulers of that time, the Tomakul."

Nedda looked up at him, her face still a block of deeply-carved stone, but there was a light in her green eyes. "You have had a very good first day, Friend Jodah."

"Thank you, Goodlady Nedda."

"*Friend* Nedda," corrected the librarian.

"Friend Nedda," said Jodah and hurried after Shannan, who was already barreling down the hallway as if he had to hunt down and capture dinner with his bare hands.

"You'll have to hurry if you're going to dress," said Shannan, as Jodah caught up with him.

"Dress?" said Jodah. "What's wrong with what I'm wearing?"

"Nothing," said Shannan, "if you're going to be working through the dinner, the servants will bring you sandwiches and cold soup. Go to your room. Your evening outfit is probably already laid out."

Indeed it was, placed there by the same invisible servants who had transformed his trail-spattered gear into silk finery. Leggings of a rich, royal blue. A short tunic of similar material edged in golden thread. A long cape which closed at the neck with a golden clasp in the shape of a sea shell. Long gloves. His boots would seem clunking and heavy with this outfit, and the mystery servants had provided a set of silk slippers.

Jodah regarded himself in the thin silvered mirror inside the door, and was impressed. His hair seemed a little shaggy now, but there was probably a barber or other servant who could take care of that as well.

Shannan was waiting for him outside his room. He was dressed in an outrageous clash of multicolored checks and stripes that made it difficult to pin down exactly where he ended and the real world began. Despite his anxiousness, Shannan now said there was no real rush—dinner was a formal affair. There would be assigned seating, again arranged by the ubiquitous and invisible servants.

Shannan, of course, was seated to Jodah's right, so at least Jodah did not have to watch the ill-conceived spawn of fashion eat. To Jodah's left was a balding, much older mage who spent most of the meal talking to himself and making notes on a small tablet.

The tables were laid out like a wide horseshoe. The

diners occupied the outer ring while servants beetled around making sure the glasses were filled and the plates sufficiently laded. Jodah tested his drink with a small sip before risking a larger gulp, and as he did so, he saw the white-haired woman, Dorine, at the opposite end of the horseshoe, watching him. He offered her a small toast, and she returned it. Then she turned to her companion, a very pale man with very blond hair, and quickly locked him down in intense conversation.

Shannan said there were about two hundred and fifty mages at the Conclave at any time, with more coming and going all the time. Only about half of them would be at dinner at any one time, since many had their own work to do. They were of all levels of capability, ranging from the new fish like himself and Jodah, up to those with their own suites and private laboratories. Some were out in the field uncovering new magical items, though there were fewer and fewer of those these days. There probably were at least as many servants, though Shannan never had bothered to count them. Barl probably knew, he said, but then Barl knew everything about the Conclave Citadel.

The central area of the horseshoe was used for magical display, at the whims of the diners. Fresh apples were served with the main course, and one mage threw his core in the center of the room. Jodah wondered at it, until the seeds within the core quickly sprouted, their stalks entwining and growing thicker and more woody, until a full apple tree stood in the center of the tables, bearing golden fruit. The apples dropped from the tree, each in its turn. Each one became a shimmering bell on its way to the ground, striking the marble floor to play out a rough, chiming tune. The assembled mages applauded as the servants brought out a sherbet, dodging the roots as they wove around the tree.

The mage who had cast the core bowed deeply and cast another spell, shriveling the tree and causing it to contract on itself until it became nothing more than an apple core, which a servant deftly picked up and carried from the hall.

"Remarin does that sort of thing all the time," said Shannan, pointing with a turkey leg at the green-clad mage.

A food fight also broke out across the arch of the horseshoe as one of the wizards, filled with black mana, animated a turkey carcass and sent it on an attack spree, charging along the far arc of the table with an oversized knife clenched beneath one wing, a carving fork in the other.

Some of the diners leaned away as the half-carved corpse surged by them, but several mages organized a resistance from the bread baskets. Several long loaves, half-cut through, accordioned their way forward, supported on the flanks by waves of animated dinner rolls.

The two forces met almost directly across from Jodah's position, near where Dorine sat. The white-haired magess abandoned her seat entirely as the animated bit of poultry slammed into the doughy legions.

Shannan provided a vivid and excited description of the battle to anyone within earshot. "And the death-turkey goes wading into the middle of the dinner rolls! Their buttery interiors are no match for blazing silverware, and the poultry-geist is carving them to pieces! Oh, there are crumbs everywhere! But wait, the long loaves are now in position, and they're raising up like cobras and slamming themselves down on the reanimated turkey! They're striking it again and again and not giving the bird a chance to regain its breath! Yes, Yes! It's all over, everyone! The baked goods have carried the field. The yeast also rises! Huzzah! Huzzah!"

The servants, who wisely disappeared during the confrontation, reappeared to clean up the worst of the debris and bring out the dessert.

"There is always good entertainment when Barl and His Mage-ness aren't here," said Shannan, slurring his words slightly. He nodded toward the apex of the horseshoe, and indeed, there were a pair of empty chairs that Jodah had not noticed before.

"Is there a reason for that?" said Jodah. "Don't they approve of mages playing with their food?"

"Ah, dessert!" said Shannan, ignoring Jodah's comment entirely. "You have to try the chocolate cheesecake. It *is* to die for."

The cheesecake was the best thing Jodah had ever placed on his tongue. Its seemed to melt there in a cool sensation that passed through the rest of his body. Idly, he wondered if there were mages in the kitchen as well.

Jodah allowed himself another glass of the wine and noticed that Shannan was partial to small shots of whiskey—one after another. Then the servants opened the doors behind Mairsil's and Barl's empty chairs, and one announced that there would be poetry and spells in the smoking room.

Shannan rose from the table, trying to take Jodah with him. "The good seats always go first," he enthused.

Jodah gently disengaged his arm. "It's been a long day," he said diplomatically. "I think I want to spend some time thinking, then turn in early."

Shannan blinked at the concept of thought as a planned activity.

At last he managed, "Okay," and plowed toward the doors. "See you at breakfast!" he shouted over his shoulder.

Most of the company was heading for the smoking room. The white-haired woman was apparently stalking one of the waiters, and the old man next to Jodah was still scribbling on his pad, half his meal untouched in front of him.

Jodah stretched and made his way up to his small room. He passed a few open doors, from which laughter, and in one case singing, emerged.

At last he reached his for-the-moment private room. He stripped and washed and crawled between the sheets. Even more than yesterday, the soft bed linens felt luxuriant.

He was safe. He had a roof over his head. He was well-fed. He was working with mages. There were no goblins here, no city guard, no church. He had finally found a place that appreciated magic.

It *had* been a very good day, thought Jodah. As the tendrils of sleep reached up to snare him, he managed one last thought.

He thought: I could get used to this.

* * * * *

Barl knocked softly but firmly and entered the private study, expecting the Lord High Mage to be hunched over his stone calendar with his sand-filled glasses. Instead, Mairsil was at his desk, books piled high around him. At the center of the maelstrom was the thin folder holding three pieces of paper detailing the interview with Jodah.

"You called for me, My Lord Mage?" said the artificer.

Mairsil looked up and smiled at Barl, a smile that told the artificer at once that the Lord High Mage had discovered something and was very pleased by his discovery. Barl had seen the expression before—Mairsil was a master at assigning mages five separate and apparently unrelated tasks, only to take their results as a group and come to a conclusion that none had anticipated.

"How goes matters with the new arrival?" said Mairsil brightly.

"As per your instructions, he was assigned to the Library as a Scriptor," said Barl calmly. "I assigned one of my junior apprentices to help him settle in. May I ask why the interest in this particular mageling?"

Mairsil smiled again and chuckled. He tapped the report. "Jodah of Giva Province," he said, "student of the now-deceased Voska, a name that means nothing to either of us. But the transcript states that there was a mage in the family line."

Barl took a deep breath and thought for a moment, "Jarsyl. He said he had a great-grandfather named Jarsyl. You mentioned this before."

"Great-great-grandfather," corrected Mairsil. "Now take a look at this."

The taller man spun the large, open text around on the desk. It was a copy of *The Antiquities War* by Kayla bin-Kroog. Barl had only seen four original copies of the work—the one he himself had brought from the south and three later copies that he had ordered destroyed over the years to keep out of other hands.

The page in question was held open by a large brass bookmark. The passage Mairsil pointed to was toward the end of the volume. Barl read, and Mairsil waited quietly.

"It speaks of the time when the Devastation reached Argive, bin-Kroog's home at the time," said Barl, "when the great explosion that her husband Urza summoned to defeat his brother reached his homeland thousands of miles away. It still had force enough to level towers and breach stone walls."

"Look at the marginal note, the one I believe to be in Kayla's handwriting." said Mairsil.

Barl squinted, then nodded. "It looks like mention of a Jarsyl. And this one is Kayla's grandson, and no more than a child. It said the blast frightened him."

"And Giva province was once the nation of Argive," said Mairsil.

Barl looked up. "You think that the Jarsyl of the Brothers' War is this boy's ancestor."

Mairsil held his hands before him and turned both palms to the ceiling, as if he was physically weighing the options. Then he smiled.

"It seems very likely. Jarsyl of Giva Province is the boy's great-whatever grandsire. Jarsyl of Argive was Urza's grandson. Therefore . . . " He raised both palms toward Barl.

"It seems like a coincidence," said Barl flatly. He had been down this type of road with Mairsil. Usually he had been proved wrong—Mairsil would often look at a collection of facts and come up with the conclusion that was not the most likely but was usually the true one.

"A coincidence worth pursuing," said Mairsil. He sat back on his high-backed chair and folded his hands over his stomach, fiddling with his ruby ring as he did so.

Barl said, "If you wish, we could get to the truth directly. The wand of pink quartz has proved to be more than adequate in gaining answers."

Mairsil looked up at the stocky man, his brows raised in mock surprise.

"Friend Barl! Not every question needs to be answered with a hammer! And here I thought you liked that young man."

Barl replied, "I said I believed he would adapt well to our group and that he holds promise. If he also holds peril, we should be prepared to deal with it directly and quickly."

"And besides," said Mairsil, the wolfish grin returning to his face as he raised a theatrical palm, "you know that if you suggest it, I would try something else. Oh, I've known you too long, Friend Artificer!"

"You make the assumption that I know you as well as you presume to know me, My Lord High Mage," said Barl, without hint of bemusement.

Mairsil templed his fingers and touched them to his lips. "He may not know he is of the blood of Urza," he said at last, "After all, the Brothers are not the most popular of roots to anchor one's family tree to. Still, if he has some of Urza's blood, *and* he is a mage, *and* he is the descendent of Jarsyl. . . ." He let the phrase hang unanswered for a moment. "I think I want to meet this lad," he said at last.

"I can arrange to have him brought here at once," said Barl calmly.

"Not like that," said Mairsil, waving a hand in frustration. "Hammers, Barl, hammers! The boy has no family. He has no real friends. He has lost his mentor, and he falls into our laps. He is looking for someone to follow, someone to look up to."

"That someone would be you, I suppose," said Barl flatly.

"Of course," said Mairsil, the lupine smile tugging back

the corners of his thin mustache, "and once I have him, he'll be the key I need to solve my great mystery. I won't need Ith at all, will I? For I will have one of Urza's blood to unlock the door and bring me the power that is rightfully mine!"

Barl said nothing but only nodded at the Lord High Mage's wisdom.

12☾

The Apprentice Wizard

Most magical organizations of the time were cults of personality, built around one particular wizard who attracted sufficient followers. If one of those followers then attracted his own students, his group, those followers, would in turn split off from the main body and form their own magical organization. Usually such organizations fell apart with the death of their founding charismatic masters. In the case of the Magician's Conclave, the student usurped the master's position, yet its eventual destruction was not prevented, only deferred. Interestingly, one of the mages present at the demise of the Conclave was an individual named Jodah.

—**Arkol, Argivian scholar**

The first few weeks were filled with small incidents and accidents that made up life. Jodah completed scripting several histories of the various city-states of the eastern coast, a book of epic poems, and several scrolls that were no more than the complete tax records of a long-dead wizard in Zegon. There was an enchanting collection of folktales and legends, which, at the outset, the author admitted were nothing more than creations of his own mind. He checked with Nedda on these, and she told him curtly that if they were on the pile, they had value, and should be read into the record.

There were three histories on the Brothers' War itself, each disagreeing with the others on the particulars. One based itself on one of the self-created fictions that Jodah had just transcribed and treated that fictional work as the ultimate truth, even where it was countered blatantly by obvious facts in other volumes.

Nedda seemed generally approving of his work, and she checked up on him only once a day now. The huge stack of books did not grow any smaller, though Jodah put aside those he had recorded in one pile, and those that he could not read in another. If he could not read a book it was usually because the text was written in some language or code that he himself did not recognize or was so badly written or damaged that he could not make out the words properly.

As he read aloud, Jodah fought the temptation to merely speak the words, without letting them sink in. The epic poems stayed with him for a number of days thereafter, and he kept track of the varying versions of the Brothers' War. There were several mentions of a text called *The Antiquities War*, but there was no copy of this text either in the library or in the pile of books that needed to be transferred to the neat printing of the recording scarab. Jodah assumed that it had been lost in the intervening years.

There was one book that described spells. It was supposedly written by a scholar talking to a goblin shaman, and the wording and phraseology was crude at best. Yet Jodah understood the bulk of it, and, after reading it, put it aside to check again later. It was about this time that he started to take his lunches on the battlement facing the mountain range. He would spend hours in the period after dinner, before dusk, just watching them, committing them to memory.

It felt right, and in its own way, was a testament and a memorial to Voska, who never got to teach Jodah any proper red spells since Jodah did not know the mountains as well as his teacher had.

One evening, in the privacy of his small room, Jodah cleared his mind and thought of the mountains. The farmlands of his home were ground into his bones and came to him easily, but it was harder to pull the mountains to him. To be among them. To be one of them. To pull their power in.

Yet after several days of meditation he did so and called up enough of the red energy to light a single taper. The red mana had its own feel, and taste, and texture—separate and distinct from the white. It felt warmer and tasted like a campfire burning pine branches to Jodah. It also felt wilder, more uncontrollable, ready to shift off in another direction if not watched properly. After several days, he was able to produce a large enough flame to light several candles from a distance.

He could not sleep that night but stayed awake, watching the candles burn and finally gutter. He thought of hunching over a cold fire pit struggling to master the concepts that now seemed so easy, so obvious. He felt a hole in the pit of his stomach. If only Voska was there to see his accomplishment.

The library was a relatively quiet place. About four

times a day a torque-wearing servant would arrive with a message requesting a particular book. Nedda would then pull the book off the shelf or send the servant back with a note that the book did not exist. She seemed to know by memory what was on the shelves.

On a rare occasion, a mage himself or herself would come down to the library for a book, then either inform Nedda of its departure, or sit down at one of the low tables and read. Jodah's low murmuring voice beneath the great windows did not seem to bother them.

Nedda, for her part, stayed behind her desk, often going through her own arcane texts. She would sometimes look through the unreadable pile and select a volume that she recognized, and she would bring it back to her desk for personal transcribing. Most of the rest of the time she read, or wrote, or tended to her plants.

Once Jodah looked up to see her murmuring softly to one of her plants, a great, leafy monstrosity with a balled bud that had as yet refused to flower. Jodah watched as Nedda spoke to it, and a thin, yellowish mist bubbled up from the heart of the bud, sending up a streamer of smoke from the flower. As Jodah watched, the smoke coalesced into a face—not human but rather thin and elven. The face dissipated and Nedda smiled. Then she noticed that Jodah was watching her and rewarded the student with a withering glare. Jodah dived back into the book he was transcribing and did not look up again the rest of that morning. The next day, the plant with the tightly held bud was no longer among Nedda's battlement of plants.

That evening Jodah practiced his candle-lighting, and, looking at the flickering lights, thought about magic. Voska had always acted like magic was a natural talent. One either had it or didn't. Sima, on the other hand, acted as if magic was a school subject, to be bookishly studied and mastered. Barl the artificer seemed to believe it was some sort of machine that could be examined and explained by a set number of physical laws. Shannan and some of the others here acted as if magic was just the job you did when you weren't eating, or a power for jokes and entertainment. Nedda seemed to use it to tend her plants. And Jodah . . .

Jodah blinked. He wasn't quite sure what magic was or what he wanted to use it for. He had spent too much of his time hiding or running or fighting to figure such things out. He thought of what he had told Barl that first night. He was tired of being hungry, hunted, and cold, and he wanted magic to cure that.

He was no longer hunted, no longer hungry, and no longer cold. He wondered what the purpose of magic was now?

* * * * *

Two days later the sun came out. The clouds had been lightening over the past several days, and there was talk around the dinner table that there might even be some true sunbreaks in the near future. The Conclave House was high in the northern latitudes, so winter days were brief and miserable, while the current summer days lasted longer than most human activity. The clouds had been omnipresent regardless of season, and they brought cold rains and snow at the higher elevations. The idea that sunlight might finally break through was a welcome change.

When it did, it took everyone by surprise. Jodah was at his table, in the afternoon, pouring over a text on comparative military tactics of the various city states, when a small, bright blotch appeared on the book he was reading. He blinked and stopped, the scarab pausing at the exact same moment. He tried to wave the bright blotch away, but it did not move. Indeed, when he moved the book the blotch stayed where it was, falling to the table when he pushed the book aside and residing on the back of his hand when he tried to grasp it.

He looked at the rest of the table, and it was covered with similar bright blotches. Many of these were multi-hued, small rainbows warped in curved patterns against the warm finish of the table.

Only then did Jodah look up and look outside.

The great window was alive with light and color. The sun was out for the first time since he had arrived at the Citadel, and it shone with a fury to make up for lost time. The various prisms and panes in the great glass window caught the sunlight and threw it against all the surfaces around. Where it hit, it hit with such impact that the light itself broke up into colors—blues and reds and greens and colors in between.

Beyond the window was the world. Not the gray world that Jodah had suffered through for so long, but a brilliant world, freshly washed by the continual rains and now intensely limned by the long-absent sun. The forests at the base of the mountain were a riot of greens. There were more shades than Jodah thought possible, ranging from a dark sullen conifer jade, to an explosion of bright green that threw back the sunlight with such an intensity that it hurt the eye.

The forests spilled down the hills, vibrant and alive, and even the plains seemed brighter. The large, grassy wastes caught the wind and rippled like an ocean. In the distance, Jodah cause sight of thin wisps of smoke rising from the plains. There were towns out there, Barl had stated weeks earlier, yet this was the first time Jodah had any clue that they were present.

"It is a beautiful view," said a rich, fluid voice behind him.

Jodah jumped at the sound and wheeled.

Lord High Mage Mairsil had appeared behind him, as if he had suddenly manifested out of nothing or removed a cloak of invisibility. Jodah assured himself that the Lord High Mage merely moved when others were not watching, but the pit of his stomach told otherwise. Mairsil seemed to enjoy surprising people, and doubtless he used his magics to aid in that surprise.

For his part, the leader of the Magician's Conclave did not deign to notice Jodah's reaction to his voice. Instead he said, "It's such a pity that the sun comes so rarely. During the winter months, it's only marginally clearer, but we are at such a high latitude that the days are short, and snow usually keeps the mages indoors."

Jodah nodded, no longer thinking about the sunlight outside. He looked past Mairsil to see if Nedda had noticed the Lord High Mage's arrival, but her battlement of plants, usually manned throughout the day by her stony, silent presence, was now empty.

The sun passed back behind its veil of clouds, and the multihued blotches disappeared from the table surface. Mairsil took a deep breath, closed his eyes, and exhaled. When he opened his eyes again, he was looking directly at Jodah.

"So," said Mairsil, "I trust your studies are going well?"

"I'm getting a lot of books recorded," said Jodah, motioning at the large "done" pile. "Of course," he motioned to the larger pile of unread tomes, "there is a lot more to do."

"So I see," said Mairsil, settling down in the chair opposite Jodah. Jodah took this as a sign that he should sit as well. "But that's not what I meant, is it?"

Jodah blinked. "I'm sorry?"

"Apology accepted," said the Lord High Mage with a grin, as if smiling at some private joke. "I mean, *these*," he made an expansive motion at the collected books, "are your *tasks*. Everyone has *tasks*; things that must be done. I have mine. You have yours. I was interested as to how your *studies* are going?"

Jodah shifted uneasily. The Lord High Mage was very comfortable sitting across from him, as if he regularly had this type of conversation, making small talk with the lesser mages. That made Jodah all the more uneasy.

"Don't tell me that you haven't had a chance to do any real magicking on your own!" said Mairsil, his dark eyebrows arching in apparent concern. "They haven't been keeping you so busy with *tasks* that you haven't had a chance to discover anything or to cadge a spell or two or to get to know the land around here?"

Jodah suddenly was afraid that his lack of spell research would be taken as an indictment of Nedda's overseeing of his work.

"No sir. I found a book on red mana in the collection and was working with it to develop in that area." He stammered for a moment, then added, "Sort of on my own."

"Excellent!" said Mairsil, pounding the table-top with the fleshy part of his hand. "And have you come up with anything?"

"Well, I've been studying the mountains," said Jodah, carefully, "and I know . . . well, I can make a flame."

It sounded so weak, so pathetic. This was the Master of the Conclave, the most powerful mage in the citadel, and

Jodah was telling him about how he worked the simplest of red spells.

Mairsil stroked his bare chin and said, "And you did this on your own?"

"Yes, sir." said Jodah.

"No one told you to study red magic or gave you the book or told you to study the mountains until you felt like they were your own?"

"No, sir," said Jodah.

The sunbeam of Mairsil's face reappeared, and Jodah allowed himself to relax.

"Good. Very good indeed." He leaned over toward the boy. "Have you noticed something about this place, Friend Jodah?"

"I've noticed many things, sir," said Jodah carefully. "Which thing do you mean?"

"We have no teachers here," said the Lord High Mage. "No mentors, no masters, no superiors. We strive to be a society of equals, all gathered together for one purpose— magic!" He said the word as if he were summoning the energy to him. "Just in case you think otherwise," he said, "you're doing exactly the right thing. You're completing your *tasks* while you work on your *studies*. And your *studies* are exactly what you yourself choose them to be. Don't let yourself be limited." He looked at Jodah for a long moment, then added, "You normally use the white, don't you?"

Jodah nodded and said, "Most of the spells I know are white, yes."

Mairsil nodded. "Healing. Light. Building. Social skills. These are white hallmarks. The citadel of white magic is carved of snow granite and smells of fresh-mown hay. At least that's the way its always felt to me. But you're studying red, now? Why not green, since the forests almost run up to the window outside?"

Jodah felt embarrassed, but managed, "My teacher . . . I mean my former teacher was a red mage."

"Yes, old Voska," said Mairsil, his face clouding slightly.

"You knew him?" said Jodah, surprised.

"Knew *of* him," said the Lord High Mage, keeping the same tone, as if he was walking down a path of memory. "I am sorry for you, and I share your loss. I've lost enough colleagues to the church and its bloody inquisition over the years." He shook his head, then added, "He'd be proud to know you were investigating his path as well as yours."

"Yes, sir," said Jodah. "Thank you, sir."

"And let's do without that 'sir' nonsense," said Mairsil. "Society of Equals, Friend Jodah."

"Yes, si . . . I mean, yes, Friend . . . Mairsil," struggled Jodah.

"I know it feels odd," said Mairsil, and the smile was back again. "Even Barl, whom I've known forever, prefers Lord High Mage. And if you need to call me that in public, use that title. But when it's just you and me, call me friend."

Jodah nodded, then said, "Yes, Friend Mairsil." He was rewarded with a radiant smile.

"Good, good," said the Lord High Mage, leaning back on his chair, "and I hope you won't ignore the other colors. Press on, into the rest of the spectrum! The first mages connected particular types of spells with particular colors, particular effects. Black with darkness, red with fire, and so on. It just seems natural. But remember that colors themselves are a limit, and one only proves oneself when one presses against those limits, and exceeds them!"

"Yes, si . . .yes Friend Mairsil," said Jodah, wondering if he dared press his newfound friend with a question.

His face must have betrayed him, because Mairsil said, "You wish to ask something?"

Jodah nodded and said, "Friend Mairsil, what color are you?"

Mairsil smiled again and held up his hand, its back to Jodah. He blinked, and a jet of flame appeared at the tip of each finger and the thumb. White at the pinkie, then red, green, blue, and finally an ebon-hued flame from the thumb.

"Most people believe that magic is broken down into five colors, correct?" quizzed Mairsil. "Each of those colors is tied to a particular type of memory of the land."

Jodah agreed, thinking of his discussion with Barl on the parapet that first day, before he was officially welcomed into the Conclave.

Mairsil still held his flaming hand in front of him. "But what people don't know is that there are certain basic temperaments that are tied to the colors themselves, and that, in many ways, determines the type of mage one becomes." The Lord High Mage motioned with his non-flaming hand, pointing at the pinkie. "White's tend to be healers, fixers, and social individuals. Those who want everyone to agree in an argument. Those who like order. Neat people are attracted to white mana—its simplicity is appealing to them." Mairsil nodded to the younger man, "No offense for your own casting."

Jodah thought for a moment, then said, "None taken."

Mairsil curled down the pinkie, and the flame extinguished itself. "Red is almost the opposite—volatile, destructive, disorganized, and chaotic. Red mages tend to have explosive tempers and also sharp tongues. They are not planners but impulsive. That's one reason I was surprised by your studies and am impressed by them."

Jodah thought for a moment. Voska was never violent, except to goblins and the church, of course. But impulsive and disorganized . . . yes, that applied to him. He nodded in agreement.

Mairsil curled down another finger. "Green is akin to white," said the Lord High Mage, "it believes in life, but it takes a much more long-term approach. Careful planners are green mages. They do well with animals, and plants, and other living things. They are patient, but they are also judgmental." He wrinkled his nose when he said this.

That seemed a fair description of Nedda, thought Jodah.

"Blue," said Mairsil, and his face clouded just a bit. "They are controllers. Illusion, the air, the sea, all changeable, mercurial elements these are blue's domain. Blue is used to doing things its way and will brook no argument. Argue with a blue mage, and you'll find the very basics of your argument slipping away like a cliff being eroded. There are very few pure blue mages in the Conclave, and for good reason."

Jodah thought of Sima, and suppressed a shudder. Mairsil curled the last finger down and left his black-burning thumb.

"And lastly black, which if you ask the church is the color of all magic. Misunderstood, black is, for it examines those parts that most of us would rather not think about—fear, death, and madness. Only by facing them do we gain strength. Black mages tend to be loners, and more secretive than the others, for fear of being chastised. They deal with dead things, but then not so much as healers but as hunters. Black mages carry that stigma with them."

Jodah thought about Mairsil's words, but realized that the mage had not answered his question. "But which color are you?" he asked again.

The Lord High Mage opened his hands, and both of them were bathed in a torrent of multihued light that dimmed even the lightening sky outside. It seemed to permeate the entire library and reach into every page of every book.

"I am the rainbow," said Mairsil, with a hearty laugh and a secretive grin, posing like an actor on the stage in those last seconds of an act when the lights are banked and the curtain drops.

Jodah blinked back the colors, wondering if it would be rude, or even possible, to try to disenchant a more experienced mage's work.

"And you can be the rainbow too," said Mairsil. "Remember that the colors are not goals. They are a framework by which one can attain one's goals." Mairsil's voice dropped slightly, and he said in a knowing voice, "So many of the others here have forgotten it—they think that by becoming a *black* wizard, one can do everything any other wizard can do, just in a different way. Black is merely one set of tools, and a true master knows all of them."

"I see," said Jodah. "I never thought about it that way."

"Oh, but you should," said Mairsil. "Always try to think in new ways! Now, I know for a fact that you're ahead of Nedda's plans for transcribing these books. I recommend you spend a lot more time studying the mountains, and the forests, and the bogs, and even the islands. Broaden your horizons and get out of the library more. You'll be a better person and a better wizard, for it."

Then Mairsil was up and gone from the table, leaving

Jodah blinking at the lights and mentally churning through everything that the older mage had said.

Shortly after Mairsil disappeared, the sky darkened and a chill drizzle laced with hail started to pelt the great window. Nedda reappeared and sat at her desk, making no comment on the Lord High Mage's appearance or her own disappearance.

Jodah turned himself back to the volume he was reading but found that he was distracted the conversation— both by what the Lord High Mage had said and by the fact that he had just "dropped in" to say it. It made no sense to Jodah that the most powerful wizard in the Conclave stopped by the library for an impromptu lesson on colors.

The entire encounter made Jodah feel uneasy, as if he was a child and Mairsil some clumsy, overbearing adult trying to be friendly. Perhaps, thought Jodah, that was exactly what it was. Shannan said that Mairsil and Barl were continually working on things that no one else had knowledge of. Perhaps one of those things involved the library.

Jodah also noted that the page he had been recording was ruined now as a result of their conversation. He had neglected to turn the scarab off, and it continued to write as Mairsil spoke, stopping at the bottom of the page, its eyes flashing silently. Jodah did notice that when Mairsil spoke, his words were written in red ink, as opposed to the neat, black block letters that Jodah had previously seen. Perhaps Mairsil was the inventor of the scarabs, thought Jodah, and they recognized his voice.

Jodah started a new page, but instead of consigning the old parchment to the foolscap bin, he folded it and placed it inside his leather vest. Perhaps a later review would reveal something that he had missed in their discussion.

Jodah found he still could not concentrate, and after a few false starts and stops, surrendered for the day. He put his materials away and told Friend Nedda that he would be stopping early. She nodded at him, but it was a wary nod. There was something in Nedda's manner that was not there before, as if suddenly the planets had moved into new orbits as a result of his public meeting with the Lord High Mage.

He went to the parapet overlooking the mountains but found his mind too cluttered to concentrate on anything, let alone study the land. Besides, the chill rain was turning heavier, and he could hear the shouts below of those who had been lured outside by the brief sunshine, only to be cruelly reminded of the true nature of the weather after they had walked far from the citadel. He watched the rain for a long while, trying to let it wash his mind clean, but he found that it did not.

Dinner that evening was curious as well. Mairsil and Barl were at the head table, at the apex of the horseshoe. As was normal when they were in attendance, there was no hijinks or horseplay, no food fights or sudden apparitions. But there was something else. There was laughter, but it was nervous laughter. There was conviviality, but it sounded tinny to Jodah's ears, forced and artificial. Several people came up to Mairsil's chair during the meal, but they seemed stiff and formal, with none of the "Society of Equals" that Mairsil spoke of.

There was fear. That was it, Jodah decided. There was fear in the air.

Jodah looked at Mairsil, but this time the Lord High Mage did not look up or even recognize Jodah's presence. Instead, his head was tilted slightly down, and he was speaking with Barl. The chief artificer was writing quickly on a tablet as Mairsil spoke. Ingles, the mage in red whom Jodah had met the first day, stood on the opposite side of the chair, shifting nervously until Mairsil deigned to notice him. Another consultation, short and to the point. Ingles was dismissed and returned to his place at the table. Mairsil rose, bowed to the assembled group, and wafted out of the room, Barl in tow. Only then did the group seem to relax completely, and something that resembled life flowed back into the conversations.

They were afraid, decided Jodah—afraid of Mairsil, or Barl, or both of them. But Barl had been kind to him the first few days, if abrupt, while Mairsil seemed to have gone out of his way today to be chatty, friendly, and informative.

Which made Jodah even more suspicious. He needed to find out more about the masters of the Magicians' Conclave, but could not figure out who to ask.

Then his eyes fell on the sloppy, overweight figure of Shannan, flirting unsuccessfully with Drusilla while a torqued waiter filled his glass again with rum. The waiter moved off, and Shannan paused in mid-witticism to instruct the man to leave the bottle.

Despite himself, Jodah smiled, and as the rest of the gathering broke up, made a beeline to Shannan's side.

13 ☾

Dangerous Knowledge

The knowledge of the Dark, and of all the ancient eras, comes down to us in dribbles and drabs. Only a few volumes survive, and those often disagree with each other, or refer to still earlier, now-lost texts. The reasons for this lack of knowledge are myriad, including the long cold gap of the Ice Age. But one basic reason for this lose of knowledge is that each age, indeed each generation or regime, wishes that its version of history be the only one that survives to tell the tale. The Church of Tal was merciless in expunging volumes that did not agree with its version of history, and mages and scholars since then were little better. Though they couched their censorial habits in terms of "modern validity" and "historical revisionism," both church and scholar spoke the same language—It would be the victors who would set down how history truly happened.

—Arkol, Argivian scholar

"Sorry about your shoes," slurred Shannan.

"I can get new ones," said Jodah, navigating the weaving assistant of artifice down the hallway to an unblemished spot. Already servants behind them were removing

Shannan's dinner from the wallpaper and rug.

"You still have the bottle?" said Shannan, turning toward Jodah, but neither eye quite focusing.

"Right here," said Jodah, holding up the bottle and glasses, clinking them together.

"Good." Shannan's head dropped down on his chest. "I'd hate to think it was a total loss." He looked up again. "Sorry about the shoes."

"Don't worry," said Jodah, steering his drunken companion to a small, overstuffed couch. He suddenly had empathy with a sea captain trying to moor an over-laded vessel against contrary winds.

Jodah got Shannan close enough to the couch that a good push and gravity carried the tipsy artificer the rest of the way. Shannan landed with a crash and raised his arms and legs as he hit the couch.

"That's better," said Shannan. "Less spinning this way."

"Good," said Jodah, pouring another drink for his companion.

"Shouldn't drink," he said. "Leaves me fuzzy in the morning. Have to do another gear for Barl's mystery machine in the morning. Got one done, but the next three cracked, right down the middle. Nothing but problems, that nephrite. You gonna drink that yourself?"

"No, this is for you," said Jodah, handing over the full glass.

Shannan smiled at the glass, then frowned at Jodah. "Aren't you going to join me?"

Jodah waved his empty glass at Shannan, shaking its nonexistent contents. "Right here."

"Good." Shannan concentrated on his drink. He raised it and said loudly, "Confusion to our enemies!" and managed to get most of it down his throat, some of it on his shirt, and only a bit on the upholstery of the couch. "You're a good person, looking out for me. Not a lot of people do around here, you know."

"That's good," said Jodah.

"No, I mean it," said Shannan, lurching forward in his seat. "It's 'friend' this and 'friend' that, but really they're all just vultures. Just waiting for you to trip up. They're sooo impressed with being wizards, that they forget they're people. And people . . ." Shannan smacked his lips and gathered his thoughts. "People are just selfish sometimes."

"Uh-huh," said Jodah. "Actually, I wanted to hear about a couple of the people around here."

"Good, 'cause I know," said Shannan. "I know just about everything. Nobody likes me, I mean, nobody likes anyone, but they all talk about each other."

"I want to know about the Lord High Mage," said Jodah, "and the Chief Artificer, too."

Shannan's eyes cleared with remarkable speed, and Jodah realized that the apprentice was staring at him in terror, as if Jodah had suddenly spat flame. Then he was struggling to his feet, "I gotta go," he said.

Jodah placed a hand on Shannan's shoulder and steered him back to the couch. "I'm just curious."

"Curious is bad around here," said Shannan. "They tell you it's good, but as soon as you get curious about the wrong thing—Whammo!" He made a chopping motion with his free hand, still managing to spill part of his drink in the process.

"That's why I'm asking you," said Jodah. "I'm asking someone trustworthy."

"Trussworthy," slurred Shannan, trying the word on like a new vest. "Yes, that's true. I am trussworthy. But I can't tell you."

Again the half-rise, and again the hand against the shoulder. "Let me tell you something, then."

Shannan was looking both trapped and peeved but said, "Go ahead."

"I talked with the Lord High Mage today," said Jodah.

Shannan's face screwed up in a tight little ball. "Did not!" he managed at last.

"Truth," said Jodah, looking exasperated and, he hoped, honest. "He came by the library today, and we had a long chat."

Shannan's eyes dropped a bit. "What did he want?"

"Ah," said Jodah, "that's the problem. I don't know. We talked about the weather, and magic, and colors, and how my studies were going. But I don't know what he *wanted*."

Shannan's brow furrowed, and Jodah could almost imagine the intuitive engines within desperately struggling to engage with cognitive thought.

"That's odd," was all he could manage. "Deucedly odd."

"My thoughts exactly," said Jodah. "Mairsil is a powerful mage, right?"

"Right," said Shannan.

"And very busy, as well," continued Jodah.

"Busy to boot," said Shannan.

"So why is he talking to me?" said Jodah.

"Maybe he sees something in you he likes," said Shannan. "Maybe something about his own youth."

"Maybe," said Jodah, biting his lower lip. "Which is why I wanted to turn to a font of knowledge. That would be you."

"Me," said Shannan, letting the words sink in. "No. Can't help you. Sorry." The drunk artificer tried to rise from his chair, and this time Jodah did not stop him.

"Fine. I'll go ask someone else. Like Barl. Maybe *he* can tell me why Mairsil wants to talk to me."

That halted Shannan in mid-rise. Slowly, like a pierced balloon, he sat back down.

"Talking to Barl is like talking to the High Mukketty hisself. Bad idea." He paused for a moment, gathering either his courage, his wits, or both. Finally, he said, "Okay, but you didn't hear this from me."

"I didn't hear it from you," said Jodah.

"I mean, its an open secret," said Shannan. "Everyone knows, but nobody says anything."

"Open secret," repeated Jodah.

Shannan held up his now-empty glass. Jodah refilled it. Shannan leaned close, and Jodah almost leaned away from the cloud of alcohol the artificer exuded. Almost.

"Mairsil is also called the Pretender," said Shannan, in a low, confidential voice that could not be heard more than twenty feet away. "I mean, behind his back."

Jodah shook his head and said, "A pretender?"

"Shh!" said Shannan, scanning up and down the hall for spies.

"You mean he isn't a mage?" said Jodah.

"Nonono!" said Shannan, "he's a pretender to the throne. He's not supposed to be leading the Conclave. He took over for the first leader, who was *his* teacher. He's an usurer."

"Usurper," corrected Jodah.

"That too," said Shannan. "His own teacher built this place. Wanted to make it a big haven for wizards. Brought in the first ones, the old guys. Then he turned his back on Mairsil, and—Whammo!" He made the chopping motion again.

"He killed him?" said Jodah. "His first master. Mairsil

killed him and took over?"

Shannan shrugged his shoulders. "Dunno. Some think he killed him. Some think the teacher got away. Some think he turned him into one of the Fallen."

"Fallen?" said Jodah.

Shannan looked at Jodah hard. "I never told you how I ended up here?"

Jodah had been wondering that himself but just nodded.

"Heard about the place and bribed a ship captain to take me here," said Shannan. "They don't recruit here, since Mairsil took over. You have to get here on your own power to prove you're worthy in the first place." Shannan shook his head. "Anyway, my challenge was to fight one of the Fallen. You know what they are?"

Jodah shook his head.

"When a mage holds too much mana for too long he gets burned, right?" said Shannan, not waiting for Jodah to respond. "You burn out too much, you hold too much mana for too long for too many times, you become the Fallen. Nasty thing. Wild and untamed. No eyes, just burning little bits of mana. They still know their spells, but have no control. Move like weasels, real fast. Fight like wolves." Shannan shook himself.

Jodah tried to imagine Shannan defeating such a creature, and found it impossible. "How did you beat it?" he finally asked.

Shannan brightened. "I had built a crossbow that fired four broad-headed bolts at once. I hit him from ten yards away."

Jodah nodded. "That would do it."

"Had to reload. Twice." said Shannan, draining the last of his drink. He held out his glass, but the bottle was empty now. Jodah showed it to him, and he just sighed deeply.

"So you think this has something to do with the Fallen?" said Jodah. "That the first mage became one by holding too much mana too long? Or that Mairsil turned him into one?"

"I don't think nothing," said Shannan. "I know that everybody walks on eggshells around the Lord High Mukketty because they're afraid that he'll do to *them* what he did to their *first* leader." He sighed. "And I think they're afraid of Barl because he's the only one who the Lord High Mukketty talks to."

"Except the Lord High Mage was talking to me today," said Jodah in a low voice.

"Uh-huh," said Shannan, hoisting himself to his feet, "so if I were you, I'd be real careful what I say to him. About yourself, and especially about me. Or else . . ." He made the chopping motion a third time.

"Whammo," said Jodah, softly.

* * * * *

There was no sign of Shannan at breakfast the next day, which was small surprise to Jodah. The large apprentice had managed to weave his way down the hall under his own power at the close of their discussion, but Jodah was fairly sure that Shannan would end up sleeping on some hallway couch.

As it was, breakfast was a quiet affair, and for the first time Jodah realized that he knew very few people here. Most he knew by face, but only a handful had he had more than a few words with, and never about magic itself. Moreover, he rarely heard people discussing magic, either at breakfast, or dinner, or in the halls.

Maybe that's what Mairsil was looking for, thought Jodah, someone to talk to about magic. Maybe everyone else is just too respectful and downright scared, so he picked on a new arrival.

Maybe. It still didn't sit right.

The library was a relief, and Jodah was pleased for once to get back to his work. His tasks, as the Lord High Mage had called them. Nedda nodded at him primly as he came past her desk, and he started to think that things would return to normal after yesterday's oddity.

He looked out the window, briefly, and saw that the clouds were heavy and gray, like inverted puffball mushrooms in the sky. It would likely rain again by midday.

Jodah opened his drawer and pulled out the scarab, quill, ink, and parchment from within. He also pulled out the folder containing the manuscript to date, and the tome unfinished from the previous day. Suddenly the prospect of reading through the various descriptions of how pikemen maneuvered into a square on sloping terrain did not seem as promising as it had the morning before.

As he prepared himself, another mage came from around the stacks. He had apparently been in there already, and he was one whom Jodah did not recognize. This mage had a high forehead and was wearing wide-lensed spectacles over his eyes. He turned briefly toward Jodah, and the lenses made him look like a surprised frog.

The new mage looked at the shelves and shook his head, then walked over to the semi-organized pile of books. He lingered over Jodah's stack of finished tomes.

"Those have been recorded," said Jodah helpfully. "The second pile is for ones I don't understand. The rest we haven't gotten to yet."

The mage looked up at Jodah with an icy glare and what might have been a sneer. Jodah took the hint and set up the scarab to record.

The wizard selected a book from the top of the unread pile. It was a huge volume, bound in leather, with a circular disk of azure mica mounted on the cover. Its pages were expensively gilt, and a red velvet bookmark hung from the bottom along the spine, looking like a flopping tongue.

The mage sat down at a nearby table, and Jodah began reading aloud about the growth of hereditary knighthood in the southern cities. That was when the new arrival began screaming.

At first Jodah did not understand what was happening. The mage sat down at the table, opened the book, and started to read. Now he was screaming and holding onto the book with one hand, waving it back and forth.

No, he wasn't holding onto the book. The book was holding onto him. It had somehow grown teeth along the covers and had a firm hold on the mage's wrist. The bespectacled wizard was now waving his arm frenetically, but the book would not relax its grip. If anything, it was trying to bite farther up the wizard's arm, using its bookmark-tongue to drag itself forward.

Jodah was stunned for a moment but only for a moment. He leaped up and ran to the mage, who was now performing a one-man dance in the center of the library, his hand trapped in the book, blood spattering on the tiles around them. Jodah tried to grab the mage and wrestle him to the ground, to pry the book from him. He was rewarded by the mage slamming Jodah with the book itself, the spine catching him in the cheek.

Jodah dropped to one knee and cursed himself. He was trying a physical solution to a magical problem again.

Now he took a deep breath, effortless calling up the memories of his home. Then, as he had on the floor of the challenge arena, he unleashed a small, negating package of white mana.

The book stiffened, then dropped off the mage's hand. Its teeth had vanished, its tonguelike bookmark just a bookmark again. The mage was still screaming, and he dropped to his knees, freed of his attacker. Nedda was there with some leaves pulled from one of her plants and a handful of berries. She shoved the berries past the mage's lips and made him swallow, and that seemed to calm him down a bit. Then she wrapped the leaves around the streaming wounds. The leaves glowed with a greenish aura and stanched the flow of blood.

Others arrived, servants and a healer who took the mage out. He left the library under his own power, cursing in some language Jodah did not understand. Nedda handed the offending volume over to another servant, with instructions to put it in a secure place until it was investigated.

She turned to Jodah. "Did you cut the mana from it?" she asked.

Jodah shook his head and wiped sweat from his brow.

"I removed the mana entirely. It didn't seem like something we wanted to see come back."

Nedda looked at him for a moment, then nodded. She told the servant that the book should be locked up but did not need to be guarded. Then she told the other torqued servants to grab mops and clean up the floor.

Jodah looked down at himself. His shirt was spattered with the mage's blood. Nedda looked at him and told him to take the rest of the day off.

Jodah nodded, then looked over at the pile of the unread books. "You think there are more like that?"

Nedda shrugged. "Possibly. Sometimes books are just brought in and dumped here. No telling where it came from."

Later Jodah thought about the comment. They were trying to record all the information in the books but did not know or care where they came from. Of course, they had an expendable junior mage do the recording, just in case there was something wrong with the book.

That was one way it could have happened, but Jodah could not be certain that the book with the blue mica oval on the cover had been there the day before. It had been on the top and would have been the next book he would have reached for.

Had someone been in the library overnight and left the book there for him to find? Or, worse yet, did Nedda, or the Lord High Mage himself put the book there? That would explain Mairsil's sudden odd appearance? But why? As a test? Or a punishment? Or a warning?

Jodah took the rest of the day off, but his thoughts were jumbled and confused.

* * * * *

Shannan was late to dinner, and upon seeing Jodah, the sloppy artificer flew into a rage.

"You rat!" he said, "you got me drunk last night!"

"You got yourself drunk," said Jodah. "I merely held the bottle."

"Don't get cute with me, young pup," snapped the overweight man. "You're to blame for this." He waved a bandaged hand in Jodah's face.

Jodah took a step back. "What happened?" he managed.

"An *accident*," hissed Shannan. "I cracked another cog today because I was up all night, because you kept giving me rum through a funnel. Next thing I know, one of the saws is accidentally running and—Whammo!"

Jodah winced at the image, but Shannan continued. "Of course, we have enough magical healers to reattach a few fingers, but still, I'm out of work for the next four weeks! Four weeks as the damned muscles retrain! They've got me gardening as therapy. Gardening! For four weeks! That's only one step above being given a torque and made a servant! And it's all your fault!"

"More than you know," said Jodah, and he quickly explained his own adventure of the day.

Shannan took a deep breath and looked more serious than Jodah ever remembered the Happy Juggernaut ever appearing before.

"Two accidents on the same day. The fates are trying to tell us something."

"The fates," said Jodah, "or someone else."

"Was there anyone else in the hall last night?" said Shannan.

"Not that I saw," said Jodah.

"Meaning that it could have been anyone," concluded the wounded apprentice. "Curse me for trusting you!"

"It could have been an accident," said Jodah hollowly.

Shannan made a rude noise and said, "I'll be sure to remember that when a tree falls on me out in the garden. In the meantime, let's try something different. I don't know you. You don't know me. And we both watch our own backs, Okay?"

Jodah frowned, but nodded.

"Speaking of our own backs, watch yours right now," muttered Shannan.

Jodah turned slightly and saw that Chief Artificer Barl was bearing down on their position.

"Friend Jodah. Friend Shannan. Your hand is better, Friend Shannan?"

"Much better, Friend Barl, much better indeed. I apologize for my clumsiness." Shannan gave a smile that was a bit too broad, as if he had a secret delight in losing fingers.

"You'll be more careful next time," said Barl smoothly.

"Much more careful," said Shannan with a pronounced bow. "Now, if you'll excuse me . . ." He left the apology unfinished and slid over to the other side of the room.

Barl turned to Jodah. "Friend Jodah," he began.

Jodah took a deep breath and said, "I must apologize, Friend Barl."

"Apologize?"

"Friend . . . Shannan was telling me about his accident, and I feel responsible. I fear I was with him yesterday evening and let him drink too much. That might account for his clumsiness this morning." Jodah finished his apology with a shrug.

Barl looked at Jodah as if Shannan's clumsiness, or his drinking, or his health for that matter, were the furthest things from his mind.

"Think nothing of it," he said. "We are all responsible for our own actions, regardless of who is in the area at the time. I came to you on a different matter."

Jodah waited patiently. All he could think of was Shannan chopping his bandaged hand through the air, and saying, *"Whammo!"*

"The Lord High Mage would like to see you in his study following the meal," said Barl. "If you do not have other plans."

* * * * *

Needless to say, Jodah did not touch dinner. Across the horseshoe, Shannan dug into his meal, though Jodah noted that he stopped at only three glasses of wine. Barl vanished immediately after giving Jodah the message, and with neither Barl nor Mairsil present, the proceedings quickly degenerated to several risqué illusions and creative things done with the mashed potatoes.

After a reasonable interval, Jodah rose. leaving his meal untouched, and made his way up to the Lord High Mage's office. Barl was waiting, and, touching a small golden rune set into a black door, escorted him into Mairsil's study.

"Friend Jodah," said Mairsil, smiling and rising from his desk, "I heard of the excitement in the library yesterday. I trust you are well."

"Well enough, Friend Mairsil," said Jodah, much less sure of himself.

"Good. I suppose there's a lesson there. Even in our secure home, there is danger in magic," said the Lord High Mage, and, having addressed the subject, discarded it. "I suppose you are wondering why I've asked for you."

"I am curious," replied Jodah, speaking as sparingly as possible.

Mairsil sat on the corner of his desk.

"You have a mage in your family tree. You mentioned it to Barl your first day here."

Jodah nodded. "Jarsyl," he said.

"Jarsyl," said Mairsil, and his eyes lit up as if he had just remembered the name himself. "What do you know of him?"

Jodah shrugged as politely as he could. "I am afraid I don't know much. Most of what I know was from my grandmother, who was but a child when he disappeared. She said he was a powerful magician and could work great spells, and that he was responsible for many of the early improvements on the manor, but I am afraid that is all that has lasted from then to now."

Mairsil templed his fingers in front of him. "He was a mighty mage," he said, "but you don't know anything he's done?"

Jodah blushed slightly. "Such has been our family history. He engaged in a number of studies and kept a tower at the corner of the family lands."

"And that tower?" said Mairsil.

"Long since gone," said Jodah. "I played among the few remaining stones when I was a child."

"Hmmmm." said Mairsil thoughtfully, "and Jarsyl's library? His notes? His writings?"

"He had an apprentice, my grandmother said," replied Jodah. "When he disappeared, there was no one else interested in his studies, and the apprentice took most of his work."

"Took it where?" asked the Lord High Mage.

Jodah shrugged, and added, "There were some books, but they were lost over the years—given to other mages. Once an agent of the Church of Tal came to the manor, before I was born. Apparently there was a great concern that the inquisitor would find something about Jarsyl and his work, but in truth he arrived, searched the place that had been Jarsyl's tower, and then left without saying a word."

Mairsil nodded and said, "You said your twice-great grandfather disappeared. He ran off?"

"I don't know . . ." Jodah paused, wracking his brain for the stories his grandmother, by then an old and bent woman, had told by the fireplace when he was a child. "He didn't die, and he wasn't fighting another mage, or the church, or anything. He was involved with some type of research and went off in pursuit of something to help him. Some far-off land, my grandmother said, but I always thought that was something that she added, since no one knew what happened to him."

"I see," said Mairsil, reaching beside him to touch a thin volume, bound in black leather, that was sitting on his desk. With a single finger he pushed the book in front of Jodah. "I want to find out," he said. "I want to find out what happened to him. And what he was working on. And I want you to help me."

Mairsil tapped the cover of the book with a long, tapered finger.

"After I read about your ancestor in your interview, I started digging through my texts and through the texts of other friend-mages in the Conclave. I went looking for your great-great-grandfather." He tapped the book again. "And I found him."

He tapped the black cover again. "Friend Jodah, this is the diary of Jarsyl the Mage, your ancestor, who discovered the Dark Lands of Phyrexia after the Brothers' War," said Mairsil, clearly pleased with himself. "With his help, and with yours, I intend to discover that land again."

14 ☾

The Gate to Phyrexia

Jarsyl has always been a transitional figure in most of the respected histories—born too late for the Brothers' War, born much to early for the most interesting parts of the Dark. Yet he has been a key piece of the puzzle. What is known by modern man about the legendary dread lands of Phyrexia, comes from Jarsyl's personal notes, and though there are those who dismiss his legend as a folktale or moral fable, there are those who continue to seek out his truths and attempt to find Phyrexia for themselves. When they do not return, everyone assumes that they have finally found it.

—Arkol, Argivian scholar

The journal was the original, not a transcription or a later reprinting. Jarsyl placed his hand on the weathered cover. The black leather was cracked in places but still unpeeled and whole. The thin tome's corners were shod in gold, and, touching it, Jodah could feel something. Perhaps it was just the ghost of long-cast magic, or perhaps it was a spiritual connection between his ancestor and himself. He could almost feel Jarsyl reaching out to him through time.

Jodah held his breath when he first opened its cover and turned its thin pages. He was afraid, from its age and import, that the volume might fall into dust at the first touch. The book's pages were made of vellum, pounded and worked so thin as to become translucent, and the rich, multicolored inks had faded with the passage of time.

He had handled older books than this in the library, and ones in worse shape, too, but this one held great power, not only because Mairsil had entrusted it to him personally but more because of who supposedly wrote it.

"Take it with you," the Lord High Mage said. "I want your opinions on the text."

Over the next ten days Jodah poured over the volume. He transcribed everything he could read in the text and then held each page in front of the light to see if there were any pen scratchings that had lost their ink. There were many. There were also various notes in the margin, some no more than scribbles. Jodah had to determine if they were written by the same writer but could only guess as to when the marginalia had been written.

The journal was crammed with information—very little of it useful from a magical approach. It was written at the manor—of that much Jodah was certain. The text was an odd mix of magical theory and local gossip, of daily affairs and deep thought. A note of the purchase of several geese was right next to a long column of numbers, their purpose unknown. A drawing of weights and balances, of the placement of mirrors and lenses, was interrupted by a remembrance of Jarsyl's visit to his own grandmother's funeral pyre. There was a detailed proof, with no preamble, that continued for a page and a half and finished with the conclusion, "Of course it works!" written in a florid hand, but there was no indication of what it was he was trying to prove in the first place.

There was nothing about colors and barely anything about the power of the land itself. Jarsyl assumed much, Jodah realized, about how magic really worked. Perhaps he was following the artificers of the era, trying to define magic in terms of physical mechanics and not as it seemed to function in reality. The journal would not say either way.

Mairsil asked for daily reports. At first Jodah was nervous, unsure he could add anything that was not already obvious to the Lord High Mage. He made mention of what was written of Jarsyl's grandmother, who originally founded the family line in Giva, but that was lacking. Even Jarsyl referred to her only as Gran-mama, without clue as to her identity. She had been powerful once and might have been nobility from another nation that had fallen in the Brothers' War—an exile spending her life in a place that was not her home.

Jodah's first draft of his initial report was flowery and fawning. Jodah read it, realized that Shannan or Lucan could have written it, and ripped it up. The report that Mairsil received had something of what life was like in Giva, both from Jodah's own memory and the stories of his grandmother. The Lord High Mage sent a brief note back encouraging Jodah to continue working in that line.

Jodah pressed on. He started pulling books from the library and asking Nedda about how life was when she was young. The old woman indicated frostily that she was not *that* old but did direct Jodah to some texts that were written over a century ago. Jodah discovered that there was much on rulers and battles and little on daily life and private matters. Still, he pieced together enough by the second day to know the size of the beast referred to when Jarsyl spoke of a crosspiece the size of an ox yoke. Jodah knew which species his ancestor would have used to plow the fields—the larger, hardier breed that had long since gone feral in the mountains and now had longer hair, as opposed to its timid cousin, which had become weaker and more in bred with the passing centuries. From that he could calculate what the distance Jarsyl mentioned truly was.

By the fifth day, Jodah began to understand Jarsyl's basic concepts. There were worlds beyond this one, he was saying. Imagine the world as a house without doors. If you were within such a house, you would never be able to discover what was "outside." Indeed, the "outside" might be filled with water, or poisons, or fierce creatures. Let's say that you could make a door and discover that there was a house next door to yours, as big as yours, with other people living there.

That was what Jarsyl had done. He had found a way to open a door to another place—not another part of the same house but another house entirely. That house was called Phyrexia.

Jodah sent a quick message to the Lord High Mage and went to bed. When he awoke later in the day there was an enthusiastic response and the question: How do you open that door?

Jodah took to eating in his room or the library. He saw little of Shannan, but that was apparently to both their satisfaction. Jodah would prowl the library for various references and then look for references mentioned by those references. If he could not find them, Jodah would send a short note to the Lord High Mage, and the books would appear, as if by magic itself.

Jodah became more sure of himself as well. His reports to Mairsil were less tentative and more direct, and the responses were in turn encouraging while not effusive. Slowly he stopped thinking of the Lord High Mage as the most powerful spellcaster in the Conclave, first among equals. Indeed, comparing Mairsil's behavior to most of the rest of the Conclave, he was the one adult among children, the only individual who seemed to think beyond practical jokes and gossip and dinner.

When his brain was filled beyond capacity, Jodah would walk the parapets and walls of the Citadel. During the day he would study the mountains themselves, in those periods when the clouds lifted and allowed a brief view of their majesty, marching row after row southward. In the evenings, the battlements were lit by magical flame that spewed from the stonework itself, the fires that Jodah had seen upon his arrival.

Jodah watched the lights and by the eighth day found he could summon the fire in the way Voska had. He understood why the battlement flames functioned and could now duplicate it. He placed that spell among the others, among the light spells and healing spells and power-removing spells he had put in his mind's manor.

On the ninth day he unlocked the greater secret of what his ancestor was talking around, the greater spell that let him into this other universe, this other house. It was in many ways worse than Voska's definition of describing a dance. Jodah felt as if he was studying the reactions of the audience and from that trying to deduce the movements of the dance.

Now at last, Jodah though he knew the dance. On the tenth day he send a brief message to the Lord High Mage saying he wished to try Jarsyl's spell. An immediate reply, carried by Barl himself, scheduled the attempt for after the dinner hour.

Jodah missed dinner that evening in his preparations and arrived at the door to Mairsil's private study. Barl was not present this time, and the door was locked. Jodah tentatively touched the gold rune in the black door, and the bolt shot open. The heavy door swung open a crack from its own weight.

"Come in," came the fluid voice from within. "I've set the wards to admit you."

Jodah pushed the door the rest of the way back, and Mairsil was seated on a low footstool, hovering over a collection of wheels and gears made of metal and stone. When he had been in the room the first time Jodah had not inspected it, being at first too intimidated by Mairsil and then too surprised by Jarsyl's tome. Now he realized that this must be the "mystery project" that Barl was having his artificers create. He thought of Shannan, laboring in the gardens, and hoped the unkempt artificer avoided any other accidents while recovering.

Mairsil looked up at the younger mage's arrival. The magical light from his desk lamps reflected off the shining, glowing bits of his calendar of stone and metal, illuminating his face from beneath and giving him a weird, unearthly appearance, like some goblin creature stretched into a human form.

Mairsil smiled, and in the unnatural reflection of the machine's light the smile looked more like a snarl. "Are you ready to try?"

Jodah nodded.

Mairsil said, "Are you sure that this opens into the other world?"

Jodah nodded again, and added, "What little he

describes seems to be like no place on this world—rains of acid, rich jungles made of metal leaves, and machine-creatures more complex than any of Urza's or Mishra's legendary clockworks. He calls it Phyrexia, though that word is not found in any other reference volume and may itself be the name provided by natives he encountered there."

"But he does not mention any natives," said Mairsil, "other than the machines."

"No," said Jodah, "though I found similarities between the great beasts he found there and the *mak fawa* of Fallaji legend, but the connection may be coincidental. No mention of natives, but if there were no natives . . ." His voice trailed off.

"Then where did the name come from?" Mairsil finished the thought.

Jodah started at the words, then nodded. Of course Mairsil had read the book. Of course he had seen the few, faint references to Phyrexia, this supposed world next door. But, wondered Jodah, did Mairsil's conclusions match his own?

Jodah suddenly felt like a small child at the family religious ritual. Everyone else had seen and heard the ritual a hundred times. Only Jodah, the child, was new to it, and nervous.

He looked at Mairsil, and the High Lord Mage was smiling, but Jodah could not figure out the reason why.

"Are you ready to start, Friend Jodah?" the taller mage said.

Jodah set out the various components he knew he needed, from the descriptions given in Jarsyl's tome. Some were scientific in nature, such as a set of five crystals set in a precise, evenly spaced pattern, or a glyph of a particular shape carved in a dark metal. Some of the components were mystical in nature, such as a goblin-skin bag of powdered bone, or the runes marked on the slate floor in chalk. Some Jodah did not know what purpose they served, save that they were mentioned and might be important.

On the sideboard he set out his recording scarab and three sheets of parchment, each overlapping the other at the bottom. He had discovered in the library that this way he did not have to change sheets as often, and he did not want to miss anything that was said during the casting.

Mairsil had by this time retreated to his stone calendar and lingered over it a long while as Jodah prepared. At last the Lord High Mage asked, "Are you ready?"

Jodah bit his lip and nodded.

"Then begin," said Mairsil, his hand snaking out and inverting a small hourglass.

Jodah closed his eyes, opened his mind, and imagined farmland, the area around Jarsyl's ruined tower. It had been abandoned after the wizard's disappearance and emptied of its contents by his apprentice and servants. That had to have been when the book Mairsil had given to Jodah was taken. The tower itself was used as a quarters for workers picking cranberries, then just for storage of farm implements. Then, about a century ago, a savage windstorm caved in the sides, and all but the great foundation stones were used to build walls between the fields.

Jodah had climbed over the great foundation stones as a boy. They were wide and flat and inscribed with rain-carved runnels that he always thought of as forgotten runes. Jodah stood on those stones and imagined himself the hero that repelled all attackers and broke all sieges.

He thought he felt the power within that land even then. The air felt somehow thicker there than elsewhere on the manor, and now the mana he pulled from it seemed heavier and more viscous than the energy from other memories. He wondered, briefly, if it was the result of his own youthful attachment to the place.

He pulled that mana and slowly began to work the spell. It was a rough spell, worked completely from the hints within his ancestor's journal. First one crystal made a high-pitched, whining sound, then a second, a half-tone off, then a third, and then the final two, all vibrating to their natural frequencies. Jodah touched the glyph-covered plate, and it already felt warm.

Jodah cast a healthy sprinkling of the bone out in the air and the crystals changed their pitch. Jodah smiled and cast another sprinkling. Again the crystals changed their pitch, vibrating at a still higher frequency. The glyph-plate now glowed of its own heat. The mana in Jodah's mind was an intense, white ball now, and he opened that part of his brain to the spell, letting the radiance flow into the framework of the spell he had created.

And nothing happened.

The whiteness at the base of Jodah's brain refused to move, refused to pass through the mental conduit into the predetermined part of the ritual. At first Jodah thought that he had not pulled sufficient mana from the land, and in a panic-stricken moment he brought forth more memories—of the gardens and wheat fields, and the ball in the base of his brain grew hotter still as it accreted the mana.

And the whiteness did not move from his mind.

Jodah could feel the sweat running down his temples now. He opened his eyes, but his vision was blurry and the room indistinct. He could hear Mairsil say something, but the part of his brain that listened would not or could not decipher the words.

The hot white ball at the base of his brain began to burn, scorching its way through his flesh. Jodah tried to force the mana into the framework of the spell, but it would not go.

Jodah felt the hairs in his nostrils begin to catch fire, and they smelled of ammonia.

He thought of Shannan's story of the Fallen.

With a cry, Jodah reached upward and cast loose the mana. He quickly pulled another spell from his memory and threw the burning ball of memories into that. Hot, white fireworks shot from each of the young man's outstretched hands, and Jodah thought he screamed.

Then he blacked out from the pain.

He awoke to Mairsil's calm, dispassionate face, framed by stars. No, not entirely dispassionate, but rather curious, as if Jodah was a frog laid out for dissection. What he had thought were the stars were instead glowing white embers that were now embedded in the ceiling of Mairsil's private study.

"What happened, Jodah?" said Mairsil. There was no "Friend" here, but rather the terse demanding tone of a disappointed patron.

"I don't know." said Jodah. "I summoned the mana successfully, but I failed to move it into the framework of the spell."

Mairsil's brows deeply furrowed as Jodah spoke.

"The physical matrix refused the mystic force." He rose and walked around the desk, each step getting tenser and angrier. "We had the matrix, but the force *refused* it!"

"Damn it to the Hells!" shouted Mairsil suddenly, and with one sweep cleared the desks of books. Heavy volumes, scrolls, and the journal itself cascaded to the floor with a thundering smash. Mairsil did not wait for the volumes to hit but slammed the desktop with a fist. Jodah was surprised the Lord High Mage did not break either the desk or his hand.

"We were so damned close!" He looked up at Jodah, and there was fire in his eyes. He started to snarl, "You must have . . ." then he stopped and took a deep breath. Then a second, letting it out like a low whistle. Then he said, in a calm, measured voice, "Are you all right, Friend Jodah?"

Jodah said he was, and added, "I'm sorry about your ceiling."

"Ceil . . ." Mairsil looked up at the thousands of small pinpricks of light now driven into the ceiling above him. The Lord High Mage gave a tired chuckle. "Think nothing of it," he said, and with a wave of his hand, each and every one of the lights went out.

"What . . ." Jodah took a deep breath, then started again, "Friend Mairsil, what do we do now?"

"*Do?*" said Mairsil, and for a moment it looked as if he would lose his temper again. Instead, he just shook his head wearily. "We do what every educated and proper mage would do. We review the facts and look for where we went wrong. Are you sure everything else was correct?"

Jodah looked at the remains of the spell materials in the room, and nodded. "I think so," he said.

"But are you *sure?*" pressed Mairsil.

"It felt right," said Jodah, which was not the question Mairsil asked.

Mairsil nodded and tugged at the corners of his mustache. "Then that's good enough." He snagged Jarsyl's journal, which had sprawled, pages open, on the floor, and closed it thoughtfully, then handed the book to Jodah. "Here. Review it again. Surely there must be something you . . . something both of us . . . missed. No, no, don't worry about the equipment—I'll get a servant to take care of it. You've been very effective, Jodah. When you have something send me a message."

With that Mairsil ushered Jodah out of his study. The younger magician paused only briefly at the door, but the Lord High Mage was already making a beeline for his stonework creation in the corner of the room. Mairsil stood in front of the calendar and tugged at the ruby in his ring.

Jodah crept out of the room like a beaten dog. Mairsil had been horribly disappointed, and he hid it badly. Jodah was disappointed as well but for different reasons. The past few days had been everything he had hoped being a true mage would entail, and it led up to this one moment.

He had failed. Failed utterly and spectacularly, and now Mairsil probably did not trust him any more.

Jodah sighed, closed the black door behind him and padded down the hallway to the small wooden door that led to his own quarters.

15 ☾

A Dance of Many
(Part II)

Were there moments, during the time of the Dark, when the course of events could have been reversed? Moments where one individual, saying "I will" or "I will not" could have altered the slow, inevitable slide into ignorance, cold, and oblivion? I like to think not, but maybe I am being charitable to those trapped within that time. The choices that the men and woman of that age made, like those of today, were based upon their own survival and their own well-being. Each had to account for their actions to their superiors and to themselves. Each had to choose the best course for themselves and those they valued. But whatever their choices were, the ice was waiting.

—Arkol, Argivian scholar

Before Sima, in the gathering dusk, the Citadel rose along the shoulder of the mountain. Those mountains, and the extensive swamps at their base, had forced a wide detour to the west, and she at last had to approach along the seacoast itself.

The Citadel of the Conclave looked like a city from this angle, a city turned on its side and stacked vertically, Buildings, actually wings of the same great castle, were stacked one atop the other and ringed with wide parapets that served as roadways threading through the mass of stone and mortar. The battlements were limned by a red-dish glow from innumerable torches, or, given the nature of the place, bits of red mana.

To Sima it was the Dark Castle, the most dangerous place on this world. Here was where the wild mages made their lair, the ones too dangerous, too arrogant, and too chaotic to ever be a part of the City of Shadows. Their power was great, great enough that the other members of the Shadow Council would not allow members to visit, much less communicate. It was a tainted place and known as such from the earliest surviving records. Drafna himself wrote of this place when it was Monastery of Gix, and he told of the treachery that broke the original Council of the Ivory Towers.

Sima suppressed a shudder. Jodah was somewhere inside there.

If he was still alive. She had heard of their barbarities, of their challenges and their violent ways. They were not scholars but violent children, who thought of themselves as the true rulers of magical power and so ignored the rest of the world. They were magic run wild, a violation of the calm, reasoned research of the Shadow Council.

She fished out the mirror from within the folds of her blouse. In the growing shadows of the darkening beach it glowed with a bluish tint all it its own. She turned it slowly, toward the great walled citadel. The bluish glow grew stronger.

He was still alive, and she would go rescue him.

She tucked the mirror securely in her shirt, hefted her walking stick and pack, and began the long trudge up the side of the mountain to the main gate. It would be nearly dawn before she arrived.

* * * * *

As she walked, four figures watched Sima from the swamp—tracker, preacher, miracle worker, and the primata.

"She is here," said Primata Delphine.

"As I foretold," said Betje, the miracle worker, gazing through sightless eyes.

"Let us take her now," said the preacher, a lean, narrow-jawed man with wavy brown hair. "Let us purge her soul before she joins with the others of her foul fellowship. 'Suffer not the Magician to live' says the Book of Tal."

The tracker, a dirty, mud-stained man, said nothing.

"No," said the primata, "let her be unaware until we drop the hammer of Tal upon her." To the mud-stained man she said, "You say this is a castle of wizards?"

The tracker nodded. For the past few weeks he had followed Sima and brought the other three here by secret ways, though with every mile he grew quieter and more circumspect. The blind woman who did not miss a step troubled him, and the brown-haired man who preached the Book of Tal at every chance, troubled him even more. The large woman did not merely trouble him, she frightened him to the core of his being, and so he merely nodded.

The primata loomed over him, and the tracker felt he needed to add a bit more to his report. "A bad place, they say. Filled with sorcerers and wizards. Best to stay clear, if you ask me."

"We should take the place ourselves," said the preacher.

"The four of us?" said the primata, sarcasm dripping in her voice. "Shall we storm the battlements, or merely pull the castle apart with our teeth?"

"The Book of Tal says, 'The righteous shall have the strength of seven,'" said the preacher.

"Then we will be outnumbered only ten to one," said the primata. To the tracker she said, "Is there a village nearby?"

The tracker nodded and said, "Up the coast, a couple of good sized towns."

"How do they feel about sorcerers?" asked the primata.

"Can't stand 'em," said the tracker, choosing his words carefully, "but they respect them. Every now and then one gets loose and carves through the area with his magic. They're afraid of 'em, 'cause they can't stand up to them."

"The power of Tal is greater than any magic," said the preacher.

"Indeed," said the primata. "Is there a Church of Tal, there?"

The tracker nodded, and added, "Small one, but influential. Tends to keep its nose clean around the wizards."

"We will see about that," said the primata. "Come, now, we shall go to this town for aid."

The three started northward, but the mud-spattered man held back. The primata looked at the tracker.

The tracker, for his part, bowed low and said, "No offense, ma'am, but you hired me to bring you here, which I've done. I have no truck with wizards, and if it's all the same to you, I'll be heading home." He paused, and added, "After I get my payment, of course."

"Of course," said the Primata Delphine. She walked up to the tracker. She towered over the smaller man, and he almost backed away from her presence. Gently she raised her hands and touched the man's temples. "Let me bless you, first, my child, before you receive your payment. Let us now hear the words of the Book of Tal."

The miracle worker did not move, but the preacher gave a wolfish grin and said, "Tal knows all."

"Tal knows all," said the primata.

"All that is known is known through Tal," said the preacher.

"Tal knows all," said the primata, joined by Sister Betje.

"All not known to Tal is not worth knowing," intoned the preacher.

"Tal knows all," said the primata, joined by Sister Betje.

"That which is not known to Tal should be cleansed," said the preacher, his voice rising.

"Tal knows all," said the primata, joined by Sister Betje.

"Let the cleansing begin," said the preacher.

"Let the cleansing begin," said the primata.

The tracker screamed. It was a short, painful scream that bubbled as it rose from his lungs. He tried to struggle, to break away, but the primata held him in place with her fingertips pressed against his temples, as if he were made of iron and held in place with magnets. He twitched, and smoke began to curl from his temples, then from his ears.

The tracker gave one last rasping gasp and perished. The primata removed her fingers, and the corpse collapsed in the soft, marshy ground.

"The sinner is cleansed," said the primata.

"Amen," said the preacher.

"Amen," said the miracle worker.

"You have been paid in full," said the primata to the corpse. To the others she said, "Come, now, we should test the fear of these townsfolk as well as their faith." She touched the holy writ inside her robes, and she smiled.

Even the blind miracle worker turned away from that horrible smile.

* * * * *

Jodah crept into his bed, but sleep would not come for him. Instead it hovered on the borders, taunting him with his failure. Something had gone wrong, but he did not know what.

He closed his eyes and willed himself to go to sleep. The uncastable spell had drained him, and the back of his neck felt hot, almost sunburned. He had held the mana too long, and it had taken its toll.

He opened his eyes and stared at the ceiling. Mairsil was obviously angry. Was it his fault, Jodah wondered. Had he been so sure that the spell would work that he had raised Mairsil's expectations? Had the Lord High Mage already gone down the same path with the same result? Was he hoping Jodah would find the way to make the spell work?

Jodah closed his eyes again and tried to breath deeply. Mairsil would calm down. He had failed only once. People apparently failed at the Conclave all the time. He thought of Shannan, cracking gears with alarming regularity.

But Shannan suffered an "accident" and was now pulling weeds in the garden in the afternoon and evenings. Jodah opened his eyes again and stared at the ceiling.

That was when Jodah realized that he was not alone. He sat up suddenly, and the ragged man was there. Jodah had not seen him come into his room, nor even felt the breeze of his entry, but now he was there, and Jodah knew he was there.

Jodah spoke a sharp syllable, stashed an offhanded bit of energy into it, and a lamp flickered to life. The ragged man was there, dressed in his tattered cloak, only his long bony fingers bare beneath the wrapping. There was something different, though it took a moment for Jodah to recognize it—the ragged man wore a sword on his belt. It was the same rune-covered blade that Barl had provided Jodah on his first day.

Was it there as a threat, wondered Jodah, or a warning? Or a message. The ragged man could go anywhere in the Citadel and take anything.

The ragged man beckoned, and Jodah rose from the bed, throwing on a shirt and pants almost as an afterthought. The tattered man-creature opened the door and glided almost effortless out to the hall, like a ghost. Jodah started to shout out that there might be others nearby, but by that time he was at the door.

There was no one in the hallway. Was the hour so late or was this some other power of the ragged man? Already the man in the tattered wrapping was moving down the hallway, away from the staircase. Jodah followed.

"What do you want this time?" hissed Jodah as he caught up to tall figure.

The ragged man turned to him and raised a finger to his shrouded lips. Jodah cursed softly and followed.

Jodah's guide took him to a dead-end passage, or what Jodah had thought to be a dead end. The passage ended in a huge alcove dominated by a great stained-glass window showing Mairsil heroically triumphing over a band of goblin raiders. To the best of Jodah's memory, he had never seen anyone in this alcove, despite benches set beneath the stained glass. The ragged man turned toward the wall on the left-hand side of the alcove and touched a stone. The stone was a part of the wall and should not have moved, but it did move, and the wall swung inward at the ragged creature's touch.

The ragged man drew his weapon, and Jodah stepped back, his mind automatically going for the memories of the land, just in case. But the ragged creature held the sword before him, and the runes burst into crackling light. The sword glowed blue, and the ragged man plunged into darkness.

Jodah followed him into the dark. He summoned a small light of his own, a white sphere in his palm that cast sharp shadows on the surrounding walls.

They were at the top of a narrow staircase, barely wider than Jodah's shoulders, which plunged downward. The types of stone used in the walls, as well as the mortar and arrangement, changed as they moved downward. The passage would often level off, then change direction and descend again. Jodah saw no other doors or side passages, but once he caught the smell of salt spray, and another time he felt the floor vibrate from some distant engines. The passage spiraled down through the heart of the Citadel.

Jodah thought of Shannan's story about the white mage mappers, and its moral. Mairsil and Barl did not allow their domain to be mapped.

Jodah also remembered Shannan's tale of the Fallen, lurking in the depths beneath the Citadel. That did not make him feel any more comfortable.

The passage narrowed now, and the walls sweated. The air grew close and tight for a moment, then the ragged man reached a blank wall. He paused for a moment, then another door swung open, into a larger space. Air, laden with dust and ancient smells, wafted over Jodah. The ragged man stepped through into that larger space, and Jodah followed.

The space was akin to a tower, if one could think of a tower as being a tube running into the ground. The ceiling was lost in the darkness above them, and they were perched on the rim of a great pit. It was ten feet from the curving wall to the pit's edge, but it felt narrow, as if the abyss below was tugging at Jodah, trying to pull him in. A warm breeze of dusty air wafted up from the depths of that pit. To Jodah's right, counterclockwise from his secret opening, a set of stairs spiraled up into the darkness.

Before them a great cage had been suspended in the center of the room by silver chains. The cage itself was made of similar silver, almost translucent, so that it looked as if it was made of ice. Jodah thought of the torques around the servants' necks, and the tracery on the church's manacles. Within the cage was darkness.

The darkness shifted and moved, and dirty hands clasped the ornate bars of the cage. A face appeared from the shadows—weathered, thin, and sallow. It had a beard, but it was ragged and matted. The face had eyes, but they were wide, and mad.

The cage swayed as the prisoner within it shifted his position. Jodah again thought of the fallen and checked to see if the door was still open to the secret passage. It was.

A thin voice issued from the cage. "Tell me," it hissed, "which is better, madness or darkness?"

There was silence for a moment, then a thin voice cackled and spoke again, clearer this time. "Have you brought me something, my Rag Man?"

The voice was almost a whisper, but it rebounded from the walls around Jodah and pressed against his ears. The ragged man—the Rag Man, bowed slowly and sheathed his sword in his belt. The light went out.

Another silence, and this one was oppressive and brooding. Jodah looked at the figure in the cage.

"What," Jodah's throat was filled with dust, so he cleared it and started again, "What is this?"

"This?" said the figure. "This is Barl's cage. Yes, that's what it is."

"Barl is the artificer," said Jodah. "Who are you?"

"Not Barl," said the figure, and he started laughing. It was a horrible laugh, rising and falling in an erratic rhythm. It slowed, then raised up again, then slowed at last to a chuckle. "I want you to know I am still sane. Oh yes, madness has been my sanctuary from the dark, but I am still sane. But it is a near thing, indeed."

Jodah did not say what he was thinking but only nodded.

The dirty, unshaven face in the darkness tried to exude some type of nobility. It stuck its chin out and moved a dirty hand back through its fouled hair. "I am Ith," it said at last.

Another long silence.

Jodah at last ventured, "And who are you, Friend Ith?"

"*Friend?*" shouted the figure trapped in the cage, "*Friend?* I am no friend of the wizards here! I am Ith, the founder, the teacher, the lord! I am the master, and no *friend* of Ith has raised his hand against the Pretender!"

Jodah took a step backward, toward the door. The Rag Man did nothing to stop him.

The figure in the cage quieted now. "I'm sorry," he said, almost sobbing, "I don't get many visitors, these days."

I can see why, thought Jodah, but he said, "You founded the Conclave?"

"I trusted him," said Ith, his voice turning snakelike and venomous. "I trusted him and he betrayed me. He took my work, my castle, my followers. And none lifted a finger to stop him! *None!*"

"You are the Lord Hi . . ." Jodah stopped and started again, "You are Mairsil's teacher."

"Mairsil, the Usurper!" shouted Ith now, "the Pretender! He is like a leech on the body, a mosquito on the flesh. All that he has was taken from me!"

Jodah took another step away. "I see," he said.

"No, you don't!" said the trapped figure. "I meant what I said! All his power he drains from me, from this cage of watersilver made by his henchman. He pulls my power from me and uses it to keep the other mages in line! Either by bribes or by threats or by violence, he maintains his power! *He must be destroyed!*"

The voice was screaming now, and Jodah wondered if it would attract others. There was a pause, as Ith panted in his cage, struggling to take a breath, but there was no sounds of approaching footfalls.

Jodah thought of Mairsil thundering his fists against the table. Yes, the Lord High Mage had a temper, and everyone seemed to be afraid of him, but the prisoner's words were confused, a jumble, fueled by rage and madness. A rage that Ith now seemed desperate to control.

"I trusted him, of course. One always trusts one's pupil. Taught him what he needed to know, brought him here, founded the Conclave. I had heard of the City of Shadows, but they were too restrictive, too old-fashioned in their thinking."

Jodah said nothing, and the voice continued. "But he changed. Everything changes. Mountains sink into the sea and become islands. Plains become overgrown and transform into forests. Change is the secret, boy! Did you know that?"

Jodah started to say that he didn't, but Ith did not wait for him.

"Change is the source of the magic! Did you think it some type of mineral, like gold, that you could pull from the ground? Change is what makes the magic! Everything changes, and everything has magic within it! Dynamic systems!"

Ith was beginning to lose his temper again. "And I was a fool to think that we were invulnerable to change ourselves." There was a laugh, a wet, weeping laugh. "I trusted him, but the boy I trusted changed. He betrayed me and locked me here in the darkness, with the things in the pit! You, there!"

Jodah stiffened as he realized he was being addressed.

Ith snapped a command, "Toss a pebble into the pit!"

Jodah paused, then kneeled down and took up a loose stone. He carefully neared the edge of the pit.

"Toss it in," said Ith, "then listen!"

Jodah did as he was told. The pebble disappeared into the darkness. Jodah counted to five. To ten.

To twenty.

He gave up at thirty.

"When I came here, I tossed something into the pit," cackled Ith. "I still haven't heard it hit. And I. Have. Good. Ears." Again the laughter.

Then the laughter came up short, and Ith wheezed, "But there are things within the pit, you know. Yes, dark, comforting things that make all sorts of promises. I've been strong, but the Pretender leeches at my strength and I wonder . . ." he paused for a moment, then added in a quiet voice, "am I still mad? Are you truly there, boy? Or are you some trick of my mind, or a taunt of the Pretender?" His voice rose, and his hands and face began to glow with their own radiance. "Answer me!"

Jodah said, "I am Jodah, goodsir Ith." As an afterthought he added, "Do not be afraid."

"*Afraid!*" shrieked the caged figure. It was grasping the bars now and swinging back and forth. "The Pretender should fear. Yes! He should! You're going to free me, boy, and I will take my revenge." An emaciated arm snaked out from between the bars, clawing at the air. "Free me! Free me, and let me destroy him and his followers!"

Jodah took a step backward, then a second.

The face and hands were glowing reddish-blue, an unearthly shade, and Ith grasped the bars of his cage and shook them. They held without rattling, and the bars themselves began to glow white, pulling the energy from him. Ith screamed, and his hair seemed to stand on end.

"*Free me!*" he bellowed, his voice becoming an almost incoherent barking.

Jodah turned and ran, back for the door. The ragged man, (No, the Rag Man) did nothing to stop him, standing like a stone sentry to one side. The screaming haunted Jodah for the first hundred stairs. After a long while, it finally stopped.

* * * * *

Down in the pit, within the cage, Lord Ith sobbed and let go of the bars. His hands had been blistered and now felt like hot plates. He tried to remember why he had been screaming, as the darkness pulled at him from below.

Then he remembered, and a single tear rolled down his grimy face, finally disappearing in his beard.

"Well," he said to the darkness, "That didn't go as well as I had hoped, did it?"

The Rag Man said nothing in reply.

* * * * *

Barl rapped on the door, and it swung open. Mairsil sat in front of his clockwork calendar made of stone and metal, his hands together, fidgeting with his ruby ring, turning it around his finger. The deep scowl on his face told the story.

"Your experiment did not go well," said Barl. A statement, not a question.

The Lord High Mage let out a long, impatient breath.

"No," he said. "My experiment did not go well."

Barl said, "Well, it was a first attempt, and he is relatively inexper—"

"*He failed!*" shouted the Lord High Mage. He almost slammed a fist down on the delicate construct in front of him, then paused, slammed the fist into his hand, and stood up.

Barl quietly shut the door behind him.

"*He,*" shouted Mairsil, "*failed!*"

"Perhaps he is not what you expect him to be," said Barl calmly.

"Oh, no," Mairsil waved an impatient hand at the artificer. "He's of Jarsyl's blood. He read the book and understood it. Within a week he knew as much as I knew in a year, and he is a *child!* I thought I had him under my control! And he *still* failed."

"Patience is a virtue," said Barl.

"We don't have *time* for patience," said Mairsil. He waved a hand at the clock. "The walls between the dimensions are at their thinnest now! We have a few days to make this conjunction. I thought that with the boy I would no longer need Ith, but the foolish child has *failed*."

"You've worked for years already," said Barl calmly. "There will be time."

Mairsil stood in the center of the room, his fists balled in rage. "I thought we were so close. The boy would open the gateway to the Dark Lands, and I would bargain with the lords of those lands to give me that which they gave Urza and Mishra—the ability to walk the planes at will."

"The legends are unclear on that point," started Barl, "and why would the lords of these Dark Lands, whomever they are, give you that power?"

"Because I was powerful enough to come to them," said Mairsil. "Like respects like. Power respects power."

"And if it turns out they are offended by your presumption?" asked the artificer.

The Lord High Mage gave a deep smile. "Then I will offer the offending boy, the one who cast the spell, as a sacrifice." The smile grew wider still. "I might offer them that anyway."

"A pity," said Barl calmly, "that the young man failed, then, with such rewards available to him."

"Do not mock me, machine-maker," said Mairsil. "I am not in the mood for jokes."

"Of course," said Barl. "I never mean offense."

"Perhaps he was not trying," said the Lord High Mage, "or perhaps there is something within preventing him from fully casting the spell. I would cut him open if I knew it would lead me to discover the magic of planeswalking."

"You have achieved much without surgery, My Lord Mage," said Barl.

Whatever achievements the artificer was going to list

were lost in the slam of Mairsil's palm against the desk. "But for every step there is a greater step beyond, my friend. A boy dreams of being a man. A man dreams of being a mage. A mage dreams of being a planeswalker."

"Do you wonder what planeswalkers dream of?" asked Barl.

There was a long moment of silence, then Mairsil asked, "Did you come here seeking to cheer me up?"

"No, I came on another matter," said Barl. "We had a new supplicant at the gates."

One of the Lord High Mage's eyebrows raised. "Another within the course of a season? Is it getting crowded here, or is the world darker and colder than even we think?"

"Her coming at this time *is* most odd," agreed Barl.

"Color?" said Mairsil

"Blue," replied the artificer, and Mairsil shook his head. Barl added, "And she has a southeastern accent."

"City of Shadows?" suggested Mairsil.

"She reeks of their manner," said Barl, "and of their spellcraft."

"I thought those scholars knew enough to avoid our haven," said the Lord High Mage.

"This one told an interesting story," said Barl, "about a plague in Ghed, about persecution by the church, about a sinking ship, and about finding her way here by chance."

Mairsil sat down and touched his fingers together. "Why does that sound familiar?"

"Why indeed?" said Barl. "It sounds similar to the tale that your young Jodah told when he arrived.

"Yes," said Mairsil, "it assuredly does."

"Friend Jodah, your young protégé, mentioned a female companion named Sima in his interview," said Barl calmly.

"Did the supplicant give her name as Sima?" asked Mairsil.

"Oddly," said Barl, "no, she did not. She gave another name.

Mairsil closed his eyes, then opened one again to regard the artificer. "Did Friend Jodah mention that his companion Sima was a mage herself?"

"No," said Barl. "I double-checked the report. He did not say, but I did not ask him directly."

"Interesting," said Mairsil, "very, very interesting." A pause, then he added, "A spy?"

"She avoided all questions about her training. She told half-truths when pressed. She lies badly and covers her misstatements even worse. I mentioned the City of Shadows and she asked me, wide-eyed, what it was. I told her it was a community of goatherds in the mountains." said Barl. "She did not seem pleased with my definition."

The smile tugged at the corner of Mairsil's mustache, and he stroked it with his thumb and forefinger. "Let us assume I wanted to send in a spy into the City of Shadows."

"Why would you want . . ." began Barl, but Mairsil held up a finger.

"I said *assume*," said Mairsil. Given a new task, all trace of his anger and disappointment vanished as he focused on the new challenge. "Assume I would. What would you say if I presented a plan in which I sent in a young mageling to become an agent in place, and sent in a more experienced mage after him, either to discover what he knows or to extract him from the castle?"

"I would say that sounds very familiar," said Barl.

"Yes, it does," said Mairsil. "So, assuming that is what we are facing, what would you do?"

"I would kill the more experienced agent at the first chance," said Barl. "Do you wish me to do so?"

Mairsil chuckled and shook his head. "Hammers, Barl, you're using hammers again! If you killed the more experienced agent, they would send another, and the first mageling would blame you for the death of his colleague as well."

"And *your* solution is?" said Barl.

"I think—" the Lord High Mage sat at the desk and twisted the ring on his finger— "that the better solution is for our mageling, Jodah, to kill our spy, Sima. Without knowing, of course, at the time that he is doing the deed. Some deception may be required."

"Some," agreed Barl, in a low tone.

"Then our surviving mageling would know that he had no one to turn to on the outside world," continued Mairsil. "The City would disown him, and he would be ours entirely, to do with as we wished." The Lord High Mage reached out a hand and grasped the air. "He would be *ours!* Completely!"

Barl nodded. "A better choice than merely ripping him to shreds," said the artificer.

The Lord High Mage leaned back and chuckled to himself. Barl permitted himself a measured smile.

In the corner of the room, a small recording scarab rested at the bottom of the third page of three parchment sheets. It had stopped moving several minutes before, and now it lay there, its eyes blinking, waiting for someone to give it a fresh sheet to write upon.

16☾

The Echoes of Battles Yet Unfought

The viewpoint of a historian is that of a surveyor on a hill-side, overlooking a river. He can see the flow of the river and has no doubt about how it runs and why.

The participants of history view that same river as would a fish, unsure where it is taking them.

—**Arkol, Argivian scholar**

The first hundred steps were scaled in a blind panic, fearing that Ith would break free of his cage and come after him. The second hundred were only slightly less hurried. Only by the third hundred, once he had passed the area of the humming floor, did Jodah start to think carefully of what he had seen and heard.

The prisoner in the cage. Mairsil's teacher. Ith. Not even Shannan had mentioned the name, and perhaps it was forgotten or forbidden in the Conclave. The young mage had no doubt now that this Ith was the one who had brought Jodah to this place. The ragged man (No, the Rag

Man, he had called him) responded to Ith's commands, and sought Jodah out.

Sought Jodah out, apparently, to have him free Ith. Brought Jodah to a place of security, rescued him from capture, and in doing so, allowing him to learn more magic, to work directly for Lord High Mage Mairsil.

Ith stated, nay, shouted that he wanted to destroy Mairsil, and with him the Conclave.

Ith was mad, Jodah considered. Perhaps he was not mad when he had first sent the Rag Man out, but he was mad now. Was his talk of Mairsil leeching his power madness as well?

Jodah paused for a moment on a landing between the narrow stairways, illuminated only by the small ball of light in his palm. Below him he could still hear the deep vibrations of whatever engines were kept beneath the Citadel. Above him he could imagine the sounds of crystal glasses clinking and laughter.

Ith was mad. Maybe his own work with magic had an effect on him, as Shannan had said about the Fallen. Perhaps instead of killing his insane mentor, Mairsil had him locked away for his own protection. That was a possibility. Where would you put a mad wizard? Somewhere close at hand but far enough away that he would not endanger others. With his tales of the cage leeching off his power and things from the pit, perhaps that was the safest place possible. Maybe the Rag Man was some type of guard or manservant.

What if Ith was not completely mad? What if everything above Jodah was built on the mind and magic of the mage held prisoner below. Mairsil had built a utopia but at the price of his teacher's sanity.

What if there was something in the pit?

Why was he here? Why did the Rag Man select him, out of all the hedge wizards, minor mages, and reclusive wizards in the world? He was a descendent of Jarsyl, but did bloodline matter as far as magic was concerned? The Rag Man appeared almost immediately when Jodah gained Voska's mirror. Was that part of it? Then why didn't the Rag Man go after Sima instead, since she had grabbed it when the ship was attacked?

No, Sima was dead, and the mirror presumably lost. Did the Rag Man bring him back only because he had been told to return with him? Or with the man who last held the mirror?

Was the Rag Man really working for Ith? Or was he Mairsil's servant? He had not freed Ith himself, nor did he stop Jodah from leaving. Perhaps he could not?

Jodah thought of Mairsil, who had encouraged Jodah's work. He remembered the smiling face he first saw in the library. The Rainbow Mage, built of all colors, but there was the angry Mairsil as well, who pounded the desk when the first experiment failed.

Was Mairsil mad as well? Jodah's stomach tightened at that thought.

No, thought Jodah, Ith was deluded, perhaps seriously ill. He would ask Mairsil. He would ask carefully and cautiously, but he would ask him. Try to find out why Ith was truly locked in his cage. Then he would decide what to do.

With a half-formed feeling of resolve, Jodah started up the stairs again. There had been no pursuit, he thought, and the Rag Man could have stopped him, could have dragged him forcibly down to the pit. The Rag Man did not. That should count for something.

Ith had to be mad. He had to have changed over the

years. Perhaps his former student had changed as well, and Ith blamed him. Everyone changes, as Ith noted, everything changes.

Mountains become islands, Ith had said. Plains become forests.

Jodah froze on the stairs, and suddenly he realized where he had gone wrong with his ancestor's spell. He had envisioned the land as it was now, not over two centuries before. Once Mairsil's tower had been out among the cranberry bogs, his grandmother had said. Then they had drained the bottomland and turned it into fields.

Mountains become islands. Plains become forests.

Swamps become plains.

Jodah smiled deeply. That was the error, of course. He was pulling the mana of the land as it was now, assuming that it had not changed. That change makes the mana in the first place, Ith had said. He was using the wrong type of mana. That was why the spell would not accept the hot, brilliant light of his white mana and why he burned himself with that light.

He should tell Mairsil immediately, he thought, his gait speeding up until he was taking the stairs two at a time. Then he slowed again. If Ith was right, and it was only an if, then should he trust the Lord High Mage at all? Why did Mairsil want to open a gate into another world? Jodah thought of the problem as a challenge, merely a puzzle to be solved. Did the man who kept his former master in a cage beneath the castle feel the same way?

Jodah shook his head. He did not know, and until he did know he would have to keep his cards close to his vest. He would gather his data together and make sure that black mana would power the spell. Only then would he tell the Lord High Mage of his work.

In the meantime, who would he ask about Ith? Shannan might know, but was avoiding Jodah. Barl would definitely know, but he had crafted the cage himself, and Barl would definitely tell Mairsil.

Mairsil would know, but Jodah didn't think he would trust the Lord High Mage's answers. Not now.

Slowly Jodah began his climb again to the Citadel above, but the world above no longer seemed as friendly and comfortable as it once had been.

* * * * *

The festival was going admirably well, thought Primata Delphine. There had to be several thousand people present, all ripe for the Word of Tal

When they arrived, they found the town typical of northern communities. It had a church, of course, but it was run by a minor priest, an asthmatic relic more interested in the daily gossip and the yearly tithe than in truly maintaining the spiritual health of the community.

Yet the town was perfect for her needs. It was heavily armed, owing to the proximity of barbarian tribes, who were considered little better than the goblins of the mountains. There were organized pikemen and a few knights, along with several huge ballistae which were kept in working order.

Better yet, they had knowledge of the Citadel and a healthy fear of the wizards within. Yes, it was a wizard's castle, and strange lights were seen there day and night. The wise shunned that place, for those who ventured there were never seen again by mortal man. There was dim, ill-formed resentment of the wizards, just looking for the right spark to promote it to violence.

The primata would provide that spark.

Using the power granted by the letter of the lord guardian, the primata had opened the temple granaries and discovered, among the dried fruits and aged meats, several large casks of properly aged wine in the cellar. The old priest complained but could not stand either against the lord guardian's seal or the primata's own towering presence.

Word spread quickly, and more townsfolk from the surrounding towns and villages came streaming in. Even the weather was cool but dry, adding to their spirits. Bonfires were lit, and oxen and goats were slaughtered and roasted.

The trap has been baited, thought Delphine, and the beast that was the multitude was already sniffing at the meat. The only thing to do was to close the gate behind it and use the whip and the goad to bring it under her control.

That was what they were doing now. Primata Delphine, Sister Betje, and the town priest waited behind an impromptu curtain as the preacher addressed the assembled multitudes. Bonfires crackled on all sides of the town's square, but the preacher's voice thundered above it.

He read from the Book of Tal. He offered prayers for the dead and dying. He offered healing to the maimed and diseased. He preached against the heathen barbarians. He preached against the subhuman goblins, and he preached against the demon-dealing magicians. In particularly, he preached against the magicians.

Primata Delphine knew the preacher's patter. Each story, each parable, each prayer would lead the assembled multitude to the irrevocable point that one cannot suffer a magician to live. That the wizards of this citadel were in a league with the barbarians. That they were stealing sons and daughters to sacrifice to their unknown gods. With each doubling back, the crowd grew angrier, more drunken, and more determined to eradicate the threat of these evil, hell-spawned wizards.

The old priest next to her sniffed and said, "All that food, wasted in one celebration."

The primata ignored him, but Sister Betje said, "Used in the better cause of the church. Better to feed people now than to let it rot in your granaries."

"We use that grain in winter and early spring," wheezed the old priest, "when the snows are too heavy and the harbor is frozen over. You have stripped us bare. We will have too little food for too many mouths in a few months."

You will likely have fewer mouths to worry about in a few days, thought Primata Delphine, a smile tugging at the corners of her lips.

"I have heard tales that these wizards have great vaults beneath their citadels, and that they eat the finest meals there. Have you not heard such tales?" prompted the primata.

The priest hesitated for a moment, then admitted that he had indeed heard such stories.

"You let these mages survive while your church was forced to horde its food?" said the primata. "Perhaps some of that food came from the wizards themselves. That wine came from a far distance, good father. Could magic have delivered it to your door?"

The priest said nothing. Beyond their makeshift divider, the preacher was shouting a responsive reading. The voices bellowed back at him and prevented any real reply from the town-priest.

The preacher was working them up to fever pitch,

thought the primata, weaving his particular form of miracles among them. He would have them lusting for wizards' blood. Every problem in their lives, real or imagined was the wizards' fault. The barbarians. The goblins. The smut that blighted the crops this past year. The lack of merchants. The dishonesty of the merchants who did show up. Yes, it was all the wizards' fault.

At the proper moment the preacher would step aside and announce Primata Delphine. She would step up, shout a few choice phrases from the Book of Tal, and then call for a crusade—a holy war she would invoke against the evil beings in the tower. Any man, woman, or boy who joined their crusade would be guaranteed both salvation and a portion of the treasure the wizards undoubtedly held in their subterranean vaults.

Of course, the lion's share would be taken back south, along with any contraband magery, to be studied and then destroyed.

"What do you see, Sister?" said the primata.

Sister Betje shifted uneasily. "I see nothing without my portents and rituals. But from the sounds I hear, I have no doubt you will soon be commanding a mighty army against these wizards."

"I have no doubt, either," said the primata. Beyond their curtain, the preacher had reached the height of his sermon, and the crowd was bellowing in response.

"I have a doubt or two," said the old priest, but the primata pretended not to hear him. The preacher called her name, and she parted the curtains, followed by Sister Betje and the priest.

The assembled crowds bellowed with one voice as she appeared, and she raised her hands to bless the multitudes and accept their undying loyalty.

* * * * *

Jodah returned to his quarters but found sleep would still not come. Of course he had nagging doubts about Mairsil and Ith, but, was now also assailed by a new conviction—he had used the wrong type of mana.

He rose, lit the lamp with a word, and went to his desk to review his notes. That was when he discovered that he was missing his recording scarab.

Jodah winced. He had set it up to take notes of the summoning, but in his haste to leave and avoid Mairsil's wrath, he had left it behind in the Lord High Mage's study.

Jodah frowned. He could use those notes now to remember fully what he and Mairsil had said, to track the course of the ritual from start to finish. He could go in the morning for the notes or perhaps ask Barl.

Or he could go himself, right now.

Jodah slipped out into the hall. The eternal lights in their sconces continued to flicker in imitation of true flame. He quietly made his way through the halls, but at this early morning hour the place was as silent as a tomb.

At last he came to the jet-black door of Mairsil's study. Jodah paused for a moment, looking around and half-expecting Barl to manifest himself in a puff of warm air, but there was no one but himself.

Jodah tried the door, but it was locked. He left out a long breath of relief. Now he would be spared the risk of being caught. He would have to wait for morning after all. He looked at the golden icon that marked the door.

The door had been locked before and had opened at his touch.

Jodah grimaced and touched the icon. The bolt popped open, and the door swung inward slightly.

Jodah cursed himself, looking around again for the omnipresent Barl. There was no sign of the artificer.

Jodah slipped into the study.

It was empty. The debris from the experiment of the previous evening, a lifetime ago, was still scattered around the area. The calendar of stone and metal whirred and chirped to itself in the corner, bathing the room in a cascade of ever-changing light. Motes of blue, green, and amber light hovered like fireflies in the room, and zipped and danced among the bookshelves and tapestries.

Jodah found the recording scarab and the three sheets as he had left them. All three sheets were inscribed with neat, angular letters, his own words in black, Mairsil's in red. Jodah didn't remember talking that much during the experiment, though without setting a lamp he could not read it in the flickering light of the calendar.

There was a sound from the hallway. Jodah pocketed the scarab and folded the parchment sheets, shoving them into his vest. He raced for the door and stepped into the hallway. He closed the door behind him as quietly as possible.

Yes, there were voices and footsteps approaching. He looked around for someplace to hide, but this part of the hallway was bare of large objects. Finally he did the only thing he could do.

He turned his back on the approaching voices and knocked on the door to Mairsil's study, the one that he had just left.

"Friend Jodah!" said the Lord High Mage, "you are up early this morning."

Jodah turned and saw Mairsil and Barl. The Lord High Mage was smiling, though Barl had a suspicious look.

Jodah shrugged and tried to look embarrassed. "I couldn't sleep after what happened," he said. "I thought I would come and help clean up the mess."

Mairsil favored him a wide smile, and for the first time Jodah thought about how that made the Lord High Mage look like a wolf.

"Ah, such dedication," he said, slapping Barl on the back. "This is what we need more of here at the Conclave. Dedication! Initiative! Loyalty!"

"All admirable traits," said Barl, looking hard at Jodah.

"Indeed," said Mairsil, "but don't worry about cleaning up. I will have servants take care of it all—that is why we have servants, after all. Have you given any thought to our results?"

Jodah thought of the revelation of the cranberry bogs, but instead shook his head. "I wonder if it was something I did, or the timing, or some outside influence. . . ."

Mairsil raised a hand, "Tut. What you need is rest, young friend. The mind works best when it is fully rested." His smile disappeared into a thin line. "Though I do appreciate your concern. Lesser mages might just walk away without reflecting on what happened. An experiment is a failure only if one refuses to learn anything from it."

"Yes, sir," said Jodah, then added quickly, "yes, Friend Mairsil." He looked at Barl, and the artificer's brows had pulled together, so that the shorter man was almost scowling.

"Good," said Mairsil, patting Jodah on the back. "Think about what happened here and get back to me. We'll try again, once you think you have things worked out."

Jodah bowed slightly and started away, but Mairsil called out.

"One last thing," he said. "I need you for one other task."

Jodah turned and said, "Whatever you need me for, Friend Mairsil, I shall do my best."

The smile returned, and it seemed very much to Jodah to be a wolf's smile.

"You're going to have to learn a few spells in the next few days," Mairsil said. "I need you to fight a duel for me."

17

A Game of
Red and Blue

The concept of dueling is almost as old as magic itself. Some point to Urza and Mishra as the first magical duelists, and while this is tempting, it should be noted that they fought with armies and artifacts, not with spells as we know them. Also, they rarely faced each other, save at the very beginning and at the very end. The concept of duels, so firmly entrenched in the period of the Ice Age, got its start at least during the time of the Dark, as a means of solving disputes.

— Arkol, Argivian scholar

Sima balled her fist and stomped, her slender boot slapping against the stone floor. For three days they had kept her confined to her room. Three days!

Room, she snorted, more of a prison cell. It was larger than her quarters in the City of Shadows, and the slaves (she refused to think of anyone wearing a metal collar as merely a "servant") were polite and prompt and brought her well-cooked meals, but there was no doubt about the fact that her quarters were intended as a cell.

The door was magically barred to keep her from leaving, and the leaded windows had watersilver within the molding, the same material the church used to keep mages imprisoned. Various vents in the walls were similarly lined with that material, and there were magical sigils around the frames. Behind the tapestries, the walls themselves were marked with runes, some of which Sima recognized, some of which were totally foreign to her.

Someone had built this room with the express idea of keeping a mage at bay. That someone was likely the diminutive, gruff artificer Barl.

She disliked the short man at once. He was one of those officious types who organized everything and tolerated nothing that happened outside his narrow purview. There were enough of them at the City, and to find one here at the Conclave was scarce consolation.

Worst of all, these officious Barl-types missed next to nothing. That was likely why she was kept in a mage-proof room until they figured out what to do with her.

"And your full name is?" Barl had said when he first sat opposite her.

"Mireille," she had replied.

"Mireille of?" Barl had pressed.

"Just Mireille," she had said.

"Everyone is from somewhere," noted Barl, his brows pursing.

"Most recently I am out Ghed," said Sima. "That city had a plague and cast out most of its foreigners."

"Then it's Mireille of Ghed," said Barl. "You were born there?"

"No," said Sima, "I am merely from there."

The entire interview continued in that vein. Sima gave

her answers partially, usually asking for a clarification or questioning the nature of the question. In retrospect, Sima thought, that was probably a bad idea for passing herself off as a would-be student, but Barl's manner had bothered her to a great degree.

She had made no mention of Jodah. She made no mention of the islands she came from. Instead she was Mireille, a blue mage (Are colors important? she had asked, darkening the shorter man's mood further), on the run from the church, looking for a safe haven. Nothing else to declare, thank you, she had said, Jodah's mirror tucked into the folds of her blouse.

"Have you heard of the City of Shadows?" asked Barl at one point.

Sima had put her best straight face on, and said, "What's that?"

"A community of goat herds to the west," said the interviewer. "They pretend they can cast spells."

Sima labored to keep her face calm, but the artificer's voice still rankled. Goat herds? Scholars! Not like this lot of dilettantes and dabblers!

She had heard the distant sounds of laughter and partying when the evening meal was brought to her, echoing down the labyrinthine corridors. These Conclave mages had no discipline, no comprehension, no understanding of their world. They celebrated while the lights went out, one after another, in the world outside.

She had not asked about Jodah. She had said, "Do you get many applicants?"

"A few," said Barl.

"Any recently?" asked Sima.

"A few," said Barl, in the exact same tone.

Sima frowned slightly. "Do all your applicants have to

go through this tiresome process?"

Barl smiled a grim, knowing smile. "No. Yours is more tiresome than most."

Then he was gone, and she was kept in her room (cell) and brought meals by servants (slaves) and asked if she needed anything for her studies while she waited (rotted). She asked for several weighty histories on the church and used them to prop her feet up while she meditated.

She did not cast spells. That would be too obvious, in this room laced with protective wards and runes. She did not take out Jodah's mirror, save to put it under her pillow each night. She considered casting a spell on it to tell her if he was still alive, but decided against it. Barl probably had this room rigged up eight ways to heaven with all manner of divination magic.

She decided to wait them out. This was fairly easy, since the food was better than most places she had been for the past three months, but if it took much longer, she would have to start reading those church histories to keep from going mad.

In the end, it took them three days to get around to her. There was a knock—not a tentative one of the serving slaves, but a confident one—of one used to giving orders.

"Enter," snapped Sima, not turning away from the window. It looked out on more roofs and walls, and in the time she had been there, it had not shown a single person.

Barl came in, officious, perfunctory, and short.

"I have good news," he said, acting as if the news was anything but good. "Your petition has been accepted by the Conclave, Friend Mireille." He paused for effect. "There is of course one more thing."

Sima turned and raised an eyebrow at the artificer.

"We have a tradition of challenges here," said Barl,

"and you must survive this duel to win a place among us."
He offered her a package. "There is ceremonial dress
involved. I will wait outside."

He was gone, and Sima shook her head. She wondered
if he had come to dislike her as quickly as she detested
him.

She dressed. Barl had given her a package of long, blue
robes suitable for hiding all manner of weapons. She
placed the mirror in a pocket directly over her breast.
Thick-soled boots in the eastern style, heavier than she
was used to, and a mask that looked vaguely animalistic,
like a lion's face, painted with blue lacquer and set with
black string around the edges in a rough mane. She shook
her head at the stupidity and put the mask on, then went
out to present herself to the artificer.

Barl led her down innumerable stairs to an oak door set
with steel bands. He pulled a sword from a nearby rack
and offered it to her. "You might need this," he said.

"I don't think so," said Sima, almost laughing. Why
would she take a weapon into a magical fight? And why
would she trust one of their weapons, even if she did?

Barl scowled more deeply and ushered her into a short
hallway, closing the door behind her. She shrugged and
slowly moved up the hallway.

There was the sound of humanity at the far side of the
hallway, beyond an open portcullis. The corridor opened
onto a narrow stadium, one with damp earthen floors. As
she entered, there was a cheer from the stands.

The stands of the area were packed. They were filled to
the brim with all manner of supposed mages in all manner
of finery. There were black, shimmering robes, and red
vests in incendiary shades and brilliant white gowns and
green-armored figures. Many were wearing masks as well,

though more ornate and less practical than hers. They cheered her entry as if she was a dancing bear that had happened on the scene.

One particular peacock had his seat along one side of the arena, dressed in black with a gold vest. Barl came down and sat alongside him. That would be the head mage. Sima had always heard there was only one master of this community.

She scanned the crowd. There was no sign of Jodah, but then, he might not be invited to this "challenge."

Across from her, another figure, similarly dressed, appeared at the other end of the arena. This one was garbed in red robes, and his mask looked like a dragon's.

A red mage, thought Sima. Excellent. She pawed through her mind for all manner of spells that were proof against red. Surely they meant this as a challenge, a test of her ability to deal with red's destructive magics.

The peacock stood and raised both hands. "Let the challenge begin!" he cried, dropping them.

The dragon and lion started pulling the mana into themselves.

* * * * *

Jodah had read the transcript the morning after his hallway meeting with Mairsil, and his stomach twisted as he read. It had recorded all of his words, of course, as they prepared the experiment. It had also recorded all of Mairsil's tantrum, and his muttered cursing after Jodah left the room. Then it recorded something else entirely.

A line of black letters read, Your experiment did not go well.

That was followed by a line in red. When Mairsil spoke,

his letters were always in red. No. My experiment did not go well.

The next line, a black one: Well, it was a first attempt, and he is relatively inexper

He Failed said the red line. Then a pause, and *He. Failed!*

Jodah read on.

I thought I had him under my control, said one red line among several that followed.

I would not longer need Ith, said another red line.

The boy would open the gateway to the Dark Lands, said a third line in crimson.

Then I will offer the offending boy, the one who cast the spell, as a sacrifice, said another line in neat red letters. I might offer them that anyway.

It continued in a similar vein through the rest of the third page. The last line was in black type, probably Barl's, and said: You have achieved much without surgery, My Lord Mage.

What had been Mairsil's response to that? Jodah wondered. The scarab had run out of paper there. What had they discussed, unrecorded, afterward? Had they come to some conclusion about him? Had they decided to punish him for his failure? Challenge him to do better? Or to test his abilities and his loyalties. Mairsil wanted him to learn some new spells so he could compete in a duel.

* * * * *

"It's a matter of settling disputes," explained Barl, "and it's similar to the challenge that you fought when you entered it."

"The Lord High Mage cannot settle his own disputes?"

asked Jodah, then immediately regretted it. Quickly, he added, "I mean, isn't it presumptuous of me to act in the Lord High Mage's stead?"

The Chief Artificer's face tensed for a moment, then relaxed. "No. The disadvantage of being both the leader and the most powerful mage among equals is that no one wishes to contest you directly. The use of proxies is preferred, actually. You will be facing a student of another powerful mage, with whom Mairsil has this disagreement."

"And this mage is?" said Jodah. "If I may ask."

"You may, but you should not," said Barl. "It might affect your ability to battle if you know you are inferior to the opponent. Similarly, if you are fighting a lesser opponent, you may get overconfident."

Jodah disagreed with the comment but did not want to challenge Barl's judgment. Jodah also failed to ask Barl about Mairsil's former teacher, and he didn't mention his possible solution to the problem of the gate spell. The entire setup smelled like a test to Jodah.

And Jodah hated tests.

Jodah did not see Lord Mairsil for the next three days, nor did he receive any notes of encouragement. Jodah did not know how to read this. Did Mairsil have confidence in him, or did he know about the recording scarab and the notes that Jodah now possessed?

A moment of panic blossomed in Jodah's breath, and he had to rationally tamp it back down. Mairsil could *not* know what Jodah had read. If Mairsil or Barl knew, they would not have left the papers there.

Part of Jodah wanted to believe that Mairsil was merely angry and was making an irrational threat (though the transcript gave small clue if this was true or not). If so, then this was just a test of his ability, and once it had been passed he would be back in the Lord High Mage's good graces. Part of him wanted to flee Mairsil and the Council and Ith and the rest and go back to surviving on his own in the wilderness.

Jodah felt suspended between the two points, unable to decide. For the moment, he would do as Mairsil asked and go from there.

Later that day Barl came and took Jodah to a tutor, a white mage named Wode who had been with the Conclave from nearly the beginning. Jodah had seen him at dinner on occasion, but the ancient, bent wizard kept to himself.

"You're Mairsil's new pup," said the wizened old man. His quarters were high in one tower, and Jodah could understand why he did not get down too often for meals. His face seemed to be frozen in a perpetual frown. "I'm supposed to teach you a few tricks for your upcoming duel. Show me what you know."

Jodah said, "I can cast lights, and fire, I can make healing draughts—"

"I didn't say *tell* me," said the old mage. "*Show* me."

So Jodah showed him his spells, one after the other, the ones that he knew. Wode sat across from him on a footstool, legs crossed, and grunted.

"Not bad," he said. "Do that yourself?"

"Mostly," said Jodah. "I had a teacher. He's dead. Killed by the church."

"Occupational hazard," said the old man. "Hope you don't care much about theory. We ain't got much time for theory. He wants results. He always does. Very well, here's the first spell you're going to learn."

That day they concentrated on a ward powered by

297

white mana, which would protect one from the effects of spells based in blue, and a circle of protection that protected the user from being harmed by blue magic. Jodah asked what the difference was.

Wode held up a hand and ticked off the reasons with his fingers. "A ward moves with you, the circle don't. Circle you gotta keep pumping mana into, but protects more. Ward keeps you from being even hit by blue spells—slides right off you. And you can toss wards on others."

Wode led him through the motions, and Jodah nodded and followed. Lunch was sent up, then dinner. Barl came to fetch him in the evening, and escorted him to his quarters.

"What did you talk about?" asked the artificer.

"We talked about magic," said Jodah. "Why?"

The shorter man made no response, but noted, "Since you missed dinner, you should know that the Lord High Mage announced the upcoming duel. There is a great deal of interest among the other mages. And, I understand, some wagering."

The next morning Wode worked him through the circles and the wards and showed Jodah how they could be expanded into other colors. He also worked with Jodah's fire spells, giving him better control, allowing him to force more mana into them. Mana from the mountains was not Wode's forte, but he knew enough to give advice. He also showed Jodah a spell by which one could bring down a blue spell by force of elemental power.

"Red and blue are called the elemental manas," said Wode. "Red comes from mountains and fire, blue from waves and air. They are natural enemies."

"Will my opponent be a blue mage?" asked Jodah.

"Likely," said Wode. "I haven't been told one way or t'other."

"Friend Wode," asked Jodah, "who would disagree with the Lord High Mage so that this challenge would be necessary?"

"No one would challenge Mairsil, directly," said the old man, a curious tone in his voice. "Not and live."

"They told me that I was going to fight to settle some argument between the Lord High Mage and someone else," said Jodah.

The old man harrumphed and said, in a low voice, "Well, if that's what you're told, that must be true, then."

Jodah nodded, and Barl again met him at the end of the day.

"What did you talk about?" asked the artificer.

"We talked about magic," said Jodah. "Why?"

Barl did not respond to the question.

On the morning of the third day, Jodah ran through the various spells. Toward noon, he asked, "Friend Wode, are you a prisoner here?"

Wode's eyes sharpened at him for a moment, then grew soft. "Yes and no. Yes, I am. I'm not allowed to leave. No, I don't have anywhere to go." He waved a hand over his tower study. "And so I remain."

"Do you wonder what Mar . . . what the Lord High Mage is up to?" Jodah tried to phrase the question as neutrally as he could.

Wode shook his head. "I gave up on that a long time ago. It ain't healthy to wonder when it comes to the Lord High Mage. Take that as a piece of free advice."

"I heard a rumor," said Jodah, "something about Mairsil keeping someone beneath the castle. . . ."

"*Where* did you hear that?" asked the old mage, his face suddenly alive and angry.

Jodah backed away. "I thought it gossip. . . ."

"Gossip . . . huh," said Wode. "You can tell Mairsil's running boy Barl that he won't get me that easily. Others have fallen for that trick and then found themselves suddenly without spells, or wearing a servant's torque, or mysteriously gone in the night."

"I don't . . ." started Jodah.

"Don't give me your 'don'ts,' " said Wode. "I see that he comes to fetch you each evening. Tell *Friend* Barl I know nothing about anything, and particularly nothing about anything that I shouldn't know about. And if you *ain't* working for Barl—" he paused here, and his eyes softened again— "then you'd best stop asking such questions. Am I clear?"

Jodah nodded, and they ran through the spells a few more times. Then Barl came to get him.

As they went down the steps, Jodah said, "We talked about magic." Barl just nodded.

Jodah rested in the early afternoon, gathering his thoughts for the battle. No, the duel. It was similar to what he had gone through before.

Wode was afraid. One of the elder mages in the Conclave and he hid in his tower, definitely afraid. Afraid of Barl. Afraid of Mairsil. Afraid because he *knew* about Ith beneath the castle and did nothing about it.

Jodah made his decision. After the duel, he would try to escape. Security or no, there were dangerous things afoot. Things no one talked about.

Things about sacrificing Jodah to the lords of the Dark Lands.

Barl sent a servant for him after dinner, and they descended down familiar stairs. The servant left him with a ceremonial costume, which Jodah donned. It was a set of brilliant red robes, topped with a smooth mask that looked vaguely like a dragon.

For the first time, Jodah was thankful he did not have a mirror. He must have looked as ridiculous as he felt.

Barl appeared, and said, "All is ready, Friend Jodah."

Jodah nodded, unsure if he could be heard clearly through the dragon mask.

Barl's face was stiff, almost lifeless.

"Our Lord High Mage thinks very highly of you, Friend Jodah. He doesn't want you to feel that there is any pressure on you one way or another."

No pressure, thought Jodah, suddenly feeling very constrained by the mask.

"But he does want you warned," continued Barl, "your opponent has a reputation for not pulling punches. Indeed, your opponent has already killed a lesser mage in combat. The Lord High Mage wants you to know that. I want you to know that. Don't seek to spare him. Do your best."

My best, thought Jodah, as a part of his mind echoed, "killed a lesser mage."

With that Barl was gone, and at the far end of the tunnel, a cry went up from a hundred throats.

Jodah moved toward the sound, and he was back in the arena. This time the stands were packed with hundreds of mages. He recognized Drusilla and Lucan and San-Lo and some of the others. No sign of Shannan or Wode. Barl came down the steps and stood next to Mairsil.

Across from him was his opponent, dressed in blue and wearing a mask that looked like lion.

Probably feeling as foolish as I do, thought Jodah. At least it was a blue mage. Jodah had feared that the wards against blue mana were all a ruse to keep him busy.

Lord High Mage Mairsil, Master of the Conclave and First among Equals, stood and raised both hands. "Let the challenge begin!" he cried, dropping his upraised arms.

The dragon and lion started pulling the mana into themselves.

* * * * *

Jodah thought to come out fast and hard with the red magics that he had learned. Blue and red were natural enemies, Wode had stated, and he tugged at the memories of the mountains beyond the Citadel. The red mana flickered in the base of his mind, briefly, then was immediately cast outward at his foe across the arena floor in the form of flaming daggers.

The opponent was fast as well, raising his hands and weaving a tight tangle with his long fingers. The red fire knives evaporated before they were even half way across the stadium. There were boos from the crowd.

Jodah took two steps forward, and the ground seemed to heave beneath him. His stomach dropped, and the bile rose in the back of his throat. He had not felt this bad since the last night he spent in Ghed, before he joined the army. Blue magic was responsible there, as well.

Jodah dropped to one knee, and the spell seemed to intensify, attacking his ears and increasing the pressure at the base of his eyes. He groped through his mental manor and found the spell to cut the energy powering the opponent's spell. With little more than a few bits of mana, he shot the spell from his mind, mentally willing it back along the conduit by which it came. There was a soft, puffing noise, and the blue mage staggered back a pace.

Jodah took advantage of the pause and scraped an arc in front of him with his toe, digging into the soft dark earth while mentally pulling one of Wode's spells to him.

The arc flickered with a white, then blue, then white radiance, and flared up all around him.

He had completed the circle of protection just in time, for a new attack blazed over him from his opponent. Something blue and fluid smashed into the circle, spattering against it like waves against a breakwater reef.

As the attack faded, Jodah was prepared. He tried fire again, this time hoping that his opponent would be worn out by the attack. A set of fire daggers arced over the length of the arena. They struck his opponent in the chest, staggering him.

But the opponent did not fall. Instead, the flaming daggers of red mana entered his opponent's robes and were flung back at their caster. Jodah dodged one, but another caught him in the arm. Cursing back the pain, he dropped to one knee.

There were more boos and catcalls from the gallery now. These were his fellow mages, thought Jodah, with whom he supped each day. Now they jeered him. He felt anger blossom in his heart and with it the knowledge that raw anger did not in itself provide the power to win.

Now there were more blue blazes of light against his shield. His opponent had to know there was no getting through his circle of protection. Then Jodah realized—his opponent was intent on exhausting his memories. The more he cast, the more he pulled from his own memories of the land. Eventually Jodah would reach bottom and be defenseless.

Jodah slowly rose and regarded his foe. His opponent had apparently thought Jodah was beaten and now stomped his foot in frustration. Jodah pulled the red mana from his mind to ready another set of fire knives. As he did, he simultaneously launched one of his light balls in the blue mage's face.

Only after he did both of these things did he recognize where he had seen that little stomp before. A small stomp, usually accompanied by a balled fist of irritation at Jodah.

Jodah cursed himself for not recognizing her with the casting of her first spell.

By that time it was too late. His opponent raised her hands to counter the light spell and could not prevent the red flame daggers from slamming into her. She screamed and went down, dark stains appearing on her robes.

The crowd cheered at the apparent victory, but Jodah was already halfway to his fallen foe. Mairsil shouted something, and Barl as well, but Jodah paid no attention to either of them.

He ripped off the lion mask, and Sima's battered face was below. She had a massive welt across her forehead, and blood trickled from the corner of her mouth. She tried to say something, but blood merely bubbled between her lips.

The other mages in attendance were shouting Jodah's name, but he was consumed by the sight of Sima. For a moment, his mind blanked, and he looked up and back, at Mairsil and Barl.

Barl was as a stone statue. Mairsil was smiling, broadly. Neither one moved from their position.

Jodah turned back and reached into his mind. There was little there, in the matter of memories of the land, but he pulled that little bit and fanned it, like a flame, trying to make one of Mother Dobbs's potions, without the potion, of course. He took the raw energy and pushed it into Sima's body.

Sima shook for a moment, but the bubbling bleeding stopped. Another moment, and her eyes fluttered open.

Jodah looked back, and Barl had turned away, and he was motioning for some mages to get down on the arena floor. Mairsil was no longer smiling. He was raising a gem-tipped wand in one hand, aiming it at Jodah and Sima.

Then the entire arena shook, and the crowd was knocked to its knees. There were screams and shouts, and whatever Mairsil had planned was lost for the moment. At first Jodah though Mairsil was responsible for this, but the Lord High Mage seemed as confused as everyone else, gripping the side of the railing and shouting now at Barl.

There was another tremor, this one accompanied by thunder, and bits of ceiling started to fall around them. Some mages responded with spells, opening them like umbrellas above their own heads. Others panicked, and still others were trampled in the attempts to leave the arena.

Jodah hunched over Sima. Her eyes were open now, and her breathing, though ragged, was strong.

She spat blood and said muddily, "It's about time you got here, Jodah of Giva Province. I'm here to rescue you."

18

The Battle
of the Conclave

The war between Priest and Mage, of inquisition and enlightenment, was mostly a war of skirmishes, fought in small villages and large city-states, but with only a few pieces on either side. The Battle of the Conclave, however, was the exception to this rule. For many it has been cited as the greatest victory of the church. Other texts says that this was the beginning of the end of church power. Interestingly enough, both sides of the issue mention a figure named Jodah as being the key to the battle.

—Arkol, Argivian scholar

"It has to be the Church of Tal behind this. They even painted their siege machines *white*," cursed Mairsil from the battlements.

Before them, on the rolling northern hillside of the citadel, was an army where none should have been. Ith and Mairsil had cowed the local tribes and towns years ago, and they should have stayed cowed. Unless something came along and stirred things up.

Something undoubtedly had. There were at least a thousand troops—slingers, pikemen, shield bearers and swordsmen, gathered on the plain. No cavalry, but they had somehow hauled up five huge ballistae, which they now used to pepper the towers. One ballista was equipped with incendiaries, and already one of the stables was on fire. Some of the servants were even now organizing a bucket brigade.

Something had stirred them up, thought Mairsil. Something like the church.

Barl was at his side. "We have the advantage of the outer walls, My Lord Mage, but they are relatively low and were not built with an organized defense in mind."

"I doubt that this is a very organized attack," said Mairsil, disparagingly.

"Still, if the mazework had been completed—" started Barl, but Mairsil stopped him with an icy glare.

"Fear is a better deterrent than stone," said the Lord High Mage. "Once we have smashed them, this rabble will never darken our walls again."

"This is no mere rabble," said Barl. "This is an army we are facing."

"Don't think of it as an army," said Mairsil with a smile. "Think of them as a large collection of targets."

Already the flaming ballista bolts were being answered by fireballs and lightning bolts from the red mages, and with high winds from the blue. Already the ragged weeds from the ruined mazework were trailing out great vines, and humped, misshapen thing were oozing out of the swamps. The mystical bolts cut a wide swatch through the pikemen, and the lines seemed to waver. Already a group of five mages were airborne, circling to cut off their retreat.

In the front line, one large warrior was dressed in white, rallying the troops. No, Mairsil corrected himself, that warrior was a priest, or rather a priestess. She seemed to glow with her own radiance in the dying light of the sun. As he watched, a flaming bolt arched from the Citadel's ramparts and caught her directly in the side. She did not wince or stagger from the attack but continued to bellow orders.

That was the first surprise. There were those among them with magical protection, and they might have the power as well. Mairsil frowned.

The second surprise was the presence of archers. A line of shieldbearers dropped their protective screen to reveal bowmen behind them, and as the flying mages neared, they let off a thick-arrowed volley. Three wizards of the five dropped from the sky, and the surviving pair beat a hasty retreat back to the Citadel. A cry went up from the besiegers. Mairsil's frown deepened.

Then came the third surprise, as the entire army gave up a cry and charged the walls.

"Madness," said Barl.

"Holy madness," said Mairsil, the frown becoming a scowl.

The units brought ladders with them, and they leaned them all along the northern walls. There were more of them than the distracted servants and mages could handle. The field at the base of the walls was littered with the bodies of townsfolk but more were climbing all the time.

Meanwhile, a large knot of troops, led by the woman in the white robes, was circling toward the main gates that faced the mountains. All manner of magical bolts, flaming daggers, and solid shards of ice rained down on them, only to shatter or extinguish themselves before they arrived at their targets.

"That one does have protection," said Mairsil. "Barl, get some units down . . ." But the Lord High Mage realized he was speaking to no one, as the artificer had already left to join the battle.

Mairsil heard a resounding crack behind him and looked down to see that the main gates of the keep were gone. Not open, but vanished entirely, spirited away by a miracle of the church. The units, bunched tightly around the figure in brilliant white, surged through the opening. The door guards were scattered in their wake, straws carried away by a powerful wind.

The church had breached the Conclave of Mages.

* * * * *

"Can you walk?" asked Jodah. He channeled the power of the plains into his own wound and watched as the bloody tear in his flesh closed up.

Sima nodded and hauled herself to her feet. "You've learned a few new things since I saw you last."

Jodah nodded. "Some things I wish I hadn't learned as well."

Sima stepped, staggered for a moment, and leaned against Jodah. He muttered a few words and pulled the mana from his memories, and she steadied.

"Thanks," she said.

"Don't worry about it," he replied. Above them, there was another boom. "What's that?"

"Nothing that I know about," said Sima, "but I think we should take our opportunities where we can. We have to leave while the leaving is good."

Sima took two steps toward the gate, then turned. "Are you coming?"

Jodah looked at her for a moment, then shook his head, "I was before. I can't now. There's something I have to do."

"You have to save yourself," said Sima. "These are *not* nice people here."

"Exactly," responded Jodah. "There's a prisoner in the basement. I think he's the reason I was brought here. I have to free him."

"Free him?" sputtered Sima. He was almost sure she was going to stomp her foot in rage. Instead she said, "This is like before, with the church prisoners?"

"Yes," said Jodah.

"And I'm not going to win this one," said Sima.

Jodah thought for a moment, then carefully shook his head.

"Then let's not waste any time arguing. We'd better get going." There was the sound of feet running overhead, and the distant sounds of screams. "Because I don't think things are going to get any easier."

* * * * *

The church forces spread out as soon as they broke through the main gates, units scattering in every direction.

The suddenness of the attack ruptured the Conclave's defenses. Those mages who were caught by surprise were overwhelmed, unable to use their abilities before being swarmed with loyal, church-fearing townsfolk. Some wizards fled entirely in the face of the attack, running for the few boats on the island side of the citadel. Those who reacted quickly enough to have some form of defense managed to first halt their assailants' charge, then to destroy the townsfolk. The walls were scorched with magical energy, and the tapestries along the main hall were already smoldering from the battle.

Sister Betje, not needing any eyes to see the evil in her foes, led a squad down one of the opulent hallways. As her force passed, it paused only to tear down the wall hangings and paintings and tip over the sculptures.

At the end of the hall was a single man carrying a crossbow. Despite his small size, he had the aura of being a large man. The sight of the weapon brought the small squad up short, and they clustered around the sister.

The sister sniffed the air. "I sense no magic about you," she said.

"I have none," said the short figure.

"Then turn on your masters," said Sister Betje, "and beg Tal for forgiveness."

"I think not," said the short figure with the crossbow.

Beneath her bandaged eyes, the sister smiled a gap-toothed grin. "You are only one. We are many. You can only shoot one of us." She raised a thin arm to signal the attack.

The crossbow twanged four times in quick succession. Sister Betje's midsection disappeared in a shower of blood and flesh.

Her squad of loyal followers hesitated, looking down at their bisected leader.

"Magic crossbow," said the short figure, raising it a second time. "Boo!"

The remnants of the squad fled, shrieking, in the opposite direction.

Barl set down the emptied crossbow, the one that his

student had built, and walked over to Sister Betje's torso. He kicked over the top half and pulled off her mask. Beneath the rag were sightless masses of scar tissue.

"I can only shoot one of you," Barl said, "so I had damned better shoot the right one."

* * * * *

The battle had spiraled into a hundred smaller battles throughout the Citadel, miniature maelstroms of destruction that ebbed and flowed through the halls. Here a group of pikemen had skewered a mage against the wall, and they laughed as they twisted their thick spear points into his guts. There another group of similar pikemen stood turned to stone, as a waiflike nature magess moved among them, whacking off pieces at random with a hammer, giggling as she worked. In one hall the carpet ran red with mage blood and green with unknown ichor. In another a squad ran in fear from some dark cloud with hell-red eyes.

There were fires scattered everywhere—the thatched roof of the stables, the tapestries along the main hall.

Through the chaos moved Sima and Jodah, aware only of the rumors of war. There was blood on the carpet, scorch marks on the walls, the occasional dead or transformed body. In the distance there was the sound of blades crashing on each other, then silence, as sudden as the shutting of a door.

Jodah led and Sima followed, gathering her strength as they moved on.

They climbed up forever, then down a long hallway. Jodah paused at a small wooden door along one hallway.

"Something there?" Sima asked.

"Nothing I need," said Jodah, grimly, and pressed on.

They moved to the back of the hall, to a dead-end alcove with a stained-glass window. Night had fallen, but flames on the parapets showed through the glass. Several of the panels had been broken out, and something large had been heaved out where Mairsil's face, depicted in the glass, had been. Jodah began slapping at the wall to the left of the window.

"Secret door?" Sima asked.

"Somewhere." said Jodah. Something behind the wall clicked, and the door swung inward.

Something tall and hunched, dressed in black tatters, loomed behind it. The thing carried a rune-carved blade, glowing blue.

Sima stepped forward, spell ready at the front of her mind. Jodah held up a hand.

"Hold," he said. "This one is a friendly. I think."

Sima looked at the figure—tall, hunched, and wrapped in black garb, its face a mystery. As she watched, the figure turned and began down the steps.

Jodah stepped forward, and Sima put a hand on his shoulder.

"Before we go any farther," she said, reaching into her blouse, "I believe this is yours." She produced the mirror from within the blouse.

Jodah frowned at the mirror. "You saved it, and not me," he said at last. "In the storm."

Sima took a deep breath, then said, "I know. I thought you could take care of yourself."

"And that was because. . . ?" Jodah raised his voice in a question.

"Because I thought you were capable enough." grumbled Sima.

"That all?"

"And Voska taught you well," said Sima, "and you have more potential than any other mage I've met. And yes, that was meant as a compliment! Anything else?"

"One more thing," said Jodah calmly.

Sima sighed deeply, "And there is more than one correct way to cast a spell. And you can breath any way you want! And you *aren't* a dunderhead! You're a competent spellcaster in your own right, and I should treat you as such. That's why I had to come after you. And why you had me worried when we fought each other in the arena. Happy now?"

"Happy enough," said Jodah, "and you had *me* worried back there, too. Good thing you kept the mirror on you."

"Good thing for both of us," said Sima. "Now let's go."

Jodah clutched the mirror, and they stepped into the darkness of the passageway.

* * * * *

Jodah and Sima traveled through the darkness, led by the glowing sword of the Rag Man. Once they passed an area that reeked with a salty tang and another where the floor vibrated. After a few minutes Sima could no longer determine how far they had descended or how far they were from their goal.

Then she heard the screaming. Loud inhuman shrieks that seemed to rise and fall with the same rhythm as the machines.

They stepped through a doorway and onto the edge of a pit. Suspended over the pit was a glowing cage. Within it, the emaciated form of a man screamed and pitched itself from one side to another. The very bars of the cage glowed with an inhuman brilliance, which traveled up the chains that held the cage and disappeared in the darkness.

The figure screamed and threw himself against the bars. They flashed as he struck them, and he bounced away, only for the bars to flash again where he struck' on the other side of the cage. The sounds that the figure made were inhuman—no more than a keening as the bars lit up around him.

The Rag Man stepped to one side.

"That's what you want to free?" said Sima.

Jodah nodded.

"He doesn't seem to be too . . ." Sima searched for the right word, "stable, at the moment."

"He said that Mairsil has been draining his power over the years," said Jodah. "Perhaps with the battle above, that drain has increased"

"Perhaps," said Sima. "I don't think it's a good time to let him out."

"I don't know of a better time," said Jodah. He sat down near the edge of the pit.

"How?" said Sima.

"Same way we broke you out of your chains," said Jodah. "By passing a wedge of infinite thinness between the seams of the bars."

"He's bouncing around a lot. Can you do it?" said Sima.

"I have to, I'm afraid," said Jodah.

Sima stared into the darkness of the pit. "Then let me help."

She stood behind him and pressed her fingertips to his temples. As she did so, she caught a whiff of freshly mown wheat. Jodah could smell the sea now and feel her power join in with his.

Slowly, a small glow appeared around the edge of one of

the bars. Its flickered for a moment, then dimmed, then gained in strength. The rocking of the cage abated as the glowing point became a line and then slowly etched its way around the perimeter of the cage.

"It's going to work," muttered Sima. "It's going to work."

The figure in the cage screamed and slammed against the side Jodah was working on. Jodah shuddered and was thrown from his perch, knocking Sima back in the process. She lost contact and felt the mana, the memories, drain away as she did so.

The figured screamed and slammed into the cage again. Then a third time.

"It didn't—" started Jodah, but the third time the cage fell apart.

It disintegrated, its bars falling away like an overturned silverware cabinet. The chains went slack, and the top and bottom collapsed in on themselves. The cage and its contents plummeted into the darkness below.

The screaming figure fell with the twisted wreckage. He was lost to view immediately, but his screams diminished only slightly.

"No," said Jodah, as the screaming became a distant wail. "I didn't mean it to happen this way."

Then the scream appeared again, first as a small echo and then increasing in volume with every moment, with each second growing louder than before. A small mote of light appeared at the bottom of the pit, and as it rose it grew hotter and brighter. It flashed sunburst white, flame red, crystal green, lightning blue, and a black so intense that it cast shadows in the remaining darkness.

Suddenly it was even with them. It was a ball of fire with a human face. The face of the figure in the cage. It hovered over the abyss, its face twisted in a mad parody of humanity.

Sima started to say, "This doesn't—"

"*Treacherous Mages! Die for your sins!*" shouted the figure, and a long, almost skeletal arm appeared from the ever-changing ball of magical energy.

The Rag Man moved forward then, lurching from his watch post and staggering between the pair of mages and the flaming figure. He had his sword raised as if to ward off a blow.

Ith's magical bolt struck the Rag Man and coursed through his body, lightning dancing and arcing at every joint. The rune-covered sword began to melt under the energies, and the Rag Man shuddered, then sagged, and finally collapsed to the ground. Sima went to his side, but Jodah only watched as the transformed figure of Ith rose up through the chamber, laughing insanely and shouting threats.

The flaming form disappeared as it struck the roof of the chamber, and thunder rolled down toward them, followed by pieces of the ceiling. Most of the debris fell into the central pit, and Jodah didn't wait to hear it strike bottom.

Jodah turned and looked at Sima. She was kneeling beside the fallen Rag Man. Water beaded at the corners of her eyes, and for the first time that Jodah had known her, she seemed confused and unsure of herself. The Rag Man lay in a twisted pose, and both his legs and one arm had been shaken loose from his body.

"He's dead," she said. "He saved our lives, and he's dead."

Jodah nodded.

"He said something before he died," she added.

Jodah looked at her, blinking. The Rag Man had never spoken before. Finally he managed, "What did he say?"

"Save Ith," said Sima swallowing hard. "He said, 'Save Ith.' " She shook her head. "Ith killed him, and he said . . ." Her voice died out as she spoke.

Jodah grabbed her by the shoulder, and she pulled away from the fallen body with its melted sword. He guided her back to the secret passageway as more of the chamber's roof began to fall around them.

19

The Lord High Mage

The Dark was a time filled with madmen, both in the church and among the mages. Yet in a mad world, is not accepting the madness the only reasonable solution?
—Arkol Argivian scholar

In the flaming wreckage that was the dining hall, Primata Delphine found her most deadly foe—the Lord High Mage of the Conclave. Or rather, he found her.

The church forces had been dispersed through the entire Citadel now, and she had no idea how they were faring, or even if they were still alive. The fact was that most of the complex was in flames now, and each dead mage would be worth at least a hundred troops.

She thought how proud the Lord Guardian would be of her when she delivered her report. While she had not found either of her initial quarry, she had created enough corpses and destroyed enough magical arcanary to please any official of the church.

There was a noise behind her, at the doorway, and she turned to face it. Mairsil was there. She recognized him at once from the ornate, decadent portraiture that her troops had torn from the walls. This was the master of the house.

He was dressed in black, with a gold vest, and held in his hands a red-tipped wand with a saber grip. His face was smudged with soot, and there was blood running down from his ear into his collar.

"The chief magician, I presume," said the primata.

"You did this," he hissed.

"No," said the primata firmly. "*You* did this. By following your hellish ways. By meddling in matters too powerful for mortals to comprehend. By interfering with the natural forces of the world. You have been weighed and judged wanting. Your destruction is your fault. I am but the instrument of that punishment."

Mairsil snarled and muttered a spell. The primata closed her eyes and the effects splashed harmlessly over her protective wards. The magical energies were reduced to bits of lights.

"I am proof against your enchantments, now, by the wisdom of Tal. If you surrender now, you will be blessed and your soul saved before you are put on the pyre."

Mairsil cursed and unleashed another spell. Red colors splashed against her wards, but left her unscathed.

"There is nothing you can do. You can fight for a while, until you wear yourself out, and then my loyal troops will find you and kill you. Just as they will find and kill any user of magic."

Mairsil straitened himself up, visibly trying to restrain his temper, "Why did you do this? Why now?"

The primata smiled, and it was an ugly smile. "I do this because I am hunting wizards and found a nest of them. I do this because the Book of Tal tells us that we cannot suffer a magician to live. I do this because magic is evil, and evil in all its forms must be eradicated. I will not rest until every spellcaster is slain."

"Even those in your holy church?" said Mairsil, circling away from the door now. He no longer cast spells, but his clasped he magical wand with a white-knuckled grip. "Even those who serve beside you and mouth the same words and sing the same hymns as you?"

"You seek to rock my faith," said Primata Delphine calmly. "Evil seeks to do that. I know there may be mages hiding among the faithful. They will always be rooted out and put to the torch. Of this I have no doubt."

"And will you be among those put to the torch, Priestess?" hissed Mairsil. Another splash of color, this time, black as the moonless night, crystallized against her protections and fell away, leaving her harmed.

"I will be holding that torch," said the primata. "I have only the desire to search out magic, search out evil, for the church."

Mairsil laughed then, and it was a horrid, mocking laugh. "You don't realize, do you? You're one of us! You use spells the same as we 'evil mages'!"

"You seek to rock my faith," repeated Primata Delphine. "Evil seeks to do that."

"You don't realize it!" howled Mairsil. "You wrap it up in religious dogma and mummery, but you don't realize that basic truth! You use magic just as we do! All your miracles and mysteries! Magic!"

The primata ignored the Lord High Mage. Instead she raised her arms and intoned, "*Bathed in the hallowed light, the infidels looked upon the impurities of their souls and despaired!*" Her entire body seemed to glow from its own light, a light that filled the room, devouring everything in its path.

When it finally diminished, Lord Mairsil was still there, inside, smiling. "I have my protections as well, your holiness. And ask should yourself, how would these protections be effective against your 'miracles' if those miracles were not themselves magical in nature."

"*And I will take a sword to the infidel and the unbeliever, and my blade shall shine with fire of righteousness.*" The primata intoned the quote from the book of Tal, and a flaming sword appeared in her left hand. She charged toward the mage.

"What were you thinking just then?" said Mairsil, raising his saber-handed wand in a mock salute. "When you did that, when you summoned that 'miracle,' were you thinking of some temple far away? Perhaps where you were let into that particular mystery of the faith?"

The primata lunged with a speed that belied her size. Mairsil beat the flaming blade back with his short wand. As he did so, the flame from the priestess's blade dimmed just a bit.

"Struck a nerve, did I?" said Mairsil dancing back from the assault. "You were thinking of a place. The place where you were taught to venerate the blade. Some shrine perhaps? Some supposedly holy place, overlooking a wide valley somewhere? Somewhere in the mountains? Is that what you were thinking of?"

The primata said nothing but brought up her sword with a violent slash. Her blade was longer than his, but again, he beat the force of the assault aside neatly and danced back. He was smiling broadly now.

"Suffer not a magician to live!" she shouted, and lunged again. Once more he turned the blade aside.

As the Lord High Mage beat aside the blow, he stepped inside her swing. He reverse his own assault, and brought up the saber-handed wand down on the primata's ribs, its ruby tip blazing with power.

The primata's side exploded in pain, and she staggered back this time.

"You are no fencer," said Mairsil. "You are no real wizard, either. The ability to cast spells is not magic. The ability to understand them *is*."

"Tal grant me wisdom," said the primata, gasping.

"Let me grant you some wisdom, Priestess," said Mairsil. "You think of a particular place when you ask for your miracles. You imagine colored light or smell a familiar smell or you feel warm when you call them into being. That's not the wisdom of Tal. That's mana, the energy of magic. And you use it as much as we do."

The primata said nothing but lunged, trying to bring her blade around for another attack, but Mairsil was too fast for her. Again, he stepped inside her swing, this time stabbing forward with his red-tipped crystal wand. Again she felt pain, this time a tearing shriek down one massive thigh.

"That's what's unforgivable," said Mairsil. "You use the mana *badly*. A real mage would have figured out what I am doing with this wand minutes ago. Let me give you that wisdom as well. I'm stripping your magic from you, pulling your miracles away from you. With every assault you lose more of your power."

Primata Delphine halted, and then gasped, "You are crafty, wizard. You have confused me and weakened me with that confusion. You seek to rock my faith. Evil does that."

"Rocked your faith," said Mairsil with a wide, lupine grin. He stepped forward, and the primata backpedaled despite herself. "Your circles and wards are failing you,

Priestess. You realize you must believe in magic in order to keep them going, but you cannot believe in magic, can you?"

The primata eyed the door beyond the Lord High Mage. "My troops . . ." she began.

"Your troops are being hunted down and slain as we speak," said the Mairsil. "Those who have not fled from this place. You got very far on surprise and good fortune. We didn't expect an attack, and we didn't expect you to get inside the Citadel. But now you are out of surprises, and every one of your troops is dead or dying or in flight. Now you will follow."

He lunged now, and the primata tried to step back. But she was too slow, and a stabbing pain lanced through her gut. Her flaming sword sputtered once, than disappeared.

"And now, I must confess, I am playing you, Priestess," said Mairsil, the smile broad and wolfish. "I have prevented you from accessing your memories, I have denied you your miracle spells. But now, alas, I must bring this to an end."

He stepped forward, lashing out with a high, upward blow with his saber-handled wand. The primata ducked, and in ducking stepped directly into the path of his second blow. Mairsil brought up the other hand, slammed it against her chest, then stepped back to admire his handiwork.

The Primata Delphine looked down and saw a broad-bladed dagger jutting out from her chest, just above the heart.

"The old ways," said Mairsil, "are often the best."

Primata Delphine tried to compose a curse with her dying breath. All she managed was a dull, rattling noise as she collapsed in the wreckage of the dining hall.

Mairsil kicked the body. "You hate wizards. You never asked why I hate the church. I'll tell you: You're narrow minded and you're dogmatic. And worst of all, you're *amateurs*."

He looked down at her fallen form, the blood forming a wide pool around her. "And may the Dark Lands damn me, you'll be the death of us all."

And at that moment the earth shook beneath Mairsil's feet, and the lights went out.

* * * * *

The climb back through the secret ways was eternal. As they passed upward, Sima realized that something was missing. The thrumming noise was gone. It was as if someone or something had shut the hidden engines down.

They had cast their own lights with their magics, white and blue, and now needed them as they passed out of the secret passage into the blackness of the main hallway. The fires outside flickered through the remains of the stained-glassed window.

Jodah halted, and Sima almost bumped into him. "It's dark," he said.

"That's a surprise?" asked Sima.

Jodah nodded. "There are usually lights on here."

Sima looked around, and said, "And I wonder who was powering the lights all those years."

Jodah nodded again, and they passed down the hallway. "Have you figured out what to do about him?" she said.

Jodah said, "No. Any ideas?"

"Is there a way to trap him?"

Jodah shook his head. "Like he was before? No, I don't think so."

"What did the Rag Man mean, Save him?"

Jodah shrugged, "Save him from Mairsil? Save him from the church?"

"Or save him from himself," said Sima.

The hallway was lit from behind by numerous fires out in the Citadel grounds, and there was smoke hanging in the air. And the smell of other things as well. Magic and fear.

"Mairsil's study," said Jodah. "If he was thinking long enough, Ith would try to find Mairsil. It's a couple floors below us, past the dining halls. Make for the main stairs."

They reached the top of the stairs when they heard the sound of a safety being released from a crossbow. Actually it was four safeties, all being released as one.

Out of the shadows stepped a short man with an ornate crossbow. In the flickering shadows he seemed larger than he truly was.

"Friend Barl," said Jodah. "Ith has been released."

"And who would have done that, Friend Jodah?" said Barl, his aim staying on a point between Sima and Jodah. "Could it have been the spies who infiltrated our conclave?"

"Friend Barl," started Jodah, "It's not like that . . ."

"Its *exactly* like that," said Barl severely. "Unlike his Lord High Mage I am not good at deceiving myself. I saw you worm your way into this place, with your innocent manners and your childlike curiosity. You had me fooled I must admit. I saw you worm your way into My Lord High Mage's good graces. I had to think at the time, Why? And now I know. This one—" the crossbow moved a fraction of an inch toward Sima— "confirmed it for me. You probably brought the church here, didn't you? Anything to keep your City of Shadows the most powerful group of mages in the land. To keep your stranglehold on magic."

"You never even gave me a chance." Sima spoke the words flatly, but her eyes flashed in anger.

"I gave you half a chance, and you took it," said Barl, "Look at what you have done to my master's house!"

"You can't take both of us with one weapon," said Jodah.

Barl smiled, and it was a deep confident smile. "Then I will have to shoot the right one, won't I?"

Sima elbowed Jodah and said, "You go. I can take him."

Jodah said, "You don't—"

Sima was sharper now. "You go. Save Ith."

Jodah nodded and dashed down the stairs. Sima took a step toward Barl at the same time, and the crossbow swung up toward her.

"Bad move," said Barl. "One target, now."

Sima nodded and raised a hand, releasing the memories of her home islands. The energies coursed through the crossbow, dismantling it as it passed along its length. In a thought, with a wave of her hand, she *unraveled* the crossbow.

Barl pulled the trigger, but it was too late—the entire device fell apart in his hands and clattered to the floor in pieces.

Sima raised both hands now, and blue flames appeared at her fingertips. "I hope you had a backup plan, artificer" she said. "For your sake, I hope you did."

* * * * *

Jodah descended the stairs, holding one hand aloft with its soft beacon of white mana. He saw lights flickering from the dining area and wondered if several of the mages had gotten the power restored.

Instead he found the Lord High Mage warming his hands over a burning human body. The figure was unrecognizable, save that it was once very large and possibly female.

"Amazing the amount of warmth one gets from one of these," said Mairsil, a hard smile on his lips, but his voice was cheery. "Must be all the fat reserves that have built up over the years."

It was the same friendly tone the Lord High Mage had taken in the library, when they first met. It was a mask, thought Jodah, a smiling mask that Mairsil could turn on or off at will.

"Mairsil," said Jodah, "Ith is . . ."

"Free?" broke in Mairsil. "Loose? Rampaging through the Citadel, killing anyone who gets in his way?"

"Free," said Jodah simply.

"And you had a hand in this, I assume?" said Mairsil.

Jodah said only, "He was being driven mad."

"He was *always* mad," said Mairsil firmly. "Mad from the start. Mad to come here in the first place. I just put his madness, and his power, to good use." He rubbed his hands again. "But that's all over now, isn't it?"

Jodah opened his mouth to argue, but Mairsil silenced him with a sharp look. "Who sent you?" said the Lord High Mage. "The church?"

Jodah shook his head, and Mairsil said, "I'll admit I thought so, briefly, when the attack first came. One visitor is a happenstance, two is synchronicity, three is dead certain, or something like that. But you should know the church failed. Oh, it killed more than a few of the mages. The weak ones, the foolish ones. But in the end there was nothing the church can do about us. We'll always be here.

We can kill them—" he looked at the burning body— "or we just wait for them to freeze, with the rest of this gods-forsaken land."

Jodah said, "You built all this place with Ith's power. You took his magic from it and used it for yourself."

Mairsil looked at him and shook his head sagely. "Is that why you freed him? Because I was unfair to him for fifteen-odd years? What would that be if he just gave me what I wanted, and I became immortal? And what is it to you? Why throw away such a promising career over a madman?"

"You tried to get me to kill Sima," said Jodah.

"A clerical error," said Mairsil, smiling broadly. "Barl's idea."

"You were willing to kill me," challenged Jodah.

"Rumor," said Mairsil, the smile fading only slightly.

"You were going to sacrifice me to your Lords of the Dark Lands," said Jodah, levelly.

The corner of Mairsil's eye twitched almost unnoticeably. He nodded slightly.

"Ah," he said at last. "Ah. So by all this I can assume there is no chance you'll be helping me in the future." His hand dipped into his vest. When it reappeared the hand held a gem-tipped wand by its saber-hilt handle.

Jodah opened his mouth, but he did not know what to say. Mairsil took a step toward him, and then the ground heaved beneath them. It felt as if the entire Citadel had been raised three feet and then dropped again.

"He's coming," said Mairsil, his voice little more than a whisper. The smile was gone now, replaced by a worried, frightened scowl.

The far wall of the dining hall began to smoke, and then crack, and then flake away entirely, like a iceberg calving off a glacier. Through the gap stepped a glowing, angry figure.

Ith had arrived.

Jodah expected Mairsil to attack his former master and pulled his mirror from his pocket, hoping to defend himself from stray mystic bolts.

Instead, Mairsil dropped to one knee and said, "Master! You're alive!"

The glowing figure snarled something incoherent and raised a flaming hand against the Lord High Mage.

Mairsil continued as if nothing had happened. "We thought you were dead! I only now discovered that Barl was working with the church and had planned to kill or imprison us all. Thank you for rescuing us!"

The glowing figure hesitated. The flaming death did not come.

Mairsil added quickly, "You've been confused. Illusions have been used against you. Come, calm down, and we can reason together."

The glowing figure of Ith snarled, and flame shot from his palm. Mairsil was bathed in the glow, but it washed over him like a wave, leaving him unscathed.

"Come, now, Master," said Mairsil calmly, "you know I am proof against any attack that you can muster. The first rule of magery is to protect yourself from your betters. You yourself taught me that. Now, believe me when I say that—"

There was another snarl, and wave of blue energy shot from Ith's outstretched arm and crackled around the Lord High Mage.

"Nothing from your hand can harm me," said Mairsil as the attack subsided around him. "Now think, Master. Please, think. You've been ill. You've been hurt by the church. I've only just now found out! You've been ill! Trust me, Master. Trust me!"

Ith hesitated, and the gigantic form looked puzzled. Jodah noticed that Mairsil clenched the gem-tipped wand tightly, and now leaned toward the former Lord of the Conclave.

Jodah found his voice, and shouted now. "Lies! He's lying to you!"

Ith turned toward Jodah, as if noticing him for the first time. A dull recognition flickered in the glowing figure's eyes, then disappeared again beneath a veil of madness.

A dragon. Ith reminded Jodah of a great dragon made entirely of mana. Made entirely of power. And without any thought to direct that power.

"That's one of them!" shouted Mairsil. "That's one of the church wizards! You can smell the white mana on him!"

The glowing figure raised a hand against toward Jodah, and the energies built in its outstretched palm.

Jodah shouted, "Stop!" and tried to pull the memories of the land into his mind. But they had fled, leaving only a few fragments of the mountains behind.

"He's the one who imprisoned you!" screamed Mairsil. "He's the one who should be punished!"

The Ith figure snarled and blue-red waves of flame shot from his palm in a solid stream.

Jodah shouted and put his hands up in front of his face, clutching the mirror like a protective talisman, this time trying to catch the force of the magical blow with it. He thought of his anger at Mairsil, and his pity for Lord Ith.

The flame bounced from the mirror and looped around the room, moving like a serpent of fire. The serpent reared and struck at last at the Lord High Mage. Mairsil screamed as the flames washed over him, igniting his fine clothing, his hair, and finally his flesh.

Jodah knew at once what had happened. Mairsil was protected against Ith's attacks, as he had said, but not Jodah's, and the attack had come ultimately from Jodah's mirror.

Mairsil screamed and beat at the flames, then fled from the room, the fire trailing from him like a comet's tail. He continued screaming as he passed through the main hall, but Jodah could not afford to worry about him.

Ith was mad now. Angry mad, as well as insane mad. No one seemed to fall down when the insane mage hit them.

Ith stepped forward, growing larger with every stride. The eldritch fires coursed through his veins, and his unseeing eyes glowed a hellish yellow.

Jodah stood his ground. He held up the mirror again, this time not as a protective talisman, but rather strongly, firmly, trying to aim the fire right back at Ith.

Ith towered over him, arcs of magical energy dancing over his flesh. He was massive as well, swollen on his own power, power that he had been drawing back into himself, draining from the Citadel and its protective wards.

Jodah stood his ground.

Ith looked down at him, down at the young man clutching the mirror. Slowly, recognition dawned in the yellowish eyes, and they began to dim, just a fraction. Then a fraction more, and Jodah realized that Ith was not staring at him. He was staring into the mirror.

"Look at it," Jodah said, almost in a whisper. "Look at what you have become. Look at what they have made you."

There was a long moment, and Jodah realized that Ith

was breathing deeply, almost sobbing. The yellowish light was fading now, and he was slowly shrinking, returning to normal size. The jagged lines of energy pulled into him, becoming nothing more than a normal glow.

Slowly, painfully, Ith became human again.

Finally, Ith raised a thin hand to his face and said, "I never looked good in a beard." His voice cracked as he said it, and he rubbed his chin. "That will have to go."

"Lord Ith?" said Jodah, from behind the mirror, "are you all right?"

Ith looked up, seeing the young man holding the mirror as if for the first time. There was a nod of recognition, and Ith said, "No. I'm not all right. I won't be all right for some time to come. But I'm back, back from the madness. Back from the borders of the Dark Lands. And I still have much to do."

Far away, something toppled. Perhaps it was one of the towers or some part of the wall. Whatever it was, it took a long time to fall, and sounded like a distant mountain avalanche.

"We should get out of here," said Jodah.

"I have things to finish," said Ith.

"We should go," said Jodah.

"Then go," said Ith, and a flash of yellow blazed behind his eyes. "You have given me my sanity back, young one. I don't intend to squander that gift. But neither do I want you pay for it with your own life. I will survive this—I want to make sure you do as well. Now go!"

"We should—"

"Go!" bellowed Ith and Jodah found himself running despite himself. Enspelled, he realized, but he could not will his legs to stop.

He was out in the hallway now, running for the front

gates. There was a flash of blue, and Sima was now alongside him, running to keep up. She had a mad, frightened look on her face, and Jodah knew that she too was under Ith's enchantment.

The grand hall was bathed in flame now, the ancient tapestries gutted by reaching claws of flame. The portraits had burned from the center out, leaving only ashes where once were pigments. The carpets were smoking from hot ash, and the remaining light-crystals exploded from the heat one after the other.

Then they were at the gate, but there was no gate, not since the church destroyed it. They were beyond the gate and into the ruined mazework. Not ruined, thought Jodah, merely unfinished. He leaped over several low walls in succession, Sima hot on his heels.

There was an explosion behind him, and Jodah felt a warm hand press hard on his back. He did not clear one of the low walls and tumbled headfirst over the foundation.

The ground came up very quickly, and then there was only blackness.

20 ☾

Devastation and Creation

A student came to me once and said, "Oh, it was better to live in those ancient times than now." I asked him why and he said that it was a better time than this one, a time when one could write of real adventure and feel the excitement of true challenges. I had to laugh and tell him that were he truly living in those times, he would have so many adventures and challenges that he would have neither the time nor the desire to write. He would be too busy trying to survive.

—Arkol, Argivian scholar

"You all right?" said a voice from deep within a well.

Jodah turned toward the voice. It was watery and distant, but it was present. He felt himself moving toward it.

"You all right?" said the voice again, cleared this time. He recognized it but wasn't quite sure from where.

"You all right?" said the voice a third time, and Jodah knew the voice. It had once said, in the same tone, "You want the rest of your ham?"

"Fine, Shannan," said Jodah, opening his eyes, "I'm fine."

Multiple Shannans (Shanni?) danced in front of his vision, then joined together to form a single mage. Overweight, sloppily dressed, with grimy white hair. Face caked in soot and mud but otherwise no different than the last time Jodah saw him.

"You all right?" said Shannan, and Jodah held up a hand, if nothing else to stop him from saying the same thing again and again.

Jodah blinked and the rest of the world swam into view. The Citadel was caved-in wreckage, its glorious towers and walls nothing more than rubble, an avalanche of smashed buildings slouching down the shoulder of the mountain. Fires were still burning somewhere within, and thick plumes of smoke rose from a dozen places.

There were survivors. Sima. Some of the servants. A few of the younger mages, now huddled among the wreckage, shaking their heads. And Shannan, protected by whatever spell it is that protects fools and children.

Shannan helped him to his feet. "I was outside when it happened," he said. "I was getting my gardening tools. I had left them behind when the dinner bell rang." He looked at the devastation. "I missed most of it."

"You were lucky," said Jodah.

Sima stood with her arms crossed, a short distance away from either group of servants or mages. She was watching the two of them.

"He wanted to know when you were up," said Shannan.

"He?" said Jodah, and looked up toward the mountainside. A lone figure was seated on the outermost stones of the mazework. It was a lean figure, its once-wild hair now tamed, dressed in tasteful, if outdated, robes. He was no longer a glowing giant of rage. No longer a dragon of uncontrolled power.

"Oh. Him," said Jodah and stood up. He staggered a few steps, and Shannan was there.

"You all right?" said Shannan.

"Stop saying that," said Jodah. He took a deep breath and said, "Yes. Now I have to go talk to him."

"Is he . . ." said Shannan.

"Is he what?" said Jodah.

"The other mages were talking," said Shannan. "Is he him. You know. Him?"

"You see any of the other mages going over to him?" asked Jodah. Shannan said nothing. Jodah added, "Then you should assume he probably is."

With that Jodah started again toward the lone figure. His legs functioned better after the first fifteen feet, and about halfway there he remembered to check to see if he still had the mirror. It was tucked neatly inside his vest, near his heart. He had not remembered putting it there.

The lone, lanky figure rose as Jodah approached.

"Friend Ith," said Jodah.

"I prefer Lord, normally," said Ith with a weary smile, "but I will accept Friend from you, Jodah. I want to thank you for bringing me back."

Jodah shrugged, and said, "You thanked me once already."

Ith bowed and said, "Then I must do so again. For saving my body. For saving my mind. For saving my soul."

Jodah shook his head. "I reacted more than I acted. I didn't make my choice until it was almost too late."

"But you were there," said Ith. "And you *did* choose."

"Your Rag Man brought me," said Jodah levelly.

Ith nodded. "I instructed him, in a moment of lucidity,

to find someone to save me. He found you. Do you wonder why?"

"Because of I was of Jarsyl's bloodline? Because there was something about Jarsyl's grandfather? Because I had the mirror at that moment?" Jodah shook his head. "I don't know."

Ith gave a tired smile. "I don't know either. But I was looking for someone to free my physical shackles. And the Rag Man sought out someone to free me from my madness as well."

"You destroyed the Rag Man," said Jodah. "Do you remember that?"

Ith nodded wearily. "I destroyed many things," he waved a hand out to the tumbled desolation ahead of them. "You sometimes have to destroy in order to create anew. Remember *that*, child. Above all else."

Jodah said nothing. Ith let out a sigh. "This place was a place of power, a weak spot in the fabric between the worlds. I thought I could master the forces that haunted it. In the end, they almost mastered me. In my vanity, I did not see Mairsil's treachery until he had slammed the cage door behind me. I think the darkness of this place got to him, as it almost got to me. A different way, perhaps, but still it got to him."

"What are you going to do now?" said Jodah.

"I am going elsewhere," said Ith. "Go into hiding. The local towns would never tolerate another Conclave here, and the church knows where we are now. And besides," and he sighed deeply, "This world is dying. It's much colder, and darker, and emptier, and it will get worse before it gets better. Do you want to come with me?"

"Me?" said Jodah, surprised.

"I could use an assistant, an apprentice," said Ith. "My

last one came to a bad end. The position is open."

Jodah thought for a moment, then shook his head.

"Why not?" said Ith. He did not seem upset by Jodah's decision.

"I have been stumbling from one position to another," said Jodah, choosing his words carefully. "I need to learn how to master my skills, and to find what makes them work. I need a little more . . ."

"Structure," said Ith, a slight smile on his lips. "Order."

"Perhaps," said Jodah.

"You're going to the City of Shadows, then," said Ith, and looked past him at Sima.

"Perhaps," said Jodah.

Ith took a long, hard look at the young man. Then he nodded and allowed himself a laugh.

"I don't know who it will be harder on," he said. "You or them." He held up a hand when Jodah began to protest. "I think you will be a powerful scholar among them. I think that's the right choice. If you want to go, then I want to tell you the secret of using the safe havens."

They stood there for ten minutes as Ith carefully detailed how one operated the transporting caves. He made Jodah repeat the secret phrases three times, and pointed out that it was important to hold the phrases in the top of one's mind, not to speak the words.

At last he said, "You won't reconsider?"

Jodah shook his head but said, "Where will you go?"

"Away," said Ith, "somewhere that I can gather my power, and my sanity. Someplace where I can finish my protective maze, and hide at its center. I want to write down what I discovered in the darkness. Write my memoirs." He laughed and added, "Perhaps even write a history or two, to confound those who follow."

Jodah nodded toward the huddled mages far away across the shattered mazework. "What about them?"

Ith's face turned stony for a moment. "They followed another path of magic. A path laid out by my student. I allowed them to live. But they are no longer my concern."

Jodah was quiet, and then said, "So you will travel alone."

Ith brightened slightly. "I never travel alone. I have my Rag Man."

"You destroyed—" started Jodah.

"A Rag Man," said Ith. "Sometimes it is necessary to destroy in order to create anew."

He waved his hand and a figure rose from where it had been sitting on the far side of the wall. It was dressed in tatters and rags, but it was shorter that the ragged man that Jodah had known. It had broad shoulders, and muscles beneath the tattered finery. It carried itself with a sense of power that made it seem much larger than it was.

The face was covered, but Jodah did not have to guess who was beneath the rags.

"Farewell, Friend Jodah," said Ith, turning toward the mountains. "May you find what you seek."

"And you as well, Friend Ith," said Jodah to the ancient mage's back.

He walked back to the others. Sima met him halfway. Shannan was still with the other mages, talking in low tones.

"What was that all about?" she asked.

"He made me an offer," said Jodah. "I turned him down."

Sima looked at Jodah, and for the first time Jodah felt she was looking at him with new eyes.

"So what are you going to do?" asked Sima.

"We," said Jodah, "should go to the City of Shadows."

Sima nodded. "I think I can get a small boat, and scavenge enough supplies for the two of us . . ."

Jodah shook his head, "I mean *we*. You, me, and the other mages. And the surviving servants. Anyone we can find."

Sima blinked at Jodah. "Are you mad?"

"Ith was mad," said Jodah, "at least for a while. Do I look like Ith?"

"We owe these people nothing," said Sima.

"Ith said that as well," said Jodah. "I disagree. We owe them what we ourselves would hope to expect if we were in their position. We are all mages. And magic, for all the definitions we want to throw on it, is nothing more than a tool. We should use that tool to keep others from suffering as we have suffered."

Sima said nothing, and Jodah added, "Besides, your city of Shadows could benefit from their knowledge and experience."

"We don't have enough supplies to reach the City with all of them," said Sima. "Or boats."

"I can use magic to reach the city, now," said Jodah. "And I can take you there. All of you."

Sima sputtered for a moment, then looked at him through serious, slitted eyes. "I'm not going to win this one, either, am I?"

Jodah shook his head. "No, you aren't"

"Can I ask at least, *why* you want to do this?" she said.

"Because," Jodah surveyed the damage, and turned back to Sima. "It just feels *right*."

Sima let out a long sigh, then said, "Then we'll do it. But I'll warn you. Once you get to the City of Shadows, you'll have to have some proper training. You have a lot to learn. All of you."

Jodah surveyed the wrecked Citadel and inhaled deeply the cold air that swirled through the ashes. It smelled of ice, and of dying magic.

"So do you," he said, smiling grimly. "So do all of you."

Invasion Cycle J. Robert King

The struggle for the future of Dominaria has begun.

Book I
Invasion
After eons of plotting beyond time and space, the horrifying Phyrexians have come to reclaim the homeland that once was theirs.

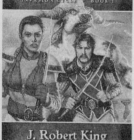

Book II
Planeshift
The first wave is over, but the invasion rages on. The artificial plane of Rath overlays on Dominaria, covering the natural landscape with the unnatural horrors of Phyrexia.
February 2001

Book III
Apocalypse
Witness the conclusion of the world-shattering Phyrexian invasion!
June 2001